British Library Women Writers

The Spring Begins

Katherine Dunning

First published in 1934

This edition published in 2025 by
The British Library
96 Euston Road
London NW1 2DB

Cataloguing in Publication Data
A catalogue record for this publication is available from the British Library

ISBN 978 0 7123 5597 1
e-ISBN 978 0 7123 6893 3

Text design and typesetting by JCS Publishing Services Ltd
Printed and bound by CPI Group (UK), Croydon, CR0 4YY

Contents

The 1930s v
Katherine Dunning vii
Preface ix
Publisher's Note xi

The Spring Begins 1

Afterword 251

The 1930s

- Following the Local Government Act in 1929, orphanages are brought under the auspices of local authorities, having previously been run by independent unions or charities. In practice though, changes are gradual and slow.
- **1930:** The average age at first marriage is 24.3 years for men and 21.3 for women.
- **1931:** The census shows there are approximately 1.7 million more women than men in the UK, about the same difference as 1921. The 1931 census was destroyed in an accidental fire in 1942.
- **1931:** The census shows there are 1.3 million women and 78,489 men employed as indoor domestic staff. About a third of women in paid employment are in domestic service.
- **1931:** 34.2 per cent of women in the UK are considered 'economically active', a term used by the Labour Force Survey to include those in work and those looking for work. The number rises by only half a per cent by 1951.
- **1932 (November):** The first book tokens go on sale in the UK.
- **1934:** *The Spring Begins* is published.
- **1934:** The first commercially successful electric steam iron is

patented. Electric irons continue to grow in popularity through the 1930s.

- **1935 (June):** Driving tests become compulsory in the UK for the first time. The initial pass rate is 63 per cent.
- **1939 (September):** The outbreak of the Second World War.

Katherine Dunning (1900–1975)

Katherine Dunning is the pseudonym of Rhona Dunning, born Rhona Catherine Rowe in June 1900, the youngest of three sisters. She was born in Ireland, in Arklow, County Wicklow, to Irish, Protestant parents. Howard Rowe was a local pharmacist with a history of political activism and writing for the Labour party, and his wife Alice (née Atkins), the daughter of a Methodist minister.

Rhona was a teenager when her father died, aged just 44, of heart failure. Her mother tried to keep the pharmacy afloat for several years, but eventually decided to move the family to England. The decision-making moment came when she found a Sinn Feiner with a drawn gun hiding out in their home. Family history tells that a map of England was brought out and, with her eyes closed, Ethel, the middle sister, put a pin into the map to choose a location. In 1921, in the midst of the Troubles, they moved to the place on which the pin landed – St Leonards-on-Sea, Sussex.

After finding work as a secretary in the local garage, Rhona fell in love with the owner's son, Guy Dunning, and they married in 1923. A couple of years later they had their only child, a daughter also called Rhona, but invariably known by her middle name, Cecil. Money was short in the household, and Dunning started writing for women's magazines under various pseudonyms – stories in certain issues were reportedly all written by her under different pen names. Her first novel, *Stephen Sherrin*, was published in 1932, followed by *The Spring*

Begins (1934), *Fortune's Yoke* (1940, under the name Katherine Ronell), *Whatever the Heart Appoints* (1950) and *The Bright Blue Eye* (1952). Her sister Ethel was also a writer, publishing six novels during the same period.

After Guy's death in 1964, Dunning moved to live with her daughter Cecil in 'the Keep', belonging to the National Trust's Grey's Court where Cecil was custodian. Dunning later developed dementia and moved to a care home, where she died in 1975.

Preface

The intertwined stories of three women seeking affection, pleasure and stability form the focus of this fascinating novel from the 1930s, set for the most part in the Kellaway household. These women represent a range of experience and assumptions in their relationships with men. Lottie the nurse-maid, orphaned and brought up in a home, has only limited acquaintance with men and is disturbed by Nurse's repeated warnings about their violent behaviour. Maggie the scullery maid is more aware of male desire and confident in her own physicality, while Hessie, a local governess, imagines a married future that would free her from her current constraints.

All the focus is on the women in this novel and the men, for the most part, are more shadowy figures. Though each woman is searching for something different from a relationship, they are all affected by considerations relating to their precarious financial position and vulnerable social standing. This is a novel in which the hierarchies of social class are palpable and sharply felt. While the position of the wealthy Kellaway family seems solid, others are less secure. Detail is everything and slight gradations signal subtle differences in status that are very evident to Hessie and her widowed mother and are reflected in the ranking of the Kellaways' 'indoor servants'. Choices are, of necessity, dictated by these limited roles.

At a time when marriage conferred both financial security and status, the engagement of Hessie's sister throws Hessie's own prospects

into stark relief and confers an urgency on her actions. Meanwhile, though the beautiful and beguiling setting of the Kellaways' home and gardens appears a haven, the emphasis on the lush vegetation and the frequent references to the stifling heat hint at underlying tensions for those living there.

From their different perspectives, Lottie, Maggie and Hessie all hope to find happiness in loving and being loved. All the perils of such a quest are here – vulnerability, disappointment, self-consciousness, lack of judgement – as well as the joys and fulfilment.

Alison Bailey
Lead Curator, Printed Heritage Collections 1901–2000

Publisher's Note

The original novels reprinted in the British Library Women Writers series were written and published in a period ranging, for the most part, from the 1910s to the 1950s. There are many elements of these stories which continue to entertain modern readers, however in some cases there are also uses of language, instances of stereotyping and some attitudes expressed by narrators or characters which may not be endorsed by the publishing standards of today. We acknowledge therefore that some elements in the stories selected for reprinting may continue to make uncomfortable reading for some of our audience. With this series, British Library Publishing aims to offer a new readership a chance to read some of the rare books of the British Library's collections in an affordable paperback format, to enjoy their merits and to look back into the world of the twentieth century as portrayed by their writers. It is not possible to separate these stories from the history of their writing and the following novel is presented as it was originally published with minor edits made for consistency of style and sense. We welcome feedback from our readers, which can be sent to the following address:

British Library Publishing
The British Library
96 Euston Road
London, NW1 2DB
United Kingdom

The Spring Begins

Chapter One

I

Each summer's day by the time the little Kellaway girls, with Lottie, their nurse-maid, were ready to go out into the garden to play, the sun was high enough to have dried the dew from the grass and the flowers had lost their look of shining fragility and the early morning gold had left the sea.

The Kellaways' house was an old one. It was white outside and it faced the garden with an air of fine quiet dignity. The garden was dignified, too, but the garden's dignity was of a different kind, for its character was dictated by the springing lightness, the variety, the profusion of its many flowers and trees. There was no real stability about the garden but the house was always the same.

The fir trees at the shore end of the grounds bent themselves darkly and benevolently over the flowers, trained by the wind to turn away from the white sand and the sparkling water.

The Kellaways were rich. There were Mr. and Mrs. Kellaway, their three children, Mrs. Kellaway's young brother, Mr. Andrew, and the servants. Next to his wife, whom he worshipped, Mr. Kellaway's passion in life lay in his garden. Maxwell, the head-gardener, was extremely efficient. There were a great many under-gardeners.

There was a shrubbery full of rare shrubs in the grounds to the right of the house. The variety of leaves there alone was astonishing. Pale green leaves; umber-coloured; scarlet-brown, the shade of virginia creeper in the autumn; clear yellow traced with bright green; and a deep cold purple green almost repellent in its strong, forbidding, varnished brilliancy. Most of these shrubs flowered at some time or other in the year unfolding waxy-looking petals of unbelievably perfect shape, or cascades of tiny sulphur-yellow flowers, or long pods that opened reluctantly and finally disgorged blossoms too stiff and strange to be flowers. Some of the shrubs were covered with clusters of minute petals as soft looking, as fragile as apple-blossom, but each cluster infinitely tiny, gay and perfect.

The foreshore, nearly two miles in length, belonged to Mr. Kellaway. Jutting headlands protected the little bay and the firm sand. The town was a mile and a half away from the ending of the Kellaways' grounds. It was a small, ugly town, with many streets of grey-faced villa houses with bay-windows and narrow steps ascending to front doors. Nottingham lace and casement-cloth shared the honours at the windows. The upper rooms had short net curtains to guard them against the inquiring eyes of the neighbours in the houses opposite. All these houses were more than respectable, they were genteel.

Hessie Price, who was daily governess to the children of the rector of St. John the Apostle, who were friends of the little Kellaway girls, lived in one of these houses in Salisbury Road. She lived there with her widowed mother and her sister, Hilda, and their house was called "Bareilly" because Mrs. Price's father had been a very military colonel who had served in the East, and traditions die hard.

The Kellaways kept six indoor servants. Nurse, Cook, Jenner the parlour-maid, Irene the housemaid, Maggie the kitchen-maid, Lottie the nurse-maid. Besides these there was a Mrs. Bartley who came in from seven in the morning till five in the afternoon to help Irene, and a young woman, the wife of one of the under-gardeners, who assisted Jenner. There were no indoor menservants.

Lottie, who had been nurse-maid to the Kellaway children for nearly a year, always slept in the room with the two little girls of the family, and from her bed she could hear them breathing sometimes. As a rule, Anne slept very quietly, but at times Isobel made little moaning noises that left a line of gentle terror down Lottie's spine. Their bedroom had windows on two sides of it, so that the beams from the sun and moon fell fully into it. Sometimes, when Isobel moaned, Lottie got out of her own bed and crossed the floor to have a good look at the little girl's sleeping yet disturbed face. On the way to the child's bed Lottie could see herself in the long mirror of the wardrobe as she went by. The glass gave her back a strange reflection, as if her white figure had sunk deep down into the mirror's dark silver, and when she paused to wave her arms up and down she looked really queer. Her nightgown floated mistily around her and, with her startled face, startled by her own appearance, she looked like a phantom figure that had blown in from the night itself, its flapping wings disturbing the pressing darkness.

But wasn't it silly, standing there waving her arms up and down and watching her big white nightgown moving so unreally in the darkness around her? If she just turned quickly on her toes like the children did when they were pretending to be fairies blown through the garden by the wind, her nightgown fled out away from her, leaving her body bare and light against the air. But it was not delicate or nice to think of herself as naked. It was all right from her head down to the top of her collar, and from her knees down to her toes she was flesh and blood again, but in between there was nothing at all—just a conveniently sized dummy's model on which to hang her blue gingham frock and white apron. How then could the night air beat against nothing? It could not, and that was that, as Nurse was always saying, and she had better get into bed and go to sleep if she was going to be good for anything in the morning.

Besides, what would happen if either of the children woke up and started asking questions? How could she explain her presence there in the middle of the dark room?

Lottie let her nightgown settle into place around her till it hung with straight full modesty from the square yoke that lay over her shoulders. The cuff-bands lingered down around her fingers. Nurse had cut out the cuffs good and long and the frills at the ends of them swamped her fingers like little tents. She looked almost comical in the billows of her nightgown. Such straight long billows concealing the whiteness and thinness of her body. The heavy gathers of the stuff swelled out strongly from the yoke and drooped like a mountain range over her breasts.

Lottie's toes began to feel a little cold, a soft touch of coldness that was pleasant in a clean fresh way. There might, almost, have been dew on the carpet, the cold had such a liquid feel. Isobel turned in bed, the slight hump of her child's body slipping over with a mysterious unawake movement. The child threw out one arm. It was thin above and below the elbow, and the joint itself looked fragile enough, too. Isobel was a lovely little thing. The sort of child it was easy to love, full of the sweetness and simplicity all children were supposed to possess.

In the huge mirror Lottie saw herself gliding with a nun-like movement of her white nightgown to the side of the child's bed, and drawing the covers up again. Supposing she bent down, feeling a little like an angel or a mother, and kissed the little girl's forehead—but supposing her lips tickled her instead and Isobel opened her eyes in fright!

Lottie's own bed felt cold when she got back into it. It had that lost crumpled feel of a bed that has been deserted in the middle of the night. But it would soon warm up for the blankets were good warm ones, slightly discoloured from use in the nursery. There was plenty of body in her sheets, too, and they were smooth for all their coarse strength. She liked the cool heavy feel of them about her thighs before she pulled her nightdress down around her knees. If she drew in a long breath and then let it out again slowly, it gave her a lovely feeling as if her body were sinking down into the bed and sleep were not far off.

To-morrow was hair-washing day. If it was nice and fine Nurse had it done in the mornings, and the little girls dried their heads out in the garden. She could almost feel Isobel's drying hair on her fingers, it was so light and strong, with a soft yet metallic firmness to it. She slipped her hand underneath the pillow with a gentle thrusting movement as if she were letting the cool wind in through the child's hair. Her fingers pressed back a little and the breath went slowly out of her body and she sank deeper and deeper into sleep.

Lottie woke to the sound of Anne's voice.

"Wake up, Lottie, you do sleep a lot! It's morning!"

She struggled into an upright position, blinking the sleep out of her eyes. She screwed up her eyes against the brightness of the sky, which was clear bright blue, a richer blue than was usual so early in the morning. The two big square windows facing east were wide open, and the sun and air were cascading into the room as if impelled there by the young vigour of the morning. It was difficult to imagine that it was night anywhere else, the day was so strong and bright here. The first and most astonishing thing Lottie had been taught when she was put into the Infants' Class at the Home was that the world was round. That piece of information was like a ray of light penetrating her infant memories. It was a searchlight to illumine herself at a time which was otherwise a blank. In a way it was a strange memory. She could not remember the room, the teacher, her small companions, or any details of substance or light or tone, but she could remember herself. She could see herself, as if her infant vision had stood apart from her body and registered for ever what it saw.

"Nurse will be calling you," Anne said nonchalantly.

Lottie slipped sideways out of bed, her nightgown bunched closely around her ankles. She was always very careful about this, conscientiously carrying out Nurse's instructions. She could expose her legs to the little girls if she was down on the beach, paddling with them, and no harm would be done, for then there was all the protective armoury of her clothes, but in getting out of bed her nightgown was her only protection. Not that Isobel or Anne ever took any notice of her legs, protected or unprotected.

"Hullo!" said Isobel, opening her eyes with a look of bright surprise in them.

Lottie smiled over at the little girl. Isobel always woke up like that—brightly, sweetly, as if her sleep had been taken in a peculiarly pleasant place that precipitated her back into the waking world with a special joyousness clinging about her.

Isobel watched Lottie's foot feeling under the bed for her other slipper. They were carpet slippers with thick white hairyish felt soles, and because quietness was so necessary she always wore them on her way down to fetch Nurse's early morning tea.

"Bother!" said Lottie, bending down as though her supple young body resented the movement, though it was not that really, it was only that Nurse would be waiting for her cup of tea, and the leaping seconds were hurtling towards the moment when Nurse would say, "You're late again, Lottie."

"It's round the other side, blind eyes," said Isobel gaily. "Aren't you silly, putting your slippers like that, one on each side of the bed."

"Hurry up and get the tea," Anne said, "and don't forget the biscuits!"

With her toes pushing their way into her slippers Lottie hurried across to the door. The white paint of the door had been washed so many times that the wood was showing through in places. Brownish islands of wood, unusual in that they were sunken in the surrounding sea of whiteness. After all, perhaps, they weren't so like islands but pools. The white paint was the land, the brown exposed wood the brackish water of pools.

Lottie went quickly down the passage, the heels of her slippers flopping on the floor like a gentle echo of her footsteps. Always dreaming, that's what she was. Matron at the Home had said so. Nurse frequently said so. "Now then, Lottie, look sharp! Dreaming again!" There were no worn places in the woodwork in the corridor to tempt her fancy away from her proper duty. Everything in the corridor, the walls, the floors, was very old dark oak.

Young Mr. Andrew came quickly out of his bedroom door, as she passed. He was trying, though not trying very hard, to gather together the ropes of his dressing-gown. The sight of his ropes swaying so easily made Lottie aware of the secure feeling around her own waist. It was all right for Mr. Andrew to come swinging out of his bedroom like that, but what would happen if she ever dared to leave her room without being neat and secure around her waist, especially if she met Nurse? Nurse would have something to say to her if she ever caught her like that! Not that she would, of course. It was impossible to be too modest. Nurse was a great believer in modesty.

But Mr. Andrew did not seem to care. The minute he saw her he forgot all about his dressing-gown and he smiled.

"Good morning, Lottie." His eyes were very bright. Really, he was rather like Isobel, or rather she was like him. They shared the same, merry, sleep-refreshed look.

"Good morning, Mr. Andrew."

He fell into step beside her.

"I'm taking a short cut out to the yard," he said pleasantly. "Those pups! The kids can come along and see them to-day. Blenheim won't be so fierce. She's always queer like that the first day or two. She won't let anyone but me look at her even." He reached out and opened the green baize door leading to the back stairs. He was going down the servants' staircase to see his big dog, which had had puppies.

Lottie's mind, under Nurse's influence, refused the word 'bitch.' Isobel and Anne were crazy to see them.

"I'll tell Nurse," she said.

"Oh, Nurse!" he exclaimed, and gave her a tiny rather shocking little smile, as if he were inviting her to laugh at Nurse, too.

In the kitchen Lottie found Maggie, the kitchen-maid, struggling with the smoky blackness of the range. Maggie was a tall, defiant girl, with a look of bitter rebellion always in her big black eyes. The kitchen fire was her avowed enemy. Irene, the housemaid, was standing by the gas-stove jealously guarding the kettle. Cook was there, too, a dark apron over her white one, a sour look on her face as she eyed Maggie.

"The dirty slut!" she remarked to Irene.

Maggie's eyes blazed up and Lottie felt her unspoken retort. Irene's face looked uneasy, but she went on with the conversation Cook's remark had interrupted.

"A nice bismuth mixture—that's what I say. Or a good dose of Epsom-salt in the morning. ..."

Lottie went about arranging Nurse's early morning tea-tray. It was a nice little set of china things, in a soft pretty pink shade. She liked spreading them out. The sugar seemed to sparkle in the pink bowl and the milk looked rich.

"Here, Lily-hands," Irene called out kindly, "you can fill up now."

Irene was very jolly and good-natured. She had a pleasant way of looking at a thing for a moment or two and then bursting out into a hearty laugh.

"Hurry up, out of my kitchen, now," Cook said curtly to Lottie.

Mr. Andrew was still out in the yard when Lottie went back up the stairs again. The night nursery was in cloudy darkness when she entered it, though there were great gashes of light when the curtains swayed with the wind. The curtains here were lined with heavy green sateen to keep the early morning sun from waking Nurse any earlier than was necessary.

Nurse was moving about in one corner of the room, moving with a soft, ponderous silence that made her movements rather horribly mysterious and intimate. She wore a dark red dressing-gown and her wisp of greying hair lay down against the red cloth like a tired, damp strand of old rope. There was an unhealthy whiteness about her skin. Fat and forty, without being fair, Cook would say, sometimes.

The baby's cradle was in an alcove close to the window. It was a very pretty cradle. There was no hood to it but the top end rose up four or five inches higher than the rest to form a screen. There were ruffles of stiff white organdie all around it and little ruchings made the hems stand out in frothy iridescent waves. Pale blue ribands gathered into posies decorated the head. This cradle was at once Lottie's anguish and her delight. It was a beautiful pale blue and white grotto, a sacred haven, and yet a responsibility almost too great to be borne. If there was a mark on its fresh spotless whiteness, Nurse held her responsible for it.

"Late again, Lottie," Nurse remarked. She turned and scrutinized the tea-tray. Nurse's breasts looked flabby and enormous without the support of her corsets, though she appeared to be neat and firm enough in the starched regalia of her uniform.

"How did the children sleep? And now what's the matter with that cap of yours?"

Looking in the mirror gave Lottie quite a shock. Against the dusky background she looked like a ghost. Her Sister Dora cap had twisted a little to one side, nothing that anyone else but Nurse would notice. She put up her hands and straightened it.

"That's right, stand there all day gawking at yourself. I suppose the children can dress themselves? And perhaps you'd like to pull those curtains for me?"

"Yes, Nurse," Lottie answered brightly. It would be a pity to let Nurse start the day in a bad temper. Such a beautiful summer's day.

She swept the curtains back and the light made the baby blink in his solemn way. He lay there looking up at Lottie from his blue and white paradise. She lingered by the side of his cot gazing down at him, loving him.

"Get on there—do," Nurse exclaimed irritably.

It was summer-time and so there were no nursery fires to light. So often her hands were powerless in the bitingly cold weather. Her fingers went white and lifeless-looking then, as though her hands were ancient things. To-day she had only to dust over the floor and the furniture, pull the curtains, open the windows, lay the breakfast, clean the shoes, dress and wash Isobel and Anne, and fetch the breakfast up from the kitchen. It was the lightest morning's work the week held. Later, when the children were out of doors, Irene, fortified by Mrs. Bartley, the daily woman, would give the nurseries their special weekly cleaning. On all the rest of the mornings it was Lottie's business to scrub over the pale fawn linoleum, and make sure she left no islands of dampness about, for that made Nurse very angry.

Lottie never forgot her early hopes that Nurse would be a big, kind, jolly sort of woman. Certainly Nurse was big and very capable, too, that was why Mrs. Kellaway kept her, but she was jolly only when someone worth being jolly with was about. She was always jolly when Mr. Andrew was with the children, and in a more subdued way with Mrs. Kellaway. She was never jolly with Lottie.

Leaving the night nursery Lottie stepped into the passage and was surrounded by old black oak-panelled walls again. Lottie knew this corridor was quite a feature of the place. It ran the whole width of the house, and was lit by windows at either end. The bedroom doors opened off it at regular intervals, and when they were all shut they looked like dark sentinels guarding the delicate privacies of the rooms beyond. The carpet was a wide soft sand-coloured one. It added to the rich subdued look of the corridor.

The door of Mrs. Kellaway's bedroom was open a little.

"Lottie!"

"Yes, Mrs. Kellaway?"

"Come in here a minute."

Going into Mrs. Kellaway's bedroom was always an occasion in Lottie's mind. She fixed her eyes on the foot of Mrs. Kellaway's bed and the hot colour moved up over her features and then went back again, leaving her face white and thin. This bedroom was always so beautiful but now there was a ruffled early-morning look about it that wanned its perfection to an unbearable degree.

"Good morning, Lottie," Mrs. Kellaway said. "I want you to take a message to the garden for me. Will you tell Maxwell that I want those flowers I spoke about yesterday—that I want them as soon as possible. He's to cut them at once."

For a frightful moment Lottie felt her eyes being drawn to Mr. Kellaway, who was sitting on the side of his own bed, dressed only in his pyjamas, drinking his tea and glancing through some papers. His eyes looked up and met hers.

"You'd better tell Nurse I've asked you to do this," Mrs. Kellaway went on. "Irene can help to dress the children."

Out in the garden Maxwell, the head-gardener, was hard to find. Lottie walked down between the flower-beds. She went beyond the formal garden and out onto the lawns. For all the brilliance of the sky and the lightly quivering sunlight there was a delicate cool dampness in the air. Beyond the trees there was a low mist, and beyond the mist lay the sea. Lottie could hear it faintly. It was singing to itself, and where the mist broke there were faint blue and gold sparkles as the sun played on the water. Nothing stirred but the mist which was rolling gently away from the wet sand, its edges faintly iridescent in the gathering sunlight. The sand came up to the ridge of fir trees at the end of the garden. Lottie stood still and she felt her body growing light and free.

After a moment's standing she turned right, and followed a path that led through the shrubbery towards that part of the gardens where the greenhouses stood. Most likely she would find Maxwell there. In a way she hoped she would not find him there, for then her search could continue, but in another way it would be better not to be too long. What would Nurse say to her when she got back? "Now then, Miss Lazybones, what do you think you're paid for? Standing round in the garden looking pretty? Trying to attract some man's attention, though I've warned you often enough about men."

There were cobwebs embroidering the shrubs, and the dew rested easily on their lacy patterns. Now and then a drop of dew, heavier than the others, fell to the ground, shaking the tips of the leaves as it dropped, and losing its round clarity in the soft brown earth. Lottie could feel herself moving through the shrubs. She could see herself in her blue frock and her stiff white apron. With a daring gesture she pulled off her cap.

At the door of the first greenhouse, she paused. The slats of the long shelves inside ran on and on, their perspectives narrowing in till the blaze of colour seemed, in the end, to meet. Every plant was in full bloom, with the green foliage of their leaves an almost hidden background for the lovely petals, the blues, the pinks, the flaming reds, the stiff wax-like whites with their proud stippled centres. The shut-in warmth and brightness of the greenhouse intensified the brilliance and profusion of the flowers.

Lottie stood in the doorway. The flowers were so beautiful that she was unable to move. She was held motionless, breathless, beneath their spell.

Then someone entered the greenhouse, coming in at the far end. For a moment Lottie believed it was Maxwell, but as the man turned and glanced at her she saw that it was not Maxwell, but George, one of the younger men who worked about the estate.

He saw her, and came towards her, walking without haste. Every now and then his arm touched an overhanging flower, so that a line of swaying blossoms marked his progress towards her.

Lottie had seen him working in the garden, or out with the horses, but never before had she spoken to him. Because of Nurse's warnings she had never spoken to any of the men about the place. She had come from the Home knowing nothing at all about men, and Nurse's immediate warnings had shocked and frightened her. She still felt sick and bewildered whenever Nurse began to talk to her. Men were horrible!

George continued his leisurely way until he was quite close to her. There was a grave pleasant look on his face. He gazed at Lottie for a moment, then he smiled.

"Can I get you something?" he asked.

Lottie relaxed her tightly-clasped hands. Whatever happened she must hide her nervousness from him.

"I've brought a message from Mrs. Kellaway," she said at last. "She wants the flowers now."

"Now?" He came a little closer to her and Lottie moved away.

"I'll see to it," he said. "You can leave it to me. I'll arrange it all right."

But as Lottie turned to go Maxwell himself appeared. He came quickly across the grass.

"Hello, what's the matter here?" he asked. He slipped his hand under Lottie's arm. "Come in and see the flowers," he said jovially.

Lottie stood still, weak and sick with fear, Maxwell's fingers were pressing so closely and strongly on her arm.

"The flowers for the house are wanted now, straightaway," George said.

Maxwell dropped Lottie's arm. "Come down soon again," he said. "I'll show you the flowers myself. Come some evening."

Released, Lottie fled across the grass and up between the flower-beds, in through the side entrance and up the stairs. Outside the nursery door she met Irene. Irene was carrying a tray laden with the nursery's breakfast.

"Been taking a stroll?" Irene inquired, pleasantly.

Inside the nursery Nurse regarded her sourly. The nursery was a big room, very sunny. There were curtains sprigged with flowers and lined with a soft pink material that had faded a little. There was a low black dado around the creamy-pink walls, and a roll-edged narrow shelf held a lot of the children's toys. The baby, in a little white smock, was sitting on a rug on the floor. He regarded Lottie with a deep solemn gaze. Isobel was busy in a corner. The nursery was full of pleasant brightness and cleanliness. Lottie began to breath easily again. She was safe in here.

And outside was the garden, and the soft cool grass, and the mist rolling away from the smooth sand to be caught up by the sunlight, and, beneath the mist, the placid sea waiting to be lit by the sun's rays.

❀

II

Maggie knelt before the kitchen fire. She hoped that, by the set of her shoulders and the very look of her neck, Cook would know that she was thinking about her. And about this kitchen range, too. It was a black monster! It was always dragging her to pieces. She was always cleaning it, and the amount of coal it used was cruel. What did Cook think her back was made of? Well, she was flesh and blood like anyone else, her body was the same as Cook's own, only less weighty, thank God!

The sun was shining when she went out to scrub the wide circular stone steps leading up to the front door. The steps were a warm soft pinkish colour. When she splashed the first drops of water on them the pink glowed with a deep liquid hue, and the soap frothed like the foam of little white waves.

It was going to be a very hot day. She could feel the sunlight beating down on the small of her back and reaching her knees as she knelt on the warm stone.

Now and then Maggie paused to look at the garden. The grass was a soft bright green and the flowers looked fresh and new, it was still so early in the morning.

She turned quickly to her scrubbing when Maxwell came up the drive. Maggie's face flushed as he walked close up to the flower-beds nearest to the steps. She bent over her work, swinging her scrubbing-brush—up and down. She hated kneeling there with a man like Maxwell watching her movements. She felt helpless and undignified beneath his gaze, and yet what could she do? She pushed her thick black hair away from her forehead which was damp and hot.

Maxwell came nearer. "Hullo, you're pretty hard at work this morning, aren't you?" he said.

Maggie squeezed out her flannel with a long slow movement, resting the thumb of her right hand firmly on the coarse stuff. This was not the first time Maxwell had come up the drive at this time of the morning, and spoken to her. Sometimes she was half afraid of him, especially when he came close to her, bracing himself backwards and forwards on his thick legs, his hands thrust into his pockets.

"Always working hard—aren't you?" he said again.

Maggie tossed back her head. "The same as you," she answered pertly.

The glint of a smile shone in his eyes. "I work pretty hard, too. Come down to the potting-sheds some evening and I'll show you what I do. Why don't you?"

Maggie sat back on her heels and glanced at him. She knew pretty well what a man of his type was after, but she could take care of herself all right. Or could she? Her arms fell to her sides. Cook hated her and the other servants, except Irene, ignored her and so the obvious admiration in Maxwell's eyes was dangerous, because it made such an appeal to her. Still, it was a change after Cook's 'You're only a bit of dirt' attitude. Supposing she went down to the potting-sheds some evening and talked to him for a bit? A little flirtation of this kind would help to restore her self-respect, for Cook saw to it that she had not much of that left by the end of the day.

"Come on—come to-night," Maxwell bent nearer, his voice coaxing. "I'll pick you some flowers! I know the very kind for a handsome girl like you."

The colour swept up over Maggie's warm cheeks, and meeting his glance she began to laugh. She laughed even when his gaze left her face and passed down over her strong white neck and the close-fitting bib of her apron that lay firmly against her breasts.

When he had gone she finished the steps in a leisurely way, sweeping the grey flannel before her in wide easy sweeps that brought the whole of the upper part of her body into play. She felt free and light in herself. Liberated by the new consciousness that her body was young and attractive. There was a heady warmth in the sunshine. When she was finished she stood at the foot of the steps. Her bucket pressed lightly against her knees and her thumb rested in the little inverted runnel of the curved handle. It had that soft cool greasy feel that belongs to cast-iron pails of its type. She looked around the garden, admiring the flowers.

She felt almost dizzy now. It was standing up after so much bending down. But it was not only that, it was the sun and the look of the flowers and grass and trees around her, and this new sense of freedom running all through her. A little bit of admiration—that's what was making her feel so different, like a human being once more.

The inside of the house was dark compared with the sunshine outside. The steps were half-dry already. The dried bits looked very hot, but the wet bits were cool, the colour of them still liquid and deep. The clock in the hall chimed the hour. Maggie liked the sound of that clock. It had a rich full chime, and the echo of it made the hall seem twice as big as it really was.

Cook and Irene were already at breakfast when she entered the kitchen.

"You're always one for a laugh," Cook was saying. Irene threw back her head and laughed again.

"Well, you might as well keep smiling," she said.

"That's what I always say—if you can manage to do it. It isn't always those who need it most who get the chance."

"No, I suppose not," Irene agreed.

Maggie sat down as far away from Cook as possible. Cold pickled pork for breakfast, and the fat end left for her as usual. Oh, well, what did it matter, plenty of mustard took the greasy taste away and a cup of strong sweet tea was a help, too. Presently the door opened, and Jenner, the parlour-maid, came in. Maggie went on with her breakfast. Nobody spoke to her. When they were all finished it would be her job to clear away and wash-up with Cook nagging at her, and the bits of pickled pork floating dismally in the water.

III

Lottie always made Isobel's bed first. Fine linen sheets for the little girls, and they had the smooth cold feel of running water when she spread her hands over them. Mrs. Kellaway was very particular about the children's beds. The bed linen was always being changed, even though it was hardly crumpled. As if Isobel's soft little body, fresh from her bath, could soil anything!

Now for Nurse's bedroom. That was a different matter. Lottie could not loose herself in the blue and white prettiness of the cradle while Nurse's bed lay open beside her. Touching it was like touching Nurse in her nightgown. Not that she ever had touched Nurse like that, but every morning it was her duty to smooth out the tepid, crumpled sheets, and, in a way, that was like touching Nurse. The bedspread at least was cool and impersonal. Now she could turn to the baby's cot. Its delicate frills ran over her fingers as she tucked in the blankets.

"Lottie!"

Isobel was at her side.

"Don't crush the frills, Isobel, dear."

"When are we going down to the beach?"

"Soon now."

"Hurry up, Lottie."

"Oh, yes." There, the pillow was in its place. The soft pale blue blankets, the little satin quilt. Oh, it was lovely.

"Now, then ..." Isobel clung to her, trying to suit her steps to Lottie's. Out in the corridor Mr. Kellaway was passing down. Lottie flattened herself against the wall. She must never be disrespectful, she must always stand still and make herself as small as possible when the master of the house went by.

But Isobel was his own flesh and blood. She could stand before him balancing herself with delicately sturdy legs right in his way.

"Hullo, Daddy!"

He put out his hand and ruffled her head. "Hullo, Monkey!"

Then he turned and looked gravely at Lottie. It was a mutely questioning gaze, intent yet entirely impersonal. She felt the blood coursing up over her face, and she hated it.

"Do you like the sea, Lottie?" He spoke in a kindly voice.

"Oh, Lottie loves it," Isobel answered negligently.

That saved Lottie. She was able to smile a little in answer to his smile.

With Isobel still clinging around her she reached the nursery door. Nurse was at it again—making a great fuss about everything, bustling about and ready to send her off on a dozen errands at once, with enough instructions about each to confuse anyone. And something else was the matter, too.

"Lottie—oh there you are! I wondered when you were coming back—can't you ever hurry over the beds? And by the way—what's happened to the milk? When did you spill it?"

"Spill it?"

"Oh, perhaps it wasn't spilt—perhaps it was … Anyhow, I'm sure a good half-pint has gone. I thought perhaps you could tell me where?"

It was difficult to know which way to turn when Nurse got at her like this.

But at last she was ready to take the children out. This was one of the good moments of the day. Going out into the sunlight with the little girls. Isobel and Anne darting ahead, their straight little bodies running so lightly and easily amongst the flowers. The sunshine closed around Lottie and she felt the shadow from the brim of her hat lying darkly across the tip of her nose. Her apron strings were close around her waist, and she was conscious of the criss-cross of them over her shoulders. The blue of her frock was very blue in the sunlight, and her stiff white apron puckered out a bit with every step. There was a density of sunlight over the garden, the flowers stood still in it. She was carrying a basket with some towels for drying the children's feet, and Nurse's sewing. Nurse was a wonderful needlewoman.

The children were still a little way ahead of her when they passed through the belt of trees that sheltered the garden from the beach. The trees were tall firs, rugged and bent a little from the sea-wind. They leant over the grass skirts of the garden and tossed their ragged plumes like the manes of tired ancient chargers. There were patches of undergrowth between the trees but mostly it was long coarse grass lying over as if flattened by the wind. Standing in the darkness of the trees Lottie looked out at the brilliance of the sea and the million faint shimmerings of the white sand.

Isobel could never resist the fir cones that lay scattered about amongst the tufts of grass. She had to fill her hands and pockets full of them, and later she would place them in little heaps on the sand and forget them. She was busy at it now, her dark wavy hair sweeping down around her face as she bent over, her short pink frock frilling out about her brief knickers. Her ankles were round and soft, where the knee joint came was a delicate creamy white. When she stood up her hair fell back and tumbled widely away from her forehead. She held the cones in her hand and looked at them with deep yet brief satisfaction.

"Here, Lottie, put these in your basket."

"Careful—mind the sewing!"

"Can I put them in your pocket, then?"

The pocket in Lottie's clean starched apron had not been used before, and it pulled open with a crackling sound as Isobel's impatient hand plunged down into it.

"Don't lose them, Lottie."

Lottie wondered what Nurse would say if she saw all those brown cones in her clean pocket. But they were clean, woody things, and anyhow Nurse was not here yet. For the moment she and the children were free from Nurse.

Once on the sand Anne sat down and pulled off her shoes. Lottie knelt and helped Isobel to unbutton hers.

"Why don't you take off yours, too, Lottie?"

"Later."

Isobel darted away over the sand, running on and on towards the sea. She was running on tiptoe, her arms spread out. She stopped at the water's edge and waited for Lottie to come up, her eyes fixed on the little waves that swept so smoothly, so tantalizingly up the flat sand.

"It's tickling my toes." Isobel squirmed her toes about in the damp sand. "It is cool, Lottie."

"Yes, I'm sure it is, darling," Lottie tried to put such tenderness into her voice that Isobel would realize her love.

"Take off your shoes and stockings now."

"Yes, I will."

Lottie sat down in the sand and drew off her black shoes and stockings. When her feet were liberated she realized what a dreadful weight her shoes had been. They were not really very heavy, but the day's warmth exaggerated the sense of freedom that being bare-legged gave to her. When she stood up her gingham frock beat coolly against her knees, and she felt fresh and light.

"Look—look here's George with the horses!" Anne called.

Lottie shaded her eyes. Two horses were coming down towards the sea. Anne rushed wildly along the wet sand to meet them, Isobel behind her. Lottie followed. But they had not far to go. The horses came prancing through the shallow waves, and George wheeled them to face the sea just before he reached the children. The animals looked dark and beautiful and yet alien against the sea and sky. With their swishing tails and tossed-back heads they dominated and enhanced everything.

Isobel, full of joy and delighted fear, clung round Lottie's skirts. Smiling at them, George dismounted and led the horses close up to them.

"Ever ridden a horse?"

Lottie shook her head. She felt unlike herself standing there by the sea with the horses close to her and George smiling down at her like this. She felt happy and natural. She met his glance for a moment, then turned away. When she looked at him again his eyes were still on her.

"I'm learning to ride," said Anne. "You couldn't ride a horse, Lottie!"

"I'm learning, too," Isobel put in joyously.

"Like a ride now?" George asked.

Anne jumped forward, but Isobel hung back, yet Lottie knew that she was longing to go, longing to be caught up and taken for a ride through the sea. But what would Nurse say to this? No, it wouldn't do. She couldn't let them go.

"I don't think—there's Nurse, you know. Another time, Anne, when we've asked Nurse. To-morrow, perhaps."

"I won't be down here to-morrow," George said regretfully. "Never mind."

"I want to go now."

"So do I," said Isobel.

"Well, just for a moment, then. Only a moment," Lottie looked at George for help. He nodded reassuringly.

"I'll take you both together." He swung Anne up into the air and placed her on the horse, while Lottie came close with Isobel. Isobel was tense and silent, her body shaking with excitement.

"One—two—three," Lottie began, "jump now!"

George walked the horse slowly along the sea's edge, and then he broke into a gentle trot. The little girls rose and fell lightly, their hair blown away from their faces. Coming back to Lottie Isobel's face was white with joy and excitement. The horses came clip-clopping along the wet sand, and the water slipped quickly into the holes made by their hooves.

Reining in, George helped the children to alight. Anne slipped easily into his arms. When it was Isobel's turn her hands clung tightly round his neck, and even when she was firmly placed on the ground she still clung to him. He laughed good-naturedly. Lottie came and stood close to the little girl, and Isobel, satisfied by Lottie's closeness, released George.

"You're down now, darling. You're quite safe," Lottie said.

Lottie pressed the child close to her skirts, and looked at George. One of the horses shook its head and the reins jingled loudly.

"Well, I must be off!" George mounted again.

Lottie and the children stepped back, and the horses pranced and wheeled, and then stretched out in a gallop along the sand.

"Wasn't that lovely!" Isobel sighed.

Nurse looked cross when she arrived down with the baby.

"Lottie, move the rug over this way—no, this way, I said, to the left—no. I said left—your right, then. Really. … And now where's my sewing? I hope the children haven't been playing with it. And that reminds me, Lottie, Mrs. Bartley has just found the baby's spoon at the back of that chest of drawers. That's an extraordinary place for a spoon to be! You must be more careful in future."

"Yes, Nurse."

"And it was dirty, too. Sticky. I must say I was surprised. … Look at those children, Lottie, Anne's going out much too far."

"Yes, Nurse."

With the tide receding as it was now a child could walk a long distance in perfect safety out towards the sand bank which was already appearing beneath the water. Little waves were breaking over an invisible shore and rolling in towards the land. In another hour or less there would be a backbone of sand spreading right across the bay, and between it and the shore a sheet of water not more than two feet deep at its fullest spot. It was a lovely safe place for the children, and Anne was in no danger.

Besides, Lottie was watching her carefully. Lottie was always a little bit nervous and alert when the children were paddling. She watched them, ready at any moment to fling herself into the sea to rescue them if the need arose! She could sense this feeling in her backbone, a cold, happy, mysterious, inevitable feeling, the kind that drove her out of bed, shaking, the pupils of her eyes enlarged against the darkness, if she heard unaccountable noises coming from the hidden corners of the bedroom.

Nurse jerked the baby's white linen hat farther over his eyes. He put up his hands to catch at her wrist and his whole body rocked. His eyes crinkled up with fun. He swayed over till his hands came down flatly on the rug and he appeared to be all hat and full white round behind. He did not wear napkins in the daytime now, but there was a comfortable looseness about his pants that made that part of him look out of proportion in a childish way.

Lottie straightened him. Everywhere she touched him his body yielded helplessly to her hands. He could be stiff enough if he wanted to, but now he was playing. He caught hold of the bib of her apron and held himself upright.

"Would he like a little paddle, Nurse?"

Nurse was sewing rapidly. "Yes, but don't get his frock wet."

Isobel came running up to watch. Lottie folded the baby's smock up under his armpits, and held him so that his feet touched the sand lightly. His feet threshed away at the waves.

"Darling!" breathed Isobel rapturously.

IV

Really, in a dashing way, of course, Maxwell, that head-gardener of the Kellaways, was a very fine-looking man! Hessie Price glanced quickly around the Kellaways' garden. He was a bit stocky, perhaps, but so often stocky men were very powerful, and a powerful man appealed to something inside a woman's heart—something—but she'd be plunging herself back into the primitive past if she went on with this thought, and so many primitive things were not quite nice. Not quite lady-like, and nowadays a girl had not much to cling on to but her lady-likeness. As Mother was always saying it was a definite asset to be a lady. Really, the modern girls made Mother shudder, and quite rightly, too. Mother certainly was a real lady—a real gentlewoman. It was a pity that Father had not been, well, just as much a gentleman as Mother was a gentlelady.

Still, poor Father was dead and one always spoke reverently about the dead. The dead have no faults—at least a gentlewoman's dead have none. She'd heard dreadful people, common people, criticizing their dear departed ones, but Mother always put her handkerchief up to her eyes when Father's name was mentioned. When there were visitors to tea and Hilda or she saw Mother fumbling for her handkerchief they knew what she was going to say, and even if they were being chatty and laughing a little it gave them time to sober down before Mother began the details of dear Father's passing away.

The Kellaways' head-gardener was still following them. She had better walk slowly and keep Mabel and Flossie well in to one side of the path. After all, it was not their own garden. It was very kind of Mrs. Kellaway to give them permission to come and play on the Kellaways' private beach, and to take this short cut through their grounds.

"Keep in, Flossie! Mabel, don't touch the flowers."

She could not help saying that in a loud kind voice so that the gardener would realize how careful she was not to let the children abuse this privilege.

"Why must we keep in, Miss Price?"

"To let—to let this," well, she could not very well say "gentleman" about a head-gardener, and yet she did not wish to use a word that would sound unrefined—so she compromised tactfully. "To let other people pass, my dear."

Perhaps Maxwell, in the course of a respectful conversation about the garden with Mr. Kellaway, would mention that the little rectory children were very well behaved whenever they came through the grounds, and Mr. Kellaway, who looked so distinguished, would nod his head and say, "Ah, yes, that's the way they've been brought up. That governess of theirs is such a refined lady." Or, no, would he say 'refined'? It would be nice if he would, for it was still a beautiful word when properly used. And then perhaps Mr. Kellaway would repeat the conversation to Mrs. Kellaway, and Mrs. Kellaway might look thoughtful and say, "Well …" now what did she call Mr. Kellaway—his name was Leonard? "Well, Leonard, we'll soon be wanting a governess for Anne and Isobel—I wonder …"

Not that she'd like to desert poor dear Mrs. Benson who relied on her so much, but to be employed by the Kellaways—

That gardener certainly was a powerful-looking man, a bit florid perhaps, but then his work kept him out in the open air so much. She had heard he was a very clever gardener. That was to be expected, if he was head-gardener of the Kellaways' place. Gardening was a passion with Mr. Kellaway and he had not to think about money. They said he paid his head-gardener a ridiculously large salary—a common man like that, too! Mr. and Mrs. Benson had been discussing it at lunch-time the other day.

"Far more than one of God's gardeners gets," Mrs. Benson had said in that beautiful resigned way of hers, and fortunately she, Hessie Price, had been able to murmur, very appositely, something about God rewarding his servants in the gardens of the hereafter. She'd been sorry that Mr. Benson had moved away as she spoke, but Mrs. Benson had pressed her hand gently. It was nice to be able to say suitable things. She could not always do it, but there were times when the right phrases just popped into her head.

Certainly that powerful-looking gardener kept these gardens in a beautiful condition. The flowers were wonderful and the lawns really did look like green velvet. So different from the rectory lawn, although she often stayed late in the evenings helping Mrs. Benson to cut the grass. Pushing the noisy lawn-mower made her very hot but she looked her best when she was warm. Her circulation was none too good but once she got flushed her cheeks went a really pretty pink—wild rose pink, Hilda had once said!—and with her hair rather prettily ruffled, negligently ruffled, she looked, well—she'd seen Mr. Benson gazing at her the other night. Of course she had pretended not to notice his glance, she'd just gone on laughing and talking quite gaily and easily with Jackie. That was one good thing about her, she always got on well with boys of Jackie's age—schoolboys. She treated them in a free, easy, chummy manner, while doing her best to influence them nicely. After all, an older woman could do a lot in a chummy way to uplift a boy's—well, moral tone. Talk about patriotism, and their mother, "honour your mother and father," etc., and about "playing the game." She knew Mrs. Benson was glad to have her there during Jackie's holidays. She thought her a good influence. That was nice.

They were crossing the open end of the Kellaways' garden now, and had a full view of the house. It did not look very much from the front, just a long low white-faced building, a sort of farmhouse affair, but inside was a different matter. She never missed an opportunity of sighing with rapture at all the beautiful old woodwork inside the house. Really, it was impressive. Of course everyone knew the Kellaways had perfect taste, but for that—well you might consider so many bits of glass and silver and cushions and flowers just a little bit—what was the word?—'flamboyant', but then she'd heard it said that Mrs. Kellaway liked luxurious things about her. Perhaps that explained it. Mr. Kellaway—Leonard—looked as though austerity would be more congenial to him, but he was so much in love with his pretty little wife that he let her fill the house with as many gew-gaws as she liked.

That was rather beautiful, wasn't it? The strong intellectual, rather austere man, abandoning his wishes to please the lovely frail woman who bore his name and was his to protect. Indulgent—yes, strong and indulgent.

"Walk hand in hand, children!"

It was a pity Mabel and Flossie had such stodgy little legs. Yes, the beautiful butterfly safe in the sweet shelter of her husband's home. "My dear, all I want is your beauty. Just be happy and beautiful, my dove." That was poetry almost. Well—now, would Mr. Kellaway talk like that? Those quiet reserved-looking men were often the most poetical and yes, passionate, when they were alone with their beautiful wives.

Ah, here was Mrs. Kellaway herself. What a good thing the children were walking hand in hand. Surely Mrs. Kellaway would notice that— "How well your little charges behave."

"Good morning, Miss Price."

"Good morning, Mrs. Kellaway. Mabel dear, Flossie ..." That was the way to speak to children, gently, kindly.

"Hullo, children—don't you want to run across the grass?"

Well now—really! But she was quick to take a hint.

"Oh, may they, Mrs. Kellaway, really? Their mummy and I thought— but of course—if you give permission. Mabel dear, would you like a scamper?"

Well, why wouldn't they run? They were such stupid little things, more like their father than Mrs. Benson—though everyone said his sermons were very clever. Flossie took an uncertain step or two on the grass and then stood still, her mouth open a little.

Mrs. Kellaway laughed. "What obedient children they are!"

Hessie smiled again. This was better. "Yes, aren't they?" she exclaimed. "Their mother and I—you see, obedience is one of Mrs. Benson's ideals, mine too, sweet obedience. Talk to the children gently, point out things, you know, little stories with morals in them. ..."

Perhaps that was said a little gushingly, but she did want Mrs. Kellaway to get a good idea of her principles about a child's upbringing. Of course she would hate leaving dear Mrs. Benson, but to be employed by the Kellaways. ... And the little Kellaway girls were—were so different from Mabel and Flossie. Anne was such a slim aristocratic child, Isobel too, but she seemed a vaguer type, not quite so easy to get on with, perhaps. She would need tactful handling. "Would you like to hear a fairy story,

Isobel dear? All about a little girl who was sweet and good and very, very obedient and so one day the fairies …"

Really being a governess was like having a mission in life. A sort of sacred mission. You could make a child's mind such a beautiful garden. Child psychology was such a deep, interesting subject, so profound.

Mrs. Kellaway had taken Flossie round to the other side of a cluster of flowering shrubs, and was showing her some splendid blossoms. Ought she, Hessie, to go round, also? Or would that be pushing herself forward too much?

"Well, good-bye, Miss Price. I'm so glad you're taking the children to the beach. Don't hesitate to bring them down every fine day, and use these gardens as much as you like."

Mrs. Kellaway and Flossie—why must the child gape like that?—were out on the path again.

"Really, that is kind of you, Mrs. Kellaway. The children do love playing on the sand."

"And we've monopolized all of it, haven't we?"

"Oh, no—no!" Mrs. Kellaway mustn't think she meant anything like that! "There's the cove by the harbour, you know, but the town children use that so much, and Mrs. Benson, well, you have to be so particular about children, haven't you …?" that was the sort of thing she could say with that little shrug that Hilda always said was so French. Expressive, too. Mrs. Kellaway caught her meaning at once.

"Well, I mustn't keep them from the beach any longer. Good-bye. Nurse and the children are down there now."

"Oh, are they? That's lovely! Mabel, Flossie—Mrs. Kellaway's little girls are down on the beach already! Let's scamper down to them!"

That ended the encounter on a nice easy gay little note. Be a child with the children sometimes—without loss of dignity, of course. But why couldn't Mabel and Flossie run after her?

"Run, children, run!"

Ah, there was that gardener again! Evidently he had been there all the time. Just hovering about amongst those shrubs. Well, really now, and he was looking at her, too. Still, he wasn't a gentleman. …

"Come along, children—who'll be down to the water first?"

It was a very hot drag across the sand to the sea.

"Good morning, Nurse!"

"Oh, is that you, Miss Price?"

"Yes! How hot it is!"

"I like the heat myself. It's always suited me."

"Yes—yes. I like it, too. Up to a point, that is!" Hessie sat down on the small camp stool she always carried. What a big lumpy woman the Kellaways' nurse was, and not very intelligent either, and certainly not a lady nurse. Still, a nurse was a sort of upper servant whom you could treat with a pleasant confiding familiarity.

"My dear old Nannie!" She and Hilda had had long talks as to whether it would be really right and truthful to refer like that to the "help" who had come in to assist dear Mother in the house when they were little, and they had come to the conclusion that it was all right, and really quite truthful. "After all, she did dress and wash us." What a pity Hilda hadn't said 'bath us.' 'Washing' gave the Saturday night bath in the round bath before the kitchen fire really unnecessary prominence.

Mabel and Flossie were sitting down pulling off their square-toed black shoes. Their gingham frocks looked clumsy compared with the dresses the little Kellaways were wearing. And, yes, Mabel's frock did droop at one side, though she and Mrs. Benson had been so sure it was straight. When Isobel Kellaway bent over she seemed all frills and freshness—not that she was wearing frills really, but she was the sort of child who gave you the impression that everything about her was clean and sweet. Besides everyone knew the way Mrs. Kellaway dressed the children. Silks and laces and white ribbons run in their underclothes. Nurse had shown her some of the baby's layette eight months ago, and really she'd gone home and told Mother and Hilda that it was wicked. …

"With so many poor dear little children needing clothes," Hilda had said, smiling gently. It was a pity Hilda's teeth were so prominent.

Nurse did not seem very talkative this morning. Well, that did not matter, she was not feeling so very sprightly herself. It was a bit unsettling passing through the Kellaways' grounds. It made the little house in

Salisbury Road seem mean, and to see the little Kellaway children so beautifully dressed did not seem quite fair—did it?—when she and Hilda had to struggle so hard for even the few underclothes they had. After all that treasured petticoat of Hilda's was only artificial silk, and even their winter vests were a cotton mixture. It was cheaper to buy a cotton mixture for there was less risk of shrinkage then. Cheap wool shrank so dreadfully.

Flossie and Isobel seemed to be getting on very well together, digging away like that in the sand. She would be able to tell Mrs. Benson all about the pretty way they had played together. It would make a nice topic of conversation at lunch-time. Even Mr. Benson always looked interested when the Kellaways were mentioned.

How hot the sun was! It made her head ache. Supposing she had to have glasses after all? Would she—would she look intellectual in glasses or would they merely accentuate the long thin line of her nose?

"It'll soon be lunch-time," Nurse said, gathering her sewing together in her lap, and resting her hands on it.

"Lunch-time? Oh, yes, I suppose so!" Hessie acquiesced.

That meant boiled beef, and carrots with the cores still hard, and flakes of onions, and the opaque jelly from the dissolved suet dumplings floating in the gravy, and Mrs. Benson, with the tip of her nose an agitated pink, and Mr. Benson, with his podgy hands, and his cheeks that seemed to fold in reverently about the curves of his mouth as he said grace.

Neither Nurse nor Hessie Price took any notice of Lottie. But Lottie was used to that. Standing with the baby in her arms she looked left and right along the line of the shore. At both ends of the little bay there was a cluster of rocks and the land rose up behind them. There were fields at the top, wide fields flaunting their sloping sides of grass or bracken against the restless water below. But there was no sign anywhere of George and the horses. Lottie sighed.

Chapter Two

I

"I was just going to lock up," Cook said sourly. Maggie, coming in through the kitchen door, gave her a long straight look. Maggie's eyes were dark and enormous. She stood in the middle of the kitchen and something of the coolness of the night outside still clung about her. She felt as if she had only that minute stepped out of a pool whose water, crystal clear, reflected faithfully the high black sky. The night outside was very dark, and richly scented. Maggie looked around the kitchen and felt herself to be unfamiliar with everything there. The night had severed her connexion with the sink, the table, the floor, even with Cook. She remained a new Maggie Anderson, poised lightly in the middle of the kitchen, looking round at a strange scene.

"Tut-tut!" said Cook, in an effort to assert herself, "if you want to mix yourself some cocoa, hurry up and do it. Smart now. I can't stay up all night."

Maggie turned lightly and went out of the kitchen. Her body, still companioned by the cool black night, ignored the passage which to-morrow it would scrub.

"Impudence!" said Cook loudly, and snapped off the kitchen light.

Upstairs, Maggie sat down on the side of her bed. Well, a kiss or two was no harm, was it? And he had not been hard to manage on the whole. So long as a girl respected herself she was all right, and after Cook's 'You're only a bit of dirt' attitude, an evening of that kind did increase her self-respect. It made her imagine that she was someone again.

Feeling, at the moment, instinctively akin to the darkness, she put out the light and got into bed. She had made it badly that morning but a properly made bed was no real necessity to her in her present mood. A heave or two and there were the clothes heaping down over the side of her shoulders, and held in firmly by the pressure of her hip.

The curtain was not drawn across the window. She could recognize the black square of it by the greater limpidity and purity of the darkness there. In the intense silence she could hear the sea and the soothing noise of the small waves rushing in over the sand.

II

Hessie Price was on her way home from the rectory.

Supposing Mr. Saul, Mr. Benson's curate, had said, just as she was leaving the house, "I'm going back to the town, Miss Price, may I accompany you?"

"Why, I'd be charmed!"

And now they might be walking along together. He might be saying:

"What a lovely evening it is, the moon behind those trees—hanging in the evening sky. Can you see it?"

He might even put out his hand and draw her a little closer to him. His hand was so white and strong-looking coming from the black of his clergyman's coat-sleeve.

"How beautiful it is!"

"Ah, yes, beauty everywhere this evening," and his hand, thin, white, yet so masculine, lingering on her arm.

Oh, God, what was the matter with her these days? It was Hilda's fault. Hilda with her blushes and that funny bright look in her eyes, and that shrill little note in her voice, if she had come home from the office with Albert Baker. And she, Hessie, was prettier than Hilda, everyone said so always. Had not she once heard Mr. Saul call her 'the better-looking Miss Price?' Mr. Saul, himself, had said that!

Hessie was walking beneath the trees in the wood behind the Kellaways' house, for this was a short cut from the rectory to the town. There was a cart track here that led to the back gardens, but she was alone on the footpath now. It was a very hot still evening. She was wearing her costume coat open and her thinnest blouse. It was almost too hot to hurry, but she was late going home and she knew Hilda wanted to go out to a free lecture this evening. Mr. Baker was going to the lecture, too. That was why Hilda was so eager not to miss it. But Mr. Saul had been up at the rectory seeing Mr. Benson about something and—no, strictly speaking she had not lingered there on purpose, Mrs. Benson had needed her, and it was not her fault if Mrs. Benson had come to the front door and kept her there chatting for a few minutes. But the study door had not opened at all, and she had had to go at last. She had thought she had heard men's voices when she was half-way down the drive, but she had not liked to turn back then. Besides, there was Hilda waiting at home, growing more and more impatient with every minute that passed.

It was rather a pity, though. Perhaps if Mr. Saul had known she was waiting he would have hurried through his business with Mr. Benson. He had often before walked home with her from church, especially after week-night services, and several times he had come in and sat in the parlour chatting with Mother, and there was always something—something special in his manner when she showed him to the door. And the way he pressed her hand!

It was not very dark yet, but inside the wood the tree-tops were close overhead, and there were mounds of thick undergrowth too, that broke the flat ground with their weird close-lying shapes.

The road leading from the end of the Kellaways' property to the town was treeless on the sea side. A stone wall ran along it, and then came the first dingy streets of the town. Holly Street, Laburnum Row. What was there to suggest laburnum about this ugly squalid terrace?

By the Congregational Chapel someone hailed her. "Good night, Miss Price." Who was it? Oh, yes, it was Ella Johnson, and that tall girl who sometimes came to church with her. She did not know her name.

"Oh, good night, Ella," she answered brightly.

The two figures melted away down Holly Street. A little further on she ran into Rosie Bates. The Bates sisters! The Price sisters! Oh, no one could talk about Hilda and her as they talked about Rosie and Lily Bates. She and Hilda were dignified girls, cheerful, too, of course, but Rosie Bates was just ridiculous. A woman should behave with a certain amount of reserve once she was forty.

"Nice night, Hessie." Rosie Bates herself came suddenly out of a doorway. "Out seeing the shops?"

The shops? Hessie flushed. What did Rosie mean by that? It had not been her fault if Mr. Spencer, who owned the drapery stores at the corner of the High Street, had been so—so attentive last spring. Seeing her home from the Bible class, and matching the silk for Mother's dress himself. He had taken the piece of material right out of her hand and carried it about the shop, and been so particular. It had been almost embarrassing.

"Have you seen the new Mrs. Spencer yet, Hessie?" Rose asked maliciously.

"Oh, no," she must sound very bright and interested. "But we're so hoping to see her on Sunday. And if Mother's better we're planning a little tea-party soon—"

"Has your mother been ill, then?"

"Well, no—not so very. You see ..."

"I see," Rosie nodded. It wasn't difficult to see right through Hessie Price. "Well, good night, Hessie. I'm sorry your mother hasn't been well. Remember me to her, will you?"

"Thanks, that's very kind of you. Good night."

Hilda was waiting on the doorstep. "Here you are at last! I thought you were never coming."

Well, that was no sort of a greeting after a day spent working in someone else's home.

"Well, I'm here, now. You can start off straight away." She disliked Hilda in this mood. "What's that you've got round your neck?"

A pink scarf? When would poor Hilda realize that pink did not suit her. Blues did not either. She was too sallow. She ought to stick to browns with a dash of orange—that could be very smart.

"Mr. Saul came to see Mother this afternoon," Hilda called up from the street. "He stayed for tea."

Hessie closed the front door firmly. The hall was narrow, with glazed green and orange paper on the walls. This paper had been there for as long as Hessie could remember. It stretched up and up into the dark regions above the narrow steep stairs—on and on, repeating its green and orange flowers right up to the skylight landing at the top of the house, where the water tank gurgled, the worn paint on its sides dropping from flaky blisters. She put her bag and gloves down on the narrow mahogany table with the carved bulbous legs. This was the second time Mr. Saul had called to see Mother when she, Hessie, was out. What could it mean—what did it mean?

"Can't you come in out of there, Hessie? What's delaying you?"

"Coming, Mother. I'll just slip out into the kitchen and see what Hilda's left for supper."

There was a damp sour smell in the kitchen, and the tea-things were stacked in the sink. Hilda had not done a thing. Really, it was too bad. There was not anything much in the larder, either. Stale cheese and a tomato or two. Hessie pondered. She'd have to keep the bacon for breakfast. Was Hilda meeting Mr. Baker to-night? Wouldn't it be awful if Hilda married Mr. Baker? Hilda married! Mr. Baker could afford to give his wife a servant. Mrs. Benson had a servant, too, and as for Mrs. Kellaway—oh, life wasn't fair.

Which one of those cups in the sink would be his? His—her lover's, her husband's—Mother's son-in-law. "My daughter Hessie, her husband's a rector now. He was the curate here when they got married. Oh, yes, very happy. Two dear little ones. … Hilda, pass me those snaps of Hessie and the babies. …"

Well, the kitchen was the best place to cry in. Mother would not come out here, and otherwise the house was empty. And now she would look dreadful, with red eyes and nose, but she could tell Mother that she was not very well. That was true enough. She did feel wretched.

When she went back into the sitting-room, Mother said:

"My goodness, Hessie, what's the matter with your nose to-night?"

This was just what she had expected. She fixed her gaze on one corner of the room. "I've got a headache." Her voice sounded tired and sullen.

"Is that why you were late coming home?"

"Mrs. Benson wanted me. There was a lot to be done."

She hated Mother's way of sniffing. If Mother were not such a real lady she would think …

"Mr. Saul came here this afternoon."

Hessie clenched her hands a little. She was beginning to feel desperate.

"Yes, I know."

"How do you know? Did Hilda …?"

"No, Mr. Saul told me himself. He walked home with me from the rectory." She'd said it! She could not take it back now. The words were swelling in magnitude throughout the room, the walls were pressing outwards before their onslaught. The whole house was not big enough to hold their terrible and increasing volume. Oh, what had she done? She kept her eyes fixed on the fire.

Mother was leaning forward a little, her fingers picking lightly at the shawl thrown over her knees.

"Hessie, dear, how interesting!" her voice was soothing. "Perhaps you went the longer way round?"

"We did. We took the upper road." The words shot from Hessie's mouth, unlicensed by her, utterly unowned by her.

"Well, dear, I'm sure that was very nice. And Mr. Baker walked home with Hilda from the office! Ah, it's what I've always said. Men do like sweet modest girls. Girls like mine."

"I think I'll go and get supper now." She ran out into the kitchen.

So, she was a deliberate liar! And at any moment her deceit might be found out. A long time ago Hilda and she had fixed a cheap mirror close to the sink. They had placed it there after reading the Beauty Hint page in the little weekly magazine they bought between them. A penny a week each. There was a half-lemon, squeezed almost dry, with its skin a mottled brown, placed in the chipped saucer in the bracket beneath the mirror. The notice had said: "Look to your beauty, little wives, keep a mirror above the sink and peep into it while you're washing-up, and smile at yourself now and then—remember a smile is a great beautifier!" They had pinned that bit from the article up, too, but it had flittered away years before, the greasy steam from the washing-up water had proved too much for it.

Sometimes Hilda and she still called each other 'little wife,' as they dried the dishes. It was a small joke between them. Sometimes they got quite hilarious over it, giving each other playful little smacks behind and crying out, "Smile, little wife!" and they had felt—well—almost married, but now—to gaze at herself in that mirror … what did it reveal? What was the matter with her face? Was it crying that had made her look like that? Old—old! With a long thin twisted nose, quite red, and a mouth that sank at the corners, and strands of dull brown hair looping over her forehead. "Both my girls have kept their crowning glory." How Mother loved saying that. But it wasn't true! The heavy bun at the back of her neck was no crowning glory, it was a hideous weight, forcing her head backwards so that she was compelled to gaze into that face in the mirror.

She thrust the strands of hair back from her forehead. But that was worse, for that displayed those great ugly bulges on her temples with the skin drawn shinily over them. What a sight she was, with her red-rimmed staring eyes and ugly forehead. And she was feeling terrible to-night, too. Life was not fair. So many women were beautiful and had glamorous adventures with men. Hilda and she had nothing but their gentility and there was no glamour about that. Still, she must try to think of Grandpa, who had been a real colonel. He was the prop and mainstay of their gentility, and, inadequate as that support sometimes seemed, it was better than nothing. You had to have something to cling onto in moments like this when you had proved yourself a liar—and your lie was one that might be found out.

If she were beautiful, would Mr. Spencer have?—would Mr. Saul have?—no, she was not going to think like that. She had better start cooking Mother's supper.

"Will you have cheese and a piece of toast, or would you like the cheese heated?"

She stood outside the parlour door waiting for Mother's reply. She felt she could not face Mother at that moment.

"Well, you know I like Welsh rarebit!"

"It's bad for you," Hessie made the time-honoured protest mechanically, her thoughts busy elsewhere. How dreadful if Hilda met Mr. Saul to-morrow and mentioned that walk. Hilda might, with that horrible coyness that she seemed to be cultivating these days.

"If you hear me calling in the night you can come in to me!" Was it her imagination or was Mother's voice full of coyness, too? Probably Mother was thinking of her and Mr. Saul coming home together. Walking side by side, her shoulder touching his arm now and then, his hand catching her elbow for a moment's brief emphasis of some deep important point. "Good night, Miss Price, and thank you. I don't know when I have enjoyed a walk so much." "Ah, but the night has been so beautiful for me, too." Dare she look up at him—his eyes were drawing hers, the clasp of his hand was so warm, so comforting, so protective. She could hardly breathe as he came closer. Man and woman created He them—oh, yes, yes. …

Would Hilda feel like that coming home with Mr. Baker to-night? "There's just two years between my daughters. Hessie's my big girl, and Hilda's my big baby girl." What made Mother say things like that? It let everyone know that Hilda was younger than she was, and, until they were told, everyone thought Hilda was the elder. It was not fair, and now if Hilda and Mr. Baker really did—She must not think of it.

Making toast was a great extravagance, because it used so much gas. But the toaster was not quite so extravagant as the geyser. Hilda and she always kept up a little pretence about their daily baths. A daily bath in the blistered bath sunk in its stained wood coffin in the bathroom was impossible, but it was wonderful what could be done with a jug of hot water poured into a bedroom basin. Not that standing with her nightgown tied about various parts of her body, or shivering behind a towel was very satisfactory really. But why sigh for a bathroom and the comfort of unlimited hot water? Sighing would not bring such things nearer, and Hilda and she were proud of the way they kept themselves nice even though they were limited to hot water in the cold privacies of their bedrooms.

“Would you like a game of cribbage, Hessie?” Mrs. Price inquired kindly when supper was over.

“No, thank you, Mother. I think I’ll go to bed early to-night.”

“Ah!” said Mrs. Price profoundly.

But Hessie continued to stare into the fire. She had turned away from the table. She held a cup of tea in her hand and sipped from it occasionally. Her mother’s “Ah!” had seared her deeply. There had been something ripe and—yes, almost horrible, behind that brief exclamation.

“I think I’ll go up now, Mother. Good night.”

Her lie accompanied her upstairs. If her mother or Hilda found out they would never let her forget about it. Never! And to think that all she had lied about to-night might easily have happened! It could all have come about so naturally. She could see it all so clearly. Mr. Saul and herself walking back together, choosing the longer way home, as lovers would. He might even have kissed her. Supposing it had been real?

She began taking off her clothes quickly, and the everyday movements of arranging and tidying them away comforted her a little. Well, even if it had not happened to-night it might easily happen some other day. He was often up at the rectory when it was time for her to go home. Or—she might even ask her mother and Hilda not to mention it to Mr. Saul. Oh, why had not she thought of that before? An exquisite warmth flowed all over her. She felt weak with gratitude at having thought of this way out. “Mr. Saul and I—well, you know, Mother, we enjoyed our walk so much but it was a sort of private enjoyment. It was something just between ourselves. Please don’t mention it to him. Or you either, Hilda.” Oh, she could say that easily! Thank God, she had thought of it in time!

Hessie put out the light and crept into bed. She gave a deep sigh, and stretched out her body in a long movement of unaccustomed relaxation. She felt free and light again and her surroundings were normal and familiar once more.

III

Lottie went down between the flowers slowly. Unconsciously she walked slightly on tip-toe. The flowers spread out in front of her, lines of blossoms and a grass path that converged towards a gap in the trees where the sunset blazed.

Now, could anyone in the world want anything more beautiful than that? The blazing red light against the sky, and the flowers that only assumed their own colourings where the shadows of the taller blossoms slanted down on those below. The sunset was painting one half of the flowers its own red, and the blues and whites and oranges and green stood out in pale clear bodiless colourings on the other side.

Lottie walked through all this with her head thrown back a little. She was still bewildered by her recent scolding from Nurse. In the house the nursery was recovering from turmoil.

"Always losing something—aren't you?" Nurse had stormed. "Well, my lady, you'll just go straight down to the beach after the children are in bed, and go down on your hands and knees in the sand, and don't come back without it."

"Yes, Nurse." She was in such disgrace. The baby's ivory and amber rattle, the baby's greatest joy in life, was missing. Nurse had taken it down to the beach, and she, Lottie, had not brought it back again.

Getting the children to bed had been a difficult business.

"Be a good girl now, Anne. Come, step out of your bath nicely."

"Don't pull me, Lottie. I'm not ready yet."

"Yes, you are. You're all washed!"

"But I'm not clean yet. I don't like being dirty, Lottie."

Isobel was bright and chatty in her bath. "You'll have to lift me out, Lottie. I haven't got any legs. I'm a mermaid. Put your arms well around me.

"That wets me, dearie."

"Oh, but you'll dry again."

"Look sharp now, Lottie. You can't have your time off this evening unless you find that rattle."

"All right, Nurse. Come up out of the sea, Isobel, dear."

"That's correct," Isobel said. "Come up out of the sea, mermaid."

The front of her frock and the bib of her apron were wet from Isobel's little glistening body. The big thick towel ran easily over the child's skin, and then put on the clean nightdress. A clean nightdress every night! Ivory washing satin, thick and cool. At Isobel's age, she, Lottie had been a veteran at the Home. Coarse strong calico changed once a week had been considered good enough for her young body, and the Sister in charge of the bathing had not spared her hand or the towel. Rub away, holding Lottie's wrists up high and scrubbing heartily with the coarse towel on the tender skin of her armpits. Still, Isobel was a little lady. Lottie had been taught all about the differences between little ladies and orphans. Nurse had seen to that.

"Don't cut the bread like that, Lottie. This isn't an Orphanage." "You come from an Institution, Lottie, didn't they teach you there to stand up when your betters came into the room?"

"Yes, Nurse." "No, Nurse." "Thank you, Nurse." Whatever happened she must not be sent back to the Home with a bad report from her very first place. The Authorities disliked that. And really, she liked it here very much. The sea and the gardens and the nursery and the baby's cradle. She might have been sent somewhere much worse.

"Carry me to bed, Lottie."

"Can't you walk, Isobel?"

"I can walk, but I'd rather be carried."

In her arms Isobel was sweet. Her hair was lovely against Lottie's cheek, and her limbs were light and warm. Isobel, who was easily tired, was allowed her supper in bed. A tray with a bowl of soup, or fish and a portion of pudding, and the glass of milk that shook and trembled as Lottie carried the tray from the nursery into the bedroom.

Mrs. Kellaway came down the passage as Lottie reached the door into the little girls' bedroom.

"Isobel in bed, Lottie?"

"Yes, Mrs. Kellaway."

Whenever Mrs. Kellaway came near her Lottie felt as if she were breathing rarer air. She was aware of everything in the room and though some of the objects were dim and distant, though still vitally present, one or two things always stood out exaggeratedly sharp and clear. As if all the light in the room and all her perceptions were focused on those objects. Isobel's tray was holding all her attention now, but, deeply and clearly, in some inner consciousness, she was aware of Mrs. Kellaway sitting beside the child's bed.

"Hungry?" asked Mrs. Kellaway negligently.

"Pretty nearly starving," Isobel said, her eyes gay and bright.

"Darling!" exclaimed Mrs. Kellaway with equal gaiety.

Lottie stood away from the side of the bed. She stood where she could see the group they made in the big wardrobe mirror. Isobel looked so tiny, sitting up in bed, and the mirror presented Mrs. Kellaway at an angle that was scarcely real. Lottie herself was mostly white apron and cap. Her face was lost between the two.

"Lottie—what's delaying you now?" Nurse's voice came through the door.

Lottie jumped a little. A small change crept over Mrs. Kellaway's face.

"I'm coming, Nurse. Isobel, have you got all you want?"

Only Isobel was undisturbed. She nodded slowly.

Lottie went quickly out of the rare bright atmosphere of the bedroom into the sombre passage. The black walls rose to inestimable heights above her. Nurse was fussing about in the nursery, the baby riding serenely on her arm. He was naked except for a vest, and he smiled and grabbed at everything Nurse passed.

"You'd better start tidying away in here, and don't dawdle. It won't be light for more than another hour or so, and you've got to find that rattle."

"Yes, Nurse."

Lottie began her tidying, picking up toys, folding away clothes. The nursery was a sweet place, really. So airy, and clean, and everything smelt of children—a soft, warm, clean smell.

"Shall I go down to the beach now, Nurse?"

"Yes, and mind you find that rattle."

"Yes, Nurse."

What else could she say but "Yes, Nurse"? Though it sounded silly when the issue was really very doubtful. Quite likely the rattle had dropped out of the baby's hand when Nurse carried him across the sand. Lottie had not noticed it at all when she was playing with him. She had not even known that the toy had been brought to the beach, and now Nurse was blaming her because it had not been brought back. Still it was no good saying that to Nurse. It was her duty to accept the blame and to go and search for the rattle, even though it shortened her off-duty hours. She was supposed to be free to-night from the time the children were in bed until ten o'clock.

Not that that mattered anyhow. She had nowhere to spend her leisure time. It was too late to go into the town alone for it would be dark when she came home. She could not bear that long stretch of road, flanked by the low wall and the woods behind it. Those woods made her go cold and sick inside if she had to pass through them alone. They were exquisite in the mornings, or if she walked through them with a companion at night-time. Soon after she had come to work here Nurse had told her about a dreadful thing. A man had done something frightful to a girl in those woods. He had taken her into them one evening, and later on they had found her. ... Men did dreadful things to women—even to their wives. Men were brutes. They were utterly different from women. Would the baby grow up to do awful things to some woman? He was so sweet now. It was all sex, Nurse said, and you'd better watch out for yourself, young woman.

Lottie could never forget the shock and horror she had experienced at Nurse's first hints of the terrible unguessed-of things that went on in the world. "Didn't the Matron at the Home tell you anything at all about anything?" Nurse had inquired. "Well, she ought to have then, letting ignorant girls out into the world is just asking for trouble. You look out for yourself with men—remember they're not women or girls or anything like them."

Mr. Kellaway, Mr. Andrew, they were gentlemen, but all the same they were men, too. Maxwell, the head-gardener, and George, they were men without being gentlemen. Ruthless, terrifying creatures.

Lottie walked lightly along the path, longing to walk on and on for ever between these flowers that were burdened beneath a double colouring—their own and the red of the sunset. The scents from the flowers rose up in soft rich waves, clean and fragrant. She could forget all about men in a garden like this. She could almost go back to her old belief that men were kind, like the doctor and the clergyman who used to come to visit the children at the Home.

And once she was through the gap in the hedge she would have the sea before her.

"Hullo, Lottie."

Mr. Andrew was standing beside some tall rose trees. Why hadn't she seen him there? The red of the sunset had been blinding her with its warm deep glow.

"What's the matter, Lottie?"

"I'm sorry, Mr. Andrew. I didn't see you."

"It was the sun, I expect. It's a jolly sunset to-night."

Now, what was she to do? It was not for her to push past Mr. Andrew. It was her duty to stand still while he passed her. Nurse was very particular-about that. "Stand quite still while the master or mistress or their guests go by, Lottie. Keep your eyes on the ground, don't look up at the gentry."

"Yes, Mr. Andrew."

"Lottie, I believe you like sunsets?" Mr. Andrew was looking at her with the same little smile in his eyes that there had been in Mrs. Kellaway's eyes as she had sat by Isobel's bed.

"Where are you going?"

"To the beach, Mr. Andrew."

"To the beach—at this hour of night?"

"Yes."

"Good Lord—for what?"

"For the baby's rattle. It was lost there this morning."

"No? But really, Lottie? You're sure you're not escaping down to the beach for a—for a … Well, for a sort of skip and dance along the shore? I believe you would, Lottie, if you got the chance!"

He was laughing at her now. She could hear it in his voice and feel it in the glance she was afraid to meet. But she had better say something, provided that she could speak at all! And now the colour was coming up over her cheeks, over her whole body.

Then someone else came down the path. Lottie looked up and saw Mr. Kellaway. What could she do now? Mr. Andrew in front, and Mr. Kellaway behind, and she must stand in between them till one or other of them released her. So she stood aside anxious to make herself as small as possible and to let the two gentlemen walk on together. But it was one thing to flatten herself into obscurity against a passage wall, for, in doing so, she became part of the house itself, a sort of living fixture, but the tall delicate spikes of the flowers behind her were a very different background. She could feel the insubstantiality of the petals and the sunset-coloured air. She was outlined against the blossoms.

And now what was Mr. Andrew doing? He was standing aside for her just as if she were Mrs. Kellaway herself. But could she move now, with both of them looking at her?

"Good hunting," said Mr. Andrew with a little smile that seemed to release her legs for her. She sped down the path and in under the trees to the sea.

At this time of the day the little bay appeared to be widened and lengthened by the sheer quietness of the sea and air. The tide was coming in and the sea was pressing softly and fully against the sand. The little waves at the edges were scarcely more than contented ripples, and the water shone a faint luminous silver.

At the edge of the sea Lottie halted, and spread out her hands a little. She was utterly alone, here by the sea's edge. Behind her was the sand, pale and cool-looking now, and the dark trees that guarded the house.

She drew in a long deep breath. It was heavenly here, so coolly silent, so vast and beautiful with the evening's stillness. Out further from the land the sea grew coloured with a pink that glanced lightly off the glistening water and changed and broke a little with each of the water's smooth, scarcely noticeable, movements.

Well, this would not do. This was not the way to find the baby's toy. The blessed little love! She went down on her hands and knees and began running her fingers over the sand. One of the other children might have trodden it beneath the loose surface. But she could not find it anywhere, though she searched over a large area. And now what would Nurse say to her?

She stood up and brushed the sand out of her apron. She pulled her cap off and shook out her hair. It flew out away from her head, light and fine, like Isobel's. She felt the red of the sunset, paler now, falling on her face and her hair.

An evening like this made her feel very strange. Very lonely. Isobel had her mother and family, Isobel could never be the sort of orphan that she, Lottie, was. That was a good thing, too, for Isobel needed a lot of care of the kind no one could expect to receive in an Orphanage—an Institution—a Home. Sometimes Nurse called it all three!

The sand was darkening slowly now. She could not go back through the trees and into the garden and up to the nursery without one more look at the little bay. There was a faint shadow gathering beneath the trees and spreading towards the sea, but the water itself was still full of light. All the light in the sky seemed to have gone eagerly and trustfully towards the water. It shone against the darkness inland.

Now, who was this coming up behind her? Lottie's heart ceased beating. It could not be Nurse, she would not leave the children! Could it—could it be a man? And what could a man be doing coming up behind her like this? She could not stir, either, nothing on earth would make her turn her head round to face those footsteps. Yet, she must! Whoever or whatever this was, she must face it.

The comforting sight of George made her feel quite weak, he looked so natural and nice! His eyes were smiling.

"Is this your evening off?" he said.

Lottie nodded, unable to speak, her relief from fear was still so great.

"I like you without your cap," George said.

He came and stood close beside her, and thrust his hands into the flap pockets of the breeches he was wearing. He threw back his shoulders a little and looked out to sea, the smile still on his face.

He was so close to her that Lottie could see the fine twill of the flannel shirt he was wearing. His shirtsleeves were rolled up. His arms were very unlike her own, or like those of any of the girls at the Home.

"Beautiful!" he exclaimed quietly, the utmost satisfaction in his voice.

"Yes, it is."

"Do you like it here?"

"Yes, very much."

"Let's go for a little walk together."

"Oh no—no!"

Now—what was the matter with her, for her heart was beating wildly. Thump—thump! Well, even if the sound of it reached the sea and echoed over the sand, she could not help it.

"Oh, come on," he said gently. He took a step forward and Lottie found herself still beside him. Now and then his elbow touched hers. They walked to the sea's edge in silence.

When she got back to the house it was nearly eight o'clock and Nurse was very angry.

"Well, I must say you've taken your own time all right. I suppose you've found half a dozen rattles by now?"

"No, Nurse."

"What do you mean?"

"I couldn't find the rattle anywhere."

Nurse looked at Lottie and her body seemed to grow and swell with indignation. Her bust filled the bib of her apron to breaking point.

"Well, I must say—What sort of a nurse-maid are you? Haven't I enough on my hands without seeing to all the children's toys? Besides, you may not understand such things, but that rattle was an expensive one. Yes—expensive! I know I can't expect you, coming from where you do, to have much knowledge of good things, but all the same—Well, what have you got to say about it?"

"I'm very sorry, Nurse."

Lottie could hear every rustle in Nurse's skirts as she flounced about the room.

"Where did you look?"

"Everywhere."

"So you ought to have—the time you've been out. What were you doing all that time?"

"I was down on the beach."

"Mooning about, I suppose?"

Lottie waited a moment and then stepped back a little. The worst was over—or was it? She never knew with Nurse. No, it wasn't!

"You'd better go straight along and tell Mrs. Kellaway what you've done. I expect she's down in the drawing-room. Go on, now, don't stand there gaping at me."

"But ..."

"You needn't pretend you're deaf because you aren't. You heard me all right."

Lottie stood still, and her eyes blazed suddenly. Go down to the drawing-room and report the loss of the baby's rattle to Mrs. Kellaway herself! She wouldn't do it! But she would have to. She was there to do what Nurse told her to do.

"Haven't you gone yet?" Nurse flounced round again.

Lottie went out slowly. It was generally Nurse who trafficked between the nursery and the drawing-room. Nurse brought the children down there when visitors were present. Lottie had been down there, too, of course, but never for long enough to have had a clear image of the room imprinted on her mind. It was a blur of softness and light and colour, and Mrs. Kellaway's voice, and Isobel's form appearing close to her—a small reality coming from the lovely confusion of the room.

But this was going to be something altogether different. She would not stand inside the door on the legitimate errand of fetching the children. She would not be standing inside the door as someone who had a real and agreeable duty and right to be there. She would be facing the room as a culprit.

She went down the wide shallow stairway slowly. The lights were on in the empty hall. Everything in it shone richly and deeply. The drawing-room door was closed, and it seemed twice its usual height and size. If it had been open a little knocking on it would have been easier, but demanding admittance of that great glowing slab of closed wood was a desperate affair.

Lottie knocked. No answer. Yet she could hear voices talking in there, a man's voice chiefly. She knocked again, and this time they heard her. "Come in."

She opened the door slowly, and faced the room. Mrs. Kellaway was sitting in a big chair, her hands resting lightly on its arms. Mr. Kellaway was there too, and Lottie could see his face clearly. Mr. Andrew and another man were somewhere about the room, as well, but it was impossible to say where. They might have been close to the door or far from it for all that Lottie knew, though she was acutely aware of their presences.

Now that she was here what was she going to do or say? Provided she could do either? They were all looking at her as if she were a ghost. Then Mr. Kellaway turned his head away.

Mrs. Kellaway said "Lottie!" in a pleasant quiet voice.

"If you please, Mrs. Kellaway, the baby's rattle is lost."

"The what?" asked Mr. Kellaway, turning round

Lottie gazed at him. "The baby's rattle, sir."

The silence in the room was intense. Lottie felt herself to be utterly inadequate against it, and yet part of it. They were all staring at her.

"The baby's rattle? Which rattle, Lottie?" Mrs. Kellaway asked in a low amazed voice.

"The amber one he likes so much, Mrs. Kellaway."

"Oh!"

"I'm very sorry."

"But he has so many rattles! Where was it lost?"

"On the beach."

"So you were looking for something then?" Mr. Andrew put in suddenly. His voice was surprised and friendly.

"Yes, Mr. Andrew, but I didn't find it."

"Who told you to come down here and tell me, Lottie?" Mrs. Kellaway said quietly.

"Nurse, Mrs. Kellaway."

"Oh! Was it your fault?"

"I think so."

"Why do you only think so?" Mr. Kellaway asked.

But how could she explain it to them all? What would be the use of it anyhow. Nurse would come down with quite another story, and it was not likely that they would believe her against Nurse. Why should they? The Matron at the Home had never believed the girls against one of the Sisters, and this angle of service under Nurse was only a repetition of Institution life.

Helplessly, she let her eyes meet Mrs. Kellaway's for a moment. Her hands hanging at her sides had gone dead. The background made by the beautiful room was a confused blur, only the human figures stood out with sharp clearness.

"But it doesn't matter, Lottie," Mrs. Kellaway said in the small gay alive way that was so like Isobel's. "Baby has lots of rattles! One more or less won't matter! No—it doesn't matter in the least. It's not anything to worry about, I'm sure."

Mr. Andrew lit a cigarette, and over the yellow flame of his lighter his eyes were fixed on Lottie.

"It's quite all right, Lottie," he assured her.

Lottie left the room slowly. She shut the door behind her with great deliberation. So that was over! Every object in the hall burst on her consciousness with a new and lovely clarity. She saw the dark wood echoing the lights in rich blurred patches, and smooth, stiffly fragile petals of the flowers, the colours glowing for all their delicacy. She threw back her shoulders. She was protected against Nurse's tantrums about the rattle now. Mrs. Kellaway was not cross with her.

She went up the stairs and noiselessly passed the nursery door. Let Nurse think what she liked about that interview. Let her imagine that she had been scolded and had gone to her room to cry. It might please Nurse to think she was upset, and that would help to restore Nurse to a better temper.

Creeping softly into the bedroom Lottie looked at the children's beds. There was no sound from either of them. The many windows were all wide open. It was almost as if they were sleeping out in the night with the walls of the house like the lifted canvas of a tent. She fancied she could almost hear the shifting of the dry sand as the tide crept up over the shore, inch by inch. Twice by the sea's edge she had met George. A feeling of fear and hitherto unexperienced delight shot through her whole body. Lottie felt as if she had gone pale all over, as if the blood had gone from her cheeks and her lips to flow into her breasts, leaving the rest of her unsupported.

She held on to the window-ledge and when she could move again she sat down on the side of her bed. She felt very frightened. At last the striking of a clock warned her that it was long past the time for her to go to fetch the nursery supper. She stood up slowly and patted and smoothed down her crumpled apron, and straightened her cap.

Nurse sniffed when she entered the nursery. Nurse was sewing, she was working away on a pink smock for Isobel. Her needle shimmered in the light as it dived so swiftly in and out of the material.

"Shall I bring up supper now, Nurse?"

"Oh, so there you are? I thought perhaps you'd got lost again. Yes, you can lay the cloth and then go down to the kitchen for the tray. It's very late."

"Yes, Nurse."

The kitchen was deserted but there was talking going on in the maids' sitting-room. Someone had turned on the wireless. Cook and Irene and Jenner were in there. Cook was leaning back with her arms folded over her chest. Her face was relaxed and smiling but it was not really amiable. Irene was sewing at some underwear that was evidently the subject of the laughter. She held it up for a moment and cocked her good-natured face to one side. Lottie could not hear what she said but the laughter burst out anew.

"I've come for the nursery supper, please, Cook."

Cook jerked her head towards the kitchen. "It's ready for you in there."

Irene gave her a broad pleasant smile and put down her sewing. Jenner did not look up at all, she was gazing into the empty fireplace.

Lottie went into the kitchen. It looked very clean and big There was that cool watery smell in the air that comes when floors and boards and tiles are scrubbed every day. Nurse was bad enough, Lottie reflected, standing still in the middle of the empty room, but Cook was worse. Every evening, if the kitchens were empty, she sensed this difference here. With Cook present and the day's activities in full swing the kitchen was a formidable place, but clean and empty with the strong light from the white reflector beating down onto the use-marked boards of the table the room had a severe yet kindly look. The food for the nursery supper lay on a tray with a clean cloth thrown over the cold meat and a fresh jar of pickles for Nurse.

Nurse was still sewing when Lottie got back to the nursery, her head bent forward as she sewed, her thick short neck thrust outwards. Lottie moved about as silently as possible. Everything necessary for nursery use was kept in the big cupboard close by the tiled, shut-in alcove for the sink and taps.

"The table's laid now, Nurse."

When Nurse was seated Lottie took her own place at the opposite side of the table. The meal began in silence. Supper was always a bit of an ordeal for Lottie, sitting alone in the nursery with Nurse deliberately ignoring her, or else talking away on subjects that were horrible to her. Nurse served the cold meat and pushed Lottie's plate across the table.

"Thank you, Nurse."

Nurse snapped the metal band from the pickle-jar and forced off the lid. The suction broke with a little pop. She smelt the pickles with a strenuous intake of breath.

"The pickle fork, Lottie. You always forget something."

Lottie helped herself to a piece of bread, and knew that Nurse was watching the amount of butter she took so she made the piece as small as possible. It spread over her bread in thin isolated patches, but that did not matter. She was not used to much butter anyhow. She had never had any in the Home. The children there got margarine, or "nut butter" as the Matron called it.

The silence went on for so long that Lottie almost forgot her surroundings. She kept seeing the broad hard width of George's chest. It had looked hard and firm beneath his grey shirt. It made her conscious of her own body and for the first time she thought definitely of the hitherto unnoticed whiteness and softness of her breasts and arms. Girls were very different from men. Nurse was correct enough about that.

"Lottie, do you remember your mother?"

Lottie started. "No, Nurse."

"Didn't you ever see her?"

Now what was Nurse getting at? "Not that I can remember."

"Didn't she even come to see you after you'd been put into the Orphanage?"

"I can't remember."

"No, I suppose not. The Matron told Mrs. Kellaway that you were only a baby when you were admitted. Still, it's queer that your mother never came to see you."

Lottie sat silent. Even if it was queer it was not Nurse's business. It was not queer for her. The strangeness, the forlornness were Lottie's own.

"And your father—what about him?"

"I don't know."

"Don't you know anything at all about your parents? Haven't you got any photographs or anything?" Nurse's glance was sharp and penetrating. Lottie kept her eyes on her plate.

"Well, I must say it's pretty queer. Not to know anything about your people. I can't say I'd like it for myself. Still, the world's made up of all sorts and kinds. But just you be careful, young woman. We don't want any history repeating itself here." After a moment Nurse added, "Don't you forget what I've told you about men."

Well, Nurse was off on her favourite topic now. Lottie began to tremble. But she could not stop Nurse once she was started on this subject. The rest of the meal was a monologue from Nurse. Most of it Lottie had heard before, but despite that she could not escape from the fear and horror it gave her.

Chapter Three

I

It was unbearable—unbearable! It was unbelievable and yet dreadfully true! Hilda and Albert Baker were engaged to be married!

Hessie put down the comb—the imitation tortoise-shell comb with the silver back that rattled every time she shook it—and looked at her own reflection in the glass. Yes, she looked the same outwardly, but the night spent staring into the darkness had left a never-to-be-healed scar on her heart. It was not that, in a sense, she grudged Hilda her triumph and happiness—God, no! She wasn't as bad as that, surely? It was just the thought that while she, Hessie, remained a spinster Hilda was actually engaged—would soon be approaching her marriage day, approaching her marriage night—Everything had gone before Hessie's mind in a ruthless progression during the sleepless night. Besides, what would the house be like without Hilda? Their little jokes together shattered by Hilda's legalized intimacy with a man. Oh, yes, Hilda would change completely once she was married. She had changed already. Already there was a hint of condescension in her manner.

"Can I come in, Hessie?"

"Yes, come in."

Hilda entered. She was wearing a brown sateen petticoat, hanging from her waist, and a camisole of woven cotton material. Hilda's hair was still in a plait down her back. She would have looked almost girlish but for the thinness of her neck, and the length of it, and the sharp thin, stiffish look of her legs and ankles.

"Hessie, can you come home in good time to-night? I may have to go out with Albert."

"I'll see what I can do," Hessie said tartly. "After all, it rests more with Mrs. Benson than with me. If she wants me for anything extra I'll have to stay on."

"Why, of course! It's just that Albert wants to take me over to that concert in the church hall."

"The church hall? But I wanted to go to that."

"Oh!"

Hilda began to hum lightly. "Well, if it comes to that I could run down and ask Mrs. Reed to come in and sit with Mother, couldn't I?"

"I suppose so. If Mother must have someone sitting with her."

"Well, it's nicer for her, isn't it? It makes a change for Mrs. Reed, too, and I'll buy in an extra quarter of brawn—or jellied veal—that'll only cost about threepence more. Oh, Hessie, aren't you sick of saving pennies here and there? I am! Albert gives Mrs. Hardcastle nearly three pounds a week just for food alone! Just for the two of them! The daily girl only comes in the mornings. She doesn't eat there. Of course the woman is feathering her own nest like anything. But I'll stop that! Albert is going to give her notice next month. We're just going to have one nice efficient—really efficient—maid, and I'll do all the housekeeping. Albert was saying—"

"Hilda, I'm sorry, but I'm dressing. If you wouldn't mind …"

"Good heavens, no!" Hilda drawled.

When she was gone Hessie sat down on the side of the bed and drew on her stockings. Black lisle thread with reinforced heels, tops and toes, and openwork clox. She thrust out her leg and stared at it. Did her legs and ankles look stiff and old-maidish too? After all, she was only thirty-six. That was not old these days. She was young—young! So Mr. Baker allowed his housekeeper three pounds a week just to feed the two of them? Wasn't that—wasn't that rather queer? Of course she was not really thinking such a horrible thing, but money handed out as generously as that did make you think—well, didn't it? A man as careful of his money as Albert Baker did not part with it unless he got value for it. Yes, and hadn't there been that gossip about him and Mrs. Hardcastle last year? Ridiculous gossip, of course!

The kitchen looked dark and dreary when she got downstairs. It was really Hilda's turn to cook the breakfast, but Hilda was still in her bedroom. The pantry smelt of mice, and on the stone part of the floor lay the corpse of an upturned cockroach, its black glossy legs curled in stiffly. Mother always screamed when she saw a cockroach, but Hilda and Hessie were used to the sight of them by now. The dark corners of the kitchen floor were black with them in the middle of the night. If you came down amongst them the whole floor moved away before your eyes, breaking and splitting up into black streams that disappeared down seemingly invisible crannies. Hessie did not mind an isolated beetle or two but a black army in silent flight across the floor was another matter.

"You'd better get some more bacon this morning," she said, as Hilda came in.

"Here comes the bride," said Mrs. Price. She sat at the head of the table, monumental in a light black bodice and full skirt.

"Girls, don't you think we ought to give a party—a little engagement tea? I think it would be a nice thing to do," Mrs. Price suggested when the tea had been poured out.

"Bread, Hilda?" Hessie ignored her mother.

"Not too thick a slice, please, Hessie."

"Now, Hilda, you've got to eat enough!" Mrs. Price declared playfully.

"I'm just not hungry, Mother!"

How horrible it was to see Hilda coy like that! Couldn't she see she was not the type? Hessie stood up quickly. "It's time I was going." At the door she made herself turn round and say, "You won't forget about Mrs. Reed to-night, will you, Hilda."

"What's that?" asked Mother quickly.

Hessie went out into the hall and pulled on her hat. Pulled on her hat! How nice that sounded. "She pulled on her little hat, and the bright tendrils of goldy-brown hair peeped out from beneath the brim." Bright tendrils—a woman's crowning glory! How dark and heavy and sour-looking her hair was this morning. It was very fine and the grease came into it quickly. When Hilda and she washed their heads they heated water on the stove in the kitchen and mixed half a threepenny shampoo-powder in the chipped basin in the sink. The shampoo always gave off a pleasant smell which was a help, for it dulled the odour of old damp wood and hot grease that came from the draining-board by the sink.

This was going to be another warm day. Hessie was glad not to meet anyone she knew on her way through the town. By the time she came home to-night the whole place would be talking about Hilda's engagement. What did it feel like to be kissed by a man—a lover's kiss? Hilda knew by now. Supposing Mr. Saul kissed her, Hessie, after the church concert to-night? But she must not think like this. It was not right.

How many times had she walked along by this low stone wall with the trees standing behind it? Six days a week for a pound a week, and a share in the rectory dinner and tea. Hilda was earning twenty-five shillings a week at the office.

That sounded like one of the Kellaways' horses behind her. Yes, she was right. That high-stepping young chestnut was the one that generally drew the Kellaways' dogcart. The big wheels of the dogcart spun by her, the spokes glittering in the sunlight, but, almost immediately, its speed slackened and the horse curved in to the side of the road. It came to a standstill with all the beautiful flurry of a spirited horse abruptly reined in.

The Kellaways' gardener was bending down towards her. "I'm delivering something up at the rectory, I'll drop you up there if you like!"

"Really, how kind of you! This is nice!"

But what would she do if her foot slipped on the high step? No, she was safely up! He had held out his hand and pulled her up beside him. How powerful he was. Strong and powerful. She was tipped back against the seat as the chestnut sprang off again.

"Another hot day," Maxwell said, rearranging the reins in his hand.

"Oh, yes—yes, isn't it!"

He had a strong face, too. A little bit fleshy, perhaps, but he was very handsome. And how kind of him to have stopped for her! He did not look the sort of man who would do a thing like that unless—unless he was interested in a person. She must look out for him if she took Mabel and Flossie through the Kellaways' grounds to the sea to-day. Perhaps she might suggest it to Mrs. Benson, and then if she met him she would smile. A ladylike smile, of course, and exchange a word or two about the flowers.

Mr. Benson was out on the front steps when they reached the rectory. He was wearing a grey suit, rather shabby, and spotted about the vest.

"Hullo—hullo, Maxwell. Good morning, Hessie. How are you, Maxwell? Very kind of Mr. Kellaway to send me these plants. I'm all ready to dig them in straight away. I suppose you couldn't spare a moment, Maxwell, to give me your advice about the best place to put them, and a hint or two about the depth I ought to dig in the manure for them? Thanks very much. That's very good of you. Are you sure I'm not keeping you?"

Standing up in the dogcart Hessie thought the ground looked miles away. She was not used to getting in and out of these things. Mr. Benson and Maxwell were busy at the back, tugging away at a bundle swathed in sacking. Really one of them might have come to help her, and yet, perhaps, it was better to try to manage alone. More discreet and ladylike.

Entering the hall she met Mrs. Benson, who cried:

"Why, Hessie, I believe you're blushing!"

How tired poor little Mrs. Benson looked, and no wonder either, with all that big family to look after and only one cheap young maid to help her, until she, Hessie, arrived each morning.

"Well, it's a lovely day, Mrs. Benson! And besides," she must be very bright now, "we've had some excitement in our small family."

"Isn't your mother well then, Hessie?"

"It's not Mother this time. It's—it's Hilda!"

"Hilda?"

"Yes, she's going to marry Mr. Baker!"

"Mr. Baker?"

Really, Mrs. Benson need not seem so surprised! After all why should not Hilda get engaged—why should not she, Hessie, get engaged too, if it came to that? Supposing she were standing here, saying, "I'm going to be married, Mrs. Benson. Mr. Saul asked me last night and I said ..." Oh, why couldn't she say that!

"Well, I am delighted! I must call round and see Hilda or write to her," Mrs. Benson cried. "I'll write her a little note to-day. Albert Baker. Let me see—yes, his housekeeper has been with him for many years—that Mrs. Hardcastle. Oh, yes! Why, Hilda will be quite a person in the town now, won't she? It will be your turn next, Hessie! Is your mother delighted?"

"Of course we'll miss Hilda."

"Yes, but it will be nice to have a man in the family, won't it? Albert Baker—fancy! I hope he'll be very kind to your mother, Hessie. I'm sure he's a good man."

Mrs. Benson's eyes met hers for a moment. Hessie guessed what that look meant. But, after all, it had been only gossip about Albert and Mrs. Hardcastle—malicious gossip, and Mr. Benson had been very quick to stamp it out.

"Of course he won't need a housekeeper when he's married to Hilda. He's going to give that Mrs. Hardcastle a month's notice. Hilda was telling me this morning. He's going to get a maid to work under Hilda."

"That's nice—and wise, too, don't you think?" Mrs. Benson said thoughtfully. "Servants who have been in a house a long time often resent a new wife. Oh, that's the telephone, Hessie. Answer it for me, will you, and if it's Mrs. Marson tell her—tell her that the rector is engaged."

The telephone was on the hall table. Hessie picked it up. "Hullo, is that the rectory?" A man's voice said: Why, it was Mr. Saul!

"Oh yes—yes! This is Hessie—yes, Hessie Price speaking," Hessie cried. "Good morning, Mr. Saul. I expect I'll see you at the concert to-night. Who did you say you wanted? I'm afraid Mr. Benson is in the garden, but I could take a message."

"Thanks, but I'll answer this myself."

Really there were moments when Mr. Benson was almost rude. There was no need to push her aside like that. Mr. Saul had sounded as if he had wanted to go on speaking to her. The way he had said "Hessie?" and then as though a light had dawned on him, he had added lingeringly. "Oh yes, Hessie!"

Mabel and Flossie were in the morning-room when she went back to Mrs. Benson.

"Good morning, chicks. It wasn't Mrs. Marson on the telephone, Mrs. Benson. It was Mr. Saul, but Mr. Benson was just coming in and so …" Well, she could afford to laugh a little now. After all there was the concert in the church hall to-night, and one the following week, too. Mr. Saul was sure to be there and the shortest route back to his lodgings lay past her home. Perhaps she could say to him, gaily, "Are you taking the short cut to-night …?" That was the sort of remark any girl might make to a man.

But, after all, she did not take the children down to the sea that morning. They helped their father in the garden instead and she remained in the house with Mrs. Benson. The cheap little maid was in one of her worst moods. Dirty, slovenly and slow, too. Mrs. Benson was close to tears by lunch-time.

Maxwell remained in the rectory garden for nearly an hour. Was it because?—could it have been … ? And when he did go he glanced all over the front of the house as if he were looking for something or someone. Not that she had let herself be seen, of course. Mr. Benson had walked beside the trap till they were half-way down the drive. God's gardener and Mr. Kellaway's gardener going down the rectory drive together. It might be wrong to think so, but, really, she did not care very much for Mr. Benson. His manners were often very bad, and there was a hard crude look in his eyes when he stared at her. Insolent, almost. Still, she ought not to think like this. Mr. Benson was the rector, and not just one of the Nonconformist ministers. Poor dear Father had been a Nonconformist, but Mother had seen to it that she and Hilda were church. Grandfather had been church too. Really the most important side of their family had been church, so everything was all right.

Hilda and Mr. Baker would be married in the church. Hilda as a bride! She mustn't think of it! But she couldn't help it. Hilda would choose white, of course, and she, Hessie, would be a bridesmaid. Mr. Benson, assisted by Mr. Saul, would marry them, and if Mr. Saul looked up he might see her, in her bridesmaid's clothes looking—looking—Didn't they say that one wedding in a family always led to another, that romance bred romance?

"Cold meat again, Hessie!" Mrs. Benson said, at lunch-time. The lightness, the gay apology of her remark addressed to Hessie but intended for Mr. Benson.

He moved his knife and fork together impatiently.

"Chutney, Henry?"

"Do I ever refuse it?"

"I think I've got a little touch of rheumatism in my wrist, dear," Mrs. Benson's face was flushed. "Would you mind finishing the carving?"

Why should he mind carving? It was the right thing for the man of the house to do. Really Mr. Benson left everything to his poor wife. It was a shame.

"Do let me do it for you, Mrs. Benson!" Hessie cried lightly and prettily, too, half-rising from her chair.

"Please sit down, Hessie!"

Really, Mr. Benson's manners did not last long in his own home. After all, her only wish was to help Mrs. Benson. It was not her fault if the poor woman had to wrestle with so many things. And now look at the way Mr. Benson was slashing down through that joint. There would not be much left over for mince to-morrow, and what came to the table would be thick and smooth with gravy-soaked bread. Not that she would mind that for her appetite was not a big one.

Mabel and Flossie were less well behaved than usual when she took them out that afternoon. Fortunately, Mr. Benson was not in for tea, and so she could fuss a little over poor Mrs. Benson.

"Really, Hessie, I don't know what I should do without you." It was pitiful to hear Mrs. Benson say that.

Chapter Four

I

Another hot day! Maggie felt so warm all through that it was impossible to imagine winter. From her window that swelled out from the roof like a rounded growth, she looked at the sea. It lay there, smooth and white, silver-white, with not a blue ripple on it. Against it, the tops of the trees looked rich and green, like dark crenellated battlements. At the foot of the trees lay the garden. Every flower down there was still, every dew-drop motionless. A deep bright virgin stillness lay over everything. Above the house the sky was a soft pale blue. The white sea, the dark trees, the rich bright flowers—Maggie gazed at them all. A dewy dampness lay on the old tiles that sloped away down the side of the roof, and they gave out a faint, almost metallic, fragrance.

The sleeves of Maggie's nightdress were folded back, and the window-ledge was the coolest place she could find for her arms. So, another day had begun! Well, and what would Cook's temper be like this morning once the kitchen got hot? Cook did not make things easy when her face looked like a bursting tomato. Far from it.

Five o'clock in the morning. She was supposed to be down at work not a second later than six o'clock. Start her scrubbing then. Scrub all over the place. All the steps and passages. Well, she was not going to wear a vest this morning. The less she wore in this heat the better. She did not want a vest clinging all round her body. It was bad enough to have an apron tight about her waist. It was a pity she had to wear stockings as well. In this heat they scratched and tickled her under her knees.

The sea was losing its silvery look, its delicate whiteness, and the sky's blue was reflecting on it in soft, placid spreads of colour. There was no appreciable change in the garden yet, only the sea was registering the changes in the sky as the sun crept upwards. Soon there would be faint noises coming from the greenhouses when the gardeners started their early morning watering.

Maggie leant farther out of the window. Gazing down at the garden and sea and up at the sky she felt as if she owned them all by virtue of the fact that she alone was looking at them. Her arms were damp with dew. Nothing stirred anywhere. No sound came from the sea, or from the birds either. Maggie ran her hands up through her hair. It was dark and shiny and waved naturally, thank God. She felt the back of her strong round neck. Yes, but for her hands and feet she was a girl well worth looking at, and Cook could say what she liked.

Standing close to the window Maggie began to dress. Knickers, and then her blue print dress, and the dark blue apron she wore for scrubbing and early morning work. She must be wearing her white with the blue over it, if necessary, by ten o'clock, the time it was likely that Mrs. Kellaway would come down to the kitchen. Her garters made deep lines on her legs above her knees. She had to wear them light or else her stockings wrinkled down around her ankles and she could not stand that. In cooler weather she wore a sort of corset affair, a brassiere and corset combined that hung from her shoulders and had two sets of good stout suspenders to it. She combed her hair back from her forehead, and jabbed the pins into her cap.

The attic landing was reached by the back flight of stairs only. It was a dark narrow stairway covered with oilcloth, well padded underneath. This part of the house was Irene's province, and it was swept and polished every day by Mrs. Bartley.

The green baize door on the first landing leading into the main part of the house was shut. Maggie eyed it cautiously as she crept down. The nurseries, Mrs. Kellaway's bedroom and the other rooms lay behind that door, each room serene and peaceful in the early morning sunshine; beautiful and mysterious as well, a province supposedly ruled off from Maggie's knowledge.

Well, those rooms were none of her business, and she had enough to do. The kitchen looked big and cool and almost bare from cleanliness. She knew everything there was to know about the kitchen. The cleanliness was the result of her labours, and what did it matter if her hands and back got knocked to pieces? Cook liked to see her hands all splayed out and red. She was not supposed to have any vanity or decent feelings.

With her lips tightened Maggie crossed over to the sink and filled the kettle. This morning she was not going to wait for Cook before having a cup of tea. She could have her cup and saucer cleared away before Cook came down. Thank God she had not to light that black monster of a kitchen range this morning. Because of the heat Mrs. Kellaway had given orders that it need not be used. It was only one of Cook's fads to use the big kitchener instead of the gas stove, which was large enough to cook anything for anybody. Cook liked to see her breaking her back over that range.

Maggie left the teapot and clean cups and milk on the table handy for Cook when she came down. It was just six o'clock and Irene and Jenner would not be down till half-past. Irene was always the first to arrive. For another half-hour Maggie knew she would be alone down here with the empty kitchens and long hollow-sounding back passage with the larders and pantries and vegetable-rooms and storerooms opening off it, and the thickly-padded door that led into the hall that was always so rich and glossy-looking, and the circle of rooms beyond.

Well, she had better get busy with her scrubbing, and no one would care what her knees and back felt like at the end of it. Maggie opened the back door to let the fresh air come in. There was the same stillness in the air in the yard as there had been in the garden. She set about whitening the back doorstep first, and then began the familiar progress down the passage, pushing herself and her bucket yard by yard along the stone floor. Scrub, mop up with her wet cloth, with the water splashing almost slimily over the stone, and then rub off with her dry cloth that was rapidly growing moist. If possible she always took a rest by the mistress's store-room. Sitting back on her heels and wiping her hands on her apron. The stable clock chimed a quarter past six. Maggie started as steps came hurrying across the yard.

"Is Cook down yet?"

Maggie looked up and saw Maxwell standing before her. "That's likely, isn't it?" she said softly.

Maxwell came quickly down the passage and stood beside her. There was an importunate look in his eyes. He put out his hand and touched her shoulder. Maggie shrugged it away.

"Stand up, Maggie." He peered into the empty kitchen, and walked in. Unable to help herself Maggie stood up slowly and followed him, drawn by the distress in his eyes. Inside the door he caught her shoulders roughly, his fingers pressing into her flesh. His eyes stared into hers. Maggie felt the necessary self-protective hostility melting from her own.

"Oh, come on, then," she said, smiling faintly. "Get it over."

He held her so long and closely, his lips on hers, that at last she tried to struggle away from him. But it was useless. He jerked at the tight-fitting neck of her uniform and pulled it away from her throat a little, and buried his face against her neck where her skin was white and warm. Maggie ceased to struggle and a look of tenderness softened her face. She put up her hand and touched his rough hair. Gradually his arms relaxed and he let her go. She began to arrange her collar again, her face turned away from him even when he left her. Sure that her clothes were neat once more she looked all round the empty kitchen, the tender smile still in her eyes. She felt that something immense, tremendous had happened here in this kitchen, and left her feeling shattered and yet strengthened, too. This commonplace kitchen, every tile and board of which had been scrubbed and mopped by her hands. She leaned a little against the table, her thigh heavy against the sharp edge of the wood.

Just before the half-hour Irene came in, cheerful as ever.

"The minute I open my eyes, my legs begin to twitch to be up and doing," she said pleasantly. "I ought to make my fortune one of these days. So much energy!"

Maggie went back into the passage and sank down on her knees again, and sent the water swirling over the grey stone. Well, it seemed as if things were getting a bit out of hand, and yet what could she do? She was helpless before this astounding shattering thing that had made her follow him into the empty kitchen and stand there helpless in his embrace.

She heard the clink of Irene's cup being slapped onto its saucer, and a minute afterwards Irene started back upstairs. All her work would be up there for the next hour or so, until she came down for Mrs. Kellaway's tea-tray, and, later, to breakfast. Jenner came down just as Maggie wiped the last section of the passage. Jenner was too high and mighty to notice anybody this morning. Well, she could be as high and mighty as she liked! Maggie felt herself apart from everyone, detached even from her work, though she went on performing it in the familiar way.

There was no sign of Maxwell as she scrubbed the wide circular front steps. The grounds were empty apparently, and they were different now from the gardens she had gazed down onto from her window. The flowers looked as though they were aware of the approaching heat. Midday would find the sky cloudless except for a rich heat haze. The flowers wore a solemn and guarded-looking beauty.

Cook was slapping some kippers onto a dish when she got back to the kitchen. Hot weather or cold, kippers were a great favourite with Cook. Maggie liked them, too, but not in such warm weather.

"Be quick with the table," Cook said.

Maggie glanced at her. For some reason or other Cook seemed almost amiable this morning. Well, that was a good thing, though by the time lunch was served it would be a different story. Cook's face would be bursting red by then, and her behind would heave and shake all over with every step. Jenner was late coming in to her breakfast. Mr. Andrew had come down demanding cold ham and coffee at once and Jenner had had to be high priestess to his breakfast.

"No toast ready?" Jenner snapped, looking at Maggie.

"Take your hands off the loaf—can't you!" Cook said. "I'll cut the bread."

But Maggie felt that she did not care—why should she? She knew something that Cook did not know. She knew she was not the dirt Cook tried to make out. She was apart from Cook. This morning's experience was cutting her off from all the other servants.

11

"We are going for a picnic, Lottie," said Isobel.

"Who said so, dearie?"

"I said so first. Lottie, I want to wear my blue frock."

Every window in the nursery was open and the sunblinds were out—fine green rush blinds that rolled and unrolled with a gentle rustle. A narrow strip of sunlight lay on the floor, it lay there with a strong smooth complacency. The green of the blinds shone yellow.

Lottie unpinned the apron she wore for washing-up the nursery china. She rolled it up with a quick circular motion of her hands, the way she had been taught to roll up her nightdress in the Home, and put it away in a drawer. The brass handles of the chest were warm, too.

"There!"

Isobel was standing by the window, and the sunlight fell around her neck and the waving ends of her hair, and caught the line of one cheek. The light shone through her flesh. Lottie stood quite still looking at her.

Coming in at the door, Nurse said sharply, "The children are going for a picnic. Run down and ask Cook to pack a picnic lunch as quickly as she can. Plenty of fruit, and tell her the sandwiches needn't be an inch thick this time."

"Yes, Nurse."

"Here you are—take this list. That's what Mrs. Kellaway wants packed."

"Yes, Nurse."

"And come back at once—don't start dreaming on the way up the stairs, there's nothing to dream about. You'll have to dress Anne and Isobel."

Well, she knew that—didn't she? Isobel ran beside her down the passage and stairs and followed her into the kitchen. Cook was at the table beating something against the sides of a bowl. She paused and looked at Lottie and the pale creamy stuff slid away from the glazed surface and gathered smoothly at the bottom of the basin. Despite her message from Mrs. Kellaway Lottie felt herself to be an intruder in the kitchen at this hour of day. Without bothering to speak Cook held out her hand for the list. Isobel stared around interestedly. Neither Cook nor the activities of the kitchen had any power over her. Her position in the household was unassailable and in some innocent way she knew it.

"It's to go straight into the trap," Lottie said, in a subdued voice, adding hastily, "Please, Cook."

"I'll see to it," said Cook grimly. "Maggie! Where is that girl?"

Maggie, her sleeves rolled up well above her elbows, came and stood in the doorway. Ah, so there was one of the children—standing there like a flower in the middle of the kitchen. Isobel that was. How soft, how fine her hair was. It looked as if it was always being blown lightly about her head. Her white frock gleamed against the deep tiles of the kitchen floor. For a moment Maggie's black eyes looked into Lottie's blue ones.

"What are you doing?" Cook asked.

"Scrubbing out the larder."

"You'll have to stop it. I want you here. Start getting these things."

Lottie, with Isobel ahead of her, went out of the kitchen. Couldn't Cook see how much Maggie hated her? That smouldering look in Maggie's eyes.

"Dear Lottie," said Isobel suddenly, and pressed her face against Lottie's apron.

"Isobel, dear! Come now, there's this picnic to think about. We must be smart in getting started."

The trap was at the door already, the horse pawing away at the gravel. Passing the head of the staircase Isobel stopped to look down and out through the wide circle of glass about the front door. Lottie glanced down too, and looked away hurriedly. That was George at the horse's head, standing there entirely unconscious of her scrutiny. How sober yet pleasant his face was? He stood looking at the house, one hand on the horse's neck.

"Come along, Isobel."

"I'm too interested. Thank you all the same, Lottie," Isobel said, with obstinate politeness.

"Never mind anything now, we don't want to delay the picnic."

Isobel took to her heels at that and fled down the passage. She waited for Lottie at the nursery door. Lottie followed hastily. Was George going to drive them to the picnic place? The trap meant that they were not going far, and that Mr. and Mrs. Kellaway would not be coming with them. Unless they followed afterwards. They did that sometimes, bringing their own lunch or tea-basket, and driving Mr. Andrew's car, for that was the most battered vehicle about the place. Mrs. Kellaway's own car, which was known as 'the town car,' was a great, beautiful affair that moved swiftly and noiselessly along the road with a great feeling of power in its very silence. Mr. Kellaway drove a choice of two cars. One was very big and long in the engine with room for two only in a snug little closed part behind, and the other a small unostentatious affair, roomy and shabby. The little one was his favourite.

Nurse was seeing to the baby's food when Lottie entered the nursery. Anne was waiting to be dressed. She rushed at Lottie. "Hurry up—hurry up—hurry up!"

"Get out those pink linens with the sunbonnets to match. Their shoes will do," Nurse said, placing the baby's bottle in a clean towel and wrapping the ends in firmly.

"I want to wear blue," Isobel protested, her lips drooping a little bit.

Nurse glanced over her shoulder at the child. "Why not then?" she said indulgently. "There's that blue smock, Lottie. Put it on Isobel."

"Yes, Nurse."

Mrs. Kellaway came to the front door as they set off. Nurse got in first and settled herself with the baby on her knee. The two little girls kissed their mother and then ran to Lottie to be helped in. Anne first. Then Isobel sprang up into the air, hurling her small body upwards with Lottie's hands beneath her arms.

"I flew up," she announced.

The horse made an impatient movement. When Isobel was settled up at the top of the side opposite to Anne and Nurse, Lottie got in. Nurse and the baby and Anne on one side, Isobel, Lottie and the driver on the other side. Mr. Andrew came out and held the horse, passive now, as George climbed in. The trap tilted a little with his weight, but slipped right again when he sat down. Isobel clutched Lottie's hand in ecstasy.

The picnic basket was slipped into its special place beneath the seat. "Good-bye—good-bye!"

The gravel sped beneath the horse's hooves as they bowled quickly down the drive. The flower-beds flashed past like strips of colour. When they flew in under the trees the colour of the children's frocks looked deeper and cooler. George's leg was pressing lightly against Lottie's. She kept her face turned well away, but rounding a corner he pulled firmly on the reins and Lottie felt his leg from his thigh downwards moving against hers. He made no attempt to alter his position once the road was open before them again. Lottie could not stir. Her limbs were powerless. The colour blazed in her cheeks. What could she do?

"Lottie, did you give Cook that list? I hope nothing has been left out."

With a desperate effort Lottie turned to Nurse. "Yes, Nurse." How small and bodiless her voice sounded, repeating the formula, "Yes, Nurse."

She felt George's eyes on her face, compelling her to turn round a little more. Nurse was busy with the baby. There was nothing for it now but to meet George's gaze with however brief a glance. She moved her head a little further, a very little further, and his eyes met hers. He gave her a small smile, very quiet and reassuring. All the heat flowed away from Lottie's face and her body. She felt cool and happy and light, uplifted almost. Her eyes shone.

While Nurse was still absorbed over the baby Lottie gave George another quick glance. The smile in his eyes deepened. Lottie faced the road again. Her limbs were free and under her control once more but she did not stir. George's knee pressed lightly against hers for the rest of the drive.

After a while the trap swung round into a track that went steeply downwards, bumping amongst dried ruts. The track ended in a field cropped smooth by a herd of sheep. Boulders jutted up here and there. A wide shallow stream of very clear water lay at the bottom of the field. The sea was close to them.

"Bring the baskets down to that tree," Nurse said. She pointed to the tree that grew nearest to the shore. Its branches spread out and arched themselves like a tall roof, curving upwards and then swaying down towards the ground, its leaves like green tassels. George carried the lunch-basket down there and laid it under the trees. He worked in a pleasant silence, ignoring Nurse's fussing. Then he went back up the field and turned the horse loose.

Nurse glanced at her watch. "Look, it's lunch-time! Open the basket, Lottie."

"Can't we play now?" Anne asked. "Must we sit down and eat at once?"

"No—you can start playing—both of you."

"Can't Lottie play with us?" Isobel asked.

"Run away now like good children. Lottie will play with you afterwards. Now then, Lottie, look sharp."

The dry leaves under the tree rustled as Lottie knelt down beside the big basket. It was almost cool underneath this great tree. Outside, the fields were burning in the sunlight. Anne and Isobel were wading in the stream which at this point had a flat sandy bottom to it with clusters of small stones and pebbles and one or two smooth boulders. Drops of water ran off Isobel's rounded arms as she plunged her hands into the stream, gathering stones. Her sunbonnet was tipped back. Anne was a little further up the stream, bent and absorbed in her game. Nurse sat on the ground, a rug beneath her and a cushion from the trap propped against the trunk of the tree.

The hinges of the basket creaked protestingly as Lottie pushed up the lid. A cloth lay on top. A thick strong cloth with a very gay border. Lottie spread it carefully, brushing away the limp brown leaves and tiny sun-dried twigs that sprang onto the edges of it. The pretty pale blue unbreakable cups and saucers and plates raised another little bevy of leaves as she laid them in their places. There were neat little celluloid labels in each packet of sandwiches. Chicken, tongue, sausage-rolls for Nurse and Lottie, salad, a basket of fruit, and cake. What a lunch Mrs. Kellaway had ordered for them! Nurse's eyes lit with satisfaction, too. There was no stinting of food in this place. Lottie placed each pile about the cloth, the fruit in the centre. It was almost as if she were offering the children this feast herself. To be arranging it made her feel bountiful and happy.

"I wonder if George has got his own?" Nurse began. Her glance went sharply up the field. "It's too far to call. You'll have to go and ask him."

"Very well."

George was standing in the shade of a small grove of trees and bushes. He was leaning against a fence and he watched Lottie come towards him. He made no effort to move until she was close up to him. She was the most beautiful thing he had ever seen. Her eyes were an intense warm blue, and she walked as if her limbs flowed down smoothly, yet with delicate firmness, from her waist.

Looking at him Lottie wondered if he would ever again smile at her as he had smiled in the trap. She wanted him to smile at her in that way. To give her that light, reassured feeling once more.

"Have you got something to eat? Nurse wants you to come down for some if you haven't."

He pointed to a package that lay on the grass close by. "I'm all right."

Lottie hesitated. Was he thinking of that walk they had taken down by the sea, and of the drive out? She turned away. "I'll tell Nurse then," she murmured.

The children were coming up the bank from the stream when she reached Nurse again. Dimples of light fell all over them as they stood at the edge of the tree, hesitating for some reason of their own, their heads bent together, whispering about something. Isobel shook back her hair and looked at Anne, her face full of startled delight.

"What secret have they got hold of now?" Lottie thought indulgently. "The little dears!"

They sat down close to Lottie. She had to rearrange their plates and spoons for them.

"Chicken sandwich, please," said Anne.

"Chicken sandwich, please," Isobel echoed quickly, and began to laugh.

"Now then—don't eat too quickly," Nurse warned.

"I can't help being hungry," Isobel said with great dignity, her eyes sparkling. "Are you hungry, Lottie?

"Yes, dearie!" When Nurse was helped, Lottie began to eat her own meal. The pastry of the sausage roll flecked away as she bit into it. The light over the tablecloth shone cool and green.

As the meal progressed the cloth that Lottie had spread so carefully began to sag into little hollows as the plates were moved from place to place. A pile of sandwiches tumbled over and the little girls laughed at the small cascade of them lying there. The children were ready to laugh at anything. When Lottie peeled their apples for them she had to keep the peel unbroken.

"Look—a beehive!" Anne said, winding her peel into a red dome. The baby began to crawl towards it, careless of everything but the object on which his eyes were fixed so unwaveringly.

"May he have it, Anne?" Lottie said quickly. She felt it would be dreadful if Anne snatched it away just as the baby reached it.

"Oh, yes," Anne said graciously.

"And mine, too," Isobel echoed hastily.

With the apple peelings falling about his fingers the baby sat down. He began pulling them into little bits and throwing them around with solemn carelessness. They fell onto the cloth and onto the remains of the lunch. He kept Lottie and the little girls busy picking them up. Nurse watched him indulgently. When he had finished he looked round from one to the other, but when his gaze reached Nurse he blinked.

"Saucy!" said Nurse.

Isobel lay down on the leaves and rolled over slowly, kicking her heels up in the air.

"Not so soon after eating, please," Nurse said.

Isobel lay still on the ground, her arms and legs sprawled out anyhow, the brown leaves caught in her hair.

"Oh, I'm so full!" she complained.

Lottie began collecting the things together. The sandwiches back into the white sandwich tin, and the scraps into a piece of paper to be buried later. She gathered up the plates and cups to give them a wash of kinds in the stream. She carried them down there and knelt on a little patch of sand that seemed whiter than the sand on the beach close by. In places there were little spread-out veins of earth in it. It did not look like real sand. She chose a place where the current was running quickly. Despite the heat beating down on her back the moving water was deliciously cool.

When she returned to the shade of the tree the baby was asleep. Nurse had made him a little bed of cushions. After the heat down by the stream there was a liquid quality in the shade beneath the tree. Isobel and Anne were round at the other side of its big trunk. Lottie could not see them at first but they were there all right. Deep in some game of their own.

Nurse rolled up a rug and thumped it with her elbow.

"I'll have a little snooze, I think, while he's asleep. Watch the children, Lottie. They can play in the stream if they want to, but keep them in the shade if you can."

"Very well, Nurse."

"There's some mending you can be getting on with in that bag there. No use sitting twiddling your thumbs."

Lottie sat down with her back to the tree trunk in a position where she could watch the little girls, and Nurse and the baby, too. Up in the field she could see George. He was lying on the grass, one knee drawn up. Was he asleep? He was lying so still.

Isobel and Anne were very quiet. After a while they wandered away a little. Nurse was fast asleep by now. Somehow she looked shapeless lying there, and yet helpless too. Her hat had slipped awry. Lottie looked away quickly, almost compassionately. People asleep were too defenceless, especially a grown-up who was not dear to the onlooker. If you loved a person then there was an innocence about their sleep that made it sweet to watch them. Lottie kept her back very upright against the tree trunk. The silence all around her and Nurse and the sleeping baby and George lying so still and the hot quietness of the afternoon, emphasized her own upright wakefulness. She was sitting here beneath the tree, screened from the blazing sun by the thick green leaves, guardian of the sleep-filled quietness around her. She took off her grey straw hat, with its narrow band of black ribbon and laid it on the leaves. From Nurse's sewing-bag, a holland receptacle that went everywhere with Nurse, she drew out the mending. Little bright cool pearl buttons to be sewn on one of Anne's frocks. She threaded her needle with a sense of pleasant leisure. How pink and smooth her finger-tips looked as she picked up a button and held it into place! There was no feeling of Nurse fussing about, nothing to disturb her.

And then a very faint noise came to Lottie's ears. The sound of a car coming slowly into the field. It was Mr. Andrew's car. Lottie glanced at Nurse. Ought she to wake her? The noise from the engine died away and Mr. Andrew stepped out into the field. George did not stir either, and, after a glance at him, Mr. Andrew came down the fields towards Lottie.

Lottie stood up as he approached. She could not go and prod Nurse awake now that he was so near. That would be too obvious. There was nothing she could do except stand still, Anne's frock hanging in her hands.

He came close with exaggerated quietness. He glanced from Lottie to Nurse and then to Lottie again.

"Haven't you been asleep, too?" he inquired smilingly.

"Oh no, Mr. Andrew!"

"I don't think I've ever before seen Nurse asleep," he mused. "What are you doing, Lottie?"

"Just sewing."

"Really!"

Lottie looked down. Ought she to pick up her hat and put it on? It did not seem right to be standing before Mr. Andrew without something on her head. What would Nurse say if she woke up now?

"I'm going to have a bathe," he said slowly. "Don't you ever bathe, Lottie?"

"No."

"Would you like to?"

"Oh, yes, Mr. Andrew."

"Why don't you bathe now, then?"

"Oh, I couldn't!" Instantly Lottie felt frightened at the very thought of such a thing. Bathe with Mr. Andrew there, and Nurse? Besides Nurse would not let her, Nurse would not approve of the time spent getting dressed and undressed. Lottie was of the opinion, too, that Nurse would not consider it quite decent for the nurse-maid in a good family to allow herself the liberty of bathing in the sea. Her place was in uniform not in a bathing-dress with the water swirling intimately and closely around her body.

Beneath Mr. Andrew's smiling gaze Lottie felt her cheeks flush.

"Lottie, I can't help asking you—do you know how very blue your eyes are?"

Lottie looked at him in distress. There was a teasing note in his voice. How cross Nurse would be if she woke up and heard this conversation.

"I'm sorry you won't bathe," he went on quickly. "I'm going to, now, at once!"

He smiled at her again, and went off towards the shore, his bathing things thrown over his shoulder.

Lottie sat down again, her knees trembling a little. She bent over Anne's frock, and then before the button was half sewn on, she felt compelled to glance up the field to where George lay. He was awake now. He had rolled over on one side and was looking down at her. She saw his hand reach out and pluck a long stem of grass which he began to chew, and all the time his gaze, calm and detached, was fixed on her. Lottie lowered her head again, and searched for a fresh button. Despite his alarming sex the thought of George steadied her fingers and gave her a feeling of warm reassurance.

Nurse awoke in a thundering bad temper which increased when she saw Mr. Andrew's car in the field above.

"Was he alone, Lottie?" she demanded. "Haven't you any sense at all in that silly head of yours? Letting me sleep on like that!"

But before Lottie could begin to placate her two more cars rolled into the field above. "Drat it!" said Nurse, and began to fumble at her clothes hastily, straightening her hat, tightening up her loosened belt, running her hands up the broad bands of her shoulder-straps, and then heavily down her thighs to smooth out the creases in her apron.

"Where are the children?" she demanded crossly. "I suppose you're letting them play out in the sunshine?"

But Anne and Isobel were in the shade of another tree a little way off. When they saw the other two cars they started running up the field to greet their mother and father.

"Here, give me that sewing, can't you?" Nurse grabbed Anne's frock out of Lottie's hand. "And follow the children same as if you knew your job was to look after them, Miss Ninny-face."

"Yes, Nurse."

There was a talkative group around the two cars when Lottie reached the children. She stood a little way off ready to do anything should she be needed. Quite a large party had come out. Mr. and Mrs. Kellaway, the Bensons, Mr. Saul and his brother, and Hessie Price. Standing beside the second car, Hessie darted a brief look at Lottie. That girl would never have any difficulty about attracting men. Or was it just because she was so young that she looked like that—as if she were something delicate and rare? A nurse-maid—a girl from an Orphan Asylum—and to look like that! It wasn't fair!

Mr. Saul and his brother were in the little group that had got out of the first car. Mr. Saul was wearing a most unclerical-looking suit of light fancy-coloured flannel, very well cut. Everyone in the parish knew that Mr. Saul was not dependent on the living for his income. He received a substantial allowance from his father, who was reputed to be a rich man with a nice estate somewhere up near Shrewsbury. Mr. Saul and his brother would share it between them eventually. Strangely enough the younger Mr. Saul was on the stage. On the gentlemanly side of the stage, of course. At least that was the general opinion. Rosie Bates had told Hessie that he always played a titled part, which, naturally, made everything very nearly all right. Mrs. Kellaway, Mrs. Benson and the two Mr. Sauls had driven in the first car, Mr. Kellaway and Mr. Benson together in the front seat of the second car, and Hessie and the children in the back seat. Hessie had hated that, though she'd realized that such placing was inevitable. After all, though she knew herself to be a lady, she was only the paid assistant in the Benson's home. She'd only come on this picnic in her official capacity, so to speak. She couldn't really grumble, but it did seem unfair. How different it would be if she were rich. Mr. Benson and Mr. Saul would take a lot of notice of her then, they'd consult her about parish matters, and Mr. Benson at least, would swing off his hat with that gesture of his if he saw her approaching; and yet, bodily, she'd be just the same as she was now. Her long nose, and her neck that needed fattening would not matter then. People would find it easy to overlook such things if she were wealthy. "One of those rich Miss Prices, such charming girls, a bit thin, but so distinguished-looking." And perhaps she would not be so thin, either? Not if she'd lived all her life on good food, and never had any worries. Worry was a dreadful thing for keeping your flesh down.

"Oh, isn't it lovely here, children! A day like this always makes me wish I was young again!" Hessie cried impulsively, and then regretted it. She ought not to have said 'young,' it was a misleading word, she ought to have chosen 'tiny' or 'small' or "I wish I was just a child again." That would have been best of all, there was an appeal in the word 'child.'

Hessie glanced round brightly. Nobody had taken any notice of her remark, except Mr. Benson who had turned his back to her. Well, for one of God's chosen to deliver His message to the rest of the world, Mr. Benson's manners were very poor.

The Kellaway children were having a lot of attention paid to them. Mr. Saul's brother was talking to Isobel as if she were a grown-up lady. It was a pity to spoil a child like that. Anne was jumping about in a high-spirited way, tossing her curls back, while Mr. Kellaway laughed at her. Mr. Benson was smiling, too.

Mr. Kellaway and Mr. Saul lead the way down the hill, and the others followed.

"Anne and Isobel—take care of Mabel and Flossie," Mrs. Kellaway called back.

Hessie gave Mabel and Flossie each a push forward. They were their father's children all right, no one would ever be able to teach them pretty manners.

"Run on, children, scamper along!" Hessie called out gaily.

Mr. Saul's brother turned and looked at her. She felt his glance, startled, interested. Did it surprise him that she should speak like a lady? Mother had taken great care with their accents when they were children and they'd both had what was called 'a good ear for inflexions', so they'd soon picked up only the nicest sounds.

Lottie followed last of all, a yard or two behind Hessie. Nurse was standing stiffly under the tree. Her greeting was rigidly respectful.

The peace of the afternoon was broken utterly for a few moments. Mr. Andrew appeared from the seashore, a towel thrown over one shoulder. His skin was tanned to a golden brown.

"What's the sea like, Andrew?"

"Marvellous, and the tide is just full."

"You've been in already?"

"I've been flapping about. It's too hot to swim."

Mrs. Kellaway turned to Hessie, and said kindly: "Are you going to bathe, Miss Price?"

Hessie stared at her. She had not expected this. "Oh, Mrs. Kellaway, really, I hadn't thought … I didn't bring … a bathe on a hot day would be delicious, but …"

"Haven't you brought a bathing-dress with you? That's a pity. Wait a minute, though, I think I've got a second one up in the car."

"Oh, no, please, you mustn't bother about me! Really!"

Hessie started nervously. A bathe in such company would be too difficult. Her underclothes were so shabby, and in the hot weather the dye from her cheap stockings stained her feet. She glanced anxiously at Mr. Saul. If he urged her—but could she even then? Although his eyes did not meet hers she had an idea that he would like her to bathe. Or no, perhaps that was wrong. Above all, a man prized modesty in the girl towards whom his feelings were growing attached.

"Really, Mrs. Kellaway—it's awfully kind of you, but I don't think I will! Not to-day, anyhow."

Mrs. Kellaway gave her a little smile, and turned away.

Hessie stood about in what she feared was a series of awkward attitudes as the others began to file down towards the beach. Isobel and Anne had taken Mabel and Flossie down to the stream and were introducing them to the intricacies of the miniature dams and castles they had built from the fine white sand. Obviously it was her duty to stay close to them.

Even when the grown-up party had disappeared there was still a feeling of tension in the air beneath the tree. Nurse was sewing away with quick vigorous stitches, her little finger crooked tightly because of her suppressed irritation. Lottie stood still, her eyes on the children. Hessie settled herself down beside the tree trunk.

"Really, it might be some tropical country—all this heat," she exclaimed brightly.

Nurse grunted. Hessie glanced at her. What a bad-tempered woman she was, and not even very polite. From the direction of the sea came an occasional shout of laughter. Hessie felt a wave of familiar depression descending on her. She might so easily have been down there, too, joining the others in the sea, arrayed in one of Mrs. Kellaway's bathing-suits. If only she had not had the delicacy to see that—that—well, her body exposed in Mrs. Kellaway's type of bathing attire might look a little out of place. Amongst all those men, too. Mr. Saul and his brother, and young Mr. Andrew. But why was not her body made in such a way that she could have accepted Mrs. Kellaway's invitation to bathe with the others? All their lives she and Hilda had missed so many of the things that made living gay and pleasant to other women. They had moved on a grey borderland of gentility and excessive modesty. Something had cheated them and withheld from them all the usual girlish pleasures and freedoms. They had been always outside things, filling in the gaps in their actual existences with thoughts. Oh, well, gentility as a consolation was better than nothing at all, and now Hilda had Albert Baker. Soon Hilda would begin to live, solidly, completely, as a woman.

The dried leaves beneath her crackled as Hessie moved suddenly. Wasn't it bad enough to spend the nights thinking about Hilda and Mr. Baker without giving over the daytime to it as well. But how could she help it? Stealthily, she put up her hand and touched her breasts. They felt small and shrunken. Fearing Nurse's eye upon her she ran her hand up to her throat and let it linger there in a little natural gesture. But how thin and bony her neck felt. She dropped her hand into her lap again, and looked hopelessly towards the stream where the four children played.

At tea-time the bathers came straggling up from the beach. Mr. Saul's brother and Mrs. Kellaway together. Then Mr. Andrew by himself, and then the others in a little group.,

Nurse was in a fluster directing the spreading of the cloth.

"For goodness sake, don't be so clumsy, Lottie. Put those sandwiches over there."

For Lottie, the lovely stillness of the afternoon was gone. The quietness of the trees and fields around the active group beneath the tree had a withdrawn quality, as if the woods and fields had deliberately rolled away some beautiful essential stillness leaving only an empty sunlit circle wherein the picnickers might revel, unaware of the silence they had dispossessed.

Isobel came and sat close to Lottie. "Oh, give me something to eat!" she cried.

She worked herself up against Lottie and leaned against her leg. "Oh, it's been beautiful to-day," she exclaimed.

For a moment, as Lottie looked down at the child, all the vanished stillness and beauty returned. Isobel's cheeks were delicately flushed, the colour moving beneath the fine clarity of her skin. Lottie put out her hand and smoothed back the hair from the child's forehead. Isobel's hair and skin felt like fine silk beneath her fingers.

"My little dear," she murmured. Between them the day had resurrected itself. It was surrounding them only and for a moment they lived together in the first stillness and undisturbed loveliness of the fields.

Nurse and Lottie and the children, together with Hessie Price and Mabel and Flossie Benson, drove home earlier than the grown-ups. They went in Mr. Andrew's car. George and the trap laden with all the baskets had been sent off earlier.

Lottie found herself seated in front beside Mr. Andrew himself, with Isobel on her knee. Behind, Nurse and Hessie Price and the three other children sat packed together. The air was cooling slightly, a faint merciful coolness making a memory of the afternoon's heat.

"This car'd go anywhere," Mr. Andrew remarked confidently, as they crept slowly up the field track and passed through the trees that lay like a duck ribbon along the road. Once clear of the trees the highway followed an imperious ridgy track across the countryside, the grasslands falling away in firm gentle slopes till fields merged into sand, and in little gaps between the low whitish cliffs the silvery-blue line of sea broke gently against the land. On the other side of the road fields and little copses and quiet streams were a foreground for groups of trees centred with the grey weather-beaten chimneys of farms and manor houses.

Inland, the sky which had been serene and cloudless all day was already rich with deep soft colourings, and faint misty clouds trailed like smoky skirts low down over the distant trees.

"More heat! Those clouds don't mean a thing!" Mr. Andrew remarked.

Lottie kept silent. They were driving fast through the coloured air. Now and then Isobel's hair was blown across her face. The little girl began to sing in a high clear tuneless voice. Mr. Andrew turned to smile at her and his eyes met Lottie's.

After a while the car began to sweep down hill. Trees grew thicker and the quietness beneath them had a peculiar brooding quality. Isobel fell silent and her head rested against Lottie's shoulder. Nurse and Hessie Price and the children behind them were silent too.

They stopped before the rectory gates and Hessie was genteelly profuse in her thanks. She smiled warmly at Mr. Andrew.

"Mabel, say good night nicely. Flossie—it's the *right* hand. …"

The flowers in the Kellaways' garden looked richer and more glowing than ever. The sun was a great red ball half hidden beneath the skirts of a cloud that humped itself with soft dark ragged edges across the sky.

It was easy to put the children to bed that night. They were half asleep. Lottie was sparing of the soap as Isobel's little body lay in the warm bath water. As she sponged the child the water ran off her skin in big pearly drops.

"Oh dear, oh dear," sighed Isobel as Lottie lifted her out and wrapped her in the towel. "I'm much too tired to stand."

"You needn't," Lottie said softly, and dried her cradled on her knee.

In bed Isobel lay back against the pillows. Lottie sat beside her, feeding her with spoonfuls of pudding, but before the plate was half empty the little girl was fast asleep. The bedroom windows were wide open, there was an intense yet coloured darkness lying lightly about the garden. There was new and fresher air stirring somewhere; as Lottie stood by the window she could feel it brushing past her. Isobel's bed looked white and cool when she turned her gaze from the garden, and tip-toed across the room.

Chapter Five

I

The National Anthem! Oh, she could let her voice go over that all right. Hessie's chest grew large with sound and it poured out fervently from her lips. Really, the high register in her voice was very good. Clear and strong. Yes, and Mr. Saul was looking at her as she sang. She was not looking at him, of course, but from the side of her eye she could see him gazing at her. Even as a little child she had always loved the National Anthem. That was the military side of them again, no doubt. After all, Grandfather must have heard it many times. Standing to attention before his troops, his moustache bristling to attention also. "We military folk. I want the girlies to appreciate what it all means."

Hilda and Mr. Baker were on the other side of the hall. It was the end of the second concert in the church hall in aid of the Organ Repair Fund. Hilda was wearing that pink scarf again, and her best silk stockings. Wasn't it funny to see her there, with a man beside her! From now on it would always be Hilda and Albert Baker, and soon Hilda would not come back home with her any longer, but would go on to her husband's home and she would enter the house in front of him, feeling her way into the unlit hall.

"Albert, I can't see. …"

"The switch, my dear. … It's no use leaving the electric light on while we're out."

"No, indeed. I hope the fire is in. Would you like a cup of cocoa, Albert?"

"Thank you—I would."

And then as Hilda went towards the door he might catch her arm, roughly, perhaps and—no, she mustn't think of it.

All their acquaintances were crowding around Hilda and Albert. The hall was warm, and everyone was feeling very friendly and sociable.

"Why didn't you give us a song, Hessie?"

Rosie Bates again. "Oh, why, but I can't sing!" Hessie protested laughingly.

"Can't you?—I heard you a moment ago—in the National Anthem!"

"Oh, that—but I've always liked the National Anthem! It's—it's something rather special, isn't it? And the tune seems to—well, you know—you can let yourself go over it!"

"Isn't this exciting about your sister! I must say it was a surprise! I want to speak to her. Your turn next, Hessie!"

Well, she could smile at that. It might be her turn sooner than they thought!

"I suppose you're not going home with the lovebirds? Not playing gooseberry?" How tiresome Rosie was, and it was nearly time she buttoned up her coat. It looked silly hanging open like that and everyone knew that it was open only to show off the green frock underneath. Well, if Rosie wanted to show off her frock she ought to see to it that the modesty vest part of it—coffee-coloured lace—was straight, and not dancing about on those high prominent bones of her neck. Still, poor Rosie, she was getting on. Better smile and say something kind. Mr. Saul was just behind them now, talking to Mrs. Sterling. The Sterlings were rich people and Mrs. Sterling was deeply interested in church work. She patronized everything—all the bazaars and fêtes. Strictly speaking it was really Mrs. Kellaway who ought to have been the greatest help to the church. The Kellaways were far and away the richest people in the district—in the county even, but they only came to church on Christmas day and Easter, though they were very generous with flowers and fruit and subscriptions. Still, an active interest was what the church needed, and the Kellaways certainly did not supply that.

What a beautiful voice Mr. Saul had. So mellow. And the hall was emptying fast now. Hilda and Mr. Baker had gone, but Rosie was still lingering by the door. Hessie made a business of searching for something in her bag. She walked down along the benches to the place where she had been sitting. Really, she had lost something. Was it her handkerchief? Well, perhaps, she had had a second one out with her. Sometimes she did carry a clean unopened one for use just in case she should require it in front of anyone she knew. The other, slightly crumpled but still clean one, was for private and unobserved use. Or had she dropped a penny? Something had tinkled out of her bag when she'd stood up to sing the National Anthem.

One of the lights at the back of the hall went out. That was Mr. Venner, the sexton. He was a very officious man. He had long drooping moustaches and a bright bald sweep of forehead. They said he was not very nice to his wife. Poor woman. Now the platform lights had gone out. She had better bend down a little and make it obvious that she was searching for something.

The little door leading into the changing-room behind the platform opened. Ah, Mr. Saul at last. Yes, he had his hat in his hand. He was frowning a little and bending his head forward to see down the length of the hall. How handsome he was!

"Is that you, Venner?"

Why did that man cough like that. "Just waiting to put out the lights, Mr. Saul."

"Waiting? Is somebody still here? Oh—yes—I see."

He had seen her now. He was looking down at her from the platform. Hessie straightened herself. Well, she must be philosophical about whatever it was that had slipped from her bag.

"Oh, Mr. Saul—"

"Lost something, Miss Price?" Really Mr. Venner was too officious.

"Well—oh, it doesn't matter!" very brightly. "I just thought—a copper or two maybe. But it's of no importance. No, really, it isn't! Please don't bother. Oh, dear, why—everybody's gone! I didn't notice—bending down. ..."

That was not really a lie—that was the sort of thing you said socially.

"You're sure it's nothing of importance, Miss Price?" How kind Mr.

Saul's voice was. It made her feel, suddenly, as if she would like to cry. How gentle, how protective a nice man could be.

"I'll put out the lights now, Mr. Saul?"

"Yes, do, Venner."

"I suppose you've heard about Hilda, Mr. Saul?" If she walked sideways through the benches, talking all the while, he would have to come with her. "Mother is very pleased. Of course, I suppose Hilda could have done better for herself, but poor Mr. Baker—she couldn't disappoint him. And he's really very kind."

"Yes."

"Then you have heard? Oh, but everybody in the town knows by now, I expect! A town of this size—everything is known at once, isn't it?"

"No doubt."

"Oh, Mr. Venner is in a hurry to get home, isn't he?" she said, laughing a little. "But what a lovely night. Look at those stars. Like diamonds in the sky!"

He was standing beside her now. "Yes, very pretty, Miss Price. Well, good night."

"Oh, aren't you taking the short cut to-night, Mr. Saul? But you're going home, aren't you? Well, would you mind awfully if I came with you? The road is quite deserted and, you know, once it's dark I'm so nervous. It's silly of me, I suppose."

"I don't think you need fear being attacked. I think the town is pretty free from rowdyism. But, of course, I'll accompany you if you feel nervous."

"It's just foolishness, I know!"

Men did like women to be women. Be independent, of course, but in a feminine way. Her eyes always looked best at night, too, when the pupils grew large and spread out over the pale irises. If only she were beautiful. But she was nicer looking than Hilda, and Hilda and Mr. Baker were somewhere ahead of them, and Hilda would be kissed. Mr. Baker's small hard mouth would close down on Hilda's, and then—but, really, really, she was ashamed of herself. Why did she keep on thinking of things like this? Indecent, immodest things, that frightened her with their persistence;

that seemed to come from some uncontrollable outside source and take possession of her.

"I think the concert to-night was a great success. The hall was quite crowded!"

"Yes, we had a good attendance."

"And Mr. Harvey—his songs were so funny—I had to laugh!"

"Will Harvey is our local comedian."

"Yes—he's clever at it, too!"

Silence. It was astonishing to watch their shadows as they walked from lamp-post to lamp-post. They were so dumpy to start with and then slowly and grotesquely they lengthened out. Mr. Saul's legs grew longer and longer at each step and foreshortened alarmingly just below the knee. Her figure looked very nice too, very slim and so ladylike, and she did walk carefully, with an upright swing of her shoulders.

"I was talking to Mrs. Kellaway the other day …"

"Mrs. Kellaway?" he gave her a quick sidelong glance.

Ah, she had captured his interest all right now—and just because the Kellaways were rich, and Mrs. Kellaway was so beautiful.

"Yes, I often see her when I'm taking the children down to the sea. You know, they allow Mrs. Benson's children to play on their private beach. It's very kind of them."

"Yes."

"Mrs. Kellaway is so charming, and their gardens are wonderful. Oh, but, of course, you know them! But I'm always just a little bit disappointed with the house itself."

"Disappointed? Why?"

"Oh well, you know—it's not so very big, is it? And then the inside—beautiful, of course, but all the same …"

But the conversation was going badly. Somehow, they were not getting into touch with each other. It was a pity she had said that about the Kellaways. He must not think she was lacking in taste. If only he would turn and look at her and smile. Just one smile, or put out his hand to help her off the curb. Any little touch at all—any of the little courteous things he had done on the first few evenings when he had come home with Hilda and her from some week-night service or lecture.

"Well, you're safely home now, Miss Price. No need to fear anything further."

"No—no indeed not! But won't you come in, Mr. Saul? Oh, do! Mother would be delighted to see you."

"No—I'm afraid I can't. It's getting late. Good night."

He stepped away from her, lifting his hat, his face so handsome and so serious.

"Well, Hessie, what was the concert like?" Mother asked immediately she got in.

"Oh, very nice, Mother."

"All the usual, I suppose? Did Rosie Bates sing?"

"No. Mother, isn't Hilda in yet?"

"Not yet. Did you come home alone?"

Hessie took off her hat, and passed her hand under her hair. Her neck felt damp. She waited a moment, and then said easily, casually.

"Oh, no—Mr. Saul saw me home."

"Really!" Mother's face lightened.

"He couldn't come in, though. He was very sorry but he had to get home."

"Well—well, Hessie!"

Hessie hummed a little as she went out to the kitchen. She lit the gas and put on the kettle. The remains of Mrs. Reed's and Mother's suppers lay vanquished on the tray. Evidently Mrs. Reed had carried it out before she left. Nothing very much remained of the brawn.

Well—wasn't it true? Mr. Saul had seen her home! Oh, he was interested in her, after all. He was—he must be!

She was feeling very hungry now. Dare she cut a slice off the cold meat and make a sandwich? The cold meat was looked upon as sacred, for dinners only. But perhaps Hilda, knowing Mrs. Reed's appetite, had had the forethought to put away a slice or two of the brawn. Hessie hunted over the shelves of the pantry, holding an inadequate match in her hand. The match flared up brightly when she struck it but after that first dazzling exuberance it lost its enthusiasm in the numbing darkness of the larder. But there was no crumpled greasy paper housing any brawn. A little recklessly she carried out the cold roast, and cut a slice from it, and left the meat out on the table as if she intended to cut more if she wanted it. The kettle was boiling now. She sat down at the kitchen table and ate her sandwich and drank some tea.

A commotion in the hall meant Hilda's return. Hessie went on eating and drinking slowly. A few moments later Hilda appeared in the doorway. Her pink scarf was open. She eyed Hessie and the cold meat. "Well, I never—!" she exclaimed.

11

Nurse seemed quiet this evening. After supper when Lottie had washed up, and Nurse could find nothing further for her to do, Lottie slipped out the side-door into the garden. She kept to a path that ran behind the shrubbery and entered the belt of trees that protected the garden from the sea-winds. This was an evening when she was entitled to a couple of hours of freedom. The long sea-grass rustled beneath her feet as she approached the shore. There was a drowsy aromatic scent mingling with the odours from the flowers in the garden and the faint more distant saltiness of the sea.

In a few hours' time when the moon was risen there would be sharp patches of light amongst the trees, but now there was only a faint glow, heavy still with the colour from the sunset, to guide her through the trees. Lottie walked on with a new unafraid confidence in her heart.

The sea was very silent when she reached the water's edge. The tide was going out slowly, and the small clear waves curled over soundlessly, hardly frothing at all until they swished lightly against the sand. In the present hour it was easy to imagine the outline of a horse and rider, coming slowly towards her. Not hard to imagine the faint jingling of reins and the dark gallant look of the horses against the sea.

When she turned to gaze inland again, someone was coming down the sand towards her. Lottie faced the sea once more, a gentle panic filling her heart. Even in this fading light she could recognize the slow easy walk of the approaching man. It was George. A pleasant confusion seized her when he stood beside her.

"You don't often come down here, do you?" he began.

Lottie moved her head slightly, and let her eyes look into his.

"This is the second time," she answered simply.

"And each time I've found you out?"

"Yes."

Unconsciously, with the vague idea of some future lovely protection stirring within him, George moved a step or two away. There was no harm in protecting her against himself, though every instinct towards her urged for gentleness and care.

"Won't you take off your cap?" he questioned.

Obediently Lottie put up her hand and took off the cap that hid her hair.

"There's that's better!" he smiled.

The sight of her now reminded him of that morning when she had arrived at the door of the long, flower-filled greenhouse, and stood, capless, in the sharp radiance of the early morning sun. Only now in place of that early sunshine there was the faintly coloured evening light that hung suspended over the water and shone in from the sea. Either way the sense of simplicity and gentleness that her soft clean-cut young beauty impressed on him was almost unbearable.

"Let's go for another little walk together," he suggested at last. "It's lovely at that far end of the bay. The sand is always so firm and white in between the rocks. You needn't be afraid."

Already their few brief encounters had accustomed him to her acquiescent quietness. He walked along slowly, keeping between her and the sea. If a wave bolder than the others and more reluctant to relinquish the land the tide had conquered, rolled up against his feet, he was heedless of the sibilant movement of it around him. "Look, that's the tree that marks the end of the garden," he said once.

"Are we as far as that?" Lottie exclaimed, and halted.

"But the garden isn't very wide just there," he said hurriedly, not slackening in his own walk, only anxious that she should continue with him. "That's its narrowest part. It spreads out from there and takes a big circle round the house on both sides."

"I don't think I've ever been all over the garden. I know the places where the children play mostly, and the beach …"

"Not this part of the beach," he asked, with sudden jealousy, and an absurd hope that the little coves, the stretches of white sand, the hump-shaped rocks that glistened with a profusion of colours when the sea-water lapped smoothly and softly around them, were his to show her first.

"No—not this end of the bay. I know the other end a little."

There was relief and radiance in the smile he flashed on her. He had scarcely realized until now how much he himself loved this end of the beach. He increased his speed and heard the rustling of Lottie's apron as she kept pace with him. They were reaching the outward sweep of sand now. The small jutting-out headland was coming up before them, its size increased enormously by the dark clear sky.

"There's a little stream here," he cautioned.

The clear fresh water ran rapidly and soundlessly over its self-made, shallow bed of sand. It had played childish pranks with the medium through which it had to flow to the sea that ended its journey. It had made little tunnels and deep channels in the sand, and raised glistening islands about which to throw its urgent waters. Closer in to the headland it fell with a liquid chattering over small rocks and rounded stones.

"It's easy to jump over this part." He guided her up-stream for a few yards.

"Oh, it's beautiful!" Lottie cried.

He smiled. "When I was small I used to come and wade here. On coldish days the water was like ice."

"You've always lived here?"

"Always. My mother lives in that cottage up there by—but you wouldn't know it."

"No. I wouldn't."

"It's hidden by the trees—all shut in by them."

They walked on in silence—The stream lay behind them, the headland sweeping up, dark and proud before them. Closer beside her now that they were approaching the low-lying rocks that ran into the sea like the spread-out fingers of a tremendous hand, George noticed again the light quality of her walk. He remembered that, too, from the day when she had sped so quickly across the dew-laden grass, away from the greenhouse with its load of blazing colour, and the two men who stood in the doorway of it—one of them himself.

"Here's the first cove," he said, halting her. "There's a cave up there at the end of it—away in underneath those rocks."

"I've never been in a cave!"

"The entrance to it is pretty low at first, and damp. Then you can walk along comfortably standing up."

"I'd never been to the sea, except twice on a day's outing, until I came here."

"Didn't you live in an Orphanage?"

Lottie's hands moved against her apron. "In an Orphanage."

"Poor kid," he said gently. "No parents?"

This was different from Nurse's questioning. The fact that she had no parents, no real home, nobody anywhere, became something touched, for the first time, with tenderness. Before, it had been a cold bleak fact, an immense, utterly inescapable reality, surrounding her consciousness like the smooth sides of a sheer cliff in which no foothold could be found. And it was something a little sordid, too, surprising and sordid. "What, no parents?—ah!" But now it was tender.

"Feel that wind?" George said suddenly. "That's the third gust I've felt to-night. There hasn't been a breeze like that for days now."

The wind had blown Lottie's hair from her forehead leaving her face naked against the night's warm sweetness. Her head was tilted back a little. The wind came again and swept lightly against her. Silently they stood together waiting for the wind to blow about them.

But not a breath stirred. Watching her George saw her breasts rise and fall slowly. The small, gentle curve of her apron moved a little. Gently, too, his glance went down her body, over the line of her thighs down to her feet.

"I've got to go back!" she cried suddenly. "What will Nurse say to me!"

"It isn't late," he protested. "It's not nine o'clock yet. You needn't be in till ten, need you?"

She hesitated. "No, I suppose not."

They started to walk again. He helped her over the rocks that lay scattered between the coves. The headland was only a small jutting out of earth-crowned rock, though in certain lights it looked squat and massive enough. There was a zig-zagging pathway up the face of it, and they climbed it together. At the top the wind came oftener to them as they followed the course of a narrow path. Clumps of bracken in which the faded ribbons of last year's grass still clung, were thick on either side. Brambles, too, with strong, dark leaves. They had to walk close together.

In a little hollow Lottie caught a glint of water. It was a small pool, fringed round with tall rushes, a placid sheet of water, with the rushes echoing their thin lonely ranks in its shallow depths.

Lottie stopped, enchanted. "Look at that!" she whispered.

"It takes a lot to dry that up," he said. "I've never seen it dry."

She took a step or two closer to it. He followed her. Then, very gently, as they stood together at the edge of the small silent pool, he put his arm around her.

Lottie stood very still. Her heart was beating no longer. Every function in her body had ceased. Her feet were not conscious of the ground on which she stood. She was suspended in nothingness, there beside shallow pool that looked so still and lovely, its smoothness pierced only by the narrow spires of the tall rushes. Then slowly, with ineffable sweetness, her heart began to beat again. The pool was no longer a blurred radiance before her, her body within the light touch of George's arm was intensely aware of everything about her. She had yielded instantly and unconsciously to his touch, and he had drawn her closely to him.

For a moment he held her like that. They could hear the sea below them, faint but clear. The dark light around them had a sudden strange brilliant clarity, and there was a fragrance of crushed grass and wet earth and the seaweed that the receding tide was uncovering. Then George took his arm away, and Lottie stood unsupported beside the pool. She was swaying a little, very slightly. She felt that her knees had given way altogether. Her knees had often betrayed her before but never in circumstances such as these. She felt that her eyes were fixed for ever now on the pool before her. With a little gasp she managed to turn her head away, to glance around at the enclosing slopes of coarse, grass-tufted fields. Somewhere behind her she knew George was standing, his hands in his pockets, his brown face sober. She did not need to look around actually to see him like that. She knew that was how he was.

"Well ..." she heard her own voice say.

She was able to turn away from the pool then. Her knees and her heart were behaving with a certain amount of reasonableness once more. They belonged to her in a half-hearted fashion.

"Watch out for those briars," he said gently.

"Oh, yes." She caught at the brambles holding her skirts, and the thorns fastened onto her fingers.

"Don't do that. Leave it to me."

She stood obediently while he pulled her skirts free, kicking the brambles away with his feet, trampling on them heavily. "Did you hurt your hand?"

"No, I don't think so. Only a scratch or two."

She walked quickly along the narrow path, slightly ahead of him because it was so very narrow here. Her apron brushed against the gorse and bracken and long heavy-headed grasses.

On the outer edge of the garden Lottie paused. They had better part here in case anyone should be walking about amongst the flowers and lawns.

"Good night," she whispered.

"Good night, Lottie."

Where the path twisted towards the house Lottie glanced back. George was standing where she had left him. How tall and young he looked with the moonlight shining down on him! Lottie began to run in and out amongst the shrubs, for once the path had forsaken its long straight way it curved amazingly. This was a bit the children loved. Leaving the shrubs behind it, the path crossed a wide space of lawn. Lottie fled through this open bit and in amongst the flowers. A great bed of white and pink blossoms flung their perfume at her. She steadied her wild flight to a walk. A stalk heavy with great dew-sprinkled flowers lay down across the path. Lottie bent and lifted it tenderly. The dew spilled over her fingers and trickled into the palms of her hands. She got a little stick that was lying on the path and drove it into the ground. The cluster of heavy, scented flowers rested against it, its head upright to the moon once more. Lottie gazed down at it tenderly. Night-time and the quietness of the garden had made her surprisingly bold. What would Nurse say if she saw her touching the flowers in the garden? What would the head-gardener say? What would Mr. Kellaway say, if they saw her tending the flowers like this?

She went on slowly. As she drew near the house she saw the light in the nursery windows. A frightened tremor ran through her. What would she say to Nurse, if Nurse asked her where she had been all this long while? She would not be able to say anything for the truth, in proximity with Nurse and the house, was impossible.

The side door was open, just as when she had gone out through it earlier in the evening. The stairs deserted. The heat of the day lingered in the upstairs passage where the black walls gleamed dully. She went straight on past the nursery door to the room where she slept with the two children and there she undressed rapidly. She drew her nightdress swiftly and decently over her head. Protected by its folds she stood undecided in the middle of the room. Isobel stirred a little. Lottie crept over to her. The child's sheet looked crumpled. She smoothed it gently. Isobel looked like a flower lying there, a faint pink colour in her cheeks, her hair flung out in such fine disorder about her face. She moaned faintly, and Lottie stood still in the middle of the room, scarcely breathing. But no further sound came from the child and so on tip-toe, her large nightgown floating out around her, Lottie moved across the room to her own bed.

Lying straightly between the sheets she stared up at the ceiling. Her eyes felt enormous in her head as if her eyelids could never close again. Her mind hovered either on the brink of delight or close to the edge of unreasoning fear, as she thought of the evening that was past. She touched the breast that George's hand had pressed so gently. She reheard every word that he had said to her, each syllable returned to her borne on its background of soft sea and night noises. At last her frightened urgent seeking conjured up a vision of George as he had been when they stood beside the pool, and looking into his eyes the tension within her relaxed. With a little sigh she closed her own eyes, lay over on her side, and fell asleep.

Chapter Six

I

The tea-party was a reality! A hideous reality! It was coming closer with every solemn sway and swing of the big pendulum of the grandfather clock that greeted visitors with such majestic respectability in the hall. Even her own silver watch, that really looked a little too big for its worn leather strap, was hustling on the tea hour.

Hilda was out, buying flowers to decorate the drawing-room. Mother had tottered off on some other errand of her own. She, Hessie, was alone in the house. Yes, quite alone with the unshrouded drawing-room where Hilda and Albert Baker would stand this afternoon in a pre-nuptial orgy of hand-shaking and simpering congratulations. Lily and Rosie Bates and almost all the members of the ladies' choir would be there, except the Derwent girls, who were never really friendly with the other choir members. Phillipa and Margaret Derwent. They were always very pleasant and agreeable and would share an anthem leaflet or anything like that with the other girls, their long white fingers looking like lilies with pretty pink rosebuds for nails, but they were never what could be called chatty or sociable. Not even in a Church of England sense. As Rosie Bates had once said, she wouldn't like to think what Margaret Derwent would do in a Nonconformist gathering. Sometimes Rosie went with a Methodist girl friend to one of their Band of Hope meetings or socials, where the spirit of real downright friendliness was like a good yeast working mightily in all there.

Mr. Saul would be coming in, too. He had accepted the invitation at once. "Delighted, Mrs. Price." Of course Mr. Saul would assist at the wedding. Mr. Benson and Mr. Saul would together join Hilda and Albert Baker in holy matrimony. Hilda and Albert Baker! Hilda would be Mrs. Albert Baker! When she appeared in church it would be at Albert's side, a married woman. Well, what was unnatural about that? Hessie put down her wash-rag and laid a wet vase on the draining-board. She stared out of the window. The view was limited by the wall of the house close by, scarcely ten feet away. There was a blackening crack in the grey cement of the wall and it opened and closed before her staring eyes. She gave herself a little shake. Well, if she wasn't a silly! Mesmerizing herself—or almost—by gazing at the wall opposite! Didn't they say that if you once allowed yourself to let another person mesmerize you that for ever afterwards you were subject to that person's will? But a dirty stone wall couldn't dominate you! No, indeed!

There—that was the back door bell, and somebody thumping on it as well! Really, some of these message boys were nothing but young hooligans. Wasn't it awful to think that they'd be men some day, going out with girls, walking out along the country roads, lying together in the hedges. Indeed some of the bigger ones—great big louts—they looked as if they knew the nastiest side of everything already. Yes, everything! The girls who went out with that sort of fellow must be coarse themselves. No gentility about them. Oh, well, like to like. As Mother often said, "Water always finds its own level."

Whoever it was at that door, they were thumping away again. Did they expect her to answer the bell with her hands all wet? Let them have a little patience. Other people had to learn to be patient. There, she would open the door now.

"Mrs. Price?"

"Yes—yes, that's right!"

What a pity she had not hurried! It was not an ordinary delivery boy at all, but a nice-looking young man in a white coat and a black peaked hat. Very polite and respectful, too. She flashed him the pleasant smile of a gentlewoman courteously sorry at having kept an inferior waiting.

"Have you been knocking long? I'm so sorry. Sometimes it's difficult to hear this bell."

"That's quite all right, madam. Will you just sign here?"

"Certainly." Better sign it on the scullery shelf, and then he would not see her hands, or perhaps he'd think she'd just taken her wedding ring off whilst she washed or did something like that. Or did married women ever take off their wedding rings? It was hardly likely.

"Thank you. Good morning, madam."

"Good morning."

What a pity she had been wearing this old overall and that her hair was falling down a little! It had become loosened when she was polishing the drawing-room furniture earlier this morning, and she had not bothered to take it down and pin it up again properly because Hilda and she were both going to wash their hair just before dinner. Hilda was out buying the shampoo now. Two sixpenny ones, and they were each going to use a whole shampoo at once! Usually they divided the powder up into three and so a hair-wash only cost twopence a time, and less than a pennyworth of gas heated the water. Pennies! How she hated them, and yet she was helpless before them. "Go down to the Stores, Hessie, I saw some nice lunch sausage for only a sixpence a pound there. Morgan's charge tenpence."

Where would Hilda get her groceries when she was married? "Good morning, Mrs. Baker, and what can I have the pleasure of getting for you this morning?" Mrs. Baker! Hilda, in the full importance of a married woman, shopping for her husband and a household. Albert Baker looked well fed. The manager at Morgan's would hurry forward to serve Hilda, he would not leave her to one of the assistants which was how he treated her now, which was how he would continue to treat Hessie. He had a horrid habit of looking right through her, and then moving carelessly away, even though it was obvious that he had not anything important to do. At the butcher's, too, Hilda would be respected. She would order sirloin instead of rib. She would not have to go in and say brightly, wisely, "I think I'll have a little mutton this morning. Oh, yes, a nice piece of the breast will do. It's just for stewing, you know. Well, yes, that bit of scrag-end looks nice...."

Nothing of that kind for Hilda any more. Her orders would be sent home, too, not slapped down on the counter before her while the assistant waited to see if she were going to slide them into a surreptitiously held up basket. "Will you put them into a bag, please?" How humiliating it was to have to say that, and to have to stand there trying to look as though this trifling oversight on the assistant's part had merely amused you. Money! Albert was what Mother called 'sound.' In Albert's soundness Hilda would soon have a legal and spiritual—yes, spiritual—right to share. Truly and beautifully a man and his wife were one, even the tradesmen recognized that. Last Sunday evening Mr. Saul had preached on the sacred beauty of marriage. How beautiful he had looked himself. Standing up in the pulpit with the splendid arch of the chancel behind him, his robes giving him a young, god-like look.

"Oh, my God—my God!" Hessie cried suddenly, her arms locked across her chest and pressing hard against her flat breasts, her fingers digging into the flesh of her arms, her body rigid.

Now, what was happening to her? Shocked and exhausted, she sank down on the kitchen chair. She had never experienced such an emotional upheaval before. As if something terrible and ungovernable in its strength had leapt to life within her. She stared straight ahead, her unseeing eyes staring at the girl on the calendar on the wall, gazing at the flowing gown and general sweet undressed modesty of this Victorian beauty's brief corsage, the long swelling neck, the smooth shoulders. Then, moving her hands with a fearful gentleness this time, Hessie pressed them to her breasts. Then she covered her face and began to cry.

At last she lay back in the chair, her head resting against the wall. She felt drained and empty. Alone, too. Terribly alone. Isolated by her recent experience. Was she getting upset and nervy? Perhaps she was overworking herself? There was so much to do for dear Mrs. Benson, and at home there was no real rest either. Perhaps she would feel better, less raw and strained, when Hilda's wedding was over. A marriage in the family was often very upsetting. Mother and Hilda and she had lived together for so long now, they knew each other's little ways so well. Hilda and she had the housework and everything planned out just so. No wonder she was a little upset and perhaps strange at a time like this. "The old order changeth—" How beautifully Tennyson had put it, and if a mind as noble as his could appreciate so clearly the vast consequences that follow change was there any wonder that she should feel a little unusual in the present circumstances, too? This was a soothing, a comforting thought, and its comfort must not be destroyed by doubts of its inner truthfulness. No, indeed. Truly she was worn out and tired, and once Hilda and Albert were married, and the dark square bedroom in Albert's house had grown accustomed to Hilda's presence there, then—then she'd feel herself again. It was only that she was surrounded by so many changes. Changes for herself, greater changes for Hilda, far far greater changes for Hilda. And she was very very tired.

"Good gracious, Hessie, whatever's come over you?"

Hilda in the doorway. Very bright and pleasant.

"I got a sudden headache. That's all. It's going off now. I sat down for a moment."

Hilda made a funny noise with her tongue. "T'ck-t'ck! That would happen to-day, wouldn't it! Oughtn't you to see the doctor about your eyes, Hessie?"

"Perhaps I ought."

"Well, anyhow, I think I'd better put on the water for some tea. Mother will be exhausted, you know. Oh, Hessie, have Albert's flowers arrived? Just fancy, I met him in the High Street and he said he'd sent some flowers for me to-day! Oh dear, oh dear, aren't the vases washed yet?"

"Some of them are—" There was a strange edge on Hessie's voice. "And some parcel or another has come. I signed for a box."

"Where is it?"

"There, on the chair."

Better get up and put on the kettle for the tea-lunch they were having to-day, for how could she bear to watch Hilda opening her flowers—flowers from Albert. The first flowers that either of them had ever received from a man; and they had come to Hilda, who was two years her junior. "Oh, Hessie, do look!"

"Oh, for God's sake, don't be so coy!" Had she said that out loud? No, she hadn't, for Hilda was still holding the flowers against her chest, her long neck moving from side to side, her face smiling girlishly as she glanced at the blossoms.

"Oh, lovely!" she breathed deeply. "Lovely—lovely!"

Hessie moved over to the sink, and filled the kettle. They were having tea and brawn for lunch, and they were having the meal in the kitchen. The dining-room and the upstairs drawing-room were sacred to-day. They had been cleaned and polished, and now awaited only what Hilda and she called the "titivations." Flowers here, photographs grouped a little more artistically there. Grandfather, Mother's father, in full dress-uniform placed well to the fore; pictures of herself and Hilda as children; Mother and Father's wedding group—Father unavoidable this time because of his function as bridegroom; Mother with Hessie's white christening gown flowing over the maternal knee. "What a mother you've been, Mrs. Price." "My two wee girlies." "We call this one 'Sisters' and this one 'Grandfather Riding His Horse.'"

Hadn't Mr. Saul very much admired the one called 'Sisters'? "A wonderful likeness, Miss Hessie." "Well, but I was younger then, Mr. Saul!" "Oh really!" How astonished he had been, just as if there was scarcely any difference between herself at eighteen and now! Perhaps there was not so much difference, really; except that she was a woman now instead of a girl. But weren't there some men who admired women more than girls, found them more sympathetic? After all, what did a young girl know about life, especially a girl who had led a sheltered genteel existence. No—no a woman was broader-minded.

Did Hilda think that she was a sort of vestal virgin, carrying those vases with the flowers arranged in them as though they were uplifted candles? A virgin! What a delicate, private sort of word it was! Biblical—or Catholic? Both, perhaps. But not quite polite; sacred, of course, but hardly a word you could use comfortably before gentlefolk.

"I'll just put these in the drawing-room," Hilda said in a hushed voice. "It's cooler there."

"I can't find the tablecloth," Hessie said brusquely.

"Oh, well," Hilda hesitated, her lips pursed up. "What do you think? It won't matter so much to-day. It isn't as if we were having a proper meal, is it? There's that nice piece of clean white paper. Put that on this end of the table."

With an abrupt little movement Hessie swept the sheet of white wrapping paper to the floor, and placed the cups and saucers on the bare boards. They had had meals on the bare kitchen table before this. How ridiculous Hilda was with her flowers and her pursed up lips and her new little niceties about white paper instead of a tablecloth! Hessie stared at the moist heap of sliced brawn that Hilda had purchased. Up till a few months ago she had never felt this irritation with Hilda. They had been chums, real friends! But a few months ago Hilda would have said, a little dashingly, "Oh, don't bother about the cloth, Hess, it may not be society exactly, but I don't think eating without a cloth will coarsen us too much!" After all, if you were a real lady it didn't matter what you did, so long as you did it as a lady would do it. But lately Hilda had been full of little airs and graces. So that was another thing this marriage was doing to them? Separating them in this new way.

Soon Hilda came into the room again, her head swathed in a towel.

"Whatever you do, don't ever let Albert see you like that!" Hessie cried. "You look dreadful. I suppose it's the soap that's made your nose so shiny?"

"Is my nose shiny?" Hilda asked almost dreamily.

Hessie rattled the teaspoons. "It'll be all right when you've powdered. I'm just tired to-day, Hilly. Don't mind me."

"That's all right, dear," Hilda said in such a gentle patronizing way that Hessie's irritation welled up again. For a moment she longed to say something shattering, something so horribly coarse that Hilda would be shaken out of this dreadful patronizing complacency. But, fortunately, she was able to control this impulse.

"Did you get a shampoo for me?" she asked.

"It's in the scullery. On the window-ledge."

"I'd better do my hair now, I think." She must keep her voice gentle and patient. "Then it'll be drying during dinner. Will you make the tea when the kettle boils?"

On the outside of the shampoo packet there was a picture of a girl with luxuriant hair and a sweet fixed smile. Hessie emptied the packet recklessly into the basin. There were several cracks in the cheap enamel surface and they irritated her finger-tips as she poured in the hot water, one hand swirling the powder into a froth. What a rich heavy scent this powder had! It made her think of a lot of things she had read. The soft scent about a woman's hair—her dusky hair—a dark scented cloud around her face—the little scented tendrils that lay against her neck.

The water she had poured from the kettle was very hot. It almost burnt her scalp, but she had better have it fairly warm because of the grease. Why was her hair of the fine thin greasy type? Still, hers was a lady's hair, there was nothing coarse and strong about it.

Hilda and she both lunched with towels around their shoulders. Suddenly they were laughing at each other. It was like being young again, young in the childish sense of not knowing any sort of maturity at all.

"Hilda, share this last slice of brawn with me?"

"I couldn't! Yes, I could, though. ..."

"Good heavens, it's two o'clock! We'll never have the house ready! Hilda, you finish off the drawing-room. I'll do the dining-room and stairs. Mother, you cut the bread and butter."

Oh, this was better! Being able to laugh and bustle round, whisking things into place. Hilda and she were just two girls together, getting the house ready for an engagement party. It happened to be Hilda's party, but that was only a detail. It would be her turn next. An engagement party was a natural, right sort of thing in their lives. After all, they were not different from other girls in that sense at all. Men friends, parties, little intimate gay occasions, girlish pleasures—why not? "My sister's fiancé ..." it was almost like saying "*My* fiancé!" The house turned upside down in the joyous rush of getting everything ready for an especially happy party. Men sending flowers—well, Albert sending flowers—anyhow, flowers sent by a man had arrived. They were up in the drawing-room now. "Oh, I say, look at what Albert's sent!" "Scrumptious, Hilda. What blossoms!" Surely flowers were a subject for easy happy every-day comment, too? To-morrow it might be her turn to say, "Look at my flowers!" "Oh, Hessie, *how* lovely! Who did those come from?" "I don't know. There wasn't any card or anything with them." "You can guess though, I expect!" "Well, I won't say that I can't ...!" How gay and happy life was!

"My goodness, Hessie, you're running round like a little child—and with your hair down your back you don't look grown up at all!" Mother exclaimed suddenly.

"Why—Mother—!"

She was restored again. That dreadful shattering moment in the kitchen was wiped out. Oh, God, how terrible it had been.

Up in the bedroom she still felt bright and gay.

"Would you like to wear my pink beads with that pretty frock, Hilda?"

Hilda turned from the mirror. "How do I look?"

"Awfully nice. ... Why, Hilda, what have you been doing? Curling your hair?"

"Yes," said Hilda nonchalantly. "I shall go to the hairdresser's regularly when I'm married. A wave is such an improvement."

"Well, I suppose it is! Do you know, I think I'll curl mine, too."

"Don't frizz it up too much!"

"Show me how to do it—be a darling!" Oh, they were pals again, chums, sisters! It was like old times. Mother was stiff and rustling in a new black silk frock.

"Now then, my chickabiddies, not much more time, now," she said with beaming sprightliness.

"There's Albert! Oh, go on down, Hilda, and don't be afraid! Mother and I'll give you five minutes all to yourselves! That ought to be enough!"

"Hess!"

"Oh, go on, go on, give the poor man a chance. You've got to say thank you for the flowers. Don't forget to kiss him nicely!"

"Really, Hessie," said Mrs. Price, as Hilda left the room. "Wherever have you picked up such ideas? A nice young girl shouldn't know ..."

"Shouldn't know what, Mother?" how bright her eyes were, how sparkling! Mother need not pretend to be indulgently horrified. "Why shouldn't Hilda kiss Albert? There's nothing improper about that, is there?"

"Hessie ..."

"Mother—you've got to be modern." Why was her voice rising like this, rising uncontrollably? She must keep it down. "Men do kiss girls—men do—men do! Yes, they do!"

Hessie ran out of the room trembling all over. She was still shaking a little even when the guests arrived and she had helped to serve the tea.

After a while she sat down in the comer where Mr. Saul was sitting.

"Mr. Saul, let me get you another cup of tea?"

"No, thank you."

"Oh, really you must! You've only had one cup!"

"That's all I ever take at tea-time."

"Only one cup? Are you really sure?" There was a teasing, quizzical little note in her voice that was really quite attractive.

"Quite sure, thank you."

"I can hardly believe that!" He must let her pour him another cup of tea, handling his cup gave her a sensation of being close to him. "Please let me!"

"No, thank you."

"But I think it would be good for you. Really! I'm not just teasing." Silence.

"Oh, it's true. I wouldn't ever tease you, Mr. Saul. I—I think you're so awfully interesting. The way you talk—"

"I trust I don't stutter, or do anything like that?" he said suddenly.

"Oh, how funny of you! Stutter? Of course not!"

Repartee, how easy it was, after all! In her present mood anyhow. But she was just being herself. Usually, she was tired and there were so many responsibilities in life. But she was young and carefree to-day.

This party was being a great success. Everybody was here. Mr. and Mrs. Benson—everybody. She had been the daughter of the house all afternoon, helping her mother with the tea, swishing about with cups and plates of sandwiches and cakes, dropping a word here, a smile there. But now she was alone in a corner with Mr. Saul. Mother was smiling at them. How different Mr. Saul's pale face and sharp features looked from Albert's plump red face?

Supposing she were serious for a change now.

"How happy my sister looks," she began gently. "Don't you think love is a beautiful thing? It seems to do something to a girl. Makes her look—radiant."

"Superlatively radiant, I've no doubt," Mr. Saul said with startling crispness. "And now, I'm afraid I must interrupt our little chat. I must speak to your mother."

"Oh, no—no!" her voice rose. "Mother's resting, I think, Mr. Saul, and you know how it tires her to talk too much. See, she's just sitting back, smiling at us all. At you and me, too! Mother is so romantic, you know. In her days when two young people sat together in corners people thought—they thought ..."

"Ah, Hessie, so you're doing the honours this afternoon?" Mr. Benson's voice broke in. "Well, I want another cup of tea. You know exactly how I like it! By the way, you're not to give parties every day, you know! Mrs. Benson missed you very much this morning. Ah, that's right—if you'd just move your chair, Hessie, then Mr. Saul could get out. That's it. Now, this is exactly what I want. A cup of tea in a quiet corner! No, stay and talk to me, Hessie, if you please. ..."

What a horrible, horrible man Mr. Benson was! What right had he to come and interrupt them like that, just when she and Mr. Saul were getting on so nicely. She hated him, hated him.

"I'm afraid there is no more tea, Mr. Benson, but I can get some more, of course." It was quite easy to make her voice sound polite yet frigid with dislike. She was in her own home. She was not, at the moment, in his employ, either. What an unhealthy pasty face his was, and his eyes were dark and hard. Oh, poor, poor Mrs. Benson who had to make wifely submission to a man like that. How horrible her life must be.

"Well—well, in that case I must forego my quiet cup in this nice corner. You mother is looking at me, I think. I'll just go and talk to her."

And now Mr. Saul had gone! He was not anywhere in the room. Hilda was standing by the empty fireplace with Albert beside her. Every smile, every look, every word, every gesture, of Hilda's was full of Albert. She was possessing Albert fully.

"Look at the flowers this man sent me!" she cried archly to everyone.

"Oh, do let me have a look at your ring, Hilda," Rosie Bates said shrilly.

What was the matter with Hilda's mouth? It looked different somehow. Was it because Hilda had been kissed? What did it feel like to be kissed? To be held in a man's arms and kissed, a lover's kiss. Hilda knew.

Mr. Benson was looking at her, with his nasty hard eyes. Hessie turned away. What a lot of washing-up there would be after the guests were gone. Cake crumbs, bits of sandwiches, cold tea dregs. How could she manage all the housework when Hilda was married?

But the worst time came when the guests were all gone.

"I saw you both!" Mrs. Price remarked archly.

Hessie picked up the dish-cloth. It was very wet and a faint sour smell clung to her fingers after using it. That was another thing she'd have to do this evening. Wash out the dish-cloths. They had three of them. That was all that was left from the half-dozen she had bought so recklessly at Marston's sale? Good union tea-cloths, 6d. each, 2s. 9d. for the half-dozen. But they had not worn very well after all. Nevertheless, it had given her a delicious housewifely feeling whenever she drew a clean cloth from the little pile in the drawer. They had suggested a model kitchen, with a blue and white colour scheme and pretty canisters cheerfully announcing their contents—coffee, tea, sugar, rice—to an expectant young husband, while a pretty young wife smiled tantalizingly from her graceful position before an incredibly white sink; or else the sweet-faced young woman bent confidingly before an open oven door from which escaped a gentle, indecently succulent stream of steam. And all the while the husband murmured, "Sardine savoury again—how delicious. ..."

"I saw you and Mr. Saul," Mrs. Price repeated coyly.

Hessie picked up another cup. Could sheer unresponsiveness beat Mother into silence?

"I saw you—"

"We just had a little talk together, Mother."

"A little talk, dear?"

"Yes."

"About something private, Hessie dear?"

Hessie pressed her hand to her head. Private? Yes, a gay, private, intimate, little talk. It had been that! Cosy, just the two of them together. Mr. Saul alone in the corner with her.

"If you don't mind, Mother, I'd rather not—" she smiled.

Mother was satisfied with that. After all, that was the truth, too. And Mr. Saul had looked at her in a tender way. What a beautiful thing tenderness was, the tenderness of a man towards a woman. Protectiveness, really. Hilda was experiencing that. Albert always put her on the inside of the pavement, and to-night going out of the front door he had swept Hilda before him with a courtly little gesture.

How had the party ended? At one moment the drawing-room had been full, and then there had been only Hilda and Albert and Mother and herself and the exhausted-looking tea-cups. Afterwards Hilda and Albert had gone out together.

"Would you like a little game of cribbage, when we've finished washing up, Hessie?"

"I think I'll go out for a little walk, Mother. Will you be all right? Don't you think we'd better finish up these sandwiches and things for supper? They'll be stale by to-morrow."

"Must you go out, Hessie?" Mrs. Price began sadly "Really—"

Hessie plunged the dish-cloth into the water. A little cloud of sourish steam rose up, and a line of dark grease gathered gently around the sides of the enamel pan. A moment of unexpected nausea caught her. She was going to be violently sick! But her stomach steadied.

"Really, Mother, I must go out!" she cried wildly. "I've got such a headache."

"I've got a headache, too," Mother said. "But, of course—yes, go on, Hessie. Go on and get a little fresh air. I shall be all right. You mustn't stay in for me. Maybe my other girlie will be home soon."

It took nearly half an hour to get Mother settled in the dining-room, with sandwiches and tea beside her, and her patience cards close to hand. Mrs. Price kept sighing gustily all the time the things were being arranged for her.

"Any sign of Hilda, dear?" she inquired as Hessie was leaving.

"Not yet, Mother. But she's sure to be home soon. Anyhow I won't be long myself."

"Oh, don't hurry, Hessie. I must learn what it's like to be left alone. But, if you could be back before very long. ..."

Hessie hurried out. Her head was hot and throbbing unbearably. She walked quickly through the streets towards the seashore. It was a small rocky piece of shore, cut off by sheer cliff from the beautiful sandy bay that belonged to the Kellaways. Piles of shingle were thrown against mounds of broken rocks, and when the tide was out, as it was now, pools of sea-water lay in the sunken basins of the flattened rocks. On still days the water in these natural hollows looked clear and very soft. There was a little strip of common-land to cross before the shore itself was reached, and this was dotted with old caravans and broken-down shanties, with here and there a piece enclosed by a medley of boards and crazy wire netting—homes of quaint, long-legged hens whose voices rose with peculiar harsh exultancy whenever one of their members laid an egg. That an egg should be laid by one of their community seemed a minor miracle to the rest of the brood. They were roosting now, crouching on bits of board, looking lonely and forlorn and hopeless. Here and there on the flattened grass loving couples lay entwined. It was the recognized courting-place for the poor of the town.

Hessie shivered a little as she passed through. This wasn't at all a nice place for a lady, but she must get to the sea. There would be air there and a dampness rising from the wet rocks. Besides, what would it matter if something awful did happen to her? Supposing a man accosted her, walked along beside her, pestered her, took her arm perhaps. What would she do—what should she do? Scream, of course, or else pull her arm away, and utter a few well-chosen, scathing words. That would be more dignified. Let him see that she was a lady, that he had made a wretched mistake. He would fall behind her then, humiliated before virtue. Virtue was a potent weapon against a man's hot desire—wasn't it? Oh dear, oh dear, what made her think of dreadful things like that. She had been down to the sea at this time of night on other evenings and no one had ever spoken to her, why should she imagine such a likelihood now? There was a little rustling noise beside one of the shanties. Hessie turned her head sharply and saw a man and a girl standing very close together. She heard the girl laugh suddenly, and saw her draw the man's head down against the hollow of her neck. Why, it was a maternal gesture almost! Not a bit—not a bit wicked or passionate. More like a mother fondling a big child.

Hessie nearly stumbled as she reached the first of the loose boulders that lay about the rocky shingle. Supposing she broke her ankle on the rocks and lay there, helpless, while the tide crept in? While the grey water swept in, eddying round the rocks, rising so that soon the low-lying rocks were no longer obstacles in the way of its smooth approach, no longer disturbances round which its waters swirled, till nothing at all broke the flat grey bosom of the oncoming tide, not even her own thin protesting body. Or would she protest and struggle, clutching at the slippery rocks, pulling herself and her agony inch by inch closer towards the shore? Rather, would she not lie still, stretched out, with her face to the stars and let the gentle sea close over her and this tired sickening body of hers?

Hessie stumbled again and sat down heavily. She found a foothold for the heels of her shoes in a ledge of a rock and braced her shaking limbs against it. Her hat had slipped sideways, and her hair, soft and greaseless from the shampoo, hung in little wisps about her face. Impatiently she jerked off her hat and pushed her hair back, leaving her face and forehead free. That was better. She could feel the wind blowing on her temples, cooling her, soothing her. She shut her eyes. How gentle, how soft the wind was, and how silent this part of the shore. Her body was growing quiet and still too, the painful excitement of the past few hours leaving it.

At last she stood up, and started for home. The night had darkened a lot and the first of the street lamps shone very harshly. Her way lay through a squalid part of the town with grey pavements blending into the peeling walls of the little crouching houses.

Hilda was in when Hessie reached home. Hilda's hair was awry and there was a tired flush on her face, yet, despite her burning cheeks and the coy girlish manner she adopted so frequently nowadays, she looked old and tired.

Hessie studied her calmly.

"Shall I get you a cup of tea, Hilda? You're tired."

"Oh, well, Hessie, it has been a tiring day, hasn't it? So much excitement. But wasn't it wonderful? The tea-party was a great success. Albert quite enjoyed himself. And men don't like tea-parties as a rule, do they?"

"We'll have a cup together. I suppose Mother's in bed?"

"Just gone. She said she couldn't wait up—she hoped you'd be all right."

Hessie smiled quietly. "I'm not a baby, Hilda. ..." She raised her eyebrows a little. "Mother's got to realize that now. Really she has."

Hilda stared down at the floor, her hands clasped loosely in her lap. Hessie went out to the kitchen. She was feeling very calm and still. She let the gas roar extravagantly under the kettle as she prepared a tray. She fingered the cups into place with a nice precision. Hilda was still sitting motionless when she carried the tray into the dining-room. "Here, dear, drink this up. It'll do you good."

She felt grave and sweet and maternal as she handed Hilda her cup of tea. Hilda was tired out, and she, Hessie, was still full of calm strength!

"Does Albert kiss you, Hilda?" she asked gently, impersonally.

Hilda started. Her thin face flushed an ugly, painful scarlet.

"Of course," she said defiantly.

"On your mouth?" Hessie pursued, with this same grave detachment.

"Well, we're engaged," Hilda stammered. "And anyhow ..."

"That's all right, dear. You're tired out, I know." Hessie took Hilda's empty cup gently from her. "Go upstairs now. I'll carry this to the kitchen, and put out the lights."

Chapter Seven

I

Mrs. Kellaway's presence in the kitchen brought some delicate perfume with it. How cool and lovely she looked in that pale pink frock that was made of the same stuff as the children's dresses.

"Maggie, I want you to help Irene to-day. She'll tell you what she wants you to do. The caterer's men will have the back kitchen to themselves."

"Yes, Mrs. Kellaway."

"We want the day to be a great success. I know I can rely on you to help in every way."

"I'll do everything I can, Mrs. Kellaway."

"Good."

Who wouldn't do anything in the world for Mrs. Kellaway? Maggie glanced out of the window. The sky was a faultless blue. After a week of rain and doubtful weather summer was back with them again. Getting up this morning she had looked anxiously at the sky, only to be reassured by the sight of the hazy horizon and the absence of any clouds in the sky's delicate blueness. Below in the garden the canvas of the huge tents had been damp with dew, the flags from their masts drooping in soft inactive folds. It was midday now, and they were still hanging motionless but their colours were bright and crisp in the sunshine.

The men from the big catering firm had been here since breakfast time. They had taken possession of the second big kitchen, and they were in there now, unpacking their baskets and things. Their vans were standing outside in the yard. One of the vans was really a big refrigerator, with ices and creams and salads and fruit stored waiting in it. The waiters were continually passing to and fro, their coats off, their shirt-sleeves rolled up. One of them was a very handsome young man. He went about his work with a deeply serious face, as if he were wholly unconscious of his own profile. Irene was openly in love with him. "The lovely young man!" she kept exclaiming with bursts of genial laughter to Cook and Mrs. Bartley. Irene was in one of her best, most cheerful moods to-day. "He ought to be on the films," Mrs. Bartley said. "What's he doing down here mixed up with a lot of Italians and such-like?"

The whole house was different to-day. The life of the place had extended itself to the gardens and the big marquees and because of this expansion the house was empty and unfamiliar. The men were still hammering away at the stalls and games in the meadow behind the trees. There was a track marked out for races for the children. Anne and Isobel were going to join in with the school-children. Mrs. Kellaway was to give away the prizes. This annual Garden Party was a great event with the tenants.

"He's looking at you, Maggie!" Irene cried, as the handsome young waiter passed the kitchen window and glanced in.

"Uh-huh!" Cook grunted.

Maggie tossed back her head, her cheeks flaming. Thank goodness Mrs. Kellaway had arranged for her to help Irene and Mrs. Bartley to-day. There were two extra helpers in the kitchen, wives of workmen on the estate, and Mrs. Kellaway had thought it best that she should help with the bedrooms, being one of the indoor servants. Nurse had agreed to do the nurseries herself this morning, so Lottie had helped Mrs. Bartley do half the bedrooms and passages, and she and Irene had whisked round the other rooms. They had got every bedroom in the house finished by ten o'clock.

The handsome waiter went by again. "He's struck on Maggie right enough!" Irene exclaimed generously. "You're a one for the boys, Maggie!"

Maggie laughed this time. "Oh, my head's hot!" she cried, pushing back her cap.

"Don't take your cap off in my kitchen," Cook said sourly.

Maggie turned her back on Cook. What did the old thing matter to-day? She glanced out of the window again and saw the handsome waiter coming back. She was feeling strong and vibrant. Her body was keenly alive, tingling under her clothes. She felt as if she had been naked in the wind and sunshine for days and that her skin was smooth and brown from exposure. Because of this she smiled a little with her lips and eyes, staring with a new boldness at the young man. She hoped Cook was watching her.

"Come on, now, let's get these things outside," Irene said.

Besides the two big tents for the tenants, there was a smaller one where tea would be served to Mr. and Mrs. Kellaway's personal friends.

It was very warm inside the tents. Mr. Kellaway came in just as Irene and Maggie were spreading clean cloths on the small tables. He stood there silently for a moment, glancing here and there, his tall spare figure isolated from them by his quiet dignity. Maggie and Irene spread their cloths with quick consciously-capable movements. Irene was accustomed to meeting Mr. Kellaway, her work as house-maid brought her into close touch with him and his clothes, but he was an almost complete stranger to Maggie. He never came into the kitchens, and she was seldom in the front part of the house once her early morning scrubbing was done. Maggie felt her face flush up as he walked slowly down the centre of the tent and out at the other end. He stood in the entrance for a moment and then moved from sight. But his coming had galvanized Irene into a more sober activity. Her face was serious as she twisted and spread the cloths. She was a capable experienced woman working with deft expert movements.

Then Maxwell came in. His face was shining with perspiration, and his shirt clung damply to his wide chest and shoulders. He looked strong and very powerful.

"How many tables here?" he asked.

"Goodness, can't you see for yourself!" Irene exclaimed amiably. "That's just like a man! Comes in when you're busy and stands round asking questions."

"Come on now—how many cloths did you bring out?" Maxwell grinned.

"As many as I could lay hands on. What's over go over there in case anyone spills their tea or messes things up."

Maggie was behind him and he turned to her. He came quite close to her.

"You count them for me, Maggie," he said in a low voice.

Irene gave a short laugh as she whisked out of the tent. "You arrange those cups, Maggie," she said, as she left.

Maggie stood still. She had not let him see her alone since the morning when he had interrupted her scrubbing. Her knees began to shake a little now, as though her bones were growing weak. It was very hot and close inside the tent, still and quiet, too, giving a sense of extreme remoteness from the garden where so much activity was going on.

Perhaps she ought to have let him see her between this and that swift early morning visit? Now his silence and his tenseness as he stood so close to her were almost frightening. If he took her in his arms, she'd be helpless against him and the betraying passion ravishing her own body.

A passing workman slung his hammer down onto one of the wooden pegs outside the tent and the canvas quivered a little from the suddenly tightened stay-rope. Maggie jerked up her head. That had restored her a little bit, thank goodness. She met his eyes with a touch of defiance in her own.

"Come down and see the flowers again to-night," he said. "Why haven't you come before?"

"I've been busy."

"Well, come to-night. Any hour will do. I'll wait up for you."

She began to shiver slightly. "But you can't see flowers in the darkness," she said.

"These greenhouses have electricity in them. I often work in them at night. Come to the row closest to my house."

He turned away quickly, and left the tent without a backward look. Maggie seized a cloth and spread its folds with weak violence. She wanted to be violent, but she was trembling so much that her arms felt useless. Irene came back with a tray-load of cups and saucers and plates. She started to arrange them in little groups of twos, threes and fours on the tables. Three waiters, laden with things, went by, making for the big marquees. The household servants were in charge of the small tent where the private visitors would have their tea. A man began hammering outside again and tautening the stay-ropes. The canvas trembled and quivered as if it were alive as he moved round adjusting each rope. The smell of trodden grass filled the tent with sweet cleanness.

Soon one of the under-gardeners came in with a large basket of flowers. He laid it down on the long buffet table and went out again. The perfume from the flowers stole through the tent, delicate and refreshing.

"Are we to arrange those?" Irene questioned indulgently. "Did anyone tell you what to do with them?"

Maggie shook her head. She knew what Irene meant. Irene bent over the flowers and breathed deeply. "I'd like to eat them," she said, "they smell so nice."

Maggie set the cups down on the saucers very gently. This was different from working in the kitchen with Cook. Irene was kind and cheerful and laying out this delicate china was pleasanter work than washing up the cups and saucers used in the kitchen.

"Two cups on that table, Maggie," Irene said. "Some of them will want to sit by themselves—in couples!"

The young under-gardener returned with a basket full of vases. He laid them out on the table, and began arranging the flowers diligently.

"Like assistance?" Irene inquired.

"Haven't got enough of your own work to do, I suppose?" he grinned.

"I'm a Girl Guide!" Irene returned.

He went on silently with his work, a little abashed by Irene's presence. He was quite young. He filled the vases carefully, arranging the flowers blossom by blossom. When he was finished he stood back and looked earnestly at his work.

"They're all ready for the tables, now," he said, with a sidelong glance at Irene.

"Work for us at last!" she exclaimed. Then she gave him a full pleasant smile. "Nobody could have done them any nicer," she added generously.

His face flushed, and he left the tent quickly.

It was nearly dinner-time now. Maggie blinked as she entered the kitchen, the sunshine in the garden had been so strong and bright that the house seemed dark after it. There was cold meat and potato pasties, and jam tarts for dinner. Afterwards the older women had cups of tea. Maggie sat beside Irene. For once Cook was too busy to take any notice of her.

What was she going to do to-night, when darkness came and the other servants had gone to bed? What would happen if she went down to the greenhouses close to the head-gardener's house? What would happen, indeed! She knew Maxwell and his type well enough. She'd met them before. Often. She put down her cup of tea slowly. The very thought of Maxwell made her feel queer. It wasn't as if he were really good-looking, but there was some power about him. God, she'd kept herself decent up till now, and it wasn't likely that he was the marrying sort. Besides it was improbable that any one girl could keep a man like that contented for long. It might be possible, though, to have enough hold on him to make him come back to her again and again. It would not matter much what happened in between, so long as he came back, hungrier than before.

"Time's up," Irene announced. "More work to do! Come along, Maggie."

II

"Please take us to the meadow. You've got to, Lottie."

"Now, Anne dear ..."

"Oh, for heaven's sake take those children out, Lottie. Take them to the meadow or anywhere else. But have them back by twelve o'clock. Don't forget. And then they are to lie down for half an hour. Dinner's early to-day. Don't forget, Lottie. Isobel's to have at least half an hour's rest before her food. Do you understand?"

"Yes, Nurse."

"Get along then, don't stand there gaping at me."

"Yes, Nurse."

When they were outside Anne ran ahead. "The meadow—the meadow!" she cried. "Hurry up, Lottie."

"That tent's bigger than a church," Isobel remarked casually. "I'm going to be a bishop when I grow up."

The children had been out in the garden all morning, playing in and out among the tents and the flower beds, but they had not been allowed to go so far as the meadow by themselves. They ran ahead of Lottie now, down through the shrubs and past the rows of greenhouses and the little clearing where Maxwell's cottage stood. It was a pretty house with creepers and climbing roses thick about it. Rather like a grown-up doll's house that had become slowly and gradually weather-beaten and decayed. The narrow belt of trees that circled so much of the garden, and which widened out into a definite wood by the main road, lay between Maxwell's house and the meadow where the sports were to be held that afternoon. The cart-track, dark with cinders and clinkers from the great stoves that warmed the glasshouses, carved its way into the green tunnel of the trees. The sounds of hammering and occasional shouting of the men in the meadow came sharply through the stillness of the woods. Isobel began running in and out amongst the trees that stood close to the track.

"What a nice green carpet my new house has got," she chanted, bending almost double to feel the thick moss as she ran.

A couple of workmen came walking out of the meadow. One of them had a bag of tools slung over his shoulder, his right hand holding the strap in an easy negligent way. Lottie felt herself becoming awkward as they approached. Her face was colouring up like anything. Why couldn't she pass two men without growing stiff and unhappy? What a pity it was that God had made men like He had? Why had He considered creatures with such strong, dreadful passions—yes, passions, that was the word Nurse always used—necessary? But evidently He had, and here were two of them now, approaching her, and there was nothing for her to do but go forward and meet them. It was too late to slip in amongst the trees. But that's what she'd like to do. Run in amongst the trees with their great trunks and press herself up against one of them, holding her skirt and apron well in so that no glimpse of blue or white would show behind the dark wood.

The two men had reached Anne and Isobel. The children had no fear of them. Lucky little things! But, then, they did not know what men were really like. They were young and ignorant and trusting. Too trusting, perhaps. From what Nurse said even little innocent children were not safe from men.

Isobel was actually talking to one of these workmen. With her heart beating quickly Lottie hastened to the child. Even if she got murdered for it she must take care of Isobel. That was her duty. To protect the child.

"Is the Aunt Sally up yet?" Isobel was asking, her innocent little face raised to his.

"Oh, yes, miss. It's all up. Just waiting for someone to come along and have a good shy!"

"Oh, Lottie, the Aunt Sally's up!" Isobel caught Lottie's hand.

These two men did not look dreadful. They were both young, and there was something quite pleasant about their faces, and the way they smiled. But, Nurse said, you never knew with men.

The taller of the two hitched his tools higher, and laughed at Lottie.

"You'll be busy this afternoon," he said pleasantly and harmlessly. "My own kid's coming. She couldn't eat her breakfast this morning for excitement."

Well! Surely a man who was a father would not hurt another child? Lottie's heart began to beat more naturally.

The meadow lay in brilliant sunshine when they emerged from the trees. Race-tracks for the children had been taped off and preparations made for obstacle races. There was a long narrow tent, open down all one side, where lemonade and kindred drinks would be served. There was a platform under the trees where the band would play. Poles supporting lines of flags and bunting were driven in all around the meadow. It was very gay. Isobel and Anne were greatly excited.

"Oh, look—look at the flags! Oh, Lottie, isn't it beautiful?"

"Don't go too far away, Anne. We must be getting back soon. You'll be here all afternoon, you know."

"Why must we go back, Lottie?"

"To have a nice lie-down. Especially Isobel."

"But I don't want a rest to-day," Isobel said wistfully yet resignedly. "I'm always resting. It's really curious how much I have to rest. It's a great pity."

"It's a nuisance!" said Anne brusquely.

Lottie anticipated trouble getting them to come back to the house, but they came at once. They were very good.

"Take off Isobel's shoes, frock and knickers," Nurse said, "and you needn't cover them up at all. And draw the blinds half-way down. They'll get enough hot sunshine later on."

When Lottie had brought up the nursery dinner, cold things to-day, she went to fetch the two little girls. She found Isobel asleep in a light slumber. Anne was reading a picture book. Isobel woke up at once, brightly, with her usual quick darting ease.

"Feel rested, my little love?" Lottie murmured, as she brushed the child's hair.

"Oh, delicious!" Isobel exclaimed.

The baby was in high good-humour, too. But the heat and unusual activities of the day had put an edge on Nurse's temper.

"Don't give Isobel so much juice, she'll only spill it. There now, you've spilt it yourself! Really, Lottie, how clumsy you are! Get a cloth and wipe it up at once. Can't you understand that fruit juice leaves a stain?" And later, "Hurry over the washing-up, Lome. You must dress the children then."

She'd hurry over the washing-up all right! Lottie made herself work so fast that her arms and wrists stiffened from her anxiety to be quick.

"Dress me first, Lottie," Anne cried.

"No, dress me first," Isobel wailed.

"I'll dress you both together," Lottie said soothingly. "Come along."

They both stood naked together in the sunshine. What beautiful little bodies they had, so soft and smooth, yet so strong and vital. Isobel's skin was very white, she sunburned hardly at all. Anne was a golden brown practically all over, her legs and arms were the rich brown of a nut.

Her cheeks glowed with a different pink from Isobel's. She was a very handsome child.

At last the little girls were ready. Nurse gave them a critical glance. Lottie stood by anxiously.

"Yes, they're all right," Nurse said grudgingly. "Now see to yourself, Lottie, and then don't forget that you're responsible for Anne and Isobel this afternoon."

When she had changed her apron and put on her hat, Lottie and the children went out into the garden. Coming out from the shelter of the house the sun met them with a blast of heat. The brims of the children's plain white panamas were turned down all round. Isobel's face looked like a small, faintly-moist flower.

Already the band was playing in the meadow.

"Hullo, where are you going?"

Mr. Andrew was close up beside them. Lottie started. Where had he come from?

"We're going to the meadow!" Anne cried. "Come with us."

He glanced at Lottie. "I've got to go that way," he said slowly. He swung Isobel up onto his shoulder. "Like a lift?" he asked.

Isobel clung to him, gripping the top of his hair with one hand as she sat on his shoulder.

"What a day it is!" he exclaimed to Lottie. "We'll all be dead by the time it gets cool this evening. It's like being in a furnace out here. Ever been near a furnace, Lottie?"

"I have," said Isobel.

"You haven't!"

"Yes, I have!"

"I'd like to believe you, but I can't—not really!"

"But it's true—it's very true," Isobel protested.

"Well, don't pull all my hair out. You don't want a bald uncle, do you?"

"Wouldn't it grow again?"

"Listen to that, Lottie!" Mr. Andrew turned, and glanced at Lottie. His eyes lingered on her face. "Heartless child, isn't she?"

They were under the trees now, alone there. Mr. Andrew turned round a little more, so that he stood right across Lottie's path barring her way, unless she stepped over to the right a bit. And she couldn't do that!

"I wish you'd smile, Lottie," he said gently. "You've such a very pretty smile."

III

Hessie pushed the strips of limp fat from Mr. Benson's plate. There were little lumps of potato too, stained with gravy. Shreds of cabbage as well. Mr. Benson liked cabbage. At lunch-time Hessie had watched him lift the palely dripping mouthfuls to his lips. The cabbage at the rectory always looked limp and anæmic. It was never strained properly, and the water oozed out diluting the gravy that swilled about the plate. But Mr. Benson always ate it with enjoyment.

"This is good of you, Hessie!" Mrs. Benson came into the kitchen, where Hessie was washing-up. Her face looked grey and little beads of perspiration dotted her nose and forehead. "Oh, dear, I wish it wasn't quite so hot. I can't think why Doris did not come back last night. She can't really be as sick as all that!"

Hessie pursed up her lips and shook her head. Really, it was just like that girl! Go home for her half-day's holiday and then send a badly-written note to say that she had been taken suddenly ill, and could not come back to-day. How ungrateful these young girls were. Mrs. Benson had done everything possible for Doris, and for her family, too. Why, she'd taught Doris everything she knew.

"If only we had a proper hot water supply," Mrs. Benson sighed. "But I think the kettle is warm enough now, Hessie."

"Oh, do you think it is? Yes, indeed, a proper hot water supply would make a difference."

"That's what I'm always saying. But what's the use? And, after all, I suppose the money is wanted for other things."

What a Christian woman Mrs. Benson was! Hardworking and resigned. Mr. Benson did not understand half what his wife had to go through, poor patient little woman. Here he was in the kitchen now.

"I suppose my new black shoes haven't walked down here, have they?" he remarked with superior facetiousness.

"Your new shoes, dear?" Mrs. Benson began a flurried search about the corners of the kitchen.

"Yes, my new ones. Ah, here they are—under this table. H'm, not cleaned, I see!"

"Oh dear, aren't they cleaned? That's Doris again! But I'll do them for you. No—no, it won't take a moment."

"I'm afraid I'm in a hurry. Really, my dear, couldn't we replace Doris by someone more efficient?"

"I wish we could," Mrs. Benson sighed, as she struggled with the lid of the blacking tin, "but, after all, she's cheap. We could hardly expect more for the wages we give. Oh, dear, what is the matter with this tin? I'm so sorry, Henry, I won't be a moment."

The blacking tin opened with a plop, and the polish, liquid from the heat, spread over Mrs. Benson's crinkled, knuckly fingers. She grew quite breathless polishing the shoes.

When the rector was gone, his cleaned shoes grasped firmly and held out before him, Mrs. Benson returned to Hessie's side and started drying the plates again.

"After this, Hessie, I suppose we'd better dress the children. Oh dear, it's half-past two already. They'd better wear their white muslins, of course. I expect Anne and Isobel will be in white. It's the most suitable colour for an occasion like this. It isn't as if Doris had looked ill when she went home yesterday. She ate a big enough dinner. She finished all the pudding, you know. I was so surprised when I went to the larder. The dish wasn't there at all!"

Hessie lifted her eyebrows. "How disgusting. And you sent her out such a big dinner. All those potatoes. ..."

"Girls of that age eat such a lot. Sometimes I think ... an elderly person … but then there's the scrubbing—no, I'm afraid that wouldn't do," Mrs. Benson sighed.

When the last plate was dried Hessie scrupulously wiped down the draining-board and the basin and yellow sink. A lady always left the sink clean, especially in another person's home.

"I'll call Mabel and Flossie now," she said brightly.

What red faces those two children had. Of course they had been playing in the sun. It was just unfortunate for them that they were so like their father. Big-faced, stocky children, displaying every possible physical evidence of their paternity. Really it was dreadful the way Mr. Benson had—had stamped himself on his children.

Mabel's frock had been lengthened by the insertion of a row of embroidered muslin at the place around the hips where the skirt flounced onto the body. It was getting tight for her under her arm-pits and the cuff-bands fastened half-way up her wrists. She wriggled uncomfortably as Hessie buttoned it down the back. Both the children had sandy-coloured hair, cut short, with a longer strand looped dismally across their foreheads.

"I suppose the rector has gone on?" Mrs. Benson fluttered into the room. "It's so wonderfully generous of dear Mr. and Mrs. Kellaway to give this fête. They must spend a lot of money on it. Still, in a way, it seems rather a pity … there are so many needy persons. … Are the children ready, Hessie?"

"Quite ready, Mrs. Benson."

"Now, dears, you'll both be very good. Do just as Hessie asks you. And be very polite to Mr. and Mrs. Kellaway if you meet them, which you will, of course. How nice you look, Hessie, that blue is most becoming."

How kind dear Mrs. Benson was! Hessie glanced at her own reflection. The mirror in the children's bedroom was very faulty. It gave a bilious tinge to her cheeks and the spots that appeared on her face were not spots that belonged to her, they were the mirror's. Her skin was unusually clear and pretty to-day. She had quite a good colour in her cheeks. A wild rose bloom. She gave a last peep at herself as they left the room. A little more hair coiling softly over her forehead—that was better! She must remember to keep her blue voile frock flat across her hips. A quick fingering movement assured her that the little pins holding in her modesty vest were in place and securely fastened.

"I've laid a cold supper." Mrs. Benson wrinkled her forehead as they stepped out into the overgrown drive. "Oh, dear, how hot it is! I must put up my parasol. The cold bacon and a few tomatoes, and the custard poured over the cold bread pudding. That'll be enough, I think."

"Delicious!" Hessie cried warmly.

"I really couldn't cook anything to-night. Besides, in this heat things go bad so quickly. And that bit of bacon was really quite expensive. Don't you think it ate well at lunch to-day? A little bit fat, perhaps. ... Of course, Mr. Benson may ask someone back to supper. Mr. Saul may be coming. In that case I might be able to make a little soup. There's some stock—and then a soup tablet. ... What can have happened to Doris, Hessie, do you think?"

"Just laziness," Hessie said firmly, adding playfully. "But if you're having any visitors for supper to-night I'm not going to let you do all the work. No, indeed! I can stay late to-night. Hilda will be with Mother."

"You've been such a help to-day, Hessie."

How appreciative Mrs. Benson was! She was a dear little woman, just knocked to pieces by that husband of hers. How differently Mr. Saul would treat his wife. Mr. Saul's wife! Despite the heat Hessie shivered violently. Besides, Mr. Saul was well-off, almost rich. The Bensons had no private means at all, their finances were typical of Mr. Benson's calling. You read so much about poor clergymen and their overworked wives. It was true enough in this case. Mrs. Benson had had some money once, but it was all gone now. Spent by Mr. Benson, of course.

In a way it was strange that the curate should be so much better off than the rector, but that was how it was. Not that you'd think it from Mr. Saul's manner or way of living. He had simple tastes, but all the same the money was there. As Mother said, you could always smell money. No doubt he would shower every comfort on his wife. He was that sort of man—wasn't he? Very chivalrous towards women. How carefully he would guard his wife. "My wife ..." how soft and deep his voice would be when he said those words. "My wife ... my wife. ..."

"Oh dear—oh dear—what has that child done now? Flossie! ..."

Mrs. Benson's wail startled Hessie. She swallowed quickly. What was the matter now? Ah, Flossie again. She'd fallen headlong down the side of the grass bank that bordered this part of the rectory drive. She was not hurt but she was yelling lustily because of the heavy green stain on her white frock.

"What shall we do?" Mrs. Benson lamented. "This would happen! Stop crying, Flossie! It can't be helped. I suppose she'll just have to go as she is? There isn't time to change her, and anyhow ..."

Hessie knew what she meant. Even if they did return to the rectory there was not another suitable frock for the child.

"Oh, but it doesn't matter so very much, does it?" she exclaimed helpfully, "green is such a natural colour, isn't it? Grass-green! And any child might fall and have a little tumble. There, I'll wipe it! Now everything's all right, isn't it?"

What a pity it was that Mrs. Kellaway—or—or Mr. Saul could not see her now. Soothing the child, brightly easing the whole situation.

"Run along, Flossie dear, don't climb the bank again! Take Mabel's hand and walk along like two dear little girls!"

They were entering the thick shade of the trees on the Kellaways' estate. They were using the private footpath that connected the two houses. This was the path Hessie took whenever she brought the children down to the sea. The track turned sharply to the right and led them into the sunshine once more. There was a splash of steely-blue glimmering glass on their right.

"What can Mr. Kellaway want with all those greenhouses?" Mrs. Benson observed. "They must cost such a lot to keep up, and they are all heated. Properly heated. And to think that the rectory's hot water service is—well, well—one must not complain."

As they passed Maxwell's house the door opened and he burst out. So this was where the head-gardener lived? What a powerful-looking man he was. Such strong, primitive-looking shoulders. Yes, 'primitive' was the word. Furtively, Hessie ran her hand down her hips. Thank goodness the blue voile was lying quite flat. The way that man was looking at her, staring at her! She must pretend that she was unaware of his scrutiny—just walk by easily, indifferently.

"Hark, children—there's the band!" she cried brightly. "Isn't that gay!"

That man was still following them. Hessie swayed a little in her walk, a graceful movement of her waist and hips. She was wearing her best patent leather shoes, the heels had just been straightened. Thank goodness her legs were a lady's legs, thin and straight, perhaps a little too thin above the ankle, but that was better than having great fat legs.

"Oh dear, this heat!" Mrs. Benson moaned.

Hessie threw back her head—a free spontaneous movement, young and impulsive. "But how beautiful it makes the flowers look! It brings out all their colourings. What exquisite gifts flowers are—gifts from God, I mean!"

Yes, he was still there! He was only a yard or two behind them. He must have heard her words. He was looking at her, too, he must be, she could feel his gaze on her back, going up and down her back, all over her! What a very strong type of man he was!

He disappeared down a side path before they came in sight of the house. Mr. Benson was pacing slowly around with some of the visitors belonging to the house-party. From the way he was placing his feet no one would think that poor Mrs. Benson had had to clean his shoes for him. He hardly looked in their direction.

"We must find dear Mrs. Kellaway first," Mrs. Benson panted. "Do you see her anywhere, Hessie?"

Hessie put her hand to her eyes, and that gesture threw her figure into, an exposed, slightly-arched position. She pirouetted a little. After all, there were advantages in being thin, 'slim' was a nicer word. A girl with a protruding stomach could not afford to stand as she was standing now.

"No, I'm afraid I don't see her. Wait a minute, though, I think I see her over there. No, I'm wrong!"

Then, suddenly, Mrs Kellaway was before them. Where had she come from? She was dressed in white, too, just like the children. Was not that just a little—a little well, a trifle too youthful, considering she was the mother of three children? But no, it wasn't! A wave of admiring honesty shook Hessie. After all, Mrs. Kellaway was younger than she, Hessie, was—years younger. She was rich, her beauty was protected by riches. Worry and tiredness and poverty could spoil the loveliest complexion, but Mrs. Kellaway was protected from all those things. Everyone knew how much Mr. Kellaway worshipped her, and there was no doubt about their wealth.

"Do come and see some of the flowers, Mrs. Benson," Mrs. Kellaway smiled. "Let me show them to you."

Mrs. Benson flushed happily, and rushed into flustered words.

"Anne and Isobel are somewhere about," Mrs. Kellaway turned her lovely smile on Hessie, "and Nurse and baby, too. Baby is loving the band and all the flags. Mabel, are you going to try to win a lot of prizes? Both of you be sure to come and tell me if you win anything. I shall be so pleased."

"Yes, thank you, Mrs. Kellaway," Mabel said.

Hessie nudged Flossie. What an unfortunate looking child she was—with her mouth open like that.

"Say something, Flossie dear," Hessie prompted quickly, but gently. Flossie took the hint.

"Yes, thank you, Mrs. Kellaway," she said, and started gaping again.

It was very hot in the meadow. Most of the mothers were gathered beneath the shade of the great trees that bordered it on one side. Hessie stepped daintily over the tufts of grass. Rosie Bates had once said that she was flat-footed. What nonsense! Rosie was flat-footed herself and suffered hallucinations on that subject about other people.

"There's Isobel," Mabel said, pointing down the meadow.

"Don't point, darling. Little ladies don't!" Anne and Isobel and their nurse-maid were standing by the Aunt Sally. As usual their frocks made Mabel's and Flossie's look so dowdy, though no one could say that they were anything wonderful really. Just plain white linen, the very fine uncrushable kind.

The greetings between the children were perfunctory. Hessie smiled at Lottie, ladies were always polite to the lower classes. Lottie smiled back. Really only a woman, a lady, of Mrs. Kellaway's beauty could afford to employ a girl as lovely as this nurse-maid. Isobel moved closer to Lottie and Lottie's tiny protective gesture towards the child was beautiful, too.

Hessie turned away. The old sick depression was gnawing at her again. Why had not she been born beautiful too? With exquisite eyes and lips and this girl's air of dazzling fragility and beauty. Poverty would not matter so much then. Men would look at her in the streets, follow her home perhaps. She would not be the age she was now and still be unmarried, her body untouched.

"Aren't you feeling well, Miss Price?"

Hessie stared at Lottie. Lottie's face swam before her eyes.

"I don't know—" she put her hand to her head. "It's the heat, perhaps. I don't really think. … Perhaps I'd better sit in the shade for a moment."

"I'll look after the little girls. Shall I get you something cool to drink?" Lottie asked anxiously.

"No, thank you, I shall be all right. I'll just rest a moment."

It was the heat, of course, nothing but that. Fatigue, too. There seemed so much to do at home, everywhere, these days. It was Hilda's marriage that was at the root of the whole trouble. This severance from Hilda was shattering her. They had always been such friends, but now Hilda had Albert. Hilda had marriage before her. A year ago Hilda was not engaged at all. If only one could put the clock back and keep it there.

She could see Lottie and the four little girls moving about. The band was in full swing, the music came across the meadow in sprightly waves and hummed away into the woods behind her. She was alone under the trees, the nearest group of townsfolk was a good distance away. A number of the village children were crowding round the stalls where glasses of lemonade and ginger-beer and cornets toppling with ice-cream were being served. The grass in the centre of the meadow looked yellow and stiff beneath the intense sunshine. There was a clear, green quality in the air beneath the trees.

Hessie leant back against a tree trunk. She let her hands—weren't they just a little knuckly?—lie easily in her lap. She gazed at them dispassionately. The skin was shiny from her work at the rectory that morning, particularly from the washing-up. The joint of her right thumb seemed swollen, and it hurt a little when she moved it. Her feet, too, looked big and ungainly, thrust out before her like that, with the toes pointing skywards. But Hilda's feet were even bigger than hers; nearly a half-size larger. Had Albert noticed that? Perhaps it was not true that men noticed a girl's feet, though they noticed her ankles of course, that was natural, and quite all right, too. Perhaps the very thinness of her ankles made her feet appear larger than they really were.

How cool the woods looked. At night they would be still and dark, the trees large with the fantastic dignity of night; at dawn they would be grey and sombre, with grotesque, arched boughs; with the first gleam of sunshine their leaves would flutter awake in the stillness before the birds began. There would be a ripple of movement through the wood, like a wave breaking on a misty shore. What was it like to spend a night in the open air? In a wood like this? Alone? Oh, no, no … not alone. Hessie sprang up, her heart beating quickly.

After a while, when her hands were steadied, she brushed the dried moss and broken leaves from her dress. It was a pity voile crushed so quickly. She pressed her hands carefully over her hips to feel if the thin material had creased. It was high time she joined Mabel and Flossie again.

As she passed behind the groups of villagers her composure returned. After all, marriage lay ahead of Hilda—why shouldn't it lie ahead of her, too? She was nicer looking than Hilda. Everyone knew that—even Mr. Saul had said so. She had heard him say it, so it must be true. Look at the way that head-gardener had followed her this afternoon, his eyes riveted on her back. It was ridiculous to think that she was not attractive to men. She would have been married long ago if Mother had not brought them up so carefully. Mother had shielded them a little too carefully—much too carefully. To be sheltered, protected, your virtue guarded like a frail blossom had been an attraction in the old days but now a girl's virtue was a hardier plant—wasn't it? Hessie smiled. From now onwards she was going to be modern. Of course she would not carry anything to excess. She would always remember that she was a lady.

Under Lottie's guidance Mabel and Flossie had been to the lemonade stall, and now they were joining in a game someone was organizing for the children. It was 'Here We Go Gathering Nuts and May.' Hessie pushed forward. Why, it was Mr. Saul who was arranging the rows of children!

Here and there a grown-up was holding the hand of a younger, shyer child. Hessie seized the hot sticky hand of a reluctant little boy.

"Come along—come along! It's ever such fun! Oh, Mr. Saul—may we play, too? Here's a shy little tot. …"

"The other side, please, Miss Price."

She swung the little boy across. He pulled stubbornly at her hand. "Let me go—let me go—"

"Oh, but it's fun! Here We Go Gathering Nuts and May …" she caught the little boy up in her arms, and pranced him about.

The children's voices rose in shrill raggedness. What a good thing it was that she was there to lead them in the words and music! Despite the sulky weight in her arms she was able to sing quite nicely. It was like singing 'God Save the King' only with all the solemnity gone—just a gay riot—but it gave her the same loosened feeling in her chest.

When this game was over she would suggest another to Mr. Saul, and together they would organize it. He would see what a help she was at this sort of thing. He would realize what a gay and tactful helper she was with children. Poor Mrs. Benson was no good at games, and really, a clergyman's wife should have a way with her on these occasions. It was such an assistance to her husband.

Panting a little, Hessie dropped the child, who glowered at her ungratefully and ran away. Now what should she suggest? A tug-o'-war? With her on one side and Mr. Saul on the other. That would be fine! His side would win, of course. A man was always gallant to a defeated woman. Besides, men were the stronger sex, they should domineer and win, and then be gentle towards the conquered. Strength and gentleness combined, and when it was over he would say, "That was a splendid game! Your little team fought gallantly but you need a rest now, Miss Price. Come—let me get you an ice." Then side by side they would walk off, he glancing down at her, she up at him, admiringly, intimately.

The game was ending now. Hessie ran forward and clapped her hands. But Mr. Saul was not there! He was threading his way through the outer fringe of children. The smile died from Hessie's lips. She put her hand to her head.

"It's hot—isn't it," she said to Lottie who had brought Mabel and Flossie to her. The other children were dispersing quickly. Teas were being served in the big tent. There was a rush for places. He could not have seen her, of course.

IV

"Lord, how I'm sweating!" Irene exclaimed.

Maggie felt that her own face had grown pale from the heat. At first her cheeks had been hotly flushed, but now she was tired as well as hot and so she was pale.

"The sweat's dripping all down my back and legs," Irene amplified. "Pouring off me!"

They were carrying the last tray-load of cups from the tent to the house. The violent heat had gone from the day but it was still breathless and hot. There were little groups of guests moving aimlessly about the lawns. The flowers looked tired, as if weary of having been gazed at so much, their colours grown delicate and fragile, their leaves pointed and thin.

Just outside the kitchen Maggie came face to face with the handsome young waiter who had excited Irene's interest earlier in the day. His name was Pierce.

"Hullo," he said.

Tired as she was Maggie tossed back her head.

"What a day!" he remarked, looking at her with undisguised admiration.

Maggie laughed shortly. She was so tired and wrought up that she felt angry at the way he stood there, asking for an ordinary flirtation! She pushed on past him, but at the kitchen door she turned and gave him a little smile. His face brightened curiously.

"That finishes us for to-night!" Irene said as she came into the pantry.

Maggie nodded. That was what Mrs. Kellaway had arranged. Two of the extra women were to stay late and help with the washing-up. Jenner was already putting the finishing touches to the buffet supper laid in the dining-room that was to take the place of dinner to-night.

"Wait a minute, though," Irene called. "I forgot. I'll want you later on—to help with the bedrooms. It won't take us long."

"What time?" Maggie asked.

"About half-past nine."

Maggie let her arms hang by her sides for a moment, letting them lie loosely, heavily, every muscle relaxed. Leaving the pantry she kept close beside the passage wall as she went towards the back door. Cook was quite capable of calling her in for extra work if she caught sight of her. In the yard the caterers' men were standing about. Some of them sat on upturned boxes, one or two had perched themselves on the steps that had been let down from the doors of the biggest of the vans. They were mostly youngish men. They sat in their shirt-sleeves, with their arms bare, their faces alert and good-natured despite the heat and the work they had done. Their presences there made the yard look a little like part of a circus. The cream and gold vans, the lounging men, their air of impermanence as they made themselves so easily at home in a place that would know them no more after that night. There was a faint smell of coffee in the air. As Maggie went through the yard the handsome young waiter appeared with a large tray full of cups and glasses. He carried it with grave, impersonal intentness. It struck Maggie that this unselfconsciousness of his was no pose. He paused beside the larger van and laid the tray down on a packing-case. The other men pressed round him.

Maggie walked on slowly. She slipped into the woods and lay down on the thick moss. Overhead the sky was darkening a little, a smoky heat-filled darkness. The band was still playing in the meadow, and faint cries of excitement came from the children. Maggie flung out her arms and pressed her cheek against the ground. There was not much that she did not know about men. She'd had all sorts of suggestions made to her since she was thirteen years old and younger. What had been the use of rejecting them all if to-night she went down to those greenhouses? Perhaps she wouldn't go down. She was inclined to be proud of her own decency. Stuck-up, her sisters called her. But it was not only that, there was something else as well. A reluctance, a pride. She was not as bad as Cook thought she was.

She was feeling a little more rested now. She'd lie here until it was time to go into the house to help Irene with the beds. The moss was soft and cool and little bits of it were catching in her clothes and hair. She felt them against her fingers as she pressed her hands up against her head. There was thunder about for her hair sprang away from her touch, crackling faintly. There was no air moving between the trees but the moss was cool. Maggie lay very still, striving not to think.

The fireworks lasted for another half an hour. Now and then a flare of golden rain and stars dropped over the trees. It was lovely lying there on the cool moss watching the coloured sky. The sky had grown a deep blue that bore no relation to the dazzling blue of midday. The real stars were sharp and clear, the red and green and gold of the fireworks made them look aloof and cold. How easy life would be if she could always lie like this?—no Cook, no work, no Maxwell to think about. Nothing immediate and pressing.

When the fireworks were over Maggie got up. She'd better hurry or Irene would be waiting for her, and she did not want to upset Irene in any way. She reached the back stairs just as Irene came in from the yard. She'd been out watching the fireworks, too, and flirting with some of the men. It was very hot and stifling inside the house. They moved quickly through the rooms.

Supper next. Irene made a pot of tea and Maggie stood by the window eating a thick sandwich. The caterers had packed up and gone away and there was not a sign of them left anywhere in the yard. The yard was restored to its usual big clean emptiness again. To-morrow morning one of the stable boys would swill it down, the hosepipe wriggling along behind him. The stable boy never whistled as he did this work each day. It was too early in the morning, and his whistling might disturb some of the sleepers in the house.

Cook was no longer anywhere about. Quite likely she had gone off to bed. "Resting my legs" she called it. Well, if your weight was as ponderous as Cook's you would need to show a little consideration for your legs.

Though Cook's were in proportion to the rest of her body. They ought to be equal to their task. But, evidently, they weren't.

Irene was sitting at the kitchen table, and her face looked sad. She was gazing down at the table and tracing something with her finger. Maggie glanced out into the yard again. It was a shock to see Irene looking sad, for usually she was so full of good-humour, her face always ready to smile. Looking out of the window again Maggie tried to concentrate on Irene. Why should Irene look sad? But it was no good. She could not stop thinking of Maxwell. Perhaps he was waiting for her now, this minute? Where would he be? Pottering about the greenhouses, glancing every now and then into the darkness?

A clock struck the half-hour. Irene stood up slowly and stretched and yawned.

"Bed!" she said briefly.

Maggie moved away from the window. It was terribly warm in the centre of the room, though the air in the stone passage outside was a little cooler.

"I'm going to sleep in Eve's nightgown to-night," Irene said with a little touch of her usual good-humour.

Maggie kept silent as she followed Irene up the stairs. On the top landing they paused.

"Nighty-night," said Irene.

Although her window was wide open Maggie felt that there was no air at all in her bedroom. The air coming in from the outside was, if anything, hotter than that inside.

She took off her cap and apron and threw herself down on the bed. For a moment the pillow felt as cool under her cheek as the moss beneath the trees had been, but soon it was burning hot. She sat up and pulled off her shoes and stockings and opened the front of her frock. But it was no good. She got up and went to the window. She could not see Maxwell's house from there but she knew just exactly where it was. She could see the greenhouses. How hot they would be to-night!

But if she went down they would not remain in the greenhouses for long. What would Maxwell say if she did not come? She thought of him as he had been this morning, when he had come close up to her in the tent. But thinking of Maxwell was a mistake, for that settled everything. Maggie tore off her frock, and her vest, too, and then she slipped on the only light frock she possessed. It had no sleeves and a low round neck. She drew the wide belt closer about her waist. She had a nice round waist, really quite slender, and there was something nice, too, in the line of her hips. But she'd always known that her figure was a good one. She brushed her hair till it stood on end nearly, and then let it settle down into pretty waves. Her eyes were bright and her cheeks glowing.

She knew every inch of the stairs down to the side door. This door was the easiest to unbolt, her quickest way out into the garden. At the end of the shrubbery she caught her first glimpse of the greenhouses. Their glass was a black-blue intersected by little bars of white. Coming close to them she could see the sleeping shadows of the plants within. Some of them were in full blossom and the flowers looked very lifeless locked away in their glass prison. Seen in the open they would be different, their petals able to move a little in the close night air, but shut away in that hothouse they were just like pale-faced prisoners.

As she came closer a light sprang up in front of the row nearest to Maxwell's house. Startlingly, it revealed Maxwell himself bending over some wonderful flowers. Maggie stopped, and at that moment the light snapped out and he came to the door of the greenhouse and stood gazing at the clump of bushes where she was standing. He saw her at once and came straight over to her.

"Come and see the flowers," he said. But the minute he put out his hand and touched her Maggie knew that she did not want to see the flowers any more than he wanted to show them to her. There was the same terrible hunger in her body as there was in his. It was no good trying to resist. She said nothing as he drew her in amongst the trees.

Chapter Eight

I

Nurse and Mrs. Kellaway were taking the baby away to London for a week. They were taking him to see a doctor about some tiny complaint, that was almost nothing at all. But the baby was so precious. They were to start immediately after an early breakfast. The little girls were very excited.

While Lottie was dressing Isobel the child kept on crying, "Scramble my clothes on, Lottie! Scramble them!"

She hopped about on one leg while Lottie was trying to put on her knickers. "What a nuisance these things are," she said, burrowing her head into Lottie's waist.

"That's one foot in, now the other!" Nurse would not allow any elastic anywhere in the children's clothes so there was always a lot of buttoning to do when putting on their pants. Anne was dressing herself. As a rule she did not bother to do this, but called Lottie to help her. However, to-day was a special day. She was anxious to be up and about. To please them both Lottie did their hair very quickly, just springing their curls up with a comb and brushing the tops of their heads. She'd comb them properly afterwards.

Nurse would not sit down to her breakfast. She kept fussing round, giving Lottie a great many orders, most of them contradictory, and pausing now and then to drink from her tea-cup, or to take a bite of toast. The baby was dressed in an overall. The little washing-silk smock and trousers he was going to wear on the journey were lying over the back of a chair. He was quite unruffled by all the excitement, and kept smiling at Lottie. Isobel's feeder was crooked around her neck, but she said she liked it like that and would not let Lottie straighten it. Every now and then she and Anne made desperately serious attacks on their fruit and cereal, shovelling the spoonfuls into their mouths.

"I'm thankful that's over!" Isobel said, as she pushed away her plate. "I don't think I'll have any more breakfast."

"You'll eat your egg," Nurse said, pausing for a moment to eat and drink a little herself.

But Isobel would not. Lottie picked off the top of the egg and dipped a little bit of bread in the yolk, but still Isobel wouldn't touch it. Mrs. Kellaway came in in the middle of this discussion and said that the cereal and fruit would do nicely. Isobel pushed away the egg, and it grew cold, a slight skin forming on the yolk.

"You dress baby while I fasten the suit-cases," Nurse said.

Lottie sat down with the baby on her knee. He sat up in a very sprightly way. He felt surprisingly warm and heavy on her lap. Just for a joke he kept his fingers spread out when Lottie was putting on his smock, so that she had to be very careful not to catch his thumb in the cuff-bands. He had a little tussore hat tied with a ribbon, the bow peeping saucily from behind one ear.

When Nurse came back she had her coat and hat on. She picked the baby up in her arms and went downstairs. Lottie followed her, carrying the small case containing the things that the baby might need on the drive. The biggest car of all was waiting at the front door. It stood there glittering in the sunshine. It looked very fine and powerful. The chauffeur was wearing his hot-weather livery. He took no notice of Nurse, but he smiled at Lottie. Lottie glanced fearfully at Nurse, but, fortunately, Nurse was busy with the baby.

Then Mr. Kellaway came down. He looked tall and very fine and dignified. He stood on the doorstep drawing on a pair of light chamois gloves. He turned and looked through the open front door with a sort of quiet expectancy.

Lottie stood very still. She could not go back into the house until

Nurse told her to. She had to go on standing there with the little case in her hands. Thank goodness she had something to hold!

At last Isobel and Anne and Mr. Andrew and Mrs. Kellaway came out. Isobel and Anne were clinging round their mother. She hugged them both and laughed gaily. As she was stepping into the car she beckoned to Lottie.

"You know exactly how to look after the children, don't you, Lottie?" she asked, and she looked at Lottie with a sort of gay, happy confidence.

"Oh, yes, indeed, Mrs. Kellaway," Lottie said, her voice almost desperate with earnestness, she felt so anxious to reassure her mistress.

Mrs. Kellaway glanced at her husband and smiled. "You'll have Irene to help you if necessary," she said. "Go to her if you want anything. Good-bye, Lottie."

Nurse and the baby were already settled in the back, Mrs. Kellaway in front because Mr. Kellaway was going to drive, at any rate for the first half of the journey. The chauffeur got into the back with Nurse, and he did not look any too pleased about it. He did not care for Nurse any more than she pretended she did not care for him. But Lottie knew that Nurse would be all beams and smiles if he had not made it so plain that he found her unattractive, and only drove her about because those were his orders. He smiled again at Lottie as the car drove off. The wheels crunched a little on the gravel of the drive and one or two tiny pebbles jumped lightly away. The car sped silently under the trees, and at the turn in the drive it looked like something from a fairy-tale, it moved with such powerful effortlessness.

Isobel and Anne were very silent too, and there was a little pucker on Isobel's forehead as she gazed down the drive. Lottie was glad when Mr. Andrew stepped forward and said, "Come along into the yard and see the puppies. You should see them trying to bite their own tails! They go round and round."

The children brightened at once, and ran off with him. Lottie went slowly back into the house. How strange the house felt without Mr. and Mrs. Kellaway or Nurse. Nurse's bedroom was littered with things. A discarded pair of corsets with an army of suspenders dangling from it lay on the bed. The baby's cot was a jumble of soft blankets and small clothes left for Lottie to wash.

As she was making Nurse's bed Irene popped her head around the door.

"Mrs. Bartley and I had better give this place a good clean-out this morning," she said, sniffing a little. "What do you think?"

Lottie's face flushed with gratitude. Only Irene would have bothered to ask her opinion on a thing like this. Cook or Jenner would have ordered her about, but Irene was treating her as if she were really in charge of the nurseries.

When doing the children's room Lottie went down on her knees and dusted behind the legs of the dressing-table and the chests very carefully. She must keep everything very clean. Extreme cleanliness must be a point of honour with her this week.

The sky had clouded over a little when she went out to join the children. She found them in the yard. Isobel was sitting on the hot stone flags, her small lap heaving with puppies. She sat with her legs straddled wide apart and her frock strained by its clambering freight. She had her check pressed against the smooth head of a puppy and his pink tongue worked in a frenzied effort to lick her face. Blenheim, the mother, was sitting back on her haunches, her great head drooping benevolently. Now and then she gazed up at Mr. Andrew or bent forward and nuzzled a puppy in a careless way, as much as to say "I'm still boss here." The kitchen windows were flung wide open. Lottie could see Cook at work at something on a table just inside. Jenner was sitting by the centre table nursing a cup of tea in her hands.

"I'm driving into the town now. I'll take you and the children with me," Mr. Andrew said.

Lottie hesitated. She was in no position to say no to anything Mr. Andrew suggested. Fortunately Irene appeared at that moment.

"Why not?" she said pleasantly, when Lottie explained to her.

They arrived home just in time for lunch. Irene had it in the nursery with them. She was very jolly and pleasant and made Lottie sit in Nurse's place at the head of the table.

In the afternoon Lottie took the children down to the beach. They brought their tea with them. Even the beach felt unreal because Nurse was nowhere close at hand. They stayed down there till quite late. There were clear liquid shadows in the garden as they came through it to the house. The trees were dark and silent. Lottie walked a little ahead of the children, carrying the tea-basket in her hand. Anne and Isobel were deep in conversation behind her. They were bare-footed, their toes filled with sand. When she bathed them to-night the sand would make a little dark line down the centre of the bath.

When the children were asleep Lottie tip-toed in to have a look at them. How quietly they slept! Feeling a little panic-stricken at their noiseless breathing she bent close to Isobel's bed. It was all right! Isobel's chest was rising and falling evenly, there was a soft glow of colour on her cheeks.

Lottie sat down on a chair in between the two beds. It was a hard, upright chair, suitable for the type of vigil she was keeping. Would she be able to sleep to-night with this weight of responsibility on her shoulders?

Gradually her thoughts drifted away from the children. She had not seen George for several days now. The last time had been when she was crossing the yard with the children. He had been doing something to Mr. Andrew's car. He had not seen her at all.

What was this terrible thing that men did to girls? It must be something dreadful. Nurse said that men's passions caused all the troubles in the world. Just lately there'd been another case of a motorist who'd taken a girl for a ride and later the police had found her—they were still looking for the man. That sort of thing seemed to be happening frequently. Nurse was always reading dreadful things in the papers. Men and their passions dominated everything. Lottie put her hand up, to her heart. She was feeling very sick and hollow inside for that was the way fear always affected her. She gripped the edge of the chair with both hands to steady herself.

Then Irene opened the door. "That's where you are, is it!" she whispered cheerfully. "Come on and have some supper. I've brought mine up to the nursery, too. The children will be all right."

At first Lottie felt that she could not eat anything, but gradually her stomach settled down. The nursery was brightly lit, and Irene began to tell her about her own childhood.

"We lived on a farm—there were ten of us—at Christmas-time we had one big stocking between us. …"

It must have been a lovely childhood, full of games and freedom and comradeship. Perhaps that was how Irene had learnt to smile so pleasantly.

"Cheer up," Irene said. "The world's not such a bad place, after all!"

Later Mr. Andrew came in, and perched himself on the edge of the table. He laughed and talked with Irene, and every now and then he smiled at Lottie. Although he was a man he looked almost harmless with the nursery for a background. Irene was very cheerfully respectful with him. Most of the time Lottie kept her head bent over her sewing. Of course, there must be some nice men in the world, but, as Nurse said, the difficulty was in 'knowing.' Often it was those who seemed the nicest, who were the worst. Now and then some police court proceeding uncovered a lot of nastiness. Nurse always read these cases aloud, explaining and enlarging for the benefit of Lottie's ignorance. "Drugs and all sorts of dirty work for you. It's a wonder we're not all murdered in our beds. Gentlemen, indeed! Most of them are savages! And just you look out for yourself, Lottie, you're just the type they do things to."

Irene came into the children's bedroom with her, and glanced at the little girls.

"All serene!" she smiled at Lottie. "Well, sweet dreams."

Lottie was not quite sure if she'd sleep at all that night. Now and then she sat up and looked at the children. Once she got out of bed and tip-toed to Isobel's bed. The child was turning and twisting a lot but she seemed quite all right. She even smiled in her sleep. Lottie remained at the end of the child's bed for a long time. Her nightdress billowed out around her as if supported against the night air by its own thick folds. She clasped her hands together as she gazed at Isobel. What a curious world it was that contained children and men!

Chapter Nine

I

Hilda wanted the bridesmaids to wear green. "It's so very fashionable just now, and not a bit unlucky. Really it isn't, Hessie."

Hessie sat silent. She knew she would look terrible in green. Her eyes, her hair, her skin—wait a minute though, if she could be sure of a warm flush on her cheeks perhaps green would not look too dreadful? But would she flush or would she grow pale at the most critical moments? When Mr. Saul's eyes went beyond the approaching bride and saw the chief bridesmaid—it would never do if she were pale then! No, it was too much of a risk.

"No, Hilda—not green!" she cried.

But there was something obstinate about Hilda's face.

"It'll suit you as well as any other colour, Hessie," she said curtly.

Hilda and Mother were still eating, but Hessie had pushed her plate aside. Was this sort of thing going to go on for ever in her life? These suppers with Mother? The quarter-pound of cold meat from the ham and beef shop or the cooked meat counters of the big stores. Those big stores were the cheapest, for they sold brawn, or jellied veal, or luncheon sausage for threepence a quarter or less. Sometimes Mother and Hilda and she just dipped the tops of their knives into a jar of bloater paste or shared a few tomatoes. In the winter a piece of bread fried in dripping with a drop or two of H.P. sauce was really quite tasty. Cups of tea as well, of course. Or you could buy a small tin containing a portion of boned kipper clotted with tomato sauce for 3d. Mother liked something a little savoury for supper, and in the housekeeping budget sixpence was the very limit that could be spent on the supper relish. When Hilda was gone would they still need a whole quarter of a pound of cooked meat? In a way it would be difficult to ask in the shops for anything less. But she could save a couple of slices for the next evening. It would do for one of them.

Years and years of suppers alone here with Mother. How could she bear it?

"Will you wash up this evening, Hessie?" Hilda asked coyly, as she laid down her knife and fork. "I promised Albert I'd be ready to go over to the house for a moment or two. To see those new curtains. The samples have just come in."

"Alone, Hilda?" Mother asked.

"Now, Mother …" Hilda shook her head waggishly. "Mrs. Hardcastle will be there."

Mrs. Price sniffed. "I'm glad you're getting rid of that woman."

At that the colour flooded Hilda's cheeks and she gave Mother a dignified look. Mrs. Price moved uncomfortably, and said:

"Of course—all gossip—nasty minds! I never did believe it. No one could, Hilda dear, no one who knew dear Albert."

Hilda took a sip of tea, her little finger crooked elegantly. Her gesture accepted Mother's apology. Hessie sprang up. How could she sit still and see Mother abject like this before Hilda, just because Hilda had Albert behind her? Because Albert was a man and Hilda was going to be his wife!

Hessie started clattering the cups and plates together.

"Hurry up with your cup, Hilda," she snapped. "I've got to go out, too. I promised Rosie Bates I'd call at her house this evening. She's got a book …"

"What book, Hessie?"

"Oh, just a book."

"Don't read anything that isn't nice, Hessie," Mother said.

"Rosie said it was good."

"Where did she get it—from the Young Women's Library? Can you remember its title?"

Supposing she screamed now. Just dropped the plates and opened her mouth and screamed. Hessie bit her under lip as she ran out into the kitchen. She laid the plates with a clatter onto the draining-board by the sink, and pressed her hands to her head. How could she live through Hilda's wedding, and afterwards, too? Evenings alone with Mother, while Hilda sat with her husband, and afterwards Hilda and Albert went upstairs together. Hilda would be a wife, a married woman. Hilda would come back to see them, and she'd talk about 'my husband' and Mother and she would exchange meaning glances, leaving Hessie outside the fraternity of married women. It was still incredible that Hilda was going to be a wife, Albert's wife, anybody's wife. A married woman anyhow.

How had that come about? Hessie stood with the handle of the washing-up mop clasped in her hand. Just how had all this happened? Hilda had been working for Mr. Baker for over six years now. Close beside him, for the office at the back of the shop was quite small. Was it possible that—that—Hessie felt the colour come hotly over her face and neck, and her mouth went dry. It couldn't be that, of course. Hilda would never have allowed anything horrid like that to happen. No, it must have been a slow ripening of friendship into attraction and attraction into love. So often things happened like that, in books, too. One day the hero's eyes are opened by something a little different about the girl who has been his companion for months, years perhaps, and then—well, things happen after that. Needless to say the girl has always been in love with the big middle-aged man, in love with his tweeds and his pipes and his unruly hair, even the mud on his brogue shoes. And in the end he gathers her into his arms, and her years of bright, smiling love-repressed companionship are at an end.

In real life you modified that, of course. For instance Albert wasn't very tweedy—nor was Mr. Saul, but they were both men. And Hilda and she were girls. Quite definitely girls. Hilda's marriage was proving that there was nothing queer or unsexed about them. Wasn't it proving too, that—that they were attractive to men? Not like poor Rosie and Lily Bates. Neither of those poor girls had ever had a young man. It was pitiful to see Rosie sometimes, her efforts to attract men were so obvious.

When the work was finished Hessie cut a lemon in two and rubbed the juice onto her fingers. With a little care her hands would be quite nice. Albert had come, and Mother and he were laughing together in the dining-room. Hessie could hear them as she passed through the hall. Hilda came running down the stairs with a girlish, one-two-three movement. She ran on into the dining-room, leaving the door open. Albert was standing by the empty fireplace, his hands clasped behind his back, every now and then tilting backwards and forwards on his toes and heels.

"Here she is!" Mother beamed, as Hilda ran in. "Here's our girl!"

Hilda's gay little rush brought her close to Albert's side, and there she stopped in a childish attitude, her stomach thrust out a little, her chin in, glancing up at him through her eyelashes.

When she had put on her hat and her light summer coat Hessie hastened down the street. The shops were still open, but at this hour their wares looked brightly dead. It was the lack of possible customers perhaps, but the heaped piles of dried cereals and pyramids of cocoa tins looked sterile and dusty. Even the expression on the face of the robust fisherman gloating over his rich salmon haul was apathetic, he was no longer exultant in his contemplation of his succulent middle-cuts.

One or two wives, out on belated errands, walked rapidly down the street, too preoccupied with their anxiety to reach their homes to notice what lay in the shop windows, though occasionally one of them would pause before a food shop and stare thoughtfully into the window, a little calculating frown on her forehead. Hessie knew what she was thinking. Pink salmon at 6d. or three tins for one-and-four. Big tins they were, too, containing enough to make plenty of fish-cakes for a good-sized family. Was pink salmon as nourishing as red?

The modiste shops were all empty except for the proprietresses or lady-managers, whose faces looked white in the bright light, a little hard and old and tired, too. Hessie paused at the window of one shop. Hilda was thinking of getting her wedding frock here. It was almost horrible the way Mother was loosening her money for Hilda's wedding. She was breaking into her carefully hoarded capital in the most reckless manner.

Hessie left the High Street before she reached the better shops and the big cinema. The street she was walking in now was a narrow one that followed a long circular curve, and for this reason was called 'Rosebery Crescent.' The Bates family lived here. The houses on one side were higher than those on the other, and their front doors boasted a flight of steps that gave the inhabitants of that side a sense of superiority over their neighbours on the lower level. It was quite amusing to live in one of the higher houses for the occupiers could glance across the road and, if by chance the lace curtains shrouding the house opposite had been displaced, they could see right into the usually carefully concealed life of another family. It was even more interesting from the front bedroom. Then one caught swift glimpses of beds, and wash-stands with intimate utensils on them, and perhaps a woman with her arms upraised before the dressing-table or a man in his shirt-sleeves. That was always particularly interesting. A man with his braces pressing hard over his shoulders and his shirt blousing out a little bit above the dark line of the top of his trousers. Once Rosie Bates had seen the man opposite dressed in his pyjamas. "Oo-er, Hessie—just imagine!"

There was little or no real neighbourliness in this road. Each house was secret to itself, only united in the one common impulse of genteel hostility to anything that was considered vulgar or not nice.

Rosie herself answered Hessie's knock.

"Mother's out with Lily, Hessie. I've got the book all ready for you. It's rather—rather broad, you know!"

"Oh, I don't mind that!"

"No?"

"After all, we've got to move with the times. I'm not a baby any longer. I was saying that to Hilda only the other day. Mother will have to get used to letting us do what we like now."

"I quite agree with you, Hessie," Rosie tittered. Then she added, just swiftly enough to allay Hessie's quick suspicions, "With Hilda getting married and all, your mother ought to realize that you're old enough to know your own minds. Men don't marry children, do they? Anyhow they oughtn't to—there's a law against it!"

Hessie laughed. There were times when she quite liked Rosie Bates. When the sense of rivalry between them went down before a nice girlish friendliness.

"Oh, come along out for a walk, Rosie," she cried impulsively. "Do come, it's such a nice night out."

Rosie giggled. "Now, Hessie," she said archly, "you won't lead me into any mischief, will you?"

"Go on this very minute—get your hat and coat on!" Hessie countered with a delicious severity.

She sat in the little, dustless sitting-room while Rosie ran to put on her coat and hat. She sat surrounded by photographs of Rosie and her sister, Lily, in all ages and stages. There were cascades of china and pictures and souvenirs of various holidays arranged around and about the mantelpiece. There were plush frames containing slightly-faded photographs of little plump girls dressed up in the very maximum of frills and laces and ribbons. "I made every bit of their clothes myself by hand," Mrs. Bates had assured Hessie many times.

What a ferocity of sewing must have gone into those frocks and petticoats and pinafores and pants with long full legs and drooping frills! Other photographs were enshrined in frames made from tiny foreign shells, little bright-coloured humps with minute ridges that were veritable dust-traps. Not that there was ever a speck of dust in the Bates' parlour. Every morning Mrs. Bates and Rosie and Lily pounced brightly on the room and shook and dusted and brushed and washed everything. It was the same all over the house, a bright spinster cleanliness prevailed everywhere.

Rosie came back very quickly. She had wound a knitted scarf in a loose reckless way about her neck and a crocheted cap rested on her head. Walking down the road her face maintained a look of cheerful expectancy.

"Oh, there's Mr. Simmons," she whispered. Really, Hessie, I wouldn't like to tell you! But they say he's gay! You know! Women! Horses, too! Just imagine that!"

"And he looks so quiet!"

"Still waters! Of course, it may only be gossip but all the same there's no smoke without fire, is there?"

Hessie nodded. Really Rosie was not so bad. Perhaps they could chum up a bit now that marriage was going to take Hilda away from her. She'd need somebody to go about with until—until her own marriage, of course. After all, that was the most sensible way to look at Hilda's engagement. What could happen to one of them was almost sure to happen to the other as well.

"What's the latest about the love-birds?" Rosie inquired suddenly.

Hessie stiffened a little. What a pity it was that Rosie expressed herself so—so vulgarly!

"I suppose Hilda is up in the clouds altogether," Rosie went on hardily.

"Oh, well, love is rather like that—uplifting—isn't it? At least, that's how it seems to be to me," Hessie said gently, reprovingly. She met Rosie's bright bird-like glance and stiffened the lines of her face. That would be something for the Bates' family to think about! She could almost imagine the scene when Rosie got home to-night. "Hessie Price? You don't mean it, Rosie! Well, really, those girls! I suppose they feel they've done their duty to their mother, and now they're getting nests of their own. Did she say who it was, Rosie?" "No, but it isn't hard to guess. Haven't you seen the way Mr. Saul looks at her?" "Well, yes, I have. ..." And then Lily might say, her voice shaking a little, her face desperate, "How do girls make themselves attractive to men? No, mother, I just can't help it—How do they do it?"

Rosie almost bumped into Hessie when they reached the wider street.

"Oh, I'm so sorry, but we were going to turn this way, weren't we, Hessie? I believe you were daydreaming!"

"Well, I was," Hessie smiled gently, then she gave herself a little shake and turned definitely to Rosie. "There—that's over! I'm back on earth again! What did you say, Rosie? You want to go down by Felthams? Why, certainly, dear."

She felt all gentle sweetness—the sweetness of a woman who is beloved, who can afford to be generous towards everyone else. She glanced at herself in a shop window as they went by. Yes, there was a sweet exalted look on her face and her eyes were big.

This mood persisted throughout the walk. She kissed Rosie

affectionately when they parted. Alone, Hessie walked with quick easy steps.

She was just a girl, her body cleaving the air without any restrictions. It was as if she had no clothes on at all, only, of course, she was clothed, which made it easy for her to smile a little at an irresponsive-looking policeman. Was this how the figure-head at the prow of a ship felt as it went its serene way through the dark water? Nudism was a horrid thing, of course, but if you felt like this perhaps there was something in it, after all.

At the corner of their road she nearly ran into a man. Quite instinctively she put out her hands and felt her arm gripped at the elbow. A strong, steadying, man's grip.

"Sorry!"

"It's all right—really it is!" she gasped breathlessly. "It was my fault!"

But, lifting his hat, he was gone! He was a gentleman, of course. No gentleman would embarrass a lady by standing talking to her when a circumstance of this kind had thrown them together so abruptly. Thrown them right into each other's arms, so to speak! Besides, he had lifted his hat before his tactful retirement into the night. That proved his gentle breeding.

There was a horrible airlessness about the house when she reached home. Mother appeared, moving ponderously into the hall, her cheeks hanging heavily from her face.

"Oh, it's you, is it?" she said sourly. "I thought it was Hilda."

Almost immediately Hilda arrived. Hessie and Mother were still standing in the hall when Albert's hand with the key in it felt cautiously for the keyhole. Mother's face lit up. She hastened forward. Hilda, with Albert gallant and courteous behind her, entered the hall.

"Won't you come in, Albert?" Mother pressed towards him.

"I'm afraid I must be going. No—not to-night."

Mother looked very disappointed when Albert finally disappeared but she revived as she followed Hilda into the sitting-room.

"Well, tell me all about it, dear," she said coaxingly.

Hilda pulled off her gloves, her mouth pouting girlishly. She was very pleased about something.

"We've fixed the wedding day!" she announced.

Mother was all attention. Hessie sat down slowly. The wedding day—Hilda's wedding day. Fixed, arranged, settled!

"When, Hilda?"

"The twenty-fifth of next month. That's a Tuesday. Albert looked it all out in a little calendar."

"The twenty-fifth—Tuesday," Mother echoed. "Are you sure that's all right for you, Hilda?" she added significantly.

Hilda flushed her usual, unbecoming red. "Mother!" she protested, glancing at Hessie.

"Oh, don't mind me!" Hessie said with sudden bitterness. "I know all about it! Everyone knows that the girl has to choose the wedding day, too."

Hilda jumped up, her throat working in quick gulps. She rushed from the room. Mrs. Price glared angrily at Hessie and waddled after Hilda.

Hessie sat on and on for a long time, twisting and turning her gloves in fingers that were cold and damp. So Hilda's wedding day was actually fixed? And wedding days were always followed by—by other things. After all, a man and his wife were one. "My wife." "My husband." United, possessive words! Just as it should be, of course. St. Paul—or was it?—and the New Testament generally supported such blessed unity. There were cruder bits in the old Bible, of course, but then in those days things were not so refined, and the methods fitted the necessities.

Chapter Ten

I

It had been misty all day, with a mild wind driving the mist into all corners of the garden, so that everything hung with tiny drops of delicate grey moisture. When the mist lifted a little, as it did every now and then, trees and flowers appeared in new startling places, their shapes and colours solemn and mysterious.

Lottie and the children had been out all the morning. The children's hair beneath their close-fitting caps had grown damp and curly, the pink in their cheeks deepening into rosy red as they played about. Isobel kept running in amongst the trees, and crying, "I'm lost, Lottie, I'm lost," her voice high and thin and queerly muted by the mist. Then, thrilled and frightened she would rush back to Lottie, rejoicing in this easy return from such desperate dangers.

Anne had picked up a small branch from a beech tree, and was marching along with this held out in front of her, cleaving the mist with her green shield. The children were having stories about King Arthur and his Knights of the Round Table read to them, and their allegiance was divided between Sir Lancelot and Sir Galahad. Isobel loved the way Sir Galahad—the young knight—had drawn the sword out of the block of stone. She could see the river and the gleaming knights in a solemn semicircle by the river bank, and the young Galahad coming forth from their midst, his face brighter than the sun. But then, on the other hand, take Sir Lancelot—the mightiest of them all! There was Sir Gareth too, with the little birds eating from his hands and perched so blissfully on the shoulders of his green doublet. It was very difficult to pick a hero from so many entrancing competitors.

Everything in the gardens and woods was different to-day. All the flowers had changed their flower-beds, and the trees had moved their solemn heights from place to place. It was very baffling and mysterious and interesting.

"Let's go down this path, it's quite new to me!" Isobel cried, as they left the broad path beneath the trees and came close to where the greenhouses lay hidden by the mist.

The children ran ahead, exploring the path, convinced that they were on strange ground. They were astonished when they came out at the greenhouses.

"Where are we?" Isobel cried. "We can't be really here yet!"

But the sight of Maxwell coming round from his cottage was only too convincing.

They went into the house for the children's dinner then. For once the house appeared more real than the garden. After the shiftings and uncertainties of the mist the furniture looked very firm and solid and the colours in the nursery appeared very bright. Isobel and Anne helped Lottie to lay the nursery table.

Soon after dinner the wind increased, and gained supremacy over the mist. The wind drove along in wild exultant gusts, hounding the mist before it. Suddenly one half of the garden stood out free, the colours clear and wet. The flowers looked surprised to find themselves on view once more. Outside the garden the sea was quite high, long stately waves rolling and curling over the sand, rearing their rounded crests with beautiful careless abandon.

The children played beneath the fir trees all afternoon. The rough tree trunks broke the wind a little, and they built houses for themselves, crawling into hollows in the patches of bushy undergrowth, which they decorated with tall green bracken fronds. They collected fir cones and plundered the garden for seed pods for food. Isobel was terribly industrious in this respect. She was so sure a severe winter was coming and food must be stored at all costs. "I've such a very big family," she exclaimed to Lottie, "and they've all got dreadful appetites." Lottie had great difficulty in getting them back to the house, and they went to bed planning to get up very early in the morning and to go back to their houses in time to feed their families with breakfast. Lottie promised to wake and dress them very early.

With Isobel and Anne safely in bed Lottie was free for the rest of the evening, and she decided to go out. Nurse looked up and pursed her mouth disapprovingly as Lottie left the nursery. She could not get used to Lottie's new habit of spending her off-duty hours away from the house.

Slipping on her coat Lottie went out through the yard, and into the grounds at the back of the house. The wind had died away now. She found George sitting on a pile of stakes. He had a penknife in his hand and he was whittling away at something, but he folded the knife and thrust it into his pocket with a long slow movement when he saw Lottie. He smiled at her.

"Where would you like to go?" he asked. "Let's go up over the hill and home by the shore?"

"Yes," Lottie agreed simply.

The hill path led gently up from the corner of the grounds where the woods were thickest. George set the pace and they walked along slowly. He held the dark wet branches aside for Lottie and smiled as she went by. Walking on the soft damp leaves amongst the trees whose privacy was so seldom disturbed made Lottie want to hold her breath. The quietness of the hour, the deeper silence following the triumphant bustling of the wind earlier in the clay had laid a spell upon the woods. The low cloudy sky was darkening a little as they began to climb up the small hill that led out onto the headland. For some reason or other George increased the pace as they went up the hill-path, and Lottie's face was flushed when they reached the top. She could hear her heart beating, a rather nice steady full beat. It made her feel almost like a child again, free and light, no longer burdened by all the things Nurse had impressed on her lately.

"It's grand up here," George said.

Lottie nodded and smiled. More and more she was coming to look on George as someone apart from other men. He was a man, of course, but he was something else as well, and whatever that something else was it was robbing her of her fear and selfconsciousness. He was gentle and strong, but not in the least alarming. When she was actually with George she felt no fear, it was only at night, when Nurse had been talking to her that she grew afraid, even of him.

"Not cold, are you?" George asked.

There was a damp coldness in the air now. Below them the little bay was possessed by the sea. The rocks looked darkly and tiredly forbidding. They were weary of buttressing the land, but yet what else could they do? That was their business. So they stood out in the darkening sea, strong but weary, and let the grey water rush over them. The face of the cliff received the spray from the sea, and from little crannies quite high up water dripped ceaselessly. In the heavy stillness inland it was strange to watch the sea's activity. So much noise and tremendous motion against the silent and acquiescent land.

"It's the tide," George said. "It will be extra high to-night."

Lottie knew well the sound of a high tide. At certain times, particularly in the spring and autumn, the sea appeared to swell and swell until it seemed as if the whole of the land could not hold the volume of water that came rushing in. At night the sound of the water washing about the sand kept her awake, it was so grey and powerful.

But the sea, even at its stormiest tides, always stopped short at the ridge where the fir trees grew, though once it had threatened to dash up and in amongst the tall bent trees. The children had been wild that day with a pleasant delicious fear and excitement, and expeditions from the house had been continually going to watch the water's progress. Mr. Kellaway, hatless and in a long mackintosh, had stood amongst the trees, with Maxwell beside him. This tide had become a date in the children's minds. "When the sea nearly came through into the garden, Lottie—"

But there were no alarming features about the tide that was coming in now. For all its tremendous rush and roar the little silent waiting bay would be equal to it.

The wind was beginning to spring up again. It blew against Lottie's face, soft and cold. She put up her hand to her cheeks, and felt the smooth coldness of her skin. George began talking about her life in the Home.

"You may be a princess in disguise," he said, laughingly. "You look like one, Lottie."

Lottie's heart began its loud steady beating again. This was different from Nurse's attitude towards her parentage. She was someone a little tainted, a little criminal, almost sordid, in Nurse's opinion. There had been something of that in the atmosphere of the Home, too. There was something mysterious and nasty about all the children. "Who's your mother?" "Where's your father?" The children didn't know; none of them knew! Quite frequently the older ones lied to the children at the council school which the orphans attended. "My father owned his own shop." "My mother was a lady, but she's dead now." But it wasn't much use. The other children told their parents what they had said, and came back the next day looking smugly satisfied and unbelieving. The Home children never played with the other school children. They played amongst themselves, and walked home immediately school was over, straggling along, two by two, in broken uneven lines.

And here was George suggesting that she might be a princess! She wasn't a princess, of course, but for the first time her mind caught on to the idea that she wasn't just—just dirt! Perhaps she had had a beautiful mother—a handsome father? Nice people. Why shouldn't George know as much about things as Nurse? According to Nurse men knew everything, certainly everything nasty. And if George, knowing everything nasty, placed her outside the nastiness, why shouldn't he be right?

They climbed down the slippery path to the shore. The wind was stronger now, damper and colder, too. Flecks of foam rustled softly and wetly against their faces, and hung for a frothy second in Lottie's hair. They were walking into the wind. The waves rushed up at them, eager to catch their feet, but they kept just above the water-line. But, of course, with an incoming tide it was difficult to know when a wave would come in faster than the rest. One such wave came in now, very swift and smoother than the others and raced away up the sand, past the hitherto highest mark. They started to run, but it was too late! The water caught up on them, and George swung Lottie high in his arms. The wave frothed around his ankles and sucked at his boots as it receded.

He put Lottie down on the dry sand and smiled at her. But it was no good. Lottie knew that her face was white, and that she hated herself for the way in which her blood always betrayed her.

"Did that frighten you?" George asked.

"Oh, no—no!" Lottie cried, and she felt the colour come back into her cheeks as she spoke. She could smile at George, and they stood for a moment, both of them facing the sea, prepared to rush away if another wave came hurtling towards them.

When they reached the protection of the fir trees, they halted. Lottie sighed. Well, it was over! She could see the light in the nursery window. The children's bedroom was dark. Evidently the children were sleeping all right. Lying there so small and innocent and defenceless with the sound of the tide colouring their dreams. Her own bed gleaming emptily in the dusk. Beyond, lay the night-nursery with the baby in his blue and white paradise.

"Let's go this way," George broke in upon her thoughts. "You haven't to be in yet, have you? It's only half-past eight."

Lottie started. Had they really been out for an hour and a half? By this time Nurse would have been down to fetch the nursery supper herself. She'd be eating it now, pickles, cold meats, the remains of some cold sweet pudding. That was what Nurse loved. And she had had to fetch it herself from the kitchen! But that could not be helped now. If she returned to the house immediately, or in an hour's time, her reception from Nurse would be just the same. A frightening silence, while Nurse's lips worked in and out, and her bust grew hard with indignation and swelled against her grey linen frock and tight white apron bib. But this was Lottie's evening off. She could be out until ten o'clock if she wished. The trouble was that she had so seldom availed herself of this freedom. To be back in time to fetch the nursery supper had become a habit.

"Come along," said George coaxingly. "Come along and have something to eat at my house. It's quite close."

At the touch of George's hand on her elbow Lottie gave in. She followed him along a narrow path, moving up close to him when he held the brambles or long branches aside for her. The path sagged and turned and twisted, and the hard brown knots of tree-roots stood out like worn knuckles for their feet to tread on. They were out of sight of the house, and the woods around them were almost dark. Somehow the darkness increased the height and breadth of George's figure as he moved in front of her, and the trees on either side looked taller, too, their leafy heads lost in the potent darkness overhead. But the reassuring sense of George's presence increased at every step they took. Every corner of the wood was filled with the comfort and reassurance of him, close ahead of her, within touching distance.

They crossed a tiny stream and a plank in the narrow width sagged and swayed under their feet. Lottie could just see the little stream below, its waters very thin and surprisingly, darkly bright. It tumbled quite swiftly over the wet brown stones—tinkle—tinkle—tinkle. … It was strange to think that it was going on like that, even in the deadest hour of night, when the trees dare not move, their leaves motionless in the tremendous stillness. It was tinkling away, too, when the children were playing on the beach, and the wood was all gold and green and drowsy with sunlight.

"Here we are!" said George at last. They were out of the wood, and she could see the outline of a small cottage before them.

George's mother looked at her kindly. For the first time in her life Lottie found herself a real guest in someone else's home. Kind ladies, with charitable hearts, had sometimes invited the orphans out to their houses, but they had gone in batches, so many at a time, wearing their Institution clothes. This time Lottie was an individual, just one solitary person, not a unit in a small squad of children.

At supper-time George pressed her to eat and drink. He leant over and put things on her plate. To please him she did her best. George's own appetite seemed terrific, but his mother did not appear to think it so.

"Another bite of this, George," she beseeched him, and at his refusal she looked anxiously at Lottie.

After supper they sat together round the empty fireplace. A great fern, standing in a deep pot, was placed where the bright flames would be in winter. George's mother gazed proudly at the strong feathery fronds. She was very proud of this fern. She washed its leaves every day, and in mild damp weather she placed it outside the cottage door, and let it smell the woods. There was a frisky young cat playing about the room, and an elderly dog came in, and gave Lottie a long serene look before it settled down on the hearthrug. It sat on its haunches, its head drooping forward, its eyes dim with old, dignified thoughts.

George escorted her back to the house. They took a path that was wider and more direct than the narrow one that led from the fir trees. By this time the wind had blown away the clouds, and the sky looked clear and wet. The stars had a bright, newly-washed appearance. They leaned over the tree-tops in a friendly manner.

"It's quite quick to the house this way," George said.

They saw the house immediately he had spoken. It stood sideways towards them as they came out of the trees.

"Which way will you go in?" George asked.

"The side door here. I can get up the back stairs easily then. I always go up and down that way with the children."

"You'll be all right, I suppose?"

Lottie nodded. After all, what could Nurse do to her? She was entitled to these hours of freedom.

George came right up to the door with her. "Good night, Lottie," he said.

For a moment Lottie hesitated. "Good night."

George gave a little laugh, and put out his arm and drew her close up against him. He bent his head and kissed her lips. His other arm went round her and Lottie's face rested helplessly against his shoulder. Her eyes were shut, he could see no colour in her face anywhere—lips or cheeks, but he could feel her heart beating beneath his hand. He kissed her over and over again, light restrained kisses.

"Good night," he said gently, and took his arms away.

Chapter Eleven

I

Maggie drew on her stockings. They were silk stockings, very good quality ones, with embroidered clox tapering up the sides of her legs. That was an advantage, for her calves were firm and shapely, rising from her neat round ankles. She had a pair of garters waiting on the dressing-table, soft green satin ones with a circlet of tiny bright pink roses for decoration. Maggie slipped the garters over her feet and up over her knee. She liked them above the knee better than below. She liked the firm feel of them pressing gently into her flesh. The green looked very pretty against the dark beige silk of the stockings.

She stood up and tilted the mirror of her dressing-table so that she could see the lower half of her body. How smooth and white her skin was! She tilted the mirror again. Her breasts were firm and shapely, there was nothing saggy about her figure, behind or in front. Another half tilt and her neck and head came into sight. Her hair was still damp from its recent washing and there was a dark shining quality about it. Maggie took up her hair brush and began to brush her head, the damp mild air moving happily against her bare breast and arm. Brushing made her hair settle down a bit, and improved her appearance, too, for now her hair looked darker than ever against the whiteness of her skin.

An artificial silk vest lay on the bed. Maggie drew it on, and then, abruptly, she sat down on the side of the bed. She could not help it, but she felt just like a bride, just as unsure, as hesitating as an ordinary bride! And this was as near being a bride as she'd ever get with Maxwell! He wasn't the marrying sort at all. But what did that matter? They loved each other. It was almost frightening the way she was unable to stop thinking about him the whole time. He lay, like a coloured background, at the back of everything she said or did. Her work, Cook, behind them all there was Maxwell and nothing else. It was almost like a disease, like having a constant pain that prevailed over every other feeling. Only this torment meant happiness as well. A dreadful happiness. It was scarcely probable that she would feel like this always, not when she was old, perhaps, but until then it was impossible to think of any kind of life that did not include Maxwell.

Everything she was putting on this afternoon was brand new. Maxwell had given her money to buy herself some clothes. "Get what you want, Maggie, nice things." She was wearing no corsets to-day. Her figure did not need them, and she liked the free easy feeling their absence gave to her. When she was dressed she raised her hands and felt the firm supple softness of her waist.

Irene's bedroom door was a little open. Maggie stopped outside it and called softly, but as no one answered she entered unbidden. Irene's room had a proper wardrobe in it, and she could see herself from head to foot in the long glass. She stood there bewitched by her own appearance. It was a pity she could not go down and walk into the kitchen and let Cook see her! But that might be a mistake. Cook might ask some nasty, awkward questions. No, she wouldn't give Cook the opportunity of spoiling her happiness.

"Hullo, you're all dressed up, aren't you?" That was only Irene standing in the doorway.

"Yes, I'm spending the night with my sister. Mrs. Kellaway said I might."

"I know," Irene smiled with unbelieving good-humour. "I hope you enjoy yourself. Anyhow, you're looking very nice."

Maggie carried the memory of Irene's smiling face with her all the way down the stairs, clutching on to it to protect herself from other thoughts. But that was no good either, nothing was ever any good these days. She could never get away from Maxwell. He was like a presence always inside her mind and heart.

Once clear of the house Maggie walked along slowly. She was in no hurry, and, besides, the day was so beautiful. She had never seen such a beautiful day. Such softly dazzling sunshine, such mild warm air that was just a little damp because the woods were still wet from the night's heavy rain and the morning's protective mist. Here and there where the sunlight shone strongly, little coils of steam were rising from the sodden leaves. Hob-goblins' cauldrons! Irene was always declaring her belief in witches and goblins and little people. She and her brothers and sisters had often seen them about the farm where they had been brought up. Riding on the cattle, peeping from behind the hedges, playing havoc with the milk and cream in the dairy. Irene knew all about them. To-day, Maggie was inclined to believe in them too. The woods were so beautiful.

The road into the town was deserted. She met only one person on the way in. This other walker, a woman, gave Maggie a hard, unsympathetic look. Perhaps she was jealous of her clothes, her new dress? The woman was wearing a long drab coat, buttoned right up to her neck, and her figure was heavy and shapeless. She had eyes like Cook's. Maggie walked on slowly.

Nothing could disturb the almost terrible happiness that was inside her to-day. She glanced into the squalid houses in the first mean streets of the town. She knew what lay behind those thick dirty bits of lace curtains that were slung across the narrow windows. But nothing like that mattered now.

She was meeting Maxwell at four o'clock. He was driving something in to the station, and then he was meeting her. They were going to have the late afternoon, the evening, the whole night together. Maggie moved her shoulders and felt the silk of her vest pressing softly against her skin. From open doorways women and children, and occasionally an old man, stared out into the street. The women's faces were hard and frowning. There was always so much for them to fight against. Dirt and hunger and extreme poverty—it did not give their faces time to relax. They had to be continually fighting things. They hardly bothered to glance at Maggie at all. But, thinking of Maxwell, Maggie's heart was full of soft pity for them.

She entered the High Street of the town very suddenly. Past a block of ugly storehouses, and she was there, in the busy rather soiled prosperity of the cheaper end of the street. It was not the busiest time of the day, and the fronts of the shops looked worn and dirty and unduly exposed! About five o'clock things would smarten up a bit. All sorts of people would come shopping then, but mostly youngish mothers, with anxious sober flatly-clean faces, and prams full of babies and parcels; and stout older women with comfortable figures and faces that were more robust than those of the younger women, possibly because their families were grown up now and the fatigue of child-bearing was not so close to them.

In the middle of the street Maggie began to study the shop windows more carefully. The little gown shops were beginning to be fairly numerous here. "Exclusive," "Model," with a hat or two labelled "Chic." There were shoe shops with plate-glass shelves in the showcases, and shoes displayed on elegantly-arched feet that ended disappointingly before the ankle began. A big cinema with wide steps overflowing into the street came next. Maggie glanced at the ornamental clock just inside the foyer. Twenty-five minutes past three. Oh, God, the sudden sick shaking of her whole body! The palms of her hands were moist. In thirty-five minutes she would be meeting Maxwell. The big broad-chested commissionaire was looking at her, jovial interest in his eyes. Well, let him look! He was welcome to that much.

Maggie paused again outside a lingerie shop. It was here that she had bought the garments she was wearing now. Everything white—bridal! Vest, knickers, petticoat, brassiere. She looked possessively at the windows. She was a customer here, and if things went on as they had begun, she'd be coming here again. Maggie gazed almost desperately into the window. She'd like to buy that and that and that! She was able to pass ten minutes in this fashion.

A band composed of out-of-works came down the street. Between them they had a trombone and a drum, and a thing like a flute, and a fiddle. It was the funniest-looking lot of instruments, but the men themselves were terribly serious. They had to play very loud to be heard against the traffic. Except for the angle at which he had to hold his back and stomach the drummer's job was the easiest. He had only to swing his arms and bang on the drum, while the other men's cheeks were in continual and desperate motion, blowing in and out, their lips pursed and rounded. The fiddle was doing his best, no doubt, but Maggie could not hear him at all. He was lost in the traffic and the drum and the occasionally varying boom of the trombone. The trombonist's cheeks swelled out powerfully, and he rolled his eyes whenever he succeeded in varying the sounds from his instrument. He was the most earnest of them all. The fiddler was the most melancholy.

Emerging from the inner showcases of the lingerie shop Maggie gave the bandsmen a penny. Almost immediately they burst into the strains of "Here Comes the Bride," the men taking quick short steps to fit the rhythm. This amused the passers-by very much, and a lot of pennies joined Maggie's. But the music made Maggie feel quite sick, there was such a touch of realism—for her—about it.

The station was at the top end of the street, and the clock there said three minutes to four. There was a very grand teashop up by the station and Maggie stood gazing into its windows. Maxwell would be with her at any moment now. In a sudden agony of bashfulness, she darted into a narrow side street. She'd stay hidden away in here for the next eight minutes, then, at five past four, she'd stroll out again. But as the clock struck four she went weakly back into the street.

Almost at once Maxwell was beside her. He seemed to have the same habit in the town, as he had in the country, of appearing quickly and powerfully from nowhere.

"Hullo—so you managed to get off!" he said, his face intimately close to hers.

Maggie smiled shakily. It was queer the way his presence affected her. Up till now she'd always wanted to move away when a man came close to her like this, but Maxwell's closeness made her limbs cease to belong to her at all. But he couldn't put his arms round her in the middle of the street.

"Look here—" he took her elbow, and glanced quickly about. "Let's go somewhere. What about a cup of tea? There's a quiet place round the corner here. Not too classy, but comfortable."

"All right."

"You've managed about to-night?" he asked, as they walked quickly up the street.

"Yes, it was easy."

"Good. We'll get things for supper on the way back. You'll cook it, won't you? We'll be very cosy."

There was a darkish passage at the entrance to the small café he had chosen. Maggie trembled as he glanced hurriedly around, but just at that moment two men came out of the tea-room. Maxwell's grip on her elbow tightened.

"Later!" he whispered.

In a way Maggie felt relieved. Everything, even the first kiss, was still ahead of them, keeping them both in a state of desperate expectancy.

"What'll you have to eat?" he asked, as they sat down at a table that ran close beside the wall. On one side of the table were round-bottomed cane chairs, on the other side a long plush-covered settee with springs in it, that ran the length of the wall.

Maggie and Maxwell sat side by side on the plush. Maggie was the farthest in, and the subdued light from the window fell on her face whenever she turned to speak to him. Not that she feared any light, for her skin was good, and the soft red in her cheeks was her own.

The waitress was a perky young thing with a sharp turned-up nose, and thin lively-looking legs. She eyed Maxwell with interest, only giving Maggie a quick look-over before restoring her attention to Maxwell. Maggie returned her glance with superb indifference, before glancing at Maxwell, too. But, instantly she was reassured. He had not so much as seen the other girl!

Maggie ate toast, hot and thickly buttered, and then cake, but Maxwell tackled a plate of ham and eggs. She had the tea things placed on her left, which was awkward for pouring out, but it meant that their plates were closer together.

"Sugar, I suppose?" her hand hung poised over the sugar basin.

"Two lumps," he said. "Will that be hard to remember?"

"Two lumps?" Maggie repeated innocently, her cheeks bright red.

The sugar tongs were incorporated in the lid or the sugar basin. Maggie squeezed the protrusions at the top and the claws beneath seized a lump of sugar.

"Just look at that!" she exclaimed.

"One—two," Maxwell counted.

When they had finished eating, they decided to go to the talkies.

"Bill, please, miss." Maxwell beckoned the waitress.

Maggie stood up slowly. She could see her own reflection in a damp-speckled mirror at the opposite side of the room. She was smart-looking and handsome, too. It was extraordinary what clothes and self-confidence could do to a girl.

This was the first time she had been out with Maxwell. She felt a sudden rush of deep passionless love for him as she watched him pay for their teas. The way he dug his hand into his trouser pocket, his face soberly careless, his body hitched over slightly. He drew out a handful of silver, and threw some of it down onto the counter. It was all so different from a woman's careful fumbling in her bag.

Out in the High Street again Maxwell paused before a jeweller's shop.

"You'd better have something," he pointed towards a rod hung with long strings of beads.

Maggie hesitated. She felt she loved him so much that she did not need presents from him.

"Come on in!" He advanced into the shop, leaving Maggie to follow him. "You'd better have something to go with this dress."

Maggie stood close beside another rod slung with necklaces. She kept fingering them for a while, pulling out the long strands and letting them fall back again. They made a tinkling noise as they slipped in amongst their fellows once more. The assistant stood by, with an air of pleasant hastelessness. Lady customers must not be hurried.

"What about this one?" Maxwell asked, as Maggie let a string of big red and crystal beads lie against her hand.

"That's very fine!" said the assistant, with a deferential glance at Maggie as if explaining to her that though two male opinions might be of some value, nevertheless it was the lady's choice that could be the only ultimate and right one.

But still Maggie hesitated. She was longing for this string but she had seen a tiny hard pear-shaped tag that told the price. Maxwell hadn't! But he did not seem to mind about that.

"We'll have that one," he said, and slapped a pound note down on the counter as if he knew there would be no change out of it.

Maggie walked out of the shop with the heavy beads swinging against her breasts.

"Like 'em?" asked Maxwell, as they walked on, the increasing crowd of shoppers making it impossible for them to walk side by side for more than a yard or two. Most of the time Maggie was a little way ahead, with Maxwell pressing close behind her.

"They're gorgeous!" she breathed. "Just the last touch this frock needed!"

Glancing back over her shoulder she saw that he was smiling. Her heart beat warmly.

"You're a pretty smart-looking girl," he said.

Maggie threw back her shoulders a bit. With her big firm type of figure she could not afford to slouch.

"How old are you, Maggie?" he asked unexpectedly.

"Nineteen."

"That's fine," he said.

The commissionaire at the cinema looked at Maggie with fresh interest. Her fingers plucked at her new necklace as she waited while Maxwell bought their tickets. The commissionaire's expression changed as Maxwell swung round. His face resumed its professional blankness and he stared out into the street.

"Was he looking at you?" Maxwell asked, jerking his head backwards.

Maggie laughed. "Why shouldn't he?"

"No reason at all," he smiled unpleasantly, "so long as you didn't look back at him."

Maggie checked her first natural instinct to toss her head. After all, this was their day together—it was like part of a honeymoon. It wasn't just passion between them, there was a tremendous weight of gentleness in her heart for him too. She did not want to hurt him in any way to-day—or at any time for that matter.

"I didn't look at him," she said comfortingly. She touched his arm gently, and felt his muscles stiffen in awareness of her.

He bought a large box of chocolates, and handed them to her as they sat down in the bewildering darkness of the cinema. Maggie held them carefully in her lap until her eyes were used to the subdued lights. In the little break at the end of 'the comic' she opened the chocolates, letting the rustling inside paper float away between the seats. They were almost alone in their row, the most expensive seats in the house. Maggie sniffed appreciatively at the rich creamy chocolate smell from the open box in her hand.

"Have one?" she whispered.

"Too soon after tea."

"It isn't too soon for me!"

"Fond of chocolates?"

"Oh, yes!" Maggie exclaimed. His hand slid onto her knee and rested there.

The main picture might have been made specially for them. Maggie followed it with the feel of Maxwell beside her sharpening and intensifying everything. It was terrible to think that the night was bringing their love to an even sweeter, sharper climax than the one the hero and heroine were displaying on the screen.

When they left the cinema it was almost dusk. The street lights were lit, and the people hurrying about the pavements were bent on far different errands from those of the earlier shoppers. It was like coming out into the living atmosphere of another film.

They walked slowly up in the street together. Maggie's eyes were very bright, and she was deeply and happily aware of her own physical attractiveness. She teased and flirted with Maxwell, until his face was continually smiling and his eyes followed every movement she made.

"We won't cook anything to-night," Maxwell said suddenly as they approached the fine double windows of a *delicatessen* shop. "But we'll have a good supper all the same. We'll get something here and bring it back."

He seemed to know a lot about food and housekeeping. "I can cook as well as any woman," he said. "Better than most!"

"I'm glad I'm not cooking anything to-night then," Maggie said.

"I'll teach you a lot," he said. "You leave it to me!"

Maggie touched his arm. His fierce possessiveness made her feel compassionate and gentle. But things would not be like this always. Her love for him might last, because she thought of him in every way, he was her lover and her child too, but what would be left of his love once his body grew tired of hers? Still, so long as he needed her in any way she was there to give him what he wanted.

It was dark when they drove out of town. Maggie did not go to the yard close to the station where the horse and dog-cart were stabled. She stood in a dark corner by the station wall and waited. Standing here in this darkness made her feel very alone, very cut off from the rest of the world. In the café and in the cinema, particularly in the cinema, she had been part of the life around her, richly part of it, almost the centre of it. But here it was dark and quiet, and she felt lost for a moment in the rather ugly vagueness that the darkness and quietness suggested. There was a faint smell of steam and coal and tar, too, and together they made her feel a little sick.

But the sight of Maxwell and the horse stopped all that. The horse was young and strong and very impatient to be off, and Maxwell had a job holding him in. He held the reins with both hands, his elbows on a level with his chest.

"Nip in, Maggie," he said.

Maggie sprang up beside him and instantly they were off. He was busy with the horse until they were out of the traffic, but once in the country he let the animal have its head. Maggie held onto her side of the seat. The spokes in the big wheels of the dog-cart flew smoothly round. Now and then Maxwell drew his whip lightly across the horse's flanks and the animal's ears flattened back and its stride increased until the night air was cutting smoothly and strongly past Maggie's face.

"It's dark, and if anyone sees you they won't know who you are," Maxwell said as they turned in through the open gates of the back entrance. "I often give a lift to one of the farmers' wives."

In the darkest part of the drive he stopped. "There's a cutting through there that leads to my house. I'll go on to the stables. I'll meet you up at the door. There'll be nobody about."

Maggie had a little torch in her bag, and she followed the narrow path quite easily. She passed from the high shrubs into a little clearing where the woods stretched away on cither side of her, woods that had grown limitless because of the night's darkness. She flashed her light down through the trees, and felt that the wood was unending. This was one of the miracles of the country at night. The roads in the cities were marked and limited by lights and houses but in the country there were no boundaries at all. The woods and the fields flowed onwards through the darkness for ever.

In the end Maxwell reached the house before she did. He was waiting for her at the open doorway. When she was inside he closed the door behind them.

"Where's the light?" she whispered.

"Not yet!" he said thickly. "Where are you, Maggie?"

Maggie stood still as he reached out and pressed his hands over her shoulders and down her arms. Then she turned in his arms and faced him. She felt so kind and tender towards him, so immensely, richly loving.

Chapter Twelve

I

"September is such a lovely month!" Mrs. Price put down her tea-cup. "I suppose Albert has got striped trousers and a proper coat?"

"Mother!" Hilda exclaimed, her voice trembling with indignation.

Mother wilted. "Of course, Hilda! Naturally! I only wondered. My girlie is going to be such a sweet bride—all in white!"

This mollified Hilda a little. "Hessie, Miss Bowman wants you to go down after tea for a fitting."

"Does she?" Hessie bit slowly into the piece of bread-and-butter she had cut for herself; she had cut it in a delicate precise way, the butter spread thinly and evenly over its surface.

Somehow or other doing a thing like that eased her a little these days. It was a small way of showing mother and Hilda that she was somebody. Prepare her food in a careful deliberate manner. It was a small form of self-expression—a way of projecting herself as a personality. She had to do it in face of Mother's interest in Hilda just because Hilda was going to be a married woman soon. It was almost disgusting the way Mother was pandering to Hilda. "Yes, dear …" "What's the matter with my girlie now?" Was it because Mother was afraid of Albert? Mother was very anxious to keep in with Albert. "My son …"

Hessie chewed her small bite of bread with deliberate gentility. Ladies never gulped their food. She held the slice of bread between her thumb and first finger. She glanced down at it in a calm detached way.

"Hessie," Hilda cried sharply, "you've got to go this afternoon! Miss Bowman's getting quite anxious about it."

"There's no need to fuss," Hessie said, with a gentle aloof smile. "I've got some engagements for this afternoon, but I'll see what I can do, dear."

But it was not always as easy as this. In the end it was always Hilda who held the trump card. Hilda's finger was encircled by Albert's ring, their friends looked at Hilda with a new respect, Hilda would soon be a married woman. Married—experienced! Hilda might some day even have a baby. Good God! A little gift sent down from heaven in proof of the consummation of her marriage. Albert's child, of course.

Hessie finished her piece of bread and butter, and sipped the last of her tea. This was the afternoon when she left the Bensons' early and was home in time for tea. "My little holiday," she always called it jokingly. It was only servants who said "My afternoon off." There was a square of ginger cake on the table, a dark slab, with here and there an astonishing piece of crystallized ginger. Mrs. Price had dark crumbs on her plate, she moistened the tips of her fingers and conveyed them to her mouth. Waste was such a sin.

After tea Hessie stood up. She made no move to clear away the tea-things. Surely Hilda could do that alone for once. So often lately Hilda had escaped doing her share of the work. "Hess—do this for me. Albert will be here at any moment. …" But this time Hessie felt that she did not care whether Albert was coming or not. Anyhow, she was pretty sure he wasn't.

The newspapers said that September was going to be a marvellous month—hotter than August. That meant that Hilda was likely to have a fine wedding day. Well, so much the better since the bridesmaids were to be dressed in pale green after all, and she would want all the colour that she possibly could have in her checks. Hessie felt Mother's eyes on her as she went slowly down the front steps. Mother was standing ponderously in the window and her presence there made the house look old and over-occupied.

In the High Street Hessie turned left. She stopped at the little shop that had "Elizabeth" written tastefully, elegantly on the narrow fascia board. Inside there was a little pathway made by footmarks in the depressed-looking beige floor-covering. Miss Bowman hurried forward.

"This way, Miss Price. I'm so glad you've come. What weather! It's glorious, isn't it? Yes, indeed."

Hessie entered the fitting cubicle with quiet dignity. She must hoard this moment a little. Miss Bowman's politeness, the atmosphere of "chic" clothes, a real evening gown, a pair of silk stockings curled negligently into the shape of a rose, a hat so correctly fashionable that it was almost secretive with exclusiveness—these were all hers. She was a customer! She must be satisfied, propitiated, pandered to; she was important!

But this moment could not last long. Once she took off her dress her importance would go with the exposure of her underclothes. She could sense the change in Miss Bowman already. Why hadn't she thought of this before and worn a petticoat over her shapeless cotton knickers? She was thin, awkward, ugly. Her hair was slipping down at one side of her head, and her skin looked sallow.

"Arms up a little higher, please," Miss Bowman said. "It's only tacked together as yet. That's it! Don't you think these flowing lines are very becoming, Miss Price?"

"Very," Hessie heard herself saying in a foolish conciliatory tone, almost gushingly humble, as though she could make up in this horrible way for the shabbiness of her own underclothes.

"Your sister suggested these sleeves—worn with long white gloves of course. Just turn round, Miss Price. That's better."

How very intimate a dressmaker had to be with all her clients. Almost, in a way, it was not quite nice. Still, another woman—what did it matter, although, of course, you could not allow a man to touch you like this.

There was another uncomfortable moment when the bridesmaid's dress was being removed. It refused to come over her head and shoulder, and there she stood, helpless, with her arms up and her head swathed in the folds of the frock and the rest of her body at the mercy of Miss Bowman's sharp eyes.

Hessie's face was scarlet when the frock flew off at last. She patted her own dress into place and fumbled with her hair. How awkward long hair was. The more she tried to straighten it the more it slipped away from her fingers. Her crowning glory! Supposing she had it cut some day—any day now! "A trim and singe, madam?" "No, thank you, I want my hair cut off. That's what I said. Cut off!" Snip—snip! And then the assistant's tone, a little regretful. "Your hair was beautifully long, madam. Still you'll find it so much easier to dress now. Short hair is so convenient."

That flat heavy strand at the side would not behave itself. Miss Bowman was standing by, the half-made frock dangling over one arm, a look of thinly-veiled impatience on her face.

Hessie seized her hat, and pulled it on, thrusting the obstinate strands and ends up beneath the brim. That was the quickest way, even if it left the bulges on her forehead rather too exposed and bare.

"Can you come again next week, Miss Price?" Miss Bowman asked. "You know, we want everything ready in good time. It's going to be such a pretty wedding, I'm sure, quite an important one, too. We all thought Mr. Baker was going to be a bachelor for life!"

Hessie drew on her gloves. She kept her hands well down, for these were just a light shabby pair that she was finishing off this summer.

"Well, let me see! Yes, I can come in next week. This day week? About the same time?"

"That'll do nicely. You're very busy just now, I expect, with the wedding so close. Your sister will make a lovely bride."

"Oh, lovely!" Hessie agreed with the innocently restrained enthusiasm of a sister who is reluctant to publicly praise a member of her own family and yet unable to resist a little loving spontaneous outburst.

"Good afternoon."

"Good-bye, Miss Price."

Hessie went rapidly along the pavement, irritable whenever her way was blocked by shoppers. Hilda and Albert Baker. How had Hilda done it? Albert was stocky and red-faced, but he was a man, and he was quite important in the town. Mother, Miss Bowman, everyone was treating Hilda with new respect. A year ago they'd just been Hessie and Hilda Price, sisters, companions, with their little girlish jokes together, and now Hilda had shot away from her. Oh God, if only she could follow Hilda.

"My sons-in-law. … Albert is a good man, steady and kind, but my elder daughter's husband—one of God's priests. Oh, yes, quite a big private income of his own, not like poor Mr. and Mrs. Benson, our rector here. My Hessie is so happy. If you'll just pass me that album I'll show you some snapshots. Snapshots are always so natural—aren't they? Ah, there's the baby. Yes, a boy. …"

A horrible convulsive tremor shook Hessie's body, and she felt desperately sick and dizzy. She stood by a shop window and supported her shaking knees against the boarding in front. What was the matter with her these days? Could she be going mad, or was she sickening for some dreadful disease? Ah no, it was only the excitement, the disturbance of Hilda's wedding. She'd reasoned all that out before. She'd feel calm and settled down again as soon as Hilda was a bride—a married woman—sharing her husband's bed and board—getting accustomed to Albert's kisses, Albert's arms. Well, why shouldn't Hilda know those things? That's what marriage was for, wasn't it? "It is not good that man should be alone." After all the animals did not live alone. Cats, dogs, the dear little birds with their bright little eyes. God had arranged it all so nicely for them.

Hessie began to walk forward, very slowly because her knees were still weak, but after a few yards she found she could walk swiftly again. Very swiftly. She had left the shops behind and was walking along a wide residential road. There were trees on either side of it, their dark green leaves heavy and still. This was a quiet, good road, a road just suitable for gentlefolk, real gentlemen and gentleladies. Houses where the lovely young daughters were unobtrusively protected by handsome fathers and tall brothers; the men, that solid bulwark of the family. There would be a slightly military flavour about the young men—God and the regiment and "sir" when speaking to their seniors. And the girls—the girls, beautiful, carefree young daughters moving graciously about the house and gardens, laughter-loving yet capable, of course, of a sweet seriousness, and able to rise to any height of true womanly sacrifice. Money, leisure, protection, beauty and breeding. Hessie began to feel slightly sick again. That was life as it should be, wasn't it? That was life as Mr. Saul's children, and his wife, too, would know it. Silk underclothes and evening dresses and shaded candles and dinner-parties—soup, fish, joint—frequently roast chicken—sweet, savoury, coffee. Wine for the men, though the younger girls would drink only pure sparkling water, water as pure as their delicate maidenhood.

Purity! What a beautiful word it was. Young and pure. Middle-aged and pure. Old and skinny with your body angular and flat and dull but still pure. Unless you got married, and then you were pure in another sense. Hilda would still be a pure woman even after her marriage to Albert. Not a virgin, but still pure.

Hessie turned for home, the swift nervousness had gone from her walk. Perhaps she was a little tired. She'd had quite a heavy morning at the Bensons'. Doris had never come back, and poor dear Mrs. Benson was still searching for a young maid who would be fairly clean, fairly efficient and very cheap. It was very doubtful if she would ever find a girl just like that, and in the meanwhile—well, a clergyman's home had to be kept as clean as possible, for, after all, cleanliness is next to godliness and a clergyman and his wife between them should try to supply both these necessities for a Christian life.

Mrs. Benson's side of the bargain would be easy enough if only they had a little more money; as things were she did her best. Not that Mr. Benson helped much. He just made work. Really it was dreadful what some women had to put up with. Marriage wasn't altogether an unmixed blessing. Far from it. There were ever so many unhappy married women.

Would Hilda be unhappy with Albert? She might be! No one ever knew how these things were going to turn out. "Hessie, if only I'd been wise, like you, and refused to have anything to do with a man. Ah"—mysteriously—"girls don't know what they're letting themselves in for when they give themselves over to a man." Dark words—full of strange horrible meaning. A woman was so helpless. Poor—poor women.

On the way home Hessie paused outside a sweetshop. A quarter of a pound of toffee at 4d. a quarter. She laid the pennies in a row in the middle of the hollowed glass, plate-like receptacle. She smiled intimately at the young girl assistant.

"Very nice evening."

"Oh, lovely."

"We've had a wonderful summer, haven't we?"

"Just wonderful. Thanks very much."

Hessie walked on down the street. She felt calmly, quietly reckless now. She went straight up the steps of the best picture house.

"Two shillings only—standing room one and four," the commissionaire called in a harsh deep voice.

Hessie eyed him quietly. She stepped up to the ticket office. "Two shillings, please."

There was a click and rattle and a metal disc shot out at her. She picked it up with calm indifference, and walked on into the pulsing darkness.

"Middle row, please," she said firmly when the attendant tried to guide her into the side of the house.

She settled herself very comfortably, and began to suck a toffee. Why shouldn't she come to the pictures alone, without saying anything to anybody? Of course it had cost her two shillings. For one and elevenpence she could have bought herself another pair of cotton knickers. The pair she was wearing would soon have holes in them. But what matter! The toffee was excellent and the picture—ah, the picture was throbbing with love and life, and it had such a happy ending. Love triumphant, with the heroine, a little older, a good deal wiser, secure at last in the arms of the right man.

Chapter Thirteen

I

Mrs. Kellaway sat on the edge of Isobel's bed. Now and then she stroked Isobel's head with the tips of her fingers, and each time Isobel threw her a confiding intimate little smile.

"You're the nicest mother in the world!" she said, and leaned her head against her mother feeling with her smooth check for the warmth and softness of Mrs. Kellaway's breast.

Then Anne came in and sat on the edge of her own bed and swung her feet all the time Lottie was taking off her slippers. The soles of her feet looked pink and crinkled as she turned and crawled into bed.

"We're going to start early in the morning," Mrs. Kellaway said, "and have a picnic lunch—Daddy knows a lovely place and then we'll be there in time for tea."

"I'm awfully excited!" Isobel said, suddenly springing up in bed, her hair flying lightly away from her face.

"Don't bounce like that," Anne said severely.

Isobel bounced again, higher this time, so that the wind got in under her nightdress and it ballooned about her. Then she sat down in bed with a startled, pleased expression on her face.

Mrs. Kellaway went over to Anne's bed and sat there smiling from one child to the other. Lottie picked up Isobel's supper-tray and took it into the nursery. Nurse was standing by the table sewing rapidly. Her needle ran out of thread and she tucked the garment she was sewing beneath her arm, and jabbed fresh thread at the eye of the needle. It went through at once—too frightened to do otherwise, Lottie thought—and Nurse began her fast furious sewing again. Nurse was always sewing. Her appetite for it was tremendous. Piece after piece of silk and cotton and linen came into the house and Nurse fell greedily upon them all. The little girls had more frocks than they could possibly wear out. Lovely little frocks really. To open their big wardrobe was like throwing wide the doors of a cage where a lot of butterflies slept. Whenever Mrs. Kellaway went to London she came home with yard after yard of stuff for Nurse to pounce on.

"I don't suppose those children will sleep one wink to-night," Nurse said sourly, "and they'll be cross and fretty to-morrow morning. By the way, you aren't forgetting the ironing, are you?"

"Oh, no, Nurse." Lottie dried Isobel's special spoon and slipped it into the drawer.

"Have you remembered to damp the things?"

"Yes, Nurse."

"You'd better get on with it, then."

It was mostly the baby's things Lottie liked ironing. The electric iron ran with such bright silvery smoothness over the white clothes, and there was a goffering iron for the frills. She liked the look of her own hands at this work. Sometimes she watched them, admiring their neat skill. They seemed a little detached from the rest of her, functioning by themselves, and when Nurse was not there she addressed them in little surprised congratulatory whispers.

To-morrow they were all setting off for a week's visit to the children's grandparents. Mrs. Kellaway's mother and father. They lived nearly one hundred and sixty miles away. They were going up by car and there were to be two picnics on the way to break the journey for the children. Isobel and Anne were wild with excitement, and even the baby had caught their joyousness. It had ruffled his every-day serenity. At tea-time he had sat up in his high chair and screwed up his eyes at Lottie and blown bubbles in his milk.

The children's suit-cases were packed. Isobel's case was pink, Anne's blue. When the ironing was finished Lottie collected their slippers and dressing-gowns, and folded the last piece of white tissue paper before closing the cases. A very faint whiff of lavender blew out as she closed the lids, and she heard the light crinkle of the tissue paper as the fitted blue and pink enamelled brushes and combs sank down into the softness of the clothes. It was almost like shutting a lot of flowers into a little restful darkness all their own.

Lottie felt tired by the time everything was done and the nursery tidied and the table laid for breakfast. But it was a willing tiredness. Despite the weakness in her legs and the feeling that her blood had gone a little white she was ready to go on and on if necessary.

"Be sure you don't waken Isobel," Nurse said, as she turned off the nursery lights.

Lottie undressed with great care. She drew off her vest slowly and stealthily, fearing the least rustle or movement. Isobel moaned and turned over in her bed. Lottie waited breathlessly, afraid to look at the little girl's sleeping face. At last she managed to edge her careful way into bed. Lying there so very close to sleep herself she ventured to turn round so that she could see Isobel's bed. The child's hair made a fine, misty darkness on the pillow.

Lottie woke up very early the next morning. The sea was hidden by the mist, but she could hear it, the little waves tossing sleepily against the shore. Now and then the low mist shifted about the garden, and the great heads of the dahlias, their stalks hidden, floated dreamily on top of the shimmering greyness. The flowers looked like great coloured water-lilies swimming on phantom water.

Out in the darkly cool corridor the quietness of the house seemed almost frightening. The closed doors were tall and mysterious because of the sleepers lying within.

Reaching the nursery Lottie crossed the room and noiselessly pulled the curtains and opened the windows.

The pale sunlight entered the room with an almost audible rush. It swept past Lottie and lit up the shaggy-maned rocking horse, and Isobel's group of dolls that lay around with helplessly cocked legs and skirts and startled faces. There was something tired-looking about the table that had been laid over-night. A big woolly dog of the baby's stared from the window-ledge into the garden, its glass eyes dark with thoughtful dignity. It was a very life-like dog, large and expensive. But its expensiveness had not impressed the baby in the least. He cuddled it or hurled it along the floor, or sat on its head without regard for its obvious cost.

Cautiously, for fear of a creaking hinge, Lottie pushed the windows wider open. The air outside was cool and sweet. She leant out of the window for a moment, looking down into the garden. The mist was clearing rapidly. Stretches of lawn were visible, each short blade of grass bearing its cool freight of mist drops. The flowers shone out, their colours clear and strong with moisture. The sky was completely cloudless.

For a moment Lottie longed to run out, down through the garden, under the fir trees and so on to the shore. She felt sure that the sand was beginning to sparkle now, the little waves becoming sprightly as they tossed negligently against the shore. If only she might run down, bare-footed, and stand there alone, solitary, with only the blue crinkly-gold sea and the shifting mist and soft fine sand for company.

Yes, and what would she think about down there? Lottie sat on the edge of Nurse's chair, feeling suddenly weak and hollow inside. Why must she always think of George these days? It was no good trying to escape these thoughts. He was always there, smiling a little, putting his arms around her in an embrace that was not terrifying.

Lottie jumped as the nursery door swung open. Nurse, in her dressing-gown but with her hair already coiled neatly behind her head and her shoes and stockings on, came into the room.

"Oh, so you're up!" she said. "Did the children sleep all right?"

"Yes, Nurse, I think they're still sleeping."

Nurse crossed over to the window and looked out. Her face softened and grew indecisive, and, for a moment, her large sharp features looked almost young and uncertain. She glanced up at the sky as if surprised at something herself.

Then Isobel came flying in through the open doorway, her eyes sparkling, her face incredibly bright and gay.

"Just look at the sky, Lottie," she cried, "it's all blue!"

"Don't run about in your nightgown," Nurse said mildly.

But Isobel took no notice of this. She gave Nurse a brilliant, kindly smile and ran over to the window. She seized a doll with tender haste and held it close, crying, "Oh, darling, I can't leave you behind! You're coming too; did you know that?"

Lottie went quickly into the little girls' bedroom and came back with Isobel's clothes.

"I'll dress you in here," she said.

Anne was already dressed when Lottie went back to the bedroom. The child sat on the floor buttoning her white shoes. "See how clever I'm getting," she said, as Lottie threw open the beds.

It was boiled eggs for breakfast this morning. Lottie boiled them on the nursery gas-ring. Isobel stood beside her watching the sand in the egg-glass slide smoothly down. She stood stiff with excitement as the last fine speck went through.

"Now, Lottie, now!"

By half-past eight they were all ready to go. Mr. and Mrs. Kellaway, Nurse and the baby went in the first car. Mr. Andrew drove his own car, with Lottie and the two little girls in the back seat. Irene and Jenner came to the front door to help them all in, and hand in packages and bags.

"Do be careful, Andrew," Mrs. Kellaway called.

"I can't go fast if Leonard is setting the pace," he called back cheerfully.

Mr. Kellaway drew on his driving gloves. He looked much younger than usual to-day. Generally he wore dark clothes, very elegantly cut, but now he was dressed in a pale grey suit with a grey hat pulled down on his forehead. He kept glancing at Mrs. Kellaway, a little smile crinkling the corners of his eyes. There was a gay holiday air about everyone.

Isobel and Anne knelt up in the back of the car waving to Irene and Jenner for as long as the house was in sight. This time there was a different feeling in the way the cars swung out into the road. The swift smooth rather serious way which makes the beginning of a long journey so different from a run into town, or to a picnic fairly close by. Mr. Andrew shifted down into the driver's seat, fixing his long legs comfortably. He glanced back at Lottie and gave her a little reassuring nod.

"Comfortable there?" he asked.

"Don't bother about us," said Anne, in her most grown-up voice. "Just watch where you're going."

"Brat!" he laughed.

Isobel stood up and tickled the back of his neck. He laughed again. Isobel's finger-tips were so light in their scrambling touch that he hardly felt them. She stopped almost immediately and sat down beside Lottie, her face shining. "Are we really off?" she whispered.

The blue in the sky was deepening a little. It was a clear soft blue that started high up and went on and on, up and up until the sky looked like a lake of crystal blue air. There were no clouds anywhere. The fields and hedges had a young, refreshed appearance about them, still cloaked with the coolness of dew and protected by the softness of the early sunshine.

Ahead of them Mr. Kellaway's big car rolled along, very smoothly and silently. The children watched it eagerly, calling to Mr. Andrew to hurry—hurry when it disappeared around a corner. It was agonizing when they came to double bends in the road and the big car slid round the second bend before they were properly round the first.

By eleven o'clock the sun was shining strongly. They were travelling on main roads now, and the hedges looked dark beneath their covering of white dust, the fields parched and tired, the woods aloof as if hoarding their shade and silence and dignity for themselves alone.

Then the big car began to slow down, and Mr. Kellaway's hand appeared waving gently. Mr. Andrew hooted gaily, and the next moment both cars disappeared from the wide road. Lottie shared the children's sudden excitement. She'd never been in such a narrow lane before. It was like a cool tunnel, full of green light. The cars nosed ahead slowly, both close together, bonnet to tail. Once Mrs. Kellaway looked back and waved her hand to the children. Isobel's face looked small and very white in the strange light. She stared ahead wonderingly, anxiously.

"It's all right," Lottie whispered.

Isobel nodded. At last the close, overgrown hedges widened out and flattened, and suddenly there were only the high trees overhead. Between the gaps in the trees the sky blazed away and a sheet of astonishing blue, cupped strangely between wooded slopes, appeared immediately in front of the cars.

Lottie stared at it. She could not believe it was real! So much smooth blueness lying amongst the trees and meadows, just lying there, quiet, acquiescent, yet far too sharply beautiful to be real! If she closed her eyes it would go. Nothing so beautiful could persist.

Isobel was the first to recover. "It's a lake, Lottie!" she cried.

Mr. and Mrs. Kellaway were already standing on the shore. The chauffeur was busy with the picnic basket. Nurse was getting carefully out of the car, her glance fixed on the step, the baby firm on one arm. Lottie jerked herself into motion. However stunned she might feel she had her duty to do. She lifted Isobel out first and felt the child's body taut and shaking with excitement.

A small wooden landing-stage ran out a little way into the lake. The water stirred around its black rotting piers and moving into the shadows became deep and green. Hidden amongst the trees was a small cottage. A little shabby boat lay quietly on the lake, not straining at all at its mooring rope.

The children ran down to the water's edge. Isobel bent and filled her cupped hands and stared, wide-eyed, as the drops ran through her fingers. The water in her hands looked clear and pink, but dropping back into the lake it became crystal blue again, each drop causing a tiny commotion on the smooth surface.

"Oh dear, oh dear!" Isobel sighed ecstatically.

Lottie stood very still. She was not herself, Lottie, she was someone in a dream. So long as she kept her back to Nurse this dream would go on.

"Lottie!"

"Yes, Nurse."

What had happened to the sunshine now? Lottie felt cold and sick as she turned to Nurse. "Come and help Anne into her bathing dress. And unpack this case for me. Really, even if this is a picnic there's some work to be done."

Mr. Andrew was already splashing about in the lake. Standing on the end of the landing-stage and diving off it, his body erect and decisive one moment, and at the next his legs and arms smoothly distorted as he swam rapidly under water. The bottom of the lake was firm and clean.

Nurse took the baby down for a paddle. Mr. Andrew came up and rummaged in the car for something.

"Jolly, isn't it?" he asked.

Lottie glanced at Nurse's broad back, she was too far away to hear anything. Besides, she was absorbed in the baby.

"It's wonderful," she said. "I'd never seen a lake like this before."

"Hadn't you?" He took up a towel and began rubbing his neck and arms. He stood looking down at Lottie, smiling at her. "For heaven's sake take off your hat," he said at last. "You don't want to wear it, do you? And the sunshine's good for your hair."

Lottie shook her head. It was easy for Mr. Andrew to talk. He would not have to listen to Nurse's remarks. He began to smile again. "Oh, all right," he said. "But you can take it off when we start driving again. I'll be the only one to see you then. Here, give me that cloth. I'll help you lay the things. What's in this package. Sandwiches? Not jam, I hope. No, we're saved from that."

Mr. Andrew talked on and on. Lottie was powerless to stop him even when Nurse came back and glanced sourly at her. After a while Mr. and Mrs. Kellaway came out from the woods at the side of the lake and began swimming slowly across to them. Nurse pursed up her lips expressing disapproval in a way that Lottie knew only too well. Suddenly Lottie knew that she wanted George, wanted him desperately. If she could glance about and see him somewhere—anywhere—lying stretched out lazily in one of the meadows, his own packet of sandwiches beside him! And it would be a week before she could see him again. Well, a week would pass, wouldn't it? Days did go by, and nights too, even the longest of them.

With lunch over the children grew sleepy. Back in the car again Isobel's head pressed tiredly against Lottie's arm.

"Do you mind if I go to sleep?" she murmured, and was almost too sleepy to enjoy her own politeness.

There was no astonishing blueness to startle Lottie when the cars emerged from the green tunnel of the winding lane. The main road stretched before them, grey-white, with the sun blazing ruthlessly on everything, the freshness long since sucked from the fields and hedges.

Their destination was a tall square house, very solidly built, and placed at the end of a little valley that looked too quiet and peaceful to be the site of such a house. Built on a hill with mountains rising forbiddingly behind it, or on a cliff with a wide winter sea battering its windows with its high-tossed spume and spray, it would have melted grandly into its surroundings; but here, amongst placid fields and a wide gentle river where willows grew and cattle meditated, it looked harsh and strange. The gardens surrounding it were very stiff and formal.

There was great formality, too, about their welcome. Lottie stood by while the children kissed their grandparents. The nurseries were large gloomy rooms.

"The only blessing is, it isn't winter," Nurse said. "That fireplace would never warm this room. I'll be glad when we're back home."

Chapter Fourteen

I

Only one week to the wedding day! Miss Bowman had sent up Hessie's bridesmaid's frock. Mother had delved recklessly into her capital. Hilda was to wear white satin and a veil just as if she were a young virgin bride. Of course she was a virgin all right, but wasn't the white satin just a little foolish? Not that Hilda was old, really, it wasn't that—it was only that Hilda, well, was she quite the right type for white satin and a girlish veil?

Some of the girls were coming in this evening to have a look at Hilda's trousseau. Hessie increased her pace. What a pity it was that her way to and from the rectory led through these squalid little streets. Most of the women in this district looked so aggressively at a neatly-dressed lady, and yet through all their hostility they seemed absorbed in immediate and pressing affairs of their own. The children had an impudent yet battered look about them. The old men were almost ugly, theirs was such a frayed worn-out air, but the young men—the young men had something bold and virile about them! Their eyes were insolent but it was a masculine insolence and some of them looked quite strong and dashing.

When Hessie reached home Hilda was fussing about the rooms. They were going to serve their guests with cups of coffee and little cakes at about half-past eight, and Hilda was polishing Mother's silver spoons for use on the coffee tray.

"Oh, there you are, Hessie!" she cried. "Do come and help me."

"I'll take off my hat and coat first. Is Albert coming to-night?"

"Amongst all those girls?" Hilda waved the chamois delicately. "Hessie, what an idea!"

Hilda was wearing one of her new frocks. It was a brown silk with lace ruffles on the modesty vest. Albert's ring shone on her finger.

Rosie and Lily Bates were the first to arrive. "Do come and see my pretty things!" Hilda cried girlishly. "Come and see them before the others arrive."

"Is Albert coming?" Rosie inquired, winking at Hessie.

"Oh, I couldn't trust him amongst so many girls," Hilda laughed gaily, "and besides—besides I want to show you all my trousseau things, and you see Albert—Albert ..."

"He isn't the bridegroom yet," Rosie finished indecently.

Hilda's cheeks blazed their usual ugly red. "Shall we go upstairs now?" she said frigidly.

The bedroom had been cleared out specially for this occasion. Little piles of underclothes lay on the bed. Rosie pounced on one pile.

"Nighties!" she exclaimed. "Oh, Hilda, won't you look gorgeous in these! Let's see—this day week, isn't it? Well, this time next week—" She left her remark unfinished and pounced gaily on the next pile. "Needle-run lace!" she murmured.

Fresh guests arrived then and soon the bedroom was full of local maidenhood. Hilda was sweetly gay and confidential with them all. "Here, Maisie, you haven't seen these, have you? Janet, there's something special here!"

Rosie Bates squealed in mock terror when she saw Hessie's bridesmaid's frock. "Oo-er, green, Hilda. Isn't that unlucky?"

"Oh no, just fashionable, dear," Hilda said gently.

Rosie gave her a quick glance. Fancy Hilda's getting back at her like that! "Well, rather you than me," she cried laughingly.

Hessie stood by, smiling brightly at everyone. "Your turn next, Hessie." The words seemed to assail her from all sides.

"Hessie's full of secrets!" Rosie said maliciously. "Aren't you, Hessie?"

Really Rosie was at her worst to-night. And wasn't there something almost indecent in this company of them all gathered here together touching and examining the intimate garments Hilda would wear as a married woman? Really, it seemed scarcely modest or genteel. A delicate aversion to this occasion filled Hessie's heart. She felt proudly aloof from it all.

"And so you're having your reception at an hotel? Fancy!" Rosie went on.

That was Albert's idea. Hilda's wedding was growing and growing in importance. It was rising to some horrible momentous height which would sweep Hilda away into her new estate on a series of events and experiences that would be a barrier between them always.

"Let's have some coffee now!" Hilda suggested brightly, when everyone had seen everything.

Hessie went into the kitchen to heat up the coffee. Hilda had made it in a saucepan earlier in the day and strained it through the top of a clean cotton stocking. They made coffee so seldom that they had never thought it worth while to buy a proper coffee maker.

There were iridescent lights on top of the brown liquid. Hessie eyed it doubtfully. Coffee was such a tricky thing and people, particularly people who had ever been abroad, even on a day's trip to Dieppe, shrugged their shoulders with such an experienced air on the subject of English coffee. Had Hilda made this too strong—or too weak? It smelt pungent enough. No doubt when the milk was poured in it would look quite all right. Not that she was going to mix the milk and coffee together in the kitchen, that was how the Bates served it with Rosie giggling—"Have some cafe-au-lait?"—she was going to keep them in separate jugs and murmur "Black or white?" to each guest. That always sounded so impressive and experienced.

Hilda came fluttering into the kitchen. There was a spot of brilliant colour high on each cheek.

"Albert's come," she whispered, "and Mr. Saul!"

Hessie stared. "And Mr. Saul?" she exclaimed.

"S-sh—don't shout about it! Yes. So put on two extra cups. Oh, dear, we haven't got them, have we? Never mind. I won't drink any, nor you either. Oh, Hessie, isn't Albert terrible—to come in like this!"

Hessie held the coffee jug over the sink, and the saucepan in the other hand. Could she pour it in without spilling it? She felt so dreadfully sick and shaken with excitement.

"Hilda, is my hair all right?" she asked weakly, putting down the jug and saucepan.

A flash of the old sympathy passed between them. "Ever so nice!" said Hilda gently.

At last Hessie had the tray ready. Smiling she entered the drawing-room. How should she greet him? With a little smile, perhaps, a little gay intimate smile, no spoken word till she reached his side with the coffee-tray and could murmur "Black or white?" But how awful if he said 'Black,' this coffee looked so strange.

Chapter Fifteen

I

Lottie stood before Nurse, her hands gripped together behind her back. If she were going to be sick what could she do? She would never be able to reach the lavatory in time.

Nurse's voice went on. "And right in the very place where you took the children for their play yesterday afternoon. Under those big oak trees. But the blood began further down the path—great clots of it! Stevens told me about it himself. He said it turned his stomach over but it was nothing to what he found under the trees. Murder! And she was quite a pretty girl, though I hadn't noticed her particularly. Silly, of course, to go out with a strange man—that is, if he was a stranger. What am I always telling you, Lottie? You can't be too careful. Thought she was out for a lark, I suppose, but he made a fine mess of her. Now, what's the matter with you?"

Lottie made a wild, helpless gesture with her hands, and ran to the window and was sick. Fortunately the window was open and the paved yard immediately below was empty. After a while she drew in her head and leaned shaking against the window.

Early that morning one of the gardeners had come running down to the house, his face colourless, his eyes haunted, and instantly the house had been full of whispered horror. It had run sharply, silently, through the very air in the great formal rooms and the dark lofty passages of the house where the murdered girl had worked as house-maid. There was a hushed activity about the place, too. Policemen in uniform, plain-clothes men with tiredly, casually alert faces and voices, press-men horribly avid even when they strove to be polite, their politeness tainted by the ruthlessness their profession demanded, swarmed about the place. When the servants left their own familiar quarters they talked in whispers. There were frightened hints and murmurings everywhere.

The news had filtered through to the nursery just before breakfast. The head house-maid had rushed in, her hands beating helplessly together, and told Nurse. Lottie, coming in with the children, had caused an awful silence to settle down on the two shocked and excited women. With a warning glance at the children Nurse had gone out of the room to join the horrified group in the servants' hall. Lottie and the children had eaten breakfast alone, Isobel's face a little grave and concerned over Nurse's absence. At that time Lottie was still in merciful ignorance of the exact nature of the horror assailing the place.

Afterwards, Lottie had been questioned by the police. The police were using the library as their head-quarters in the house and the sombre dignity of the room was an impressive background for the ideals of justice and protection that these almost too-human men represented. It was terrible to think of justice handicapped because these men were not infallible. Their minds were trained to question and consider each possible clue, to weigh each word and look of the people who came before them, to consider the keyless fabric of all that they had heard or seen or deduced, and all the time they were handicapped by the measure of their own common humanity.

Lottie had been very frightened at this interview though the man who questioned her had been kind, almost gentle. He had asked her if she had seen anyone in the woods when she and the little girls had played in the very spot where the body had been found. But no, no one had disturbed them. So far as Lottie knew the children's cries and laughter had been the only sounds beneath the spreading trees.

Nurse had flounced past Lottie as Lottie left the library. Nurse was indignant because Lottie had been called before she was and also because her own evidence could not possibly be as necessary as Lottie's, for she had not been in the woods at all yesterday.

A little later Mrs. Kellaway ran in to the nursery and caught the little girls to her as the black ambulance with the town's crest on it made its slow authoritative progress across the stable-yard.

"Darlings!" Mrs. Kellaway cried, with an attempt at gaiety, for the little girls knew nothing of the tragedy that had happened in the place where yesterday they had played their intent, untroubled games.

"Lottie, a story book!" Mrs. Kellaway cried anxiously as the ambulance stopped. She pressed the children's soft faces to her breast for a moment, and then she began to read to them. But at a fresh sound from the yard, her voice faltered. She took Isobel on to her knee and drew Anne close against her.

Nurse and Lottie had packed the children's clothes and their own, too. No one knew when the police would let Lottie and Nurse and the children leave the house, but the general opinion was that they would be released some time that afternoon, though their car would have to be driven by a hired chauffeur.

It was afternoon now. The little girls were downstairs with Mrs. Kellaway, and the baby was asleep. It was the first time Lottie had been alone with Nurse since the gardener's discovery. Lottie leaned against the side of the window with the sunlight falling powerlessly on her shivering body.

Nurse was quite at home in this terrible atmosphere. Her manner all day had been the triumphant one of someone whose prophecies have come true. She was like a priestess of black magic who sees the rites of her ghastly faith celebrated with full panoply.

She came in from the bedroom and glanced at Lottie. "Let this be a lesson to you," she began again. "If young girls had any sense they wouldn't let men hoodwink them. Powdering up their faces and giggling, and then getting into a mess of this kind. What am I always telling you? Don't let any man get familiar with you—they're all the same kind underneath. Still, if girls weren't fools enough to give them their chance they couldn't do very much. All the same, though, I blame the girl. I'd like to see that man getting what he deserves, too. And ten to one the police'll find no trace of him though he must have plenty of blood about his clothes and his hands and things. But these sex murders never do seem to get cleaned up these days for the simple reason that there are too many men in the world, and most of them have pretty nasty minds. Just give them the opportunity and see what will come out. I know!"

Lottie closed her eyes. Every word Nurse spoke went through her painfully. They were like sharp hammer-strokes on an aching nerve, and she was helpless to get away from Nurse.

The door opened and Mrs. Kellaway came in. Her face had been colourless all day. She made a weary fluttering little gesture with her hand. "There's no chance to-day," she said helplessly. "But you and the children can go to-morrow—that's almost certain."

Nurse's face grew bland with relief. For the first time in her life she was close to a murder, and to-night when the children were in bed she could share the horrors and excitements of the servants' hall or the housekeeper's room.

Afterwards Nurse and Lottie took the children out to play on a stretch of lawn at the side of the house farthest from the library. Mrs. Kellaway and her mother sat on the terrace watching them. Sitting out in the sunshine eased the chill fear in Lottie's heart. Isobel and Anne played with their dolls, and were very gay. They were so innocently detached from the grown-up world of fear and conjecture that was all around them. It was different with the dogs belonging to the place, particularly the older animals. They were uneasy and one old dog lay close to the children, stretched out on its belly, its head resting on its paws, its eyes staring ahead mournfully.

Mr. and Mrs. Kellaway joined the children at tea-time. They sat in low chairs placed close together and they watched their little girls the whole time. Halfway through tea Mrs. Kellaway was called back to the house.

"That'll be her mother," Nurse whispered to Lottie. "That's the car that went to meet her at the station."

When Mrs. Kellaway came back she knelt on the short richly-green grass and gathered Isobel and Anne into her arms. Isobel's hair tumbled all over the child's surprised, delighted face and her mother swept it back and kissed her swiftly.

"I'm having supper with Mrs. Field," Nurse said to Lottie when the children were in bed and asleep. "Don't go to bed until I come up."

Lottie was thankful to be alone. When she had eaten she went to the window and stood looking out into the half-darkness. She tried to keep her eyes on the yard, but inevitably she found herself staring at the slope of splendid trees that surrounded the back of the house. There was a line of flowing amber, the last echo of the sunset, warming the darkness of the sky, and the tree-tops rose up into this fading colour with fine impassive dignity. It would be quite dark beneath those spreading branches, the old thick tree trunks going down and down till they reached the ground that was soft with moss and ancient leaf-mould. And it was at the foot of the highest finest tree that the house-maid's young body had lain all night. Lottie drew in her breath in sudden terror. What could she do to escape before Nurse came up again, primed with further horrifying details and warnings?

A sound behind her made her start round and she saw that Mr. Andrew was in the room with her. He was standing beside the table. There was a look of wear and strain on his face, too, but Lottie's frightened mind ignored the young appeal in his eyes as he came swiftly towards her.

She put her hand to her mouth and uttered a stifled scream.

"For God's sake, stop that!" he cried. He stood close beside her, and stared at her in sheer amazement.

Gasping a little Lottie stared back at him.

"Never mind!" he said in easier tones. "I expect we're all a bit like that to-day. It's all so beastly, isn't it?"

"It's awful!" Lottie cried shakily.

"Yes, it is—it's awful. I don't wonder you feel queer. But you're going home to-morrow. That's practically certain. You and Nurse and the children. They won't want you any longer."

"I'm glad."

"You're lucky," he cried bitterly. "I wish I was going too. We may get off later on to-morrow, though, Mr. Kellaway and I. You see, they've sent for Scotland Yard. The police aren't interested in women. This was a man's job, so we're all under suspicion at the moment. All of us! My God!" He passed his hand quickly over his face. "To be suspected of a thing like that!"

Lottie gazed at him. How white his face had gone, and his eyes looked like Isobel's when she was frightened or unhappy. In many ways Isobel and Mr. Andrew were alike, the resemblance now was startling. He turned away.

"He was a madman, of course," he said wearily. "No sane man would do a thing like that. I wish I could stop thinking about it. Well, good night."

But at the door he turned round. "Supposing it had been you!" he cried.

Impulsively Lottie went over and touched his hand. In a way it was like touching Isobel. He put his arm round her and drew her close. Her cap slipped off, and he rested his face against her hair. Lottie felt that her body was very strong and upright against his; it was the same feeling she had when Isobel clung to her in fright. That she was strong and equal to the task of comforting him, that she was equal to anything! At last he took his arms away.

"You've lovely hair, Lottie," he smiled. "It's so soft. Well, good night."

Alone again, Lottie went back to the window. There was still a deep glow of colour in the air behind the trees. Night had come to one half of the sky and the stars shone with a distant warm radiance. The leafy tops of the trees rose up in dark benign outlines against the coloured sky, their branches motionless, each leaf soundless and asleep in the quiet air. Lottie fancied she could hear the river that ran close beside the house, its waters moving hastelessly between its still banks, the long grass and water-weeds swaying helplessly with the current.

Suddenly Lottie was intensely aware of the beauty and stillness around her. The wood with its great trees, their branches arching high into the sky, the stiff beauty of the garden which was cased by the lightness and delicacy of the flowers themselves, the fields that lay beyond the garden, their hedges heavy with tall grasses and wild flowers, and the cattle lying so cumbrously, so awkwardly on the wet ground. And in the house itself, Mr. and Mrs. Kellaway and Mr. Andrew and the children, all of them, except the children who knew nothing, stunned and shocked by the abnormality that had sent such horror in amongst them.

Nurse came back primed with fresh details.

"Stevens himself was down there. He's spending the night here in case these new detectives want him. He said he didn't know what all the red on the path was at first. It didn't sort of strike him for a moment and then …"

Lottie stood quite still, watching Nurse. She clasped her hands tightly behind her back, and, remembering the quiet, patient beauty of the night outside, and inside Mr. and Mrs. Kellaway and the sleeping children, she was, for the first time, spared the full force of the old sick trembling that always assailed her after a conversation of this kind with Nurse.

Early the next morning she and Nurse and the children started for home.

Chapter Sixteen

I

Mother and Hilda were staring at Hessie's head. Mother's mouth was open and her breath came heavily. Her high flaccid breasts, buoyed up by her shapeless corsets, moved with ponderous agitation. Hilda's eyes popped unbecomingly from her thin nervous face.

Hessie moved slowly from the door to the table, her face disdainful with the weight of her elaborate unconcern, her head shorn of its crowning glory. Small wonder that Mother and Hilda were looking at her! Well, let them look!

"No post to-night?" Hessie asked languidly. No letter in the world would have interested her in this supreme moment as she held Mother's and Hilda's full and horrified attentions, but it was wise that her voice, languid, uninterested, should be the first to shatter this silence. At last Mother recovered speech.

"Hessie—your hair—it isn't possible! Surely no child of mine—" she gasped incoherently. She collapsed onto a chair and her dingy, generous skirts flowed out around her.

"My hair?" Hessie exclaimed, with startled innocence. "Oh, I see—you mean—why, yes, I slipped into the hairdressers' on the way home this evening. I had it cut short."

"Hessie, you might have spared Mother this just now!" Hilda burst in. "Mother, I'll get you a cup of tea."

"No—no!" Mother clutched hold of Hilda's arm; her eyes still fixed on Hessie's head. "Stay with me, Hilda."

Hessie moved slowly and carelessly across to the window. Let them get the full effect of this gesture of hers! She stood there before them, aloof, separated by this action of hers, this gesture of emancipation, and yet she was the focus of their full and horrified attentions. Hilda, Albert, Hilda's wedding, were all forgotten at this moment. She, Hessie, held the centre of the stage.

"Where is your hair, Hessie?" Mrs. Price demanded, her voice trembling.

"Well, really, Mother I didn't ask what they were going to do with it! Hardly!"

"I brushed it so often when you were little," Mrs. Price wailed suddenly, "it looked so nice when it was plaited at night and then in the morning when it was combed out over your shoulders."

For a moment there were genuine tears in Mrs. Price's eyes; they shone in a way that made the rest of her full face look old and soft and grey. She laid her tremulous hands on her knees and rocked slightly.

Looking at her, Hessie's heart was assailed by her mother's emotion. Poor Mother! She ran over to her and dropped on her knees beside her, covering her mother's hands with her own. This was a sorrowful yet jubilant moment, deeply touching in its sad, evitable pathos, and she, Hessie Price, had created it in all its harrowing completeness.

"Mother, dear, you've got to look at it my way! Really and truly. Just think! How easy for me in the mornings! And really my hair was so heavy and just a little too greasy. Think how smart I shall be now! No long hair. …"

Poor Mother! From her kneeling position by her mother's side Hessie threw back her head with a little gesture that was appealing, sad and gay all in one. It was an almost pathetic gesture, too. Hessie felt her own eyes filling with tears. Supposing she bowed her head on Mother's knee and Mother's hand touched her short hair.

"Anyhow you've made yourself look ridiculous," Hilda broke in sharply, shattering all the emotion and regret and intimacy of this moment.

"Dear, do you think so?" Hessie answered gently. After all, she could afford to be generous. The tears were still rolling down Mother's cheeks.

She patted her mother's hands again and then she jumped up and said with bright gaiety, "Mother, I'm going to get you a cup of tea! Yes, I will! I feel I need one, too, and I'll have time now for all sorts of little extra things. Think of having no long hair to pin up! No, Mother, you mustn't cry! Really and truly! It'll be ever so much better for both of us. You'll see!"

In the kitchen, waiting for the kettle to boil, Hessie stood before the small mirror hanging above the sink. There was a freshly cut lemon in one compartment of the little rusty, chipped soap-holder. Hilda was getting reckless with the lemons these days. Perhaps she was thinking of her wedding day, and her hand held out for Albert's ring. But Hessie knew that she must not think of Hilda's marriage now. This was her own evening, the straight tassels of her hair tossing with each movement of her head recalled her to her own importance to-night. "It will hang better at the second trimming, madam," the girl at the hairdresser's had said. "If you would care to have it shampooed and waved now, I'm quite sure you would be satisfied." Ah, shampooed and waved by a professional! She had not had enough money for that this evening. It would have cost her four shillings and sixpence. The cheapest shampoo—'Pine Tar,' what a dark, heavily smelling name that was—cost two shillings, and a wave was two-and-six. Add that to the frightening price demanded for the first cutting of long hair and the result was something appalling. No, it was impossible now, but on the day of Hilda's wedding she would abandon herself into the hairdresser's hands, and even pay the sixpence extra that was required for a shampoo with a more rosily fragrant name than 'Pine Tar.'

When she carried the tray into the sitting-room Mother was still sitting on the high, uncomfortable chair, her skirts drooping in the same melancholy folds around her legs. But her skin had resumed its customary sallow colour.

Hessie poured out the tea and brought it over to her, arranging it prettily on a small table.

"Two lumps and a half, Mother!" she said, soft playfulness in her voice. "Come, drink it up!"

It was terrible to have had to hurt Mother like this, but somehow it was sweet to be comforting her now. After all, a mother looked to her daughters for comfort. Sometimes the younger generation, their feet stepping forward bravely along the path of progress, had to wound their elders a little, but let them do it gently—kindly—comforting and soothing with their young strong bodies, as they stepped out to face the future. Ah, how beautiful thoughts could be! Hessie brushed the back of her hand across her eyes. She smiled shakily at Hilda. "Do come and have a cup of tea, Hilly," she urged.

Mrs. Price drank her tea in soothing gulps. "And I was so happy this evening," she said mournfully. "Hilda and Albert had just made me so happy."

Hessie felt her lips tightening. Always Hilda and Albert!

"I'm only too glad Albert had gone before Hessie came in," Hilda put in tartly. "He hates short hair."

"Men do!" said Mrs. Price mournfully.

But Hessie knew that she was equal to this argument. "Don't you think that's rather an outworn shibboleth, Hilda? After all, look at the number of women—married women—and attractive girls who have short hair. Practically everybody, you know! No, no, that's not going to frighten me!"

"But at heart, Hessie, men do like modest girls and they love to see a woman's crowning glory—a woman's hair! Look at Hilda. She has won a good man's love, and Albert admires long hair. He admires it very much."

"Perhaps Albert is just a little old-fashioned, Mother," Hessie said, with gentle daring.

There was a horrified silence. Then Mrs. Price's voice, full and robust with indignation said, "Albert is a good man, Hessie! He is a real son to me already. You don't know—you couldn't, or you wouldn't say such things—all that Albert has done for me, and for you, too."

Hessie stirred her cup of tea slowly, watching the graceful crook of her little finger. But she felt that her pose of easy nonchalance was slipping from her. There was something freshly menacing behind Mother's indignation.

"Albert is going to give me a fixed allowance!" Mrs. Price went on with gloomy impressiveness. "A generous one. And he's settling a lot of money on Hilda—a marriage settlement. He told me the terms of it all this evening. Hilda is marrying a good man, Hessie."

Hessie put down her cup slowly. It was no good! Nothing she could do was big enough to stand against the power and importance of Albert's money and the fact that he was a man. Albert, Mr. Saul, both of them men, and men with money, too. They could do what they liked in life, choose what woman they wanted, have freedom and importance of a kind utterly denied to girls like Rosie and Lily Bates and herself, too. Girls stultified by poverty and plainness and a pre-War upbringing in a provincial town.

Hessie put up her hand and touched her short hair. It had availed her nothing. She had only made herself look ridiculous. Albert and his marriage settlement and his allowance to Mrs. Price had reduced her to the old position of inferiority. Her little moment of triumph had been brief, indeed!

What truly wonderful importance the possession of money gave to you. It wasn't what you were yourself that counted, it was what you had. Look at the poor King of Spain for instance. What was his position now that he was throneless and outcast? Goodness, bravery, long hair, short hair—nothing but your possessions really mattered.

"If you could only see yourself in the glass Hessie," Mother said lugubriously, after a long silence. "The back of your neck looks dreadful."

Chapter Seventeen

I

Maggie drew her flannel slowly over the soft pink of the steps. She paused at the lowest step of all, and looked out over the garden. There was no one in sight. It was September now and the weather was still unbroken. Except for the older, maturer quality of the sunshine and the new dark immobility of the trees, it might have been early summer.

Maggie felt a new devotion for the garden these days. It was here that Maxwell worked, this was his domain and consequently her love for him gave her a vicarious sovereignty over it, too. The mere sight of the flowers, of the lawns that ran in so remotely beneath the low branches of the trees, brought her into contact with Maxwell. To Maggie the garden belonged to her lover, not to Mr. Kellaway.

Maxwell's appearance among the flowers was important to-day. It was over a week since she had last been down to his cottage and then she had had the place to herself. For ten days now he had been away on business connected with the garden. Mr. Kellaway had gone with him, but had returned the night before.

Standing there Maggie let her flannel slip down into the grey water in her pail. Her hands were damp and there was a soft pink and whiteness about her skin. The pores on the backs of her hands were distended from the scrubbing she had done already this morning.

Ever since that first night of hers spent in Maxwell's cottage the sullenness had gone from Maggie's eyes and mouth. She felt warm and generous towards everyone, even towards Cook! Nowadays, when Cook was at her worst, Maggie had a refuge within her own mind. She could ignore Cook and the kitchen, she could become oblivious to them, because, really, she was stepping out into the silent misty garden, her body still warm from Maxwell's embrace, her heart full of the new overwhelming tenderness of her love for him.

The clock in the hall struck the half-hour. Its chimes came out through the open door, and following them came another sound. Maggie looked round. Isobel was standing on the top step, the expression in her eyes very solemn and her hair looked as though she had rushed so quickly along the corridor and down the stairs that her flying speed had blown it out into a fine cloud around her face. She was bare-footed. She appeared surprised and startled to find herself where she was.

"Oh, hello!" she said to Maggie. "I haven't had my breakfast yet."

"You haven't?"

"But I'm not hungry." She came down the steps slowly, seeking with her toes the damp places left by Maggie's flannel. She found a spot damper than the rest and stood there with both feet placed close together, her face filled with delight.

"I wish you hadn't stopped scrubbing," she said regretfully. "It's a pity I wasn't down earlier."

"I don't suppose Nurse knows you're down here?" Maggie asked.

"Nobody knows where I am." Isobel began to walk along the wide step. At the end of it she jumped down onto the fine gravel of the drive and over onto the grass. The minute her feet touched the soft turf she threw up her arms and sped away, the muslin of her frock fluttering wildly as she ran.

All this seemed part of her new life to Maggie. It was in harmony with the love and gentleness filling her own body.

When she got back to the kitchen Cook stormed at her. "I hope everything in the garden's growing nicely," she said bitterly, adding to Jenner, "the lousy bitch!"

Irene, coming in at that moment, glanced hastily at Maggie's face, but Maggie's expression was quite serene. She was far away from Cook. She could feel Maxwell's arm flung over her, and sense the terrible, wonderful power her body had over his. The immensity of her love for him, and his need for her, clothed her in a happiness that no words from Cook could shatter.

11

The garden, the woods, the little bay, the house, the nursery itself, were parts of a new kingdom to Lottie. She and Nurse and the children had been back for a fortnight now. They had been glad to leave that big sombre house standing so awkwardly, so grotesquely, at the head of the placid valley where the river ran with such a wide untroubled sweep and the grasses bending from its banks moved easily and tranquilly in the gentle current.

In the end Mr. Andrew had been free to drive them home. They had driven back in his car, leaving the bigger car for Mr. and Mrs. Kellaway and the chauffeur.

Irene had had the nursery ready for them. The windows wide open, the curtains drawn back, the table laid for tea. The children had been delighted to get back home. They had run about, touching their toys, too excited to play with any one thing for longer than a few minutes at a time. Isobel had met the kitchen cat coming up the back stairs for a sleep in Irene's bedroom, and she had embraced him fondly, pressing her cheek to his shining fur. He was a big cat with solid limbs, pale green eyes and a long tail. "I think we'll have to have a cat like that in the nursery," she had said to Lottie.

This was the fifteenth day since they had come home. It was early yet, and there was still a delicacy, a fragility about the sunlight shining in through the window close to Isobel's bed; there was no fullness at all to it, it just lay there very bright and clear, like pale golden liquid. Isobel lay sleeping, unaware of the golden light spreading closer and closer to her bed.

After breakfast Lottie took the children out to play in the garden. A couple of young gardeners were clipping the edges of the grass close to the house. They were very serious about their work, their faces absorbed and intent. Isobel stood watching them, her face very grave, too. After a while she started to help them, bending down to gather up the little handfuls of clipped grass. Mr. Kellaway came out from the house and stood watching her. Isobel pretended not to see him but continued her work with re-doubled energy. She worked furiously, staggering beneath the weight of her labour. At last she sat down on the edge of the lawn and looked severely at her father.

"I'm just exhausted," she told him, "this garden takes up so much of my time."

Mr. Kellaway felt in his pocket and drew out a penny. "You'd better have some wages," he said.

Afterwards the children went into the shade of the fir trees and played houses. Lottie sat with her back against a tree and watched them. The stream in the little wood to the left was tinkling away. The sunlight was dropping down through the leaves and here and there a leaf, turning yellow, looked like sunshine caught and held in mid-air.

Every now and then Lottie fancied she heard footsteps coming through the woods. Once a gardener did appear, but most of the time it was just her imagination. She began to wonder why she had not seen George since her return. She felt him all around her, but yet he never actually appeared before her. She let her hands lie together in her lap and watched the tips of her fingers touching each other lightly.

She was late bringing the children in for lunch and they had to hurry across the hot still garden where the flowers stood dignified and resigned in the intense sunshine. The garden had changed a lot lately, such different flowers were blooming there. The roses were out again, but their blooms had the air of experienced people now, they had lost that look of lovely startled surprise at their own fresh magnificence which had given their beauty such an intense, arresting quality earlier in the year.

In the bathroom Lottie kept the cold tap running all the time she was washing Isobel's face and hands. The cold water was always inclined to be slightly warm at first because the hot pipe ran close beside the cold one. Anne washed her own face and hands while Lottie dried Isobel.

"Late again," said Nurse as they entered the nursery. "Will you ever learn to be punctual?"

"Yes, Nurse."

Lunch began in a horrid silence. For the first time since their return home Lottie felt the old sick fear of Nurse troubling her again.

"They've caught him!" Nurse exclaimed suddenly in the middle of lunch.

Lottie put down her knife and fork and gazed across the table fascinated and terrified by the look on Nurse's face.

"At least, they've caught somebody. It was in the paper this morning."

"Have they?" Lottie whispered painfully.

"If he's the right man he's done his last trick of that kind," Nurse went on with grim relish. "The police will take care of that."

"Yes."

When it was time to fetch the nursery pudding Lottie went slowly along the passage. She had been so close to freedom from the kind of fear Nurse inspired in her, and now it had all returned again. On the back stairs she met Irene. Irene gave her arm a little kindly squeeze.

"My sister had a little daughter two days ago. I heard this morning," she told Lottie. "I've got to buy it something when I go into town this afternoon. Something a little bit extra! My sister wanted a little girl so much, she's got three boys already. Fancy that! Only last week she wrote and said how much she wanted a little girl. She was pretty sure it was going to be one, too, she's felt so different all along—much sicker. She was fit enough to jump a five-bar gate before each of the boys, but this time she was quite seedy."

Lottie wanted to go on talking to Irene for ever, she was so kind and nicc. "I'm awfully glad."

"Of course the little boys were welcome too—don't think they weren't, but there's something about a little girl of your own, isn't there?"

Cook was just sitting down to her dinner when they reached the kitchen. She pointed to the oven.

"In there."

Irene placed the warm plates on Lottie's tray. "Wait for the sauce," she said, as Lottie turned away. "You'd only have to come down again if you forgot it!"

She followed Lottie to the door. "I expect George'll be out in a day or two," she said unexpectedly. "His foot's much better now. Didn't anyone tell you? He hurt his foot, they thought the bones were broken, but they weren't, after all. Why don't you go up and see his mother? She'd like to see you, I know. Come up this evening with me? I'm going there."

III

This was Hilda's last night as a virgin. Hilda was in the kitchen ironing out her bridal underwear. Mrs. Price was sitting beside the kitchen table, her eyes intent on Hilda's movements. As the moments went by the miracle of Hilda's marriage was growing more and more real. It was wonderful, it was amazing! Her dear younger girlie preparing with such sweet modesty to be a bride.

Hilda drew the iron carefully across the Celanese knickers she was pressing. There was a white petticoat to match. White stockings hung with gauzy purity over the back of a chair. Hilda's long hair was freshly washed and the little soft straight ends hung wispily around her thin flushed face. Her hair would be waved to-morrow, now it must lie straight.

Hessie came into the kitchen and glanced at Hilda's absorbed face. The kitchen was full of a deep emotional tension.

"Hullo, Hess!" Hilda glanced up at her, shaking the drooping strands of hair away from her face. "There, I think everything's done." She sat down for a moment and looked across at Mother. To-night was a minor climax on the road to to-morrow's great event.

"Where are we going to have supper to-night?" Hessie asked. She felt so tired and yet rest was impossible. She must just go on and on through all the stages of Hilda's marriage to-morrow and once Hilda was Alfred Baker's wife it might be possible to rest and relax a little. At least it would all be over.

"What a mercy dear Albert has arranged for the reception to be held at the 'Phoenix'," Mother said. "He is so considerate. Hilda can just rest to-morrow morning. It would never do if she were tired out on her wedding day."

The colour ran up into Hilda's cheeks. Hessie turned to the stove. If she could get through to-night and to-morrow night things would be easier. There would be a little lull then until Hilda and Albert came back from their honeymoon.

At last Hilda stood up and laid her underclothes across her arm. She fingered them delicately, as if afraid the touch of her hands would soil them. The modesty vest of the blouse she was wearing had slipped to one side and Hessie could glimpse the little hollow between her flat breasts. It was difficult to believe that beneath Hilda's modest clothes lay a woman's body.

"Let's just have boiled eggs to-night," Hilda paused in the doorway. "There's a fresh half-dozen in the larder."

Mother's face looked anxious. "We'd better have eggs for to-morrow morning, too," she observed, "but if there are six we'll have enough."

Hessie fetched the eggs and placed them in a saucepan. When Hilda came down again there was a sweet exalted look on her face, but her lips were twitching nervously.

Mrs. Price gave her a fond look. "Everything done, dearie, the last thing packed?"

"Yes, everything, Mother."

"And now you must have your supper. Hessie, is Hilda's egg ready?"

"I'm afraid they're all a bit hard. Put a bit of butter into the yolk, it's nice that way. Well, Hilda, your last supper at home! To-night'll be your last night in this house."

Hessie was deeply horrified at the effect of her words and she tried to smile them away, but the emotional atmosphere was catching them up, hurling them, louder and louder around the kitchen. Hilda's lips twitched and then she gave a high horrible little laugh and began to cry.

Hessie put down her own egg. She was hungry no longer. She stared miserably at her sister's convulsively working face. Mother was over by Hilda's side, patting her hands, pushing the hair back from her forehead. At last she drew Hilda's head close to her bosom. It was an oddly dignified, maternal gesture. She pulled her own handkerchief from her pocket and wiped Hilda's damp cheeks tenderly. She held her daughter lovingly and closely, until Hilda's tears ceased. Then she looked over at Hessie. "Brides are often nervous," she said, with cumbrous gentleness.

IV

Irene and Lottie were up at George's home. Lottie found George able to hobble about in quite an agile fashion.

"The doctor says it's healing nicely," his mother remarked.

"Say, Mum, there's nothing there to heal," George smiled at her. "I didn't break anything! It was only a sort of a twist. I just got the muscles and all a bit mixed up."

Lottie sat in a corner and George pulled a chair over and sat close beside her, his hurt leg straight out in front of him. Irene and his mother were over by the window. They were looking at Mrs. Loder's ferns. She was very proud of them, and, because of their springing fronds, the light coming in through this window was always coloured a pale, very delicate green. Irene admired them greatly. "What a fine frond!" Her voice was full and sincere.

George smiled at Lottie and reached over and patted her hand. For a moment Lottie's fingers lay against his. They felt very soft and light and they lay so still that he guessed the nervous effort that kept them quiet like that.

"I'll be walking about again to-morrow," he said taking his hand away from Lottie's. "Let's go a little way together? When can you meet me?"

"Not till after eight."

"I'll go down to the fir trees about eight then. I'll be quite all right by to-morrow."

Mrs. Loder made tea for them before they left. She cut into a big slab of home-made cake. "Here's a piece for Lottie, George," she called.

Lottie wanted to forestall his getting up, but he got out of his chair at once. Lottie's face was half lost behind the rim of the huge mug his mother had filled for her, as she tilted it to her lips. The steam from it tickled her eyebrows.

"That's the sort of cup I like," George said. "You can get a real drink out of one of those."

Lottie held the mug in both hands and glanced down into it. She seemed to have made no impression on the quantity of tea there. George came close to her and looked in, too.

"That's no good, you'll have to take a longer drink than that," he said. "Here, I'll hold it for you while you eat some cake."

Lottie tried to eat the big slab of cake on her plate, but it seemed to go on and on for ever, too. Every time she took a bite the slice of cake sprouted another bite. As a child in the Home, the opposite had always happened. On the rare occasions when the children were given cake the slice vanished all too soon, despite the most careful eating. At last she finished it, and George took her plate from her. He put the large mug away, too, though it was only half empty. Lottie felt very grateful when she met his understanding smile.

"It was a bit too much for you, wasn't it?" he said.

Lottie looked up at him. Somehow his slight limp changed him a little. It seemed to draw him closer to the cottage, and the cottage was so small that, by contrast, he looked extra big.

"Time to go now," Irene said.

George wanted to see them through the wood but Irene scoffed at such a suggestion. "If you'd two sound legs it'd be another matter. You go and rest for to-morrow. You'll be back at work then, I suppose."

"Yes, he's going back to-morrow," Mrs. Loder answered.

George held Lottie's hand closely when they said good night.

"See you to-morrow evening," he said.

Irene slipped her hand into Lottie's arm as they walked through the wood. They passed close to Maxwell's cottage and Irene gave the unlit windows a keen look.

"Not home yet," she commented.

CHAPTER EIGHTEEN

I

Hessie opened her eyes on Hilda's wedding morning to find the sun shining brightly. At breakfast-time Mrs. Price said "Happy is the bride that the sun shines on!" and smiled.

Hessie and Mother were having breakfast in the kitchen. Why not, when there was so much excitement ahead of them? On a day like this breakfast in the kitchen was not a social lapse. It was merely a conservation of nervous energy.

Mother refused to allow Hilda to get up. She carried Hilda's breakfast tray upstairs, with Hessie following with the tea-pot in case Mother's grip on the tray should waver and the tea spill out onto the clean tray-cloth.

They found Hilda lying stretched out in bed, her eyes very, bright and nervous-looking. She lay flat on her back with her hands folded meekly on her chest. Mother sent Hessie to fetch some extra pillows, and when she came back Hilda was sitting up in bed, her two long thin plaits of hair drooping over the front of her modest high-necked nightgown, which to-night would be replaced by the silk one lying in the top layer of clothes in the already packed suit-case. The suit-case was still open on the chair beside the dressing-table, the nightdress dominating the other bridal intimacies there.

Hilda's bedroom looked neat and bare. A little raft of sunlight lay isolated in the middle of the worn square of green and fawn oilcloth that was laid in front of the yellow deal washstand. Oilcloth on that spot was better than carpet because of the rites performed at the washstand which, on so many days of the week, had to do duty as bath and bathroom. There was a deep cascade of frilled muslin draping the hideous narrow high dressing-table. Five years before Hessie and Hilda had brightened their dressing-tables with draperies of muslin frilled over blue sateen. They had read how to do this in a small weekly paper which devoted itself to tender domesticities of this kind. How gay and girlish they had felt as they had run in and out of the rooms admiring each other's work! They had felt like real girls, surrounded with such pretty, rather sweetly-foolish daintiness. And somehow the fuss of muslin around the dressing-tables had compensated a little for the ugly cheapness of the underclothing in the now rather inconveniently concealed drawers.

But that had been a fleeting solace. To-night, Hessie thought, when Hilda was alone with Albert in some strange hotel bedroom, she would tear down the muslin hanging round her own dressing-table, and leave the wood once more bare and exposed and naked in its battered ugliness.

Mother drew a chair to Hilda's bed and sat down. This day was almost as immense to Mrs. Price as it was to Hilda, the bride-to-be. A daughter was going to be married at last! There were a thousand little phrases she could use now in speaking about Hilda. Besides, in a family of three women she would no longer be the only one who knew the mysteries of consummated love. In their childhood she had often looked at her two little girls with their neat braids of hair and long faces, and murmured, "I hope one day to see them happy wives, and happy mothers!" And she had waited so long for the fulfilment of those desires. She gazed fondly at Hilda.

"Eat up, dear," she said, gently.

Hilda raised a hand that had grown damp and flaccid during the night. She began a nervous picking at her egg. Mrs. Price bent over and took off the top for her, just as if she were a small child again. Hilda began to eat it slowly, craning her long neck forward so that no egg yolk should drip onto the bedclothes. Occasionally her hand shook.

Hessie went down to the kitchen to finish her own breakfast. Her egg was only half-eaten, and it was cold by now. Not that that mattered. She began to eat it, keeping her hand firm and steady. What on earth was

Hilda making all this fuss about? Wasn't she getting married, this was her bridal day, in a few hours' time she would be Mrs. Albert Baker, complete with a home, a husband, security and experience. Why was Hilda going to pieces at a time like this ?

Hessie pushed her hair back from her forehead. Her fingers touched the two unsightly bulges that she had trained her hair to cover. She touched them reluctantly. How smooth and shiny and hard they felt! How terrible it was that she had been born like that, born like she was all over. Handicapped, now and always, because she was plain and uninteresting in her appearance. If beauty were only a personal choice what rare and perfect loveliness she would have chosen to present to the outside world as herself.

But was not there a saying that beauty was in the eye of the beholder? Oh, perhaps it was! And character, too, surely character counted for nearly everything? Some of the ugliest women had been the greatest personalities. Take Catherine of Russia for instance. So ugly, but so powerful!

After breakfast Hessie washed up. She was having two days' holiday from her work at the rectory. Yesterday and to-day. By this time to-morrow her first experience as a bridesmaid would be over, and Hilda would be a wife. Through the steam from the washing-up water Hessie gazed at her own face. Already there was a faint flush in her cheeks. If only it would deepen and deepen until it reached that lovely shade she sometimes saw there! Occasionally, when the weather was right, and her circulation was good, she was astonished at the colour in her cheeks. But it happened so rarely, and never when she wanted to look her best.

When the dishes were finished Hessie went to hang the dish-cloths up on the line in the back-yard. Were the neighbours saying, "That's Hessie Price—she's going to be her sister's bridesmaid to-day. They say she'll soon be a bride herself!"

But was she—was she? Hessie ran back into the kitchen, and leant against the table. What a useless thing prayer was! She might kneel down now on the hard flags, and fold her hands in front of her and close her eyes and throw back her head and petition God for a miracle to happen. For Mr. Saul, or anyone—anyone to take her hand in his and say,

"Hessie—Hessie, I need you. You're beautiful to me." Just for some man to forget her plainness, her age, the thinness of her body, her dullness, and take her close in his arms. It had happened to Hilda. Why—why shouldn't it happen to her? Perhaps at the wedding to-day Mr. Saul would look at her with new eyes.

At eleven o'clock Hilda came trailing down, clad in her dressing-gown.

"Will you make Hilda's bed, dear?" Mother looked at Hessie.

"Hadn't I better fold up the clothes, they won't be needed to-night?" Hessie asked. "The sheets will go to the laundry, I suppose, though the top one's nearly clean. It would be a pity to send it too soon. I'll finish it off on my bed."

The dreadful flush fled over Hilda's face at the suggestion that she would not be in her own familiar bed that night, and she turned away quickly.

At twelve o'clock they all sat down to a little snack. Slowly, but very surely, Mrs. Price's new dignity was becoming a real and formidable thing. As Hilda's nervous weakness increased so Mrs. Price strengthened. She was growing calm and strong and ponderously capable. Now she concentrated on Hilda's appetite. Beneath the impulsion of Mother's will Hilda drank some soup, a finger or two of toast, and a cup of strong coffee. Hessie, torn as she was by nervous thoughts, began to see Mother in a new light. This was the Mother of her young memories. Strong, coercive, domineering. In a way it was rather horrible.

Soon after Hilda had finished eating a young girl-assistant from a cheap hairdressers' arrived. For days Hessie had been casually mentioning this great event to Rosie and Lily Bates, and to Mrs. Benson. "Oh, but, of course, the hairdressers are sending someone to dress Hilda's hair. Oh, yes, and mine, too." It was very dashing and high society.

But with the girl actually here there seemed little romance about her. She was so matter of fact. She looked bored and there was none of the pretty subservience about her behaviour that had tinted Hessie's imaginings so rosily. She made the hair-waving a cold and practical piece of work. Didn't she know she was waving a bridesmaid's hair, and a bride's, too? While her hair was being done Hessie avoided looking in the glass. The contrast between her own appearance and the young arrogant youthfulness of this other girl was too great. No matter! When the girl and her soft youngness were gone, things would adjust themselves.

The wedding was to be at two o'clock. Afterwards Hilda and Albert, man and wife, were driving to a seaside town about sixty miles away.

It was a quarter to one before the hairdresser left, having done Hilda's hair first. Hilda was already dressing, with Mother's assistance. On the way to her own bedroom Hessie glanced into her sister's room. Hilda was standing by the washstand, cleaning her teeth. She was dressed in her vest and knickers and long white silk stockings. She looked strange and unfamiliar and pathetic. With a sick feeling in her heart Hessie observed that the small tight artificial curls at the back of Hilda's neck were a mistake. Her neck was not young and round enough for them. Hessie's hand crept up and touched the tight curls at the back of her own neck. She had been relying so much on this hair wave.

Mother stood by the bed, ponderous and unfamiliar in her new grey frock. She was hovering over the wedding dress. There seemed no relationship between Hilda standing by the washstand, and the white satin at the end of the bed. For the moment Mother appeared to have transferred her interest and concern to the wedding dress. It stood for a symbol of her great desire.

In her own bedroom Hessie began to undress. Like Hilda she was changing everything. Her hands were awkward as she drew on her clothes. It was almost impossible to believe that Hilda's wedding hour was so near. Up till even half an hour ago it had seemed more like an event still swamped beneath the greater importance of its own preparations. But now the preparations were almost at an end. The event was here!

She must be very careful now. This might be the turning point in her own life, too. When Mr. Saul saw her standing by the bride's side, lovely and still girlish but with a woman's serenity. … Ah, if only the colour would deepen delicately in her cheeks, then she could stand with downcast eyes, and raise them just for one moment to look into his, as he moved before the bridal pair.

"Hessie—Hessie!" came Mother's voice.

But she could not halt in her own dressing now. At this moment she was more important than anyone else. Everything might hinge on her appearance to-day. She studied the curls at the back of her neck. Feeling reckless and a little desperate she ran the comb up through her hair and let it settle down again. It looked soft and pretty and full of hidden lights. Her neck was white and smooth, too. She pulled the green silk bridesmaid's frock over her head, and for a long slow critical moment she gazed at her own reflection.

"Hessie!"

"Coming, Mother."

She ran lightly across the landing. "Here I am!" But Mother hardly glanced at her. Was there no one to notice the lovely colour in her cheeks, the brightness in her eyes, the way the green frock rippled and fled away from her figure which was no longer thin and ugly but slim, just slim?

But Mother was engrossed in Hilda. "Help me fasten up these," she said, pointing to the fasteners on Hilda's dress.

Hilda stood in the middle of the room, more like a dummy figure than a bride. Her face was white, and there was a nervous twitching down her right cheek.

Hessie bent down, feeling proud of the lightness and firmness of her fingers as she fastened the side of Hilda's frock. Mrs. Price straightened herself, and waited with the veil and wreath of orange blossoms in her hand. There was a tense yet pleased look in her eyes when she glanced down at the veil. She moved her hand to let the soft tulle slip over her fingers.

"Now, bend your head a little, Hilda," she said coaxingly.

They arranged the veil in silence. It was a little ceremony in itself. It changed Hilda completely. It gave her a curiously ageless look, that had nothing bridal about it.

Mrs. Price went out of the room and came back with a little brandy. She held the glass to Hilda's blue lips.

"Here's the car for you, Mother," Hessie cried.

"You go on in it," Mrs. Price commanded, "and tell somebody to send a car for me at the same time as they come for Hilda. I'll go on only just ahead of my girlie."

Mother was like a general serenely re-making arrangements at the last moment.

When Hessie went back to her own room to put on her bridesmaid's hat, and to pick up her bouquet she almost wished Mother had given her some brandy, too. Oh, what a fool Hilda was to need brandy on her wedding day.

II

Hilda was late in arriving at the church. There were tear-marks on her face as she stepped into the church porch, for the bridal procession to form up behind her. But Mrs. Price was in the porch, too, waiting for her girlie, and Mother's hand was strangely competent with a handkerchief and a borrowed powder-puff. She rearranged Hilda's disordered veil, and then she took Hilda's limp hands in hers and said in a firm low voice, "Head up, Hilda, remember—you're the bride!" And then Mother sailed up the aisle, with a white-faced, trembling, yet hypnotized Hilda, following on Mr. Ponsonby's arm. Mr. Ponsonby was Albert's friend and family solicitor.

Hessie longed to shake Hilda's drooping shoulders as the procession halted at the chancel steps, and Albert, gallant in striped trousers and correct coat, moved out to meet his bride. If she, Hessie, were the bride, how differently she would bear herself. She would be modest, of course, modest and shy, but she would not forget that she was the bride—the bride, the beloved woman being joined in holy matrimony to the man she loved.

But this was a great opportunity for her, too, for she was standing close to Mr. Saul. She raised her eyes and gave him one long beautiful serene look, her glance holding his. And surely his face softened a little? For had not the occasion and her new clothes altered her a lot? Her cheeks were a glowing pink and her frock flowed away in soft becoming lines. But then Mr. Saul stepped back behind Mr. Benson, and Mr. Benson's big soulless common face came close to hers. But, no matter, she had made her impression on Mr. Saul and her real opportunity would come at the reception afterwards.

In the vestry it was impossible to get close to Mr. Saul again. All she wanted was just to stand beside him, and exchange tolerant smiles as the bride and bridegroom kissed. But perhaps it was just as well that she and Mr. Saul were not standing side by side when Albert's neat hard little mouth pressed Hilda's slackly hanging lips. What in Heaven's name was the matter with Hilda? To look like that on her wedding day! Naturally, she would receive Albert's kiss with proper modesty, but need she shrink like that, her face white, her eyes terror-stricken? Good God, didn't she know the primary reason for marriage, the almost hygienic reason? Poor Albert.

The wedding-breakfast was served in the ballroom at the Phoenix Hotel. The Phoenix was a good-class commercial hotel, and the ballroom was part of an annex built out into the yard behind. The windows were dusty and old stale tobacco smoke lingered in the curtains, but the service was good. The waiters had the bright alert manners proper to such occasions. In the kitchens they made lewd remarks on Hilda's shrinking appearance, and Albert's bull-like stockiness. Like Hessie, they pitied him.

Mrs. Price stood close to Hilda, as the guests came in. Most of the men were jocose, middle-aged friends of Albert's. They were very jovial and hearty and slapped Albert's shoulder, and drank his health repeatedly, and grew ponderously hilarious.

A glance in one of the big mirrors at the end of the hall was enough to assure Hessie that she really was looking her best. Her eyes so bright, her cheeks so pink, the green frock so amazingly becoming. Why—she was more than pretty, she was almost beautiful! She felt happy and animated and confident! The minute Mr. Saul came in the door she would run over to him and they would begin to talk together, they would have a gay little conversation, and, after the gaiety, perhaps, they would grow serious. And while she was waiting for Mr. Saul she would practise her new sprightliness on Mr. Ponsonby, though it would be a pity if she led him on too far, for once Mr. Saul came she would have to leave him.

But Mr. Saul never did come. Mr. and Mrs. Benson were there, but Mr. Saul was nowhere to be seen.

"Parish matters, my dear Hessie," Mr. Benson said blandly, when Hessie, the palms of her hands damp and cold from suspense, asked him why Mr. Saul was not there.

Mr. Benson eyed Hessie coldly. "He regrets it very much, but I have made his apologies to your dear mother, and your sister, the bride," he went on. "And that reminds me, Hessie," his voice changed and became harsh and brutally brisk. "It is possible that Mr. Saul will be announcing his engagement soon. I understand that he is going to be married to a charming young girl, a friend of his own family's. A most suitable match. This is in strict confidence, but for reasons that are unfortunately obvious, I am informing you now of Mr. Saul's intended matrimony. Thank you, I will have another glass of champagne. I must drink the bride's health."

Hessie felt that her own lips had gone whiter and slacker even than Hilda's. She could hardly breathe for the sudden agonizingly tight pressure across her chest. Something like an iron band was pressing cruelly into her heart.

She spun away from Mr. Benson, her muscles jerking like those of a hanged body. Whatever happened she must conceal her feelings from Mr. Benson's cold bland searching gaze.

She jerked out her hands, and forced her lips to smile in a gay sprightly way. "Oh, really, really, why this is delightful news! So delightful!" Her voice was high and shrill, but, after all, the general excitement of the day might account for that.

"You'd better drink some champagne," Mr. Benson said coldly, watching the effect of his shattering but untruthful announcement. "Take this glass, Hessie. It will help you to control yourself."

It was four o'clock before Hilda and Albert drove off. A puzzled, but still gallant Albert, assisted his bride into the car. Hilda looked ghastly as she leaned back. Mrs. Price kissed her firmly, and for the first time Mother's face showed signs of strain, but the next moment she patted Hilda's hands with the bland firmness of a procuress handing a terrified virgin over to a favoured client. Only Hilda was a married woman now, and Albert her husband in the sight of God and man. Everything was correct and decent.

For the first time since Mr. Benson's news, Hessie experienced emotion of any kind. A hot anger against Hilda. What a fool—fool—fool Hilda was not to be appreciating her wedding day! She was the bride, she was married! The old frightful, frightening, passionate hunger swept over Hessie. To-night, Hilda and Albert would be together in some hotel bedroom while she, Hessie, was alone, unloved, un-desired by anyone.

Perhaps if there had been no war to rob the world of lovers for women of her age, she would not be living this lonely unnatural spinster life now. For all her plainness, her unloveliness she would have made some man a good wife. She would have cooked for him, she would have borne children gladly, she would have been normal and happy, but instead of all that she was growing sick and perverted from years and years of repressing all the natural hungers of her mind and body.

When the car swept Hilda and Albert down the street and out of sight round the corner, Mrs. Price went grimly into the house. She sat down in her special chair and rested her hands on her knees. One of her girlies was married, God had granted her a son-in-law, and in due time perhaps He would grant her a grandchild. A bouncing little boy. This was September—well, October, November ... say, in June, if all went well. She must have a little talk with Albert when the young couple returned from their honeymoon. By that time, no doubt, Hilda would be more sensible and settled-down. Still, in these days it was nice to see a really modest bride, though perhaps Hilda had been a trifle too shrinking. However, modest, shrinking and everything else she was in Albert's hands now. They were man and wife. After all these years one of her daughters was married!

Hessie came in with a cup of tea on a tray. Mrs. Bates arrived just as Mrs. Price took her first sip.

"Show her in, Hessie," Mother said, and rearranged the skirts she had pulled up above her knees. She spread out the grey silk with the measured, pontifical gesture of a prelate arranging his robes before receiving one of his lesser brethren.

"Oh, my—it was a lovely wedding!" Mrs. Bates exclaimed breathlessly. "It'll be Hessie's turn next!"

"Rosie's or Lily's, you mean," Mrs. Price said graciously.

Hessie fetched another cup from the kitchen. Long familiarity with the china cupboard and the passage from the kitchen to the sitting-room helped her to succeed in this task. Then she went upstairs and flung a light coat over her bridesmaid's frock, and ran out of the house. Walking was a poor and ineffectual way of attempting to escape from her miseries, but it was the only way open to her. She took the road that she knew best. On the outskirts of the Kellaways' estate she turned into a narrow path that led through woods and fields. She met no one on this walk of hers, and when she was tired and it was growing dark she rested in a meadow where the earth was still hot though the dew falling on the grass was fresh and cold. Hessie sat there with her fingers twisting together.

Where were Hilda and Albert now? Hilda who was a married woman. A married woman! The words ran through and through Hessie's distracted mind.

Hilda was married, and Mr. Said was about to be married. Soon he would be saying, "My wife—my wife. ..." Life was not fair nor true nor honest! Some women started with every advantage, but what advantage had she ever had? None at all, unless one could count Mother's gentility an advantage, and she had had to pay a heavy price for her share of that. Wasn't it possible to be a little too genteel and ladylike? And all this time as she sat here, Hilda was alone with her husband—her husband, and she, Hessie, was alone with nothing but the mocking ghosts of her genteel inhibitions, and the frightening, always unfulfilled demands of her body.

Whimpering a little Hessie got up and plunged through the long tufted meadow-grass. The ends of her dress grew wet and draggled, and she left behind her the marks of her crazy flight in the bowed and broken heads of the tall, helpless grasses. She went down through a little wood and out onto a cindered path that must, she thought vaguely, be part of the Kellaway estate.

Chapter Nineteen

I

Maggie sat on the side of her bed. Maxwell was still away. There was a sense of resignation in her longing for him now. He wasn't here yet, but he would come some day. Perhaps, to-morrow. He was bound to come soon, and she must be patient because, after all, she had such memories to keep her company. She sat there and wondered about him. Was he happy? No doubt at the moment he was too busy to be thinking about her at all, but at night-time did he lie awake needing her?

Her best underclothes lay beside her, but there was no necessity to put them on this afternoon. Wouldn't that be a waste? It would, in a way, and yet supposing she met him driving home from the station, then she would be sorry she was not ready for him. She had better put them on. She had bought a little box of manicure things and when she was dressed she sat on the side of the bed and manicured her nails.

Then Irene knocked at the door. "Someone to see you," she called.

Maggie jumped up. The relief was so wonderful that she felt quite dizzy, and then a quick suspicion clouded everything. He would never come asking for her at the house. No!

Irene put her head inside the door. "My goodness, he's good-looking," she said. "And you all ready to go out on the spree with him! Well, that's neat work!"

"Who is it?" Maggie whispered.

She felt frightened at the depth of her own disappointment as she followed Irene downstairs. She had forgotten that young waiter who had carried the tray of steaming coffee out into the yard that had been so changed by the growing dusk and the cream and gold vans and the lounging men on the night of the fête. And what did he want with her now?

"Hullo, Maggie," he said, when she appeared.

"He's got your name all right!" Irene laughed. "Well, I've fetched her for you now. Good-bye."

Pierce lifted his smart hat, and the echo of Irene's delighted laughter came back to them.

"Pleased to see me?" he asked Maggie. "I'm on a job close here. I thought I'd run around and look you up. You look very smart."

"I'm sorry, Cook doesn't allow anyone to come in," Maggie answered, her heart still heavy from disappointment.

"Can't you come out a stroll with me?" he said then. "You're not working now, are you? Come on into the town and we'll have a look round. I don't know this part at all."

Maggie shook her head. Irene was quite right. He was handsome and he was dressed like a prince, but he wasn't the man she wanted.

He took a step or two away, then he came close again. He looked very young and beseeching.

"Oh, come on! I'm all alone here and it'd be nice to have a friend. Just come this once."

Looking at him Maggie wavered. For all his smart clothes and good looks there was something lonely and appealing about him. He was almost too good-looking, and that set him apart from other men. She began to feel sorry for him. Besides, he belonged to that day when she had first gone down to Maxwell. He belonged to the heat and conflict and wonder of that day. He was a small thread in the pattern of the memories that were her only link with Maxwell now.

"Oh, I'll come," she said, and smiled at him.

She ran upstairs and put on her hat. She found it easy to talk with him as they walked through the woods and out onto the road into the town. It was almost like walking with another girl, a very pretty, well-dressed girl. At least, compared with Maxwell's dark terrible power and intensity he hardly seemed a man at all. After a while Maggie was glad she had come with him. It was one way of passing the afternoon. She began to be conscious, too, that other women were gazing with admiring pleasure at her escort. They always glanced at Maxwell, too, but in a strange way, as if they feared their own thoughts about him.

Walking beside Pierce everything in the town looked different, too. The shops were less exciting and Maggie could see the people much more distinctly than when she walked amongst them with Maxwell. She felt tranquil and undisturbed, able to give her attention to all she saw around her.

"You'll have a cup of tea with me?" Pierce suggested. He was very polite. He led her into a popular café and they ate thinly cut white bread and butter and cakes that were overloaded with tasteless whipped cream and mocha icing. The waitress who attended to them was greatly taken with Pierce's looks and his immaculate clothes. His manners were perfect, too.

But half-way through tea Maggie almost forgot him in her sudden longing for Maxwell. This tea compared so poorly with the first they had had in town together, when the mere physical sense of Maxwell close beside her had charged every movement that she or he made with intense importance.

She was glad when Pierce began to talk, telling her stories about his work. Exalted names tripped from his lips. He had served tea and coffee and caviare and champagne to half the nobility of the country. Maggie listened, fingering the great red beads that Maxwell had given her and she let Pierce's words drift aimlessly through her thoughts.

"Shall we go to the cinema?" Pierce asked when they left the cafe. He bent slightly towards her, his profile turned away from her a little.

Maggie hesitated. Why not? A year ago attention from a young man as elegant, as beautiful as Pierce, would have seemed an impossible dream. But her new underclothing, her smart frock, the recent tremendous changes in her life caused her now to accept Pierce without question or marvelling. After all, he was only a very poor second best to Maxwell, whom she loved.

They went to the cinema, but the picture had no real interest for Maggie, apart from the fact that it was passing the hours away. That was all.

Turning her head a little she could see the pure outline of Pierce's profile. There was the immaculate line of his collar and tie, too. He was certainly a very beautiful young man, but his tall body, his carefully manicured hands, his wavy hair had no masculine significance for Maggie. The girl who had shown them to the seats had sent a fluttered look at Pierce's glorious face, the waitresses at the cafe had been absorbed in him, Maggie alone was unstirred.

The programme was a long one and the clocks were striking eight as they left the cinema. Pierce guided her as they went out into the street. He held her arm gently, his fingers feeling softly around her wrist. He kept his hand there as they walked up the street. When he spoke to her he bent over her solicitously, the lights playing on the curve of his lips and his fine eyes. He appeared older now that it was night and they were moving amongst the evening crowds. He wheeled her into another cafe.

"We'll have a snack before I see you home. You don't want to go back yet—do you?" he asked.

11

Maxwell threw the reins to a stable-boy. It was nearly seven o'clock. The train had been half an hour late. He went, first of all, to his cottage. It was neat and tidy, but empty though there were signs of Maggie about the rooms. He halted before the table and stared down at a bowl of common-looking flowers, almost weeds, which Maggie must have picked in the hedges. His thick shoulders shook with laughter. Weeds in his cottage, when the windows looked out on greenhouses rich with exotic flowers! He could fill his cottage with flowers over and over again and no one would miss the blossoms he had cut. And Maggie had picked weeds and carried them in here, and filled a bowl with water and arranged them—thinking of him all the while!

By God, he'd show her what he thought of her flowers!

He walked to the greenhouses, and went through them, one after another, cutting the finest blossoms from each plant. Both arms were filled with flowers when he entered the cottage again, and they toppled over each other and fell on the floor as he threw them onto the table and sought for bowls and vases and jugs. When he was finished the cottage looked like a flower show, and the air was sweet and heavy with scent from the tremendous petals. And all the time Maggie's weeds stood alone in the place of honour in the centre of the table!

Maggie! Why didn't she know he was back and appear before him now, at once? He went to the door and peered out, searching for any sign of Maggie's figure in the increasing dusk.

Looking back into the cottage he grinned to himself, and rubbed his hands together. But his face altered as the perfume from the flowers, heavy, sensuous and hot reached him. After ten days and nights of separation from Maggie he could wait no longer. He clenched his hands slowly. In all his many adventures with women he had never known anything like this present hunger for Maggie. For the first time in his life he thought of marriage. To have Maggie here, waiting for him always, with her big splendid body, her generosity, her kindness. She was no longer just another adventure, she was necessary to him.

Impatiently he looked out through the open doorway again. No sign of her anywhere. But how was she to know that he was home? After all, how could she know?

Cursing softly, he plunged out of the cottage and followed the path to the house. He needed Maggie so badly that he did not care what Cook and those other bitches there thought of him. He was going to marry Maggie, and they might as well know it now as later.

He banged on the kitchen door, and flung it open. Jenner was alone in the kitchen. She jumped as Maxwell swaggered in.

"Where's Maggie?" he demanded abruptly.

Jenner put down the tray she had just picked up.

"What a fright you gave me! What's the matter now?"

Maxwell had always hated Jenner for her prim manners and her bloodless mouth.

"I've no time to waste talking to you," he said coarsely. "I want Maggie. Where is she?"

Jenner's lips went white with outraged, spinster anger. She drew herself away from his demanding arrogant figure, his domineering maleness.

"She's gone out with her boy friend. She's been out with him all afternoon. He called for her," she said venomously. "And if I may say so he's a nice handsome, civil young fellow—which you aren't!" She tried to march past him but he caught her shoulder roughly.

"You're lying!"

Jenner flinched from his touch, but she met his angry gaze coldly.

"Find out for yourself, then. Wait till she comes back and ask her. And don't ever lay your hands on me again!"

He snatched his hand from her shoulder and threw back his head and roared with laughter. "Is it likely?" he shouted. "Though you'd like it, wouldn't you?"

"I'll thank you to let me go by." Jenner spoke frigidly.

"I wouldn't thank myself to stop you," he retorted, but he was laughing no longer and his face was darkening again. "But I want Maggie—see?"

Jenner flounced primly past him. As she reached the end of the passage Irene appeared through the service door.

"Has Maggie come back from her outing with that nice young waiter yet?" Jenner asked.

"No—not yet," Irene said cheerfully, and then she saw Maxwell's broad low figure blocking the passage door. "But she won't be long now," she added hurriedly. "She didn't want to go out with him a bit."

But it was too late. Irene hastened down the passage but Maxwell was gone.

As he went through the door he was almost blind from anger and frustration. Maggie, his girl, out with another man. With another man! He stopped in his headlong rush across the yard to try to understand, to realize what he had heard. He clenched his hands, tightening them till the skin on his knuckles gleamed like fine taut grey rubber. Never before had he experienced such anger, or such a feeling of frustrated desire. If Maggie and the man appeared before him, now, he'd kill the fellow, and after that he'd teach Maggie something, too. Every vein in his body was throbbing as though his blood had gone mad.

He rushed across the yard and plunged into the bushes, fighting them as their branches caught at his clothes and face. Cursing, he beat his way through to the clearing before his cottage. His cottage with the living-room like a flower show, with the weeds Maggie had gathered in the foremost position of all.

Outside the door he halted, his breath coming fast. There was someone there in his cottage, a woman, waiting for him! It was Maggie, after all, and those women up there had been lying to him.

It was almost dark inside the cottage as Maxwell stumbled in, but the scent from the flowers was hotter and richer than before. He could see them vaguely, their petals like dark or pale velvet, their stalks hidden by the size and magnificence of the blossoms.

"Maggie!" he whispered.

The woman sitting there stood up. "Oh dear, oh dear; I'm afraid I'm trespassing," she said, with a shaky little laugh. "I was so tired and the house was open and I just peeped in and saw the flowers. … How wonderful they are. … I hope you don't mind? We've seen each other before, haven't we? At the rectory, you know. …"

He went close up to her. Her eyes were shining and there was an hysterical unsteadiness about her lips. She swayed a little, not away from him but towards him, the low front of her long, pale green frock rising and falling rapidly. For a moment Maxwell stood and stared at her. Then he began to laugh, a short coarse laugh. But after a moment his face changed. If Maggie was out in the darkness with another man, there was a woman in here with him too: this was a game that both of them could play. Hessie had closed her eyes. When Maxwell's arms went round her erotic body she gave a little high shrill laugh.

Chapter Twenty

I

Lottie and Nurse and the children were down on the sands. Nurse had a newspaper in her hand, and her hat was pulled down to protect her eyes against the strong light.

"It should start to-morrow unless they ask for another adjournment," she began. "That's the way the police always get on. Keep everyone in suspense. You haven't heard, I suppose, whether they're going to call you or not?"

Lottie felt a wave of sick pain shoot through her. "Call me?" she cried, startled. "Oh, but they couldn't! I didn't see anything."

"No, but you were the last known person to go through that wood until Spencer came down and found the bits of that girl's body lying there. Why shouldn't they call you? You never know what the police are going to do."

"They couldn't—they wouldn't!" Lottie cried again.

"Why not? Now then, Lottie, pull yourself together a bit! And don't answer me back like that."

Fortunately, at that moment Isobel came up. Her face was very pink from stooping in the heat. She pushed back her hair and sighed deeply. "Oh, this heat!"

"Sit down and rest for a moment," Lottie said difficultly.

What Nurse had suggested surely could not happen? Not now! If the police had wanted her wouldn't they have let her know long before this? But no one had said anything, that was why she was so unprepared for Nurse's suggestion.

Isobel sat beside Lottie for a moment and then she got up and went down to the sea's edge and stood there with the small waves playing around her feet. Now and then she bent and studied her toes with great interest as the receding water ran between them. After a while she ceased to wriggle her toes in the wet sand, but stood gazing out towards the horizon, her thoughts lost in dreams of her own, her body motionless, the faint warm wind coming in little rare gusts to stir a fold of her frock.

"Good gracious me!" said Nurse sharply to Lottie. "You'd think you'd be glad to serve your country a bit. It's the duty of every decent man and woman to help the police in every way they can. You ought to be glad of getting the opportunity. A real murder trial! You'd see the murderer himself!"

Lottie's hands pressed deeply into the soft sand. "I couldn't look at him," she said desperately.

"Don't be such a little ninny!" Nurse flounced her sewing with indignation. "There'll be people who'll stand for hours and hours in a queue outside the court, and half of them won't get in, but the witnesses get in all right. The police make way for them, or else bring them in through a back entrance."

Isobel was still standing at the water's edge. She had turned sideways a little. Her face was very thoughtful as though she were listening to something far away but very lovely. When the wind came it blew her fine light hair away from her face. Lottie tried to keep her eyes on Isobel, to see nothing but Isobel, and hear nothing but the sea—just to forget Nurse.

But Nurse went on. "A sensational trial like this! Why, it's years since the police found a girl left in such a mess! And you were the last known person to have been in the very place where he cut her up! Don't you be surprised if the police decide they want you, after all. They generally keep quiet about these things, but I, for one, wouldn't be astonished if they sent for you. And look at the counsel they've got on both sides! Why, people would go anywhere, just to hear those two men going at the witnesses and each other, let alone seeing the murderer himself!"

The heat from the sun beating down on Lottie's head was nearly unbearable. She put up her hand and pressed her fingers against her forehead.

"I couldn't go—I couldn't bear to see him!" she cried.

"Hoity-toity, you'll go all right if the police come for you."

"I couldn't go," Lottie repeated in a whisper. "I couldn't bear to see him."

11

After lunch Mrs. Kellaway came into the nursery. When she was going away again she said, "What's the matter, Lottie? Don't you feel well?"

But Lottie could not explain anything to Mrs. Kellaway. She could not ask her if it were true that she might be called to attend that murder trial. It was impossible to question Mrs. Kellaway on such a subject. She must just go on trying to persuade herself that such a thing could not happen. Why, the police would have notified her before this surely? They had been so kind to her at that interview on the day the murder had been discovered. But how was she to know? As Nurse had said, you never knew what the police would decide to do next in a case like this.

"Lottie, how hot your hands are," Isobel said, as Lottie brushed her hair.

"It's a hot day, darling," Lottie answered. She touched her cheeks with her own hands, but could feel no difference between the two, her cheeks were so hot as well.

"Darling Lottie!" said Isobel suddenly, and she pressed her face against Lottie's big white apron.

Mrs. Kellaway was taking Anne into the town that afternoon and Nurse and baby were going, too. Lottie and Isobel were to have the whole of the garden and the shore and the woods to themselves. Isobel was very pleased at this.

"I think we had better be two grown ups together," she said to Lottie as they set out.

It was a warm, still afternoon. Half-way across the garden, Isobel decided that they had better be French people. Lottie knew no French at all, but she did her best, and Isobel kept close by her side, walking with short stiff steps, she was so pleased with this idea of hers. She nodded her head constantly, and threw out her hands. "*Oui, oui!*" she cried in answer to Lottie's gibberish.

But she forgot that she was grown-up and French when they reached the sand. She darted off, zigzagging wildly, calling to Lottie to follow in her tracks. It took them a long time to reach the sea in this way. The water was very blue close in to the shore but as the sea rose widely and proudly away from the land the blue grew paler and paler till it reached the place where the horizon should have been but where, instead, hung a curtain of shimmering blue and gold mist. But the colours inshore made up for the misty horizon.

The sea was very calm, like the afternoon itself. Lottie took off her hat which was pressing heavily about her forehead. If only the days could go on and on like this, so quietly. But if the police wanted her, and if she had to go to the trial, and if she saw the man they were accusing, and if the jury found him guilty, and if the day came, a morning like this morning had been, for instance, and they hanged him. ... She would be branded and tainted for ever! She would never be able to forget the terrible thing he had done, and the penalty he had suffered, justly or unjustly. And if they called her could she keep her eyes away from the dock? Supposing they said "Did you see anyone like the accused lingering in the woods?" Why, then, she'd have to look at him. Look right into his eyes. There would be counsel, too. Very clever, distinguished men, their fine presences dominating the court, their assured voices kind or frightening, but, underneath all their poise, their erudition, their rhetoric, the ferocity of men demanding or protecting a human life.

Isobel was content to walk slowly along the shore. She had taken off her shoes and stockings and was paddling. The tide was about to turn so the little waves came in with a tired lazy swish and ran out again slowly and placidly.

"The sea feels very soft to-day," Isobel said.

Although they were walking slowly it did not seem long before they reached the end of the little bay. At low tide it was quite easy to pick a way over the flat rocks to the next and longer sweep of shore, but that was impossible now.

They sat down together on a rock, where the seaweed was crisp and brown from exposure to the sun. When Isobel felt rested they started home again. By this time the sea was getting a little bit more excited about itself. There was a stronger pull in the water as each wave went out. By eight o'clock to-night the sea would be lying far down on the wet sand, its murmuring very faint when it reached the fir trees at the end of the garden.

At tea-time Nurse appeared to have forgotten the murder trial. She was full of interest in the shopping she and Mrs. Kellaway had done in the town.

Isobel and Anne were both tired when bedtime came, and they went to sleep without any fuss.

But at supper Nurse had the latest news about everything. She began to read from a newspaper.

"He's pretending to be ill now. 'Man in Wood Murder Charge sent to Prison Hospital. Doctors fear Operation may be Necessary.' There, now! But that won't do him any good! If they want to they'll just cut out his appendix or whatever it is, and take good care to have the rest of him alive when the police are ready to start the trial. We'd better have out a new jar of pickles. There's one there in that cupboard."

The strong smell of vinegar and mustard filled the room for a moment as Nurse helped herself to the freshly opened pickles.

When her duties in the nursery were finished, Lottie saw that it was nearly eight o'clock. Nurse was at the table, busy cutting out some new frocks for Isobel and Anne, and for the baby, too. She was absorbed now, in the task before her, measuring and checking up lengths and widths.

"Do you want me any more to-night, Nurse?" Lottie asked.

"No, I don't. But where are you off to now? It's dark outside."

"Yes, it's dark," Lottie agreed. She did not know yet where she was going, though she remembered her promise to meet George. The pain had gone from her head but she felt tired and sick. She might go to bed.

"All right then—you can go," Nurse answered. "I can manage without you. You don't forget your time off these days, I notice."

Lottie turned and went out of the nursery. She went into her bedroom and looked at Anne and Isobel. Then she stood by the window for a moment. The night air was fresh and cool. There was no wind, but there was a crisp whispering in the air itself. Lottie leant out of the window. She pressed the back of her hand to her forehead.

Would she ever escape from fear and anxiety and the horror that lay so close to everything in this grown-up world? At the Home, life had been simple and uncomplicated. She had shared with some of the older girls a deep consciousness of the responsibilities of their age and position. There had been a delicate seriousness about Lottie's comprehension of these responsibilities. Something lay in her keeping and it was her duty to cherish it. She had set out on the adventure of this first situation with the same feeling, and suddenly found her equipment inadequate. She knew nothing at all about life. She was foolish and defenceless. She had soon learnt that from Nurse.

Out in the garden that seemed so quiet, with the flowers and the trees and the gentle darkness, anything might be happening. The stillness, the peace, were delusions. There was neither real stillness nor real peace, and the darkness was no gentle cloak but a cover for horrible things when man and Nature combined together on their predatory quests. Beyond the woods and fields lay the towns, and things were worse in the towns, Nurse said. And miles away, but covered by the same linking darkness, was the man they were so soon to try for murder. Was he a guilty man? And, if so, was he thinking of his crime now? Just thinking of the girl he had killed? Not thinking of the lovely woods through which he must have walked with her. The great trees, the little mounds of soft, cleanly-rotting leaves that had, months before, been green and then turned yellow and floated down from the high twigs and branches, the patches of moss with their myriad tiny green fronds that spread themselves over the ground with such gentle patience.

And how close she had been to all this. Removed from it only by the passage of a few hours. And how close she was to it still. At any moment, if the police sent for her to attend the trial, she would be swamped in the terror and horror of it all. There was no refuge for her anywhere.

Lottie put her hands up to her face again and pressed the palms against her cheeks. For months and months now her own ignorance and the little, distorted knowledge she had gained from Nurse's hints, had been pressing like a terrifying load on her mind. The world outside these gardens was an ugly place. Men took girls and did horrible things to them. "They're a dirty lot and mind you look after yourself, Lottie." Even marriage could be terrible. You were wholly at one man's mercy then. Poor women. The only thing to do was to keep clear of them, keep yourself to yourself, and remember that men were brutes. Even Mr. Kellaway was tainted. Behind his apparent gentleness and courtesy there were times, Nurse said, when he was as bad as anyone else. Not even he could escape this common horror that afflicted all men and changed them into something capable of anything. Even murder.

What could she do if she had to go as a witness at the trial of this man who was accused of a murder of this kind? How could she escape if the police said, "We want you. You must come with us and tell everyone what the woods looked like on that lovely quiet evening before this man came and violated the kind trees and the silence and the darkness. Did anyone accost you? Did you see any signs of this man and a girl? Did you hear anything or see anyone before you took the children home to bed?"

The pain inside Lottie's head had come back again and was sickening her, it was so intense and pressing. She was frightened, too. There was no escape for her anywhere, for she knew now, from Nurse, that life was full of cruelties and fearful dangers and horrors, all the greater to someone, who, like herself, had been ignorant of them for so long. If she had known about them always, if this knowledge had grown with her—but, no, how could that have helped when the horrors were still there?

Lottie leaned a little further out of the window seeking fresher air. Supposing she leaned so far out that her body just slipped helplessly over the windowsill and fell down into the garden below? Then it would not matter to her what terrible things men did to women. It would be quite easy, for her head felt top-heavy with pain. But how wrong and wicked these thoughts were! Lottie pressed her hands to her head to see if, by doing so, she could hold in the pain.

Almost immediately then, she saw George. He came right out into the middle of the lawn and stood smiling up at her. She could see the pleasant smile on his lips.

"Come down, Lottie," he called softly and kindly. Lottie tip-toed out of the bedroom and ran, with panic-stealth and quietness, down the stairs and out through the side door into the garden.

"I thought you were never coming," George said. He slipped his arm around her and led her down through the fir trees to the sea. They walked slowly along the hard wet sand, the pain in Lottie's head easing as the light sea-wind blew against her face, and the quietness, the reassurance of George's presence soothed her heart.

Reaching the little headland they climbed to the top and sat down in a sheltered hollow where the grass was strong and thick. George lay back, with his hands behind his head. Lottie sat beside him, her hands folded and resting in her lap. Now and then George plucked a long stem of grass and chewed the end of it slowly, his eyes watching Lottie's delicate profile.

At last he rolled over on his side and took her hand.

"Head better?" he asked.

Lottie turned and looked at him. The moon was rising, and she could see his face quite clearly.

"It's almost gone. How did you know that my head was bad when I came out?"

"I knew it!" he laughed. "Your face didn't look right, not happy, somehow. Lottie, put your head down on my shoulder and rest a bit. I'll make you comfortable. See? Is that all right?"

With Lottie's head against his arm George began to stroke her temples. Once or twice his fingers caught in her hair, and he let its waves slip over his hands.

"Close your eyes until the pain's all gone," he said again.

Lottie closed her eyes. She looked as if she were asleep, and the light from the moon that was still young and soft gilded her face as George looked down at her. Her eyelashes were long and golden and they swept innocently against her cheeks.

But after a moment or two she sat up again. This rest and quietness, this happiness with George would be over soon. Soon she would be back in the house with Nurse, and the murder trial, and all the unknown horrors of life still surrounding her.

She caught George's hand quickly and held on to it. Here was someone whom she could ask, whom she must ask.

"George, do you think the police'll want me?"

"The police?"

"As a witness at that murder trial!"

"Oh!" George sat up a little, leaning towards Lottie, resting on his elbows, his free hand covering hers. "Go on, tell me what's worrying you," he urged.

"I couldn't bear to look at him," Lottie whispered.

"You won't have to!" he said confidently. "The police haven't mentioned it, have they? Well, they won't."

"But they might!" Lottie cried despairingly.

"They won't! Not by what the papers say anyway. She didn't go out to meet that fellow until nearly eight o'clock and people were talking to him soon after seven, You took the children home at six. No one'll want you to go and say that you didn't see either of them in a place where nobody the police want could have been. See?"

Lottie turned and looked at George.

"Then you don't think they'll want me?" she asked breathlessly.

"Quite sure!" he said firmly.

Lottie sat silent for a long time. At first her release from anxiety was like a flash of vivid lightning flaring grandly and proudly across the sky, but after that first sweeping relief everything went dark again, and then slowly, one by one, the obscuring clouds moved away and she experienced a lovely sense of comfort from a source entirely unreasoned and unreasonable. Then, bit by bit, her seeking mind urged on by the memory of that first sense of comfort, she reasoned everything out step by step. Yes, George was right! She could believe now, since George had said so, that the police had heard from her all that they wanted to hear, that they would not send for her, that she would not have to face the man accused of such a frightful crime, that the fear and suspense and horror under which she was living were needless.

On the grassy slope above them something stirred a little.

"Look at that!" said George softly.

Lottie saw two bright alert eyes watching her, and the tall ears of a giant rabbit rising above the grass. It advanced a little way into the clearing where they sat, its soft nose twitching violently. If only Isobel were with them now! It remained there for a minute or two, motionless except for its nose, its staring eyes quite unperturbed by their human presences. It was part of the night and the rising moonlight and the closeness of the woods and the sea and the tufted grass of the headland fields, it was part of the wild gentle dignity of the night. At last it loped across the clearing to pursue its own important way amongst the grasses.

"They're pretty things, it's a pity they're such pests," George said.

"Oh, I wish the children could have seen him!" Lottie cried softly. Something of her new relief, her new freedom rang in her voice. She felt so free and happy, so gay! She turned and smiled a little at George.

He put out his hand and drew her down beside him.

"Do you love me at all, Lottie?" he asked, his hand moving across her forehead and up into her thick fine hair.

Lottie closed her eyes again. She was so grateful for the comfort he had given her, but as she opened her eyes and looked up to see him bending over her this sense of comfort and reassurance was submerged in a tide of feeling that was newer and stronger than anything she had ever known before. She put up her hand and touched his face, wonderingly. A little smile crept into his eyes as he turned his face and kissed the palm of the hand she had raised.

"You're so sweet, Lottie," he said. "I've loved you ever since you came down about the flowers that day."

A tender smile lit Lottie's face, too. She was full of tenderness and love for George. She had always been aloof from ordinary affections, someone apart, alone, not really needed by anyone, never, never the object of another's love and care. And alone by herself she had suffered fear. But with George there could be no fear, now or ever.

He lay down beside her, one arm thrown lightly over her. Lottie turned towards him overwhelmed by this new wonder and joy. Her movement towards him was simple and instinctive, unthinking. There was no need to think or reason when she was with George, his very presence was enough to drive away the cold unhappy fears of the past months, the terrors inspired by Nurse.

"I'm going to love you always, Lottie, I'm going to take care of you," George murmured.

Lottie's lips parted a little, but she could not say anything. George's words went on and on echoing through her mind, her heart, her body, till they filled everything with a lovely insistent happiness. "I'm going to take care of you, Lottie—Lottie, I love you."

He moved slightly, easing her in his arms till she lay close within his embrace. He kissed her cheek and her forehead and then her mouth. He held her gently and tenderly. Her eyes were wide open and the love and gratitude in them stirred him profoundly.

"You don't looked scared now," he said. "What was always frightening you, Lottie?"

For a moment her body stiffened with a vague resurgence of the old terror, but instantly the depth, the power, the certainty of her realization of George's love triumphed. She knew now, with a sense of deep tranquil certainty, that terror and injury could not spring from love of this kind, no matter what Nurse said. But she could not put all this into words. She could only lie like this, looking up at George, watching a little smile break over the seriousness of his face.

"That's better!" he said, studying her closely. "I don't want you ever to be scared, Lottie."

The sea was very quiet, it was only a murmur, a mere rustling whisper drifting up through the air, a little light sound that was almost sad and wistful at this hour of night. But it was beautiful, too, and so was the sense of the trees behind them. Their sheltered hollow lay just between the woods and the sea, and there the sounds from the sea and the stillness from the woods met and moved gently and tranquilly about Lottie and George. Now and then George talked, brave confident words, with one arm under Lottie, the other lightly over her, while her hair rested against his cheek as he talked and planned their future together. Now and then he kissed her, but always gently as if he feared to startle her. He loved her so deeply, and she was so very young and innocent, and he was overwhelmed by her quick and lovely response to his love.

He kept looking down at her face that was so radiant and trusting, and saying, "I'm going to take care of you now, Lottie. You needn't ever be afraid again."

Chapter Twenty-One

I

Hessie hurried through the woods. At first she ran with quick fluttering steps, catching her frock in the brambles, her silk stockings already ruined. But reaching the wide cart-track leading to the back entrance of the Kellaways' house, she steadied her walk, and even put up her hand to pat her hair into place. Her short hair—how fortunate that it was short!

She threw back her head and gazed at the sky. She could see the moon through the high arched branches of the trees. Never had there been such moonlight, so soft and golden! Was this what they called the harvest moon, that great triumphant globe that shone with such warm supremacy in the night sky? It was the most beautiful thing she had ever seen. And the quietness of the woods, too! Surely they had never before been so quiet with just that quality of stillness? Just as if the night were waiting, with suspended breath, for some lovely sound or revelation.

Poor Hilda, to be shut away in some hotel bedroom! Hessie walked more and more slowly, she was so anxious to prolong her journey home. Never had she felt such a sense of ease and contentment. She was no longer old and frustrated. She could go on and on in her old life now, not caring at all about Hilda and Albert, no longer sickened because of the mysteries that life had withheld from her because she was plain and poor. The gradual slipping by of the years of her life would not matter now. For however brief a while she had been a woman, living, experienced. She had something to remember, always, even when Mother and Hilda talked together in the hushed tones of married women. She would be able to smile at them, because of the secret knowledge in her own heart. She could even think with equanimity of Mr. Saul and his young bride-to-be!

Fortunately she met no one she knew in the streets of the town. The roads were fairly deserted. Now and then someone glanced at her frock, but, after all, she might be a guest at a party. She held her head high, and met their glances casually.

She was surprised to find no lights on in the house when she reached home. Only the dim hall-light. Surely, it was not so late that Mother had gone to bed? No, it was hardly half-past nine.

But the kitchen door opened as Hessie stepped into the hall, and Mrs. Bates came out. Her lips were drawn down, her face heavy with woeful importance.

"Why—Mrs. Bates!" Hessie began.

"Oh, is that you at last, Hessie?" Mrs. Bates spoke lugubriously. "Oh, your poor sister—your poor mother! Such a dreadful accident!"

Hessie stood still. One part of her feared that something dreadful had happened, but there was another part of her consciousness that could never be disturbed or fretted again. To-night's experience had silenced that self-reproach for ever.

"What is it, Mrs. Bates? Tell me!" she urged.

"Oh dear, oh dear, I can hardly say it! Such a lovely wedding, and the two of them going off like that, and now your poor sister a married woman, but not—as I said to your mother—never now a wife."

"Albert!" Hessie exclaimed tensely.

"The police have arrested him," Mrs. Bates went on, her eyes popping out of her head with horrified excitement and stimulation. "I mean the young fellow whose car run into poor Albert and Hilda. A policeman was right there when the collision occurred and they arrested him straight off, they say. And it'll be manslaughter if poor Albert dies. At the best he'll be a cripple always. Your poor sister—on her wedding day, too. It's like being royalty—these—dreadful accidents—"

Hessie caught her hands together. Hilda—Albert—Mother!

"Your mother wants you at once. She's round at Hilda's new home—poor thing. You'd better go there, Hessie!"

At Albert's house Hessie found Mother sitting beside the couch on which Hilda lay. Hilda's face looked white and drawn, but it was no longer the sick-green it had been when she started off on the fateful drive. Hessie was almost afraid to imagine that there was a sense of strained relief in her sister's grief.

Hilda—poor Hilda, weeping at her wedding, half-fainting and hysterical as Mother led her out so firmly to the waiting car, a puzzled, bewildered Albert following them. If she could have foreseen the future would she have enjoyed her floating veil, her wedding-gown, Albert's more possessive kiss in the vestry, the champagne, the soiled but gallant joviality of Albert's gentlemen friends?

With a feeling of delicious unfamiliar superiority Hessie ran across the room and dropped on her knees beside her sister.

"Hilda—darling," she cried pressing Hilda's hand between her own.

"It's a comfort to know that dear Hilda is secure. Dear Albert signed his will and the settlement this morning," Mrs. Price droned with sorrowful satisfaction. "I've sent for our things, Hessie. We must come and make this our home now. Hilda will need us. You can tell Mrs. Benson that."

Still pressing Hilda's limp hand, Hessie nodded. It was terrible to be planning all this now, but after all, Hilda would certainly need them, and this house was big and solid and comfortable enough to hold them all. There would be comfort—money. Plenty to eat, no drudgery—comfort!

Hilda opened her eyes and looked at Hessie.

"Hess," she murmured.

Hessie leant closer. Why, this was Hilda back again! Her own sister returned to her from the barrier that recent events had erected so flimsily. They were sisters, friends again! Hilda was nominally married, there would be Albert's money, Albert's house, and always, always she, Hessie, would have a memory of her own. She was the elder sister, she was the experienced one, she was strong and loving and supreme!

Life was beginning afresh for them all. What a tremendous, momentous day this wedding day of Hilda's had been!

She gathered Hilda into her arms, and Hilda's damp cheek pressed exhaustedly against hers. There was something like relief in this abandonment of Hilda's.

"Dear Hilly!" Hessie murmured, possessively.

11

Maggie paused in the clearing before Maxwell's house. Was there really a light in that window or was it just a delusion born of her longing for Maxwell's return? She stared at it, almost sorry that she had parted so brusquely with Pierce, sending him back to the town as soon as they'd reached the entrance to the grounds for she wanted someone else, now, to confirm the reality of that light.

But then the door opened and Maxwell himself appeared on the threshold. The light was behind him so that Maggie could not see his face.

She forced herself to walk slowly towards him.

"I didn't know you were coming back to-day," she said brightly, "but I wish I had known! I'd have been back sooner. It's been just awful in the town."

She was close up to him now, close enough to see the ferocity and anger in his face, and to halt in her approach. He caught both her arms roughly.

"Who was your fancy fellow?" he shouted.

Maggie gazed at him for a moment, her fear giving way to compassion.

"Oh, just him," she said with a backward movement of her head. "That waiter fellow. But it doesn't matter. He didn't touch me."

Her arms were hurting her as he held them close to her side, but she raised her head and gave him a long steady look. Then she began to smile, her lips parted, her eyes full of her love for him.

"I just can't believe you're back," she said. "I've been thinking of you all the time you were away." She moved closer to him as his grip on her arms relaxed. "I'll get you some supper," she said simply. "You must be hungry."

Suddenly-his hands dropped from her arms and he let her go past him into the cottage. She caught her breath as she saw the flowers. How queer he was, and how much she loved him! She forgot the evening spent with Pierce, she forgot Maxwell's jealous anger, she turned to him, her face alight with generous love and kindness.

"Oh, my, aren't these fine?" she said, her eyes soft and beaming with pleasure.

He laughed abruptly. "They're yours," he said. "I picked them for you. Yes—go on. Smell them!" Then his voice changed, it grew urgent and impatient and hungry. "Come here, Maggie," he said. "I need you."

III

Lottie and George came home through the woods. They walked across the little bridge where the stream ran, the water tinkling over the smooth stones. Occasionally a little eddy swirled to the side of the stream, and broke gaily and ineffectively against the bared root of a tree. Lottie stopped and looked at the stream, though she could only glimpse the movements it made here and there where the trees let the moonlight brighten the clear busy water.

There was a light in the window of George's house, but they decided not to go in and see his mother that night.

"She'd love to see you," George hesitated, "but you won't want to be late getting back."

"I mustn't be late," Lottie agreed dreamily, but there was no fear of Nurse in her reply, only a happy acquiescence with George's statement that it was her duty not to be late.

George put his arm around her when they walked on. There was a blissful quality in Lottie's response to his touch. She let her head rest against his shoulder. It was such a comfort to be close to him like this.

At the side door into the house he kissed her again.

"Good night, Lottie dear."

"Good night."

"It isn't ten o'clock yet," he said, adding, "I don't want to let you go!"

At that moment the big clock in the hall began to strike the hour. They listened to it, both saddened by its stately mellow striking that meant the end of to-night's companionship.

"Good night—good night!" Lottie whispered, the sudden pain of this parting becoming unbearable.

"I'll see you again soon," he said. "To-morrow, perhaps."

Lottie ran up the stairs to the nursery door. To-morrow was only the space of a little time away, and no separation could rob her of her certainty of George's love. She put her hands up to her face and pressed her finger-tips against her eyes. She drew in a long deep breath that was almost painful with ecstasy. George had said, "You must never be afraid again, Lottie." She put out her hand and opened the door and entered the nursery.

"Oh, so you have come back, then," Nurse said, looking up from her vigorous sewing.

Lottie bent down and picked up one of Isobel's dolls that had slipped from its place against the wall. How beautiful the nursery was, with its pale pink walls and the children's toys lying about it!

She looked steadily at Nurse, too. "Yes, I've come back," she said gently and compassionately.

But how was Nurse to know that she had not really come back at all? That this was a new Lottie, a Lottie whom Nurse could never frighten again. Smiling a little, Lottie slipped into the room where Anne and Isobel lay sleeping. She stood by Isobel's bed glancing down at the little girl's face. Isobel looked so sweet and young, and Lottie's heart was bursting with happiness. Where was George now? Was he walking through the trees, over the little bridge, pausing to listen to the water, and thinking of her all the time? Loving her? Very softly and gently Lottie bent down and kissed Isobel's forehead. Isobel opened her eyes for a moment. "Dear Lottie," she murmured, and dropped back into sleep.

AFTERWORD

In *The Spring Begins*, the women who would normally be in the background of a 1930s novel are brought to the foreground. Roles are flipped: the upper-class, well-connected families pass by incidentally, while the nurse-maid, scullery maid and a governess have the focus of the narrative.

In the hands of many novelists, these roles are filled by women whose interior lives are a mystery – perhaps not even that, since there is no sense of enquiry about what we aren't being told. In Dunning's hand, there is a rich depth to our understanding of Lottie, Maggie and Hessie and the ways in which they navigate the narrow boundaries of the lives allotted to them. While all three women are unmarried, they share something in common: a preoccupation with men. But this preoccupation could scarcely be more different. Dunning is too subtle a novelist to make this the only theme for her complex characters, but throughout the novel, even as it focuses on the routine lives of ordinary women, men loom as the common thread, representing, respectively, fulfilment, threat, and opportunity.

The most confident of the three is Maggie, the scullery maid. She believes 'There was not much she did not know about men' and she approaches them with a mixture of desire and mistrust. Particularly, she approaches Maxwell the gardener – a brooding, dangerous, almost animalistic man: 'She knew pretty well what a man of his type was after, but she could take care of herself all right. Or could she?' The

final three words undermine some of her confidence. She characterises herself by a certain wild earthiness, but no amount of attitude can alter the power balance between a man and a woman – particularly a man and a woman of their class – in the 1930s.

> "Come and see the flowers," he said. But the minute he put out his hand and touched her Maggie knew that she did not want to see the flowers any more than he wanted to show them to her. There was the same terrible hunger in her body as there was in his. It was no good trying to resist. She said nothing as he drew her in amongst the trees.

With another writer's pen, Maggie's role might be that of cautionary tale – but that is not Dunning's aim. She is an amoral writer, showing us people's actions without judgement. Maggie serves more as a tonal opposite to the nurse-maid, Lottie.

In contrast to Maggie's show of confidence and knowledge, Lottie could scarcely be more innocent and vulnerable. Having grown up in an orphanage, she has no familial connections and little understanding of the world – so a certain part of her mind is a vacuum waiting to be filled by the hints and warnings of other servants.

This was an era when unmarried women were less and less expected to be ignorant of sexual matters, and it was more widely accepted that the woman (post-marriage, at least) could be an enthusiastic participant in sex. While a 1930s guide to *Real Life Problems and Their Solutions* by R. Edynbry advised a wife to 'hold her husband and share his ecstasy', this did not filter down to unmarried women, and particularly not to working-class women who had no mother or older sister to advise her. Lottie has a fear of anything connected with this realm, to the extent that she scarcely acknowledges her own body to herself:

> It was all right from her head down to the top of her collar, and from her knees down to her toes she was flesh and blood again, but in

> between there was nothing at all–just a conveniently sized dummy's model on which to hang her blue gingham frock and white apron.

Partly, this is the propriety expected of her role, and rigorously enforced by Nurse. She must keep her legs hidden from her young charges (except at the beach), and adheres to Nurse's dictum: 'It was impossible to be too modest.' For a class of women with little power at their disposal, modesty is treated like a protective weapon. But, as Nurse hints, it is a weapon that is limited against beastly men.

> After a moment Nurse added. "Don't you forget what I've told you about men."
>
> Well, Nurse was off on her favourite topic now. Lottie began to tremble. But she could not stop Nurse once she was started on this subject. The rest of the meal was a monologue from Nurse. Most of it Lottie had heard before, but despite that she could not escape from the fear and horror it gave her.

Lottie is convinced of men's 'strong, dreadful passions', and that they 'knew everything, certainly everything nasty'. The final word might remind of Stella Gibbons' *Cold Comfort Farm* (published a few years before *The Spring Begins*) and Aunt Ada Doom's obsession with seeing 'something nasty in the woodshed' in her youth. Indeed, Lottie has her own fear about a rumour that 'a man had done something frightful to a girl in those woods'. Gibbons was satirising the vogue for hinted-at sexual unpleasantness in novels of the period, many of which took a glance at Freud's theories of repression and sexual deviancy and adapted them loosely and conveniently to give a torrid undertone to a novel. As D. H. Lawrence once commented, 'The Oedipus complex was a household word, the incest motive a commonplace of tea-time chat.'

But though there was scope for literary satire, there was also real fear that came from discussion of the possibility that ordinary-looking men

might harbour dangerous, harmful sexual obsessions. Lottie's fear is of physical danger, not psychological. Perhaps older women have always passed on this hint to the younger generation, but Nurse's prurient enjoyment in giving her warnings is something unlikely to have taken place in an earlier era.

Thankfully, despite the backdrop of these forebodings, Lottie's story follows the most traditional romantic plot with, in George, a fairly traditional romantic hero. It gives *The Spring Begins* a sweetness that offsets some of the more brutal realities facing the servant class of the 1930s.

If Lottie longs for love, Hessie longs for security. She is that recurring figure in early twentieth-century fiction and life: an impoverished gentlewoman. Though not living in total poverty, the disparity between her class and her wealth is the keynote of her life and, without the stability that wealth would offer, she must cling to her position. The genuinely upper-class characters in the novel – in any novel – do not face this preoccupation, because their respectability is not in question. Hessie thinks of little else. How else will she secure a marriage with the 'right' sort of man if she cannot demonstrate her respectability?

She lives with her mother and sister in one of the uninspiring – but beyond reproach – houses that proliferate throughout the town. The Kellaways' mansion is distinctive in its beauty and grandeur; Hessie's home is determinedly similar to all the others, 'united in the one common impulse of genteel hostility to anything that was considered vulgar or not nice'.

Her day-to-day life is dominated by a minutiae of pretensions that made sense only in a limited time period and only to a limited group of people. She can speak to a Nurse 'with a pleasant confiding familiarity' but not a lower servant; she cannot refer to the head-gardener as a 'gentleman', but doesn't want to 'use a word that would sound unrefined'; she laments sitting in the backseat of a car with children,

but, 'though she knew herself to be a lady, she was only the paid assistant in the Benson's home'. There are things she is at pains to avoid, or hates her mother or sister doing: sniffing, pointing, eating without a tablecloth, reading a book that isn't 'nice'. Like Lottie, she doesn't want to bare her feet – but, in this case, it is because others might see that cheap stockings have stained her feet.

Hessie's life is a tightrope walk of proving herself to others. The ridiculousness of her position is clear in some of her self-imposed rules.

> When the last plate was dried Hessie scrupulously wiped down the draining-board and the basin and yellow sink. A lady always left the sink clean, especially in another person's home.

The unspoken irony is, of course, that a 'true' lady would never be in the position to make this decision since she would never do the washing up herself. All these rules show the precariousness of her claim to class, and her desperate need to cling onto it.

But the rules are here for some other purpose too: acquiring a husband. Hessie knows she has to marry for long-term financial security and, equally important, respect in the eyes of others. In an era when marriage was firmly class-bound, there are very few possible candidates for that role. Hessie cannot marry above her, and she wouldn't marry below her. It is increasingly clear that she is unlikely to marry at all. She is on the shelf at the age of 36. She has not fulfilled her mother's only ambition for her and her sister: 'I hope one day to see them happy wives, and happy mothers!'.

With so many more women than men in the interwar period, the spinster is a trope of contemporary fiction – sometimes as a figure of fun, sometimes a lively, contented, free woman, and sometimes melancholy. Seldom is the reader invited into the desperation of an unmarried woman's hopeless hopes with the intensity Dunning provides:

> Supposing she screamed now. Just dropped the plates and opened her mouth and screamed. Hessie bit her under lip as she ran out into the kitchen. She laid the plates with a clatter onto the draining-board by the sink, and pressed her hands to her head. How could she live through Hilda's wedding, and afterwards, too? Evenings alone with Mother, while Hilda sat with her husband, and afterwards Hilda and Albert went upstairs together. Hilda would be a wife, a married woman. Hilda would come back to see them, and she'd talk about 'my husband' and Mother and she would exchange meaning glances, leaving Hessie outside the fraternity of married women.

But it is not simply respectable safety that Hessie longs for. She is not immune to the lusts that lurk below the surface of the novel: 'Why did she keep on thinking of things like this? Indecent, immodest things, that frightened her with their persistence; that seemed to come from some uncontrollable outside source and take possession of her.' If Lottie is fearful of the unspoken sexual nature of men, Hessie is fearful of those same things within herself. Only Maggie, of the three, is largely at peace with this drive.

Hessie looks like she may have the saddest outcome of the novel, 'alone with nothing but the mocking ghosts of her genteel inhibitions, and the frightening, always unfulfilled demands of her body'. It is a stark and haunting prospect – perhaps unexpectedly stark for a 1930s novel of this variety. But even more unexpected and daring for the period is the event that changes her future. Spontaneously and surprisingly, Maxwell and Hessie have sex. It is brief and not to be repeated but, even more curiously, treated by Hessie as a happy ending: 'The gradual slipping by of the years of her life would not matter now. For however brief a while she had been a woman, living, experienced.'

Maxwell the gardener becomes the unlikely thread connecting the three women and their guiding motivations in the novel: making Lottie 'weak and sick with fear' early in the novel, giving Maggie the

passionate partner she desires, and fulfilling a need that Hessie has hardly allowed herself to imagine. She doesn't have a husband, but it turns out that her own self-image is ultimately more important.

In hundreds of novels throughout the 1930s, women like Lottie, Maggie and Hessie appear fleetingly – perhaps accompanying the children on a trip, washing the floors, or doing good deeds in the parish. They are scarcely seen by the main characters – indeed, their role in the house may require that they are seen as little as possible. But Katherine Dunning brings them forward. She shines a light that is generous and thoughtful, revealing that their inner lives are as rich and complex as anybody else's, and their fulfilment and futures prove equally moving to the reader.

Simon Thomas

Series consultant **Simon Thomas** created the middlebrow blog Stuck in a Book in 2007. He is also the co-host of the popular podcast Tea or Books? Simon has a PhD from Oxford University in Interwar Literature.

ALSO AVAILABLE

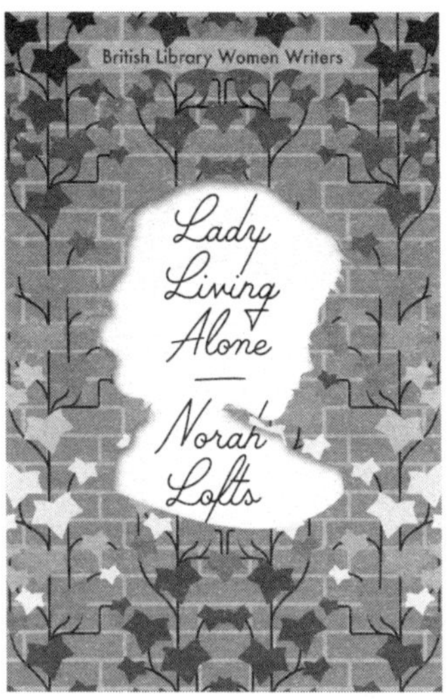

Well, then, since that has got you nowhere, stop being yourself. Beat your way out. Escape.

Originally published in 1945, what begins as a domestic novel quickly evolves into a dramatic thriller. Penelope Shadow, like her name suggests, has made very little mark on the world, until she purchases a typewriter and becomes a sensation as a romance novelist. She can now afford to buy her own house, and employs a capable and attentive young man as housekeeper. But what are his motives? Is she in danger? As events twist and turn, she must summon up the strength and ingenuity of her characters as the novel moves to a tense denouement.

ALSO AVAILABLE

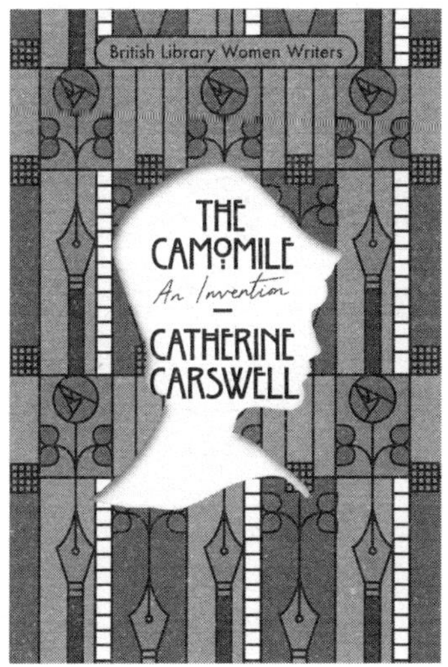

I have a Room! A room all to myself and away from home!

Set in twentieth-century Glasgow, this effervescent novel is widely considered a fictional counterpart to Virginia Woolf's feminist essay 'A Room of One's Own'. Desperate to escape her intrusive aunt and explore her creative talents, the vibrant Ellen Carstairs rents a room ten minutes' walk from home in which to find the peace and solitude to focus on her music and writing. Written as a 'journal letter' to her good friend Ruby, Ellen reveals her fluctuating ambitions and dreams as she endeavours to negotiate her place in the world.

ALSO AVAILABLE

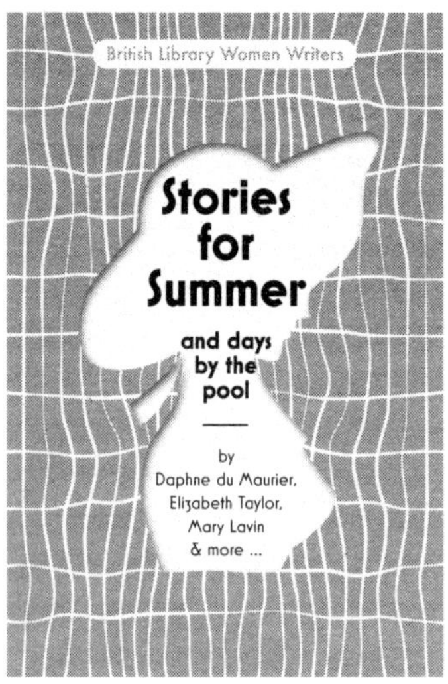

There were fewer boats now down in the harbour. She got into bed. Her sunburned body was fiery between the coarse sheets; she felt wonderfully lulled and, turning her cheek at once to the pillow, she let out a long breath like a contented sigh, and fell asleep.

Recline on a sun lounger with *Stories for Summer*, a collection of seasonal tales to idle away the hours of a long summer's day. This new anthology includes the talents of Daphne du Maurier, Elizabeth Bowen, Virginia Woolf, Muriel Spark, Elizabeth Taylor, Katherine Mansfield, Mary Lavin, G. B. Stern, Mary Norton and Phyllis Bottome. Don't forget to re-apply the sunscreen...